I0823983

PENDERGAST

THE BEGINNING

DOUGLAS PRESTON &
LINCOLN CHILD

GRAND
CENTRAL

New York Boston

Also by Douglas Preston and Lincoln Child

Agent Pendergast Novels

*Angel of Vengeance** • *The Cabinet of Dr. Leng** • *Bloodless** • *Crooked River* • *Verses for the Dead* • *City of Endless Night* • *The Obsidian Chamber* • *Crimson Shore* • *Blue Labyrinth* • *White Fire* • *Two Graves*† • *Cold Vengeance*† • *Fever Dream*† • *Cemetery Dance* • *The Wheel of Darkness* • *The Book of the Dead*‡ • *Dance of Death*‡ • *Brimstone*‡ • *Still Life with Crows* • *The Cabinet of Curiosities** • *Reliquary*§ • *Relic*§

*The Leng Quartet †The Helen Trilogy ‡The Diogenes Trilogy
§*Relic* and *Reliquary* are ideally read in sequence

Nora Kelly Novels

Badlands • *Dead Mountain* • *Diablo Mesa* • *The Scorpion's Tail* • *Old Bones*

Gideon Crew Novels

The Pharaoh Key • *Beyond the Ice Limit* • *The Lost Island* • *Gideon's Corpse* • *Gideon's Sword*

Other Novels

The Ice Limit • *Thunderhead* • *Riptide* • *Mount Dragon*

By Douglas Preston

Extinction • *The Lost Tomb* • *The Lost City of the Monkey God* • *The Kraken Project* • *Impact* • *The Monster of Florence* (with Mario Spezi) • *Blasphemy* • *Tyrannosaur Canyon* • *The Codex* • *The Royal Road* • *Talking to the Ground* • *Jennie* • *Cities of Gold* • *Dinosaurs in the Attic*

By Lincoln Child

Chrysalis • *Full Wolf Moon* • *The Forgotten Room* • *The Third Gate* • *Terminal Freeze* • *Deep Storm* • *Death Match* • *Lethal Velocity* (formerly *Utopia*) • *Tales of the Dark 1–3* • *Dark Banquet* • *Dark Company*

PENDERGAST

THE BEGINNING

This book is a work of fiction. Names, characters, places, and incidents are the product of the authors' imagination or are used fictitiously. Any resemblance to actual events, locales, corporate or government entities, facilities, or persons, living or dead, is coincidental.

Grand Central Publishing
Hachette Book Group
1290 Avenue of the Americas, New York, NY 10104
grandcentralpublishing.com
@grandcentralpub

First Edition: January 2026

Grand Central Publishing is a division of Hachette Book Group, Inc. The Grand Central Publishing name and logo is a registered trademark of Hachette Book Group, Inc.

Library of Congress Control Number: 2025946428

ISBNs: 9781538765746 (hardcover), 9781538765777 (ebook), 9781538779156 (large print)

Printed in the United States of America

LSC-C

Printing 1, 2025

PENDERGAST

THE BEGINNING

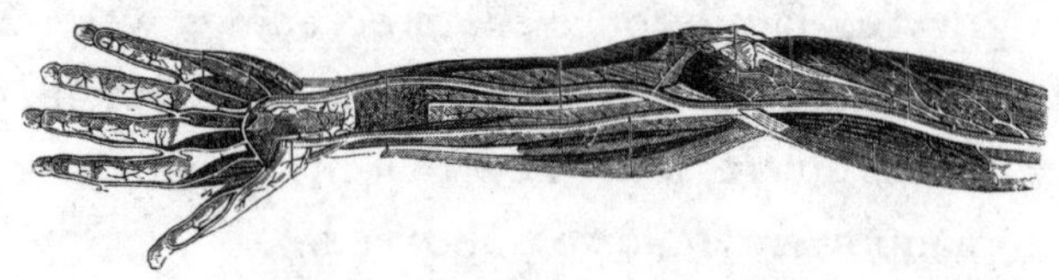

Prologue

Grosse Tete, Louisiana
1989

It was a sweltering October morning when Austin Landry and the rest of the crew drove through the gates of Savior's Rest Cemetery, the rust-black of the wrought iron spikes almost invisible under a coating of lichen and moss. The cemetery wasn't large, and Landry could see, ahead and to the right, the burial party: a black-clad cluster of people, heads down, bowed either in grief or by the relentless sun.

He steered the van left, off the cobbled lane and down a dirt path, so he could approach the ceremony from the rear. "You boys ready?" he asked.

Various murmurings and mutterings from the passengers. Landry glanced over at them. "Heaven's sakes, will you tidy up? All y'all look like the Three Stooges."

As he watched from the corner of his eye, the others—Stanley Trahan, Ned Fontenot, Martego Unpronounceable-Last-Name—made half-assed attempts to straighten their ties, tuck in their shirts, and in general make themselves as presentable as the cheap black suits would allow.

This wasn't Landry's full-time job, thank the Lord. He and his acquaintances only got called by Albert Kroker—director of Kroker Brothers Funeral Home—when the bereaved couldn't assemble a group of their own pallbearers to carry the coffin. Kroker didn't mind *that*, of course: it gave him another line item for the bill he'd present the grieving family once the proceedings were over. Eight men, $150 each. Except Kroker just hired the four of them, paid them seventy-five dollars apiece, and knew that in the general trauma the difference in manpower would go unnoticed.

Unnoticed—except by Landry and the other three, who had to heft the coffin from hearse to grave with a semblance of dignity.

As the van came around the rear side of the cemetery, he got a better view of things through the shimmering curtains of heat. Hearse; escort car for the priest; flower van; Kroker's six-door black Caddy for the grieving family at three hundred dollars an hour. The group of mourners was relatively small, about a dozen—a family named Montcalm, mostly white-haired and balancing on walkers, and a couple of younger men who'd probably been fellow workers. The family had chosen Parson Jessup to officiate: he liked the long, old-fashioned rites, though Landry suspected even the stringy, bad-tempered man of God would hurry things up today, with the humidity hovering around 100 percent. He could see the cemetery workers had already prepared the grave site, metal supports in place on both sides and a granite headstone set into the earth. Granite, must have cost some bucks. Clearly, the family wasn't hard up for cash... and the funeral director would have taken full advantage of the fact.

Landry wound down his window just enough to hear what the parson was intoning.

Man, that is born of a woman, hath but a short time to live, and is full of misery...

Wasn't that the truth. Shoot, they were further into the proceedings than he'd expected. Leaving the window open and nodding to the others, he turned off the engine. All four got out and gathered behind the van, out of view, making final adjustments to the Woolworth's-grade suits Kroker had provided them with. Landry looked them over one last time. Fontenot's eyes were red and sunken, and he swayed ever so slightly. Up close, he stank of beer.

"Goddamn it, Ned—drink your breakfast again?"

Fontenot looked away, mumbled something. Landry glared at him another moment, then took a deep breath. "All right. Let's get this over with."

"What kind of coffin they using?" Stanley asked.

"How should I know?"

"That last one was so heavy, my back hurt for a week."

"Don't worry about it. Thirty minutes and we'll be gone. Fontenot, you'd better keep it together."

They made their way in a funereal line toward the open-backed hearse. As they walked, heads bent in simulated solemnity, Landry tried to recall the details of this particular burial. Not that it made any difference, but he remembered the deceased was young, about his own age. The guy had worked in construction, crushed his head when he'd slipped off a girder and fell half a dozen stories. That meant a closed coffin—too bad for Kroker, who could make a lot more dough fixing up faces with superglue, Nair for the nostrils, and tampons in the mouth to wick away moisture. Not that Landry felt bad for the funeral director—he had a dozen other ways, legal or otherwise, to aid the bereaved in parting with their money along with their loved one.

Thou knowest, Lord, the secrets of our hearts...

The four approached the hearse and took up their positions, two on each side of the open rear doors. Landry raised his head and, like a general preparing strategy, took in the field: about ten feet from the hearse to the grave, on good level ground. No problem.

Then, glancing back at the coffin for the first time, his heart sank. It lay in the shadow of the hearse, but he could nevertheless see the mourners had chosen the heaviest of Kroker's offerings: the Mahogany Requiem, with SlumberSafe brass appointments. It figured: Kroker always did his best to push this particular coffin onto families in no condition to think sensibly about such details. In the Viewing

Room, where the various coffins were laid out under soft light and piped-in organ music, the Mahogany Requiem was always the shiniest of the lot. Kroker had made damn sure the top and sides were heavy as hell, so the bereaved knew they were getting their money's worth. Of course, nobody ever asked to look *under* the coffin, where the mahogany stopped and the plywood began.

A muttered curse from Fontenot: he'd noticed the coffin, too.

Landry looked back at the graveside and the small assembly surrounding it. Kroker was giving him a surreptitious stink-eye, warning him to do a creditable job. Next to him was Kroker's assistant director, three months on the job, youthful and radiating a lot more life than the rest of the group. Seeing Landry, he gave a sympathetic nod. Unlike Kroker, the assistant was a friendly, stand-up guy: Landry hadn't spoken to him much, but he knew the man didn't care for the way Kroker took shortcuts, bilked customers, and ignored the rules. He'd once heard an argument between Kroker and the assistant in which the younger man had warned the funeral director that, with all the new environmental regulations President Reagan was pushing through in his second term, he'd better get his act together. It was no longer okay to just dump formaldehyde, phenol, and a boatload of other carcinogens straight from the embalming room into the Atchafalaya River and then downstream into Bayou Chene. The assistant meant well, but Landry knew Kroker was too old and cheap to change his ways.

The parson raised his arms over the empty grave, and his voice rose: that was the signal. Landry and the others lined up along the back of the hearse, another cursing as he, too, recognized the casket. With Landry murmuring instructions, they grasped the brass handles, gently pulled the coffin forward—Jesus, it was even heavier than he remembered—and, with a few gasps and additional curses, balanced it on the rear lip of the hearse. All eyes swiveled toward them: showtime.

"On three," Landry said.

They lifted the coffin free of the hearse and began moving—front bearers stepping first, rear bearers after—in the shuffle-procession they'd learned was the easiest way to lug a dead person toward an open grave.

"Shit fire," Trahan muttered through gritted teeth. "I thought this stiff was fit. He must weigh three hundred pounds."

"Save your breath." Landry was concentrating on the job—one step ahead; wait for the rear guard to move; then the other foot forward. The coffin did seem even heavier than usual. He guessed Kroker had begun installing extra-thick lids so he could jack up prices still further.

They were halfway to the grave when Landry heard a cracking sound.

He was struggling with the weight and, at first, wasn't sure where it came from. But then he heard another: *snap*, like a pistol shot. It was coming from the underside of the coffin.

Oh Jesus—had Kroker replaced the plywood base with frigging balsa wood? Speaking of the funeral director, his face had suddenly gone gray.

No time to worry about it now—another step, and they'd have the coffin positioned over the framework of metal poles that paralleled the grave, with heavy green lowering straps extending across the deep hole in the earth. They'd lay the coffin on the straps, transfer the weight to them, then crank both the straps and the casket down into the earth—and when it was all over, he'd have a few words with Mr. Kroker.

We commend the soul of our brother departed, and we commit his body to the ground; earth to earth, ashes to ashes, dust to dust...

Just as they were placing the casket onto the straps, and Landry was preparing to expel a breath he'd held too long already, he saw something that made his insides turn to ice despite the heat: the front left strap assembly, the one used to crank the coffin down into the grave, wasn't seated properly. The cemetery workers hadn't fixed the strap securely to its banding clip. As Landry grunted with effort, straining to get a better look around the edge of the coffin, he realized that, if they set the casket down, the straps would slip right through their fairings, drop into the grave... and the whole mess would give way completely.

Sweet mother of God...

If they had the normal eight pallbearers, or if the casket wasn't so heavy, he could briefly one-hand the coffin and secure the strap into position. But the four of them were struggling as it was. How the hell was he going to fix this?

He glanced at Kroker, but the funeral director seemed to have seized up—as if that cracking sound was still echoing in his brain. It probably was. *Cheap-ass skinflint son of a bitch...*

"Lower it!" Fontenot, who could not see the problem, gasped.

"Hold on!" Landry overruled him. Could they move the coffin back to the hearse, fix the lowering framework? A quick look at his three associates, purple-faced with effort, told him they couldn't.

A third crack sounded, louder than the first two, causing even Parson Jessup to pause mid-intonation. It was the unmistakable sound of wood giving way.

"I can't hold it!" Fontenot half spoke, half gurgled.

"Wait!" said Landry. "*Wait—!*"

The next set of events came in quick succession. Fontenot let his portion of the load slip down onto the framework. The other three, finding their own loads now intolerable, had no choice but to do the same. As the friends of the deceased, realizing the situation, prepared to lend a hand, Landry grasped for the lowering strap, praying he could fix it in position... but with the sudden introduction of hundreds of pounds it slipped immediately from its axle and curled down into darkness like a thick, flat snake. The coffin tilted; righted; tilted farther, and then—with another cracking noise, this time accompanied by a groan of metal and a rising gasp from the onlookers—fell into the open grave.

Landry stared, paralyzed by horrified fascination.

The head of the coffin slammed into the base of the freshly dug hole with a terrible thud, shivering the entire casing. At the same time the bottom of the casket gave way, splitting into several pieces and allowing the body within to flop out. Gasps and curses rose as the deceased was exposed: crushed head, strips of hospital tape holding the bits of jaw in place; corpse nude from the waist down and already an eggplant purple; body cavity seals popping loose from the impact, followed by a gush of fluids.

Shrieks erupted around Landry. Parson Jessup was calling for order and praying at the same time. The funeral director was, quite suddenly, nowhere to be found.

As the scene grew increasingly chaotic, Landry suddenly heard a scream, louder than the others, and an elderly woman collapsed to his left. A few seconds later, he heard a chorus of dismayed cries, followed by the sound of retching. Another person collapsed on the far side of the grave, fainting dead away and falling prostrate over the remains of the metal scaffolding, already badly askew.

Distantly, as he stared down into the open grave—shocked by how quickly things had gone from normal to nightmare—he wondered what had caused the fainting and delayed screams. The worst imaginable had *already* happened—a coffin had accidentally been dropped into its grave, and the ill-prepared remains dumped unceremoniously from beneath it—what could be any more awful than that?

And then—as he stared down into the hole yawning before his feet—he saw . . . and understood.

PART ONE

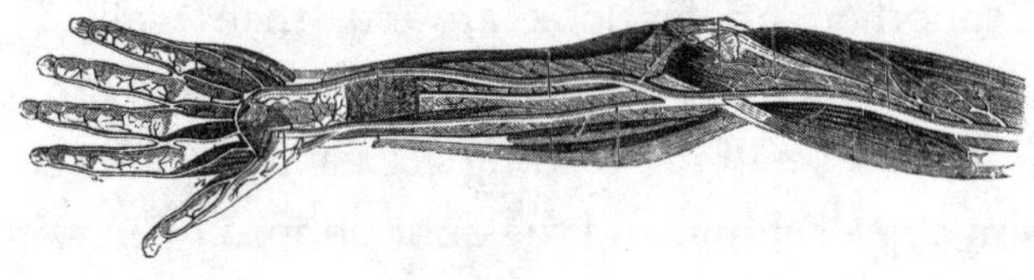

I

August 7, 1994

The Expedited Medical Transport company occupied the rear of a nondescript building in an equally nondescript industrial park in East New Orleans. Although a few tech start-ups were sprouting up here and there, attracted by low commercial rents and easy access to downtown, the area remained a monochromatic landscape: squat buildings of corrugated steel amid a welter of chain-link fences and shabby one-way streets.

As J. F. Foreman pulled into EMT's parking lot and eased his Cadillac DeVille Concours into his space, he felt—as always—that he liked the industrial wasteland just the way it was. Talk of a new "tech corridor" being established here was just that: talk. Silicon Valley had a lock on that enterprise, and he didn't see things changing anytime soon. Besides, the computer industry was never going to cause much of a change, beyond a lot of secretaries and accountants losing their jobs: look at Gateway, its stock way overvalued and headed for a fall. Apple, already moribund, would be next.

By force of habit, he glanced around before killing the engine. He grabbed his briefcase and stepped out into the overpowering humidity of a Louisiana summer. He shut the door, locked it, and gave the new Caddy an affectionate pat. The Japanese could try taking over the luxury segment with their Acuras and their Infinitis, but Foreman had always bought American and always would.

He took another, briefer look around, then walked up to the smoked-glass entrance to his business, which instead of a company sign merely bore a small tag reading PLEASE PRESS BUZZER. But Alice had seen him approaching, and the door popped open with the hush of a well-oiled lock just as he raised his hand toward it.

"Morning, Alice!" he said cheerfully to his secretary-receptionist-accountant. EMT was a small outfit, less than a dozen employees. "Is everybody there?"

"Yes, Mr. Foreman. They're all waiting for you."

"Thank you." As he passed her, heading for the reinforced metal door of his office, he looked back to give her one last smile—noting approvingly as he did so that the short-barreled 12-gauge was in its proper place below her desk, easily accessible.

He entered his spartan office, shut and locked the door behind him, hung up his suit jacket, and placed the briefcase—which was empty—on his desk. Then he slid behind the desk, accessed a safe behind a wooden panel, and withdrew a thin folder. Closing the safe, he walked toward a second door set into the rear wall of his office.

It opened into a conference room, with a table around which six men were already seated. He looked at them in turn. Each glance was brief, but his highly tuned instincts could spot anything even remotely out of place. The men all looked calm and alert, with nothing in either their dress or expressions to alarm him. Anybody else might find such a motley aggregation—some dressed as plumbers or electricians, others as businessmen, one in a cheap tank top—peculiar. But all J. F. Foreman felt was satisfaction.

He placed the folder at the head of the table, then took a seat behind it. "Gentleman, we're on for August 9."

He was pleased at how this announcement was greeted. Eagerness gleamed in their eyes, not unlike what he'd seen in the marines when he'd told his squad a new mission was in the offing.

After leaving the armed forces, Foreman had spent a few years as a guard in a private bank, then as armed escort for Middle Eastern billionaires visiting the United States. In their own ways, both jobs had opened his eyes to the state of the security industry—and within it, a niche that seemed ripe for exploiting. So he'd taken his small inheritance and founded Expedited Medical Transport.

Despite the name, EMT had nothing to do with health care. Rather, it acted as a courier service—a kind of bespoke armored car company—for high-value customers and corporations who wished to move their assets, in whatever form they took, as inconspicuously as possible.

Over the last three years, Foreman had built a client base sufficient for his operational needs. He had two heavily reinforced medical transport vans—armored cars, with their high visibility, were precisely what he didn't want—along with a small fleet of backup and escort vehicles. He was careful in choosing which clients to take on and ensuring the goods transported were legal, not weapons or drugs: he did not wish to attract the attention of the authorities or get involved in a gang war. His few employees were carefully curated and vetted. Most were ex-military or ex-police; all were well trained in the use of weapons and had concealed carry permits. All were single. All dressed for "work" in their assigned ways, be it businessman or blue-collar. And all lived far apart from each other and did not fraternize.

This last element was vital to Foreman. It was easy to guard against one bad egg trying to steal from his boss. An internal conspiracy among several, however, to hijack a delivery was more difficult to prepare for. That was why Foreman took on only one job at a time and always used the entire team; why he paid them extremely well—and why he'd carefully drilled into them an ironclad rule: if one of his men went rogue during a delivery, the rest were to incapacitate him without hesitation. This was also why he always assigned four men to the delivery vehicle, and three others to the escort car that followed. He had a perfect record, and he intended for it to remain that way.

He had just been given the green light for a new delivery, and now it was time to brief the team. He gave one more quick look around the table, his gaze stopping at Arnold Carson, whom he'd met during the Gulf intervention and considered his informal second-in-command.

"A Gulfstream G-IV SP will be landing at the Lakefront Airport at approximately twenty-one hundred hours the night after next," he said, opening the folder. "Our package will be aboard. We are to deliver it to a location within a three-hour drive from the airport, over interstate and primary roads."

Everyone knew Carson would be handed an envelope with the precise location on the actual day of the op.

"The package itself will be unusual. It will be a woman—in fact, the client herself."

This raised a few eyebrows.

"Naturally I have no photographs. But she is Asian, about five feet tall, and thirty years old. A small attaché case—Hermès, brown, crocodile—will be handcuffed to one wrist, and will remain there until she reaches the destination."

He took a deep breath. "Other than that, there should be nothing out of the ordinary. She will ride in the transport vehicle, inside the safety chamber. There will be no need to speak with her. Now: are there any questions?"

Carson shook his head. The rest remained silent.

Foreman nodded. "Good. Then make the usual preparations. We'll meet back here at fifteen hundred on the ninth. I'll inform you of any updates should it be necessary."

As they rose to leave, Foreman spoke to the man in the tank top. "Proctor? Got a minute?"

Proctor halted and waited for the others to leave.

Proctor was Foreman's most recent hire. He was promising but inscrutable. He'd been with EMT half a year and had performed his duties flawlessly. Foreman wasn't the kind to fully accept somebody until he was absolutely sure of their qualities—but Proctor was not an easy one to pin down. He'd provided excellent references from his most recent employment as a security guard. He was an excellent shot and was accustomed to taking orders: obviously ex-military. He was six foot four, ripped as hell, but he also carried a quality of litheness and grace that seemed God-given rather than the product of a gym. Yet he'd declined to specify what branch of the military he'd been in, or in what capacity, and he was evasive regarding details of his personal life. When asked, he'd shown Foreman discharge papers that were equally imprecise, indicating he'd been involved in classified work, which he had nothing to say about. He had little to say, period. While this might have put off a more traditional employer, Foreman sought out qualities like these.

Since his hiring, Proctor had reported for work, accomplished his duties faultlessly, and left when the op was done. Foreman sometimes worried about his men getting too chummy with one another—but with Proctor, it was the opposite. He had none of the swaggering, jocular tough-guy attitudes his other men had. Foreman had kept a close eye on Proctor, worried that the reticence might be from PTSD, but in the end he realized the man was just quiet.

"You know Rodriguez is still out." This was Foreman's seventh employee, missing from today's meeting. He was currently in the hospital with diverticulitis. That meant Foreman was a man short—one risk of running so tight a ship.

Proctor nodded.

"That means I'll need to shift you from the escort car and give you Rodriguez's position in the van. That leaves only a driver and navigator in the tail vehicle, but it's more important the asset be fully covered."

"Understood."

"I'm glad to hear it. Because this is an opportunity, Proctor: a high-value transport. Do a good job, keep it clean, and there'll be a nice bonus for you at the end."

Proctor nodded again.

"That's all. Come by the office tomorrow at three for your briefing."

The man rose and left the conference room the way the others had taken. Foreman stared at the door as it closed behind him, chewing his lip meditatively, for a long time.

2

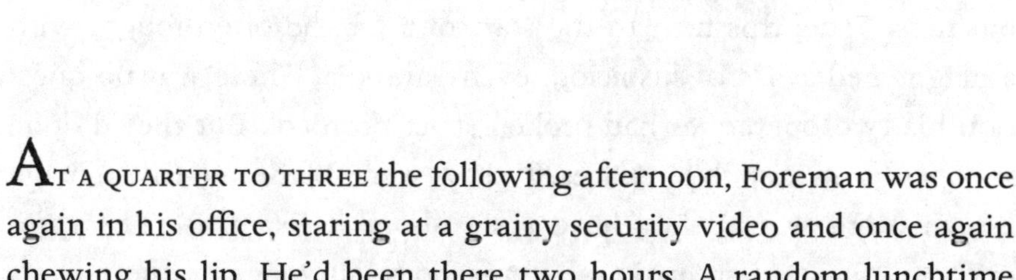

AT A QUARTER TO THREE the following afternoon, Foreman was once again in his office, staring at a grainy security video and once again chewing his lip. He'd been there two hours. A random lunchtime sweep of the security cameras installed throughout the office—and, in a few cases, at the residences of his employees, unbeknownst to them—had revealed something alarming.

He'd isolated the two videos that most concerned him and replayed them, zooming in until the screen was more noise and grain than recognizable image. Then he'd gone back over all the other videos, carefully. But no: it was just those two moments, captured on camera—first a friendly punch in the arm and a few exchanged words as two men left the office parking lot the day before; and later the same two, in the plaza outside one's apartment, eating a quick meal from a po'boy vendor.

Foreman isolated each video to its relevant five-minute segment and watched them in turn. A little banter between the two as they left the office was of no concern. But their meeting outside the parameters of work was a conduct violation. The place of their meeting suggested they both knew where the other lived—another violation.

Foreman snapped off the monitor and took a moment to prioritize his thoughts. First was a sense of betrayal, given the breach of protocol. Second was concern for the next day's job. Although he had not mentioned it yet with his team, this was a particularly important assignment. Not only did it come with an unusually large payment, but—perhaps more important—it would cement his position of trust within a certain wealthy circle, ensuring a flow of remunerative jobs in the future.

He could cancel or try delaying the assignment. But one did not abandon jobs like these, sometimes involving the transfer of gemstones, gold, or tens of millions of dollars, and expect to remain in business. True: this near to the start of a job, he often fought with a heightened sense of suspicion, even paranoia. There was no question his two operatives had broken strict protocol. But they'd done so openly, in a public space. If they were planning to sabotage the mission, would they have gone about it like this? The camera view was a distant one, but the body language of the two as they relaxed over a meal didn't show any obvious signs of guilt or complicity.

Of course, that could be by design. As careful as he was to keep all his delivery jobs legal, or at least in a legally defensible area, that didn't necessarily make his employees saints. It might be—probably was—nothing. When the mission was successfully completed, he would deal with the violation. For now, the only option was to proceed... under advisement.

His intercom buzzed. "Sir? Mr. Proctor has arrived."

"Thank you, Alice." Rising from his chair, Foreman stepped into the outer office and passed through a smoked-glass door into a corridor. At its end, another door led into a vast, echoing garage. Inside were two medical transport vans emblazoned with EMT logos, first-aid crosses, and a caduceus. The only signs they might not be what they claimed were the tinted (and bulletproof) windows, oversize engine manifold, and bonded polyurethane tires upon which the vehicles—weighted down as they were with over a ton of shielding and interior armor—rode low. The small embrasures, sized to accommodate automatic weapon muzzles, were form-fitted and nearly invisible. It had never been necessary to use them—yet.

Also in the garage were three escort cars of innocuous makes and colors, fitted out in similar fashion. At the far corner were a few other vehicles kept for unusual situations—an old school bus, a pickup truck, a taxi.

Proctor waited quietly in his work-specced uniform of T-shirt and jeans.

"Proctor!" Foreman called out with a joviality he didn't feel. He stepped up and they shook hands. "Glad to see you."

"I appreciate the opportunity." Proctor had a low, gravelly voice—not because he was trying to be a badass, Foreman assumed, but because his vocal cords were the one part of his body that didn't get regular exercise.

"Good man. Since you'll be taking rear lookout for the first time, I wanted to make sure you were up to speed. Feel free to ask any questions, and don't worry about sounding stupid—it's more important you feel 100 percent comfortable. Ooh-rah?"

"Understood."

Even after six months, Foreman occasionally poked at Proctor like this, more out of curiosity than anything else. The way he'd responded just now meant he hadn't been a marine. Or perhaps he simply chose not to reveal that he'd been one. Anyway, he knew how to shoot a gun, and if there was a fix on with this job, he wasn't involved.

They made a slow circuit of the vehicle, Foreman pointing out various features and explaining instructions to follow in emergency situations. For the most part, Proctor listened in silence, his questions limited to minor details.

They stopped at the side of the vehicle and Foreman opened the door, pointing out the explosive bolts as he did so, along with the stun and gas grenades attached to the interior roof in neat Velcro rows. They both stepped inside, and Foreman quickly went over operation of the safety chamber: a four-by-four-foot metal cube secured to the ceiling and floor of the vehicle's midsection by redundant fastenings. A chair was placed in the middle.

"This is the moneymaker," Foreman said, wrapping up the tour. "Everything we do is about getting the contents of this chamber from point A to point B. It's never held a client before—and she won't exactly be comfortable—but you can see the air vents along the top and bottom, and there's plenty of room for both her and her briefcase. So: any questions about opening or securing the chamber?"

"No, sir."

"The three—I mean two—guys in the escort vehicle will be responsible for taking point during the time that the, ah, package is being placed inside the chamber. That's an obvious vulnerability. Over time, we've shaved down how long it takes to move and secure a dead load to around twenty-five seconds. Since a person is involved this time, it will probably take longer."

Proctor nodded.

"Once rolling, primary responsibility for safe delivery is transferred to you four in this vehicle."

Foreman pointed out each position: driver, shotgun, payload master, tail lookout. He asked Proctor to take up position in the swivel seat of the last to make sure he was familiar with the recon fields, and he pointed out where the ammo for the chopped-down M240 were stowed. He went over a couple of minor errors Rodriguez had made when manning tail lookout over some past runs, and how they'd been rectified.

As he spoke, there was no fear or doubt in Proctor's gaze—just quiet attention.

Foreman finished up and, after a hesitation, decided to share his misgivings with Proctor. "Listen," he said, taking a seat on an armored panel behind the safety chamber. "Something's come up. It may be nothing."

Proctor remained motionless, waiting.

"I'm telling you this out of a hyperabundance of caution. Hopefully, tomorrow's run will go without a hitch. If that's what happens, you're to forget what I'm about to tell you and never mention it again. Understood?"

Proctor nodded.

"I've come into possession of some unreliable intel that the shotgunner and payload master might attempt to subvert tomorrow's action in some way. Beyond that, I know nothing. I want to emphasize this intel is highly questionable. But with Arnie Carson as wheelman, you're the obvious choice to keep watch on those two guys."

Proctor nodded, more slowly this time.

"I'm fairly sure that if they're planning to make a move, it won't happen until the package is secure and you're rolling. On the other hand, they wouldn't wait until you reach the delivery point—especially since they don't know its location yet." He paused. "Carson's likely not in on it, so shotgun might just take him out while you're on the road or stopped at a light. If that happens, the payload master would be tasked with snuffing you. Your job is to prevent that. Carson wears no armor; you do. If shit goes down and they drop you, we've failed. Take out payload, then shotgun—if Carson is killed, make sure the others are neutralized, then take over as driver and complete the mission. You'll find the envelope with the location in his breast pocket."

He stood up again, shoulders bent beneath the reinforced roof. "You don't need to worry about the package—no small-arms fire is going to penetrate the safety chamber. But in this case, the 'package' is also our client—so any problems en route, even small ones, will reflect badly on us. Like I said: consider the scenario I've just outlined to be just left of paranoid. But keep your pecker up."

Foreman sighed, then cursed under his breath. "You know what the most fucked-up thing is? On the one hand, I can't just let this go without preparing. On the other, I can't afford to alert *anybody*—even you, new man. If two people are dirty, I guess six could be, too. But it's because you haven't buddied up yet, and because of the field of fire that rear seat affords you, that I have to trust you." He paused. "How's my signal coming in, mister?"

"Five by five, sir."

And somehow, this response—as clipped and emotionless as it was in delivery—made the unexpected weight Foreman had been carrying the last several hours just a little lighter.

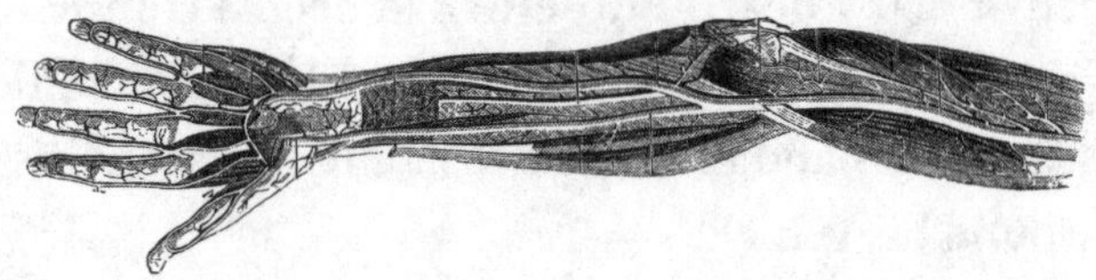

3

PROCTOR SAT AT THE BREAKFAST TABLE of his kitchen, sipping coffee and reading the *Times-Picayune*. He would have preferred the *Washington Post*, but home delivery to Louisiana was expensive—one of the sacrifices he'd made when he decided to spend time in New Orleans. Besides, daily events around the world were of little concern to him—he didn't even own a TV—but reading a newspaper from front to back every morning had become habitual, and, like all the habits he'd acquired over the years, he preferred to retain it.

Finally, coffee and paper both finished, he stood up, went to the sink, washed out the cup and saucer, and put them in the drying rack. Normally he ate no breakfast, but since there was a job on today, he'd had half a cup of Scottish oatmeal.

He went into his bedroom to get dressed. Foreman had assigned him casual office attire. He had no air conditioning, the windows facing the street were open, and he paused to take a long look. The scene was typical of the suburban neighborhood he'd chosen. A young woman in pink booty shorts and block-heeled mules was pushing a stroller down the sidewalk. A light-gray utility truck was parked down the street, a uniformed man beside it, peering up an electrical pole, perhaps in reaction to the short brownout caused by the intense heat of the last week. From next door, where his neighbor Otis Burdette worked on his pickup, he could hear a country singer complaining about his achy-breaky heart. Burdette had been a commercial fisherman until a chum line got loose and sliced his left Achilles tendon. Now in his late fifties and retired on disability, he spent his mornings puttering around his vehicle.

Proctor stepped over to the closet, chose a blue blazer, white pullover, and khakis. The blazer was cut wide in the shoulders. The pullover was of an artificial material that both breathed and wicked moisture.

As he dressed, he briefly ran over the afternoon ahead. Riding the rear lookout position would be a welcome change from the backup car, with the endless litany of dirty jokes, idle boasting, and arguments about sports. From his spotter's position in the car, he'd seen a dozen or so packages taken into the transport vehicle and, later, removed at their various destinations: they had come in every variety, from steamer trunks to a rolled-up paper bag. But never before had it been a person. Proctor paused a moment to consider this. Unusual, but in itself of no particular concern. More important was Foreman's worry about a possible betrayal by two of his own men. Foreman was a type A personality who overthought everything, but that didn't make him wrong. He hadn't told Proctor his source of intel, and Proctor hadn't asked. Perhaps the man riding shotgun and the vault guard were getting restless with the squeaky-clean messenger runs and had grown eager to go rogue, make a boatload of money, and vanish. But then, why with a person involved, instead of a load of gemstones or bearer bonds?

Proctor shrugged into his jacket and exited his bedroom, turning off the light. Speculation without adequate information was counterproductive. He already had all the intel he was going to get.

He glanced at his watch: twelve thirty. If he left now, he'd have time on the way to fill the tank of his indigo Taurus SHO and check its tires: the left rear was looking a little low.

As he closed the living room windows, one after another, he made another habitual glance around the neighborhood. The young mother had vanished from view. The utility man had left his van and was starting up a pole a few houses nearer, tool belt hanging low, butt crack the envy of any plumber. Burdette next door, who ran his retirement like clockwork, had turned off his radio and gone in for lunch. Proctor knew the man would spend the afternoon napping, have dinner, then watch cable channels until he fell asleep in his Barcalounger.

Proctor spent an extra moment looking still farther down the tree-lined street but saw nothing of note. As he closed the window, he shook his head. Foreman's paranoia must be rubbing off on him: if there really was an inside job in the offing, he'd be the last guy the offenders would worry about.

Foreman had said the delivery would take six hours, out and back: that meant he'd be home after dark. He pulled the shades down and turned on the outside light as he bolted the front door. Then he walked back into his kitchen and closed those blinds, as well: a young couple lived in the house to the rear, but they both worked downtown and he didn't know their names.

Grabbing his keys, he stepped into the garage and pressed the opener. As the motor hummed and the door began to rise, he wondered about the years he'd spent in prefab houses just like this, and how they had ultimately brought him to this particular neighborhood. Once again, New Orleans was temporary parking. *Every day is a journey, and the journey itself is home*, Lao-tzu had said. A rather contradictory phrase from Jung immediately came to mind: *I am not what happened to me, I am what I choose to become.*

Idly, Proctor wondered who would win in a knife fight—the poet or the philosopher.

As he was musing, he suddenly recalled he hadn't armed himself. He'd grown so used to jamming his 1911 into his jeans that, now in a suit jacket, he'd forgotten to don his shoulder holster. He went back into the bedroom, took off his jacket, rummaged around in his dresser for a holster, grabbed it and poked his arm through it. Then he put his jacket on again, took his sidearm from its drawer in the bedside table, and slipped it in place.

Stepping out into the garage again, he looked up from the holster to see somebody standing before him—the utility worker who'd been climbing the pole a few houses down. The man, holding a metal-cased clipboard, smiled. "I'm sorry to bother you, sir," he said. "But have you experienced any problems with your electrical supply? I'm having a difficult time tracking this down."

Proctor unexpectedly found himself doing several things at once: ensuring his weapon was concealed and the holster was tight, glancing over the man's shoulder in search of his utility van—and so when the man's free hand shot forward holding a two-foot cattle prod, and its twin contacts pushed an ungodly voltage through his clothes and into his body, Proctor was astonished even as he was instantly incapacitated. As he fell to the floor, head slamming against a tool cabinet on the way down, stunned paralysis gripped him. In a flash, the man flipped him on his stomach and cuffed his hands behind his back. Next, a hood went over his head and the sting of a needle pierced his neck—and a blackness fell over him.

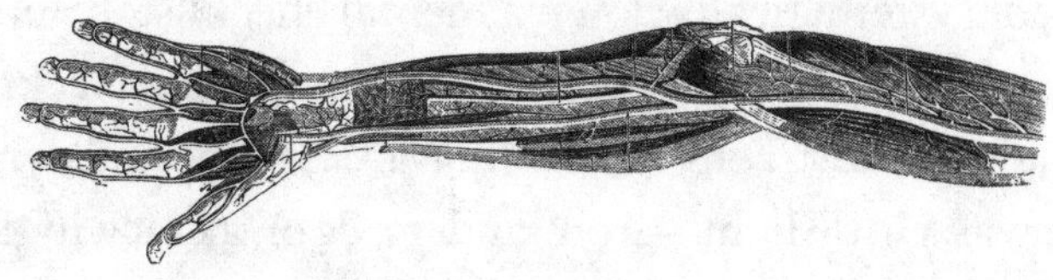

4

PROCTOR WOKE IN DARKNESS.

For several minutes, he remained motionless as he tried to piece together what had happened.

It came back to him in reverse order. He'd been injected with something that had rendered him unconscious. Before that, he'd been felled by a cattle prod, his wrists bound behind his back, and a mask slipped over his head. All this had been the work of the utility man he'd first noticed a few houses down.

Incredibly, the man had gotten the drop on him.

He took stock of his physical constraints. He was sitting with his back against a padded wall, his hands now bound in front instead of behind. Unusual: his captor cared enough for his welfare not to impede his circulation—in fact, the cuffs were relatively loose and forgiving. He moved around, testing his bindings, and realized his wrists were held by a double set of zip ties, the right slightly looser than the left, but not enough to make a difference. It was a secure and sophisticated binding system, designed to be comfortable—under the circumstances.

Interesting.

His ankles were bound as well, in a way that made it impossible to stand. As he moved his legs, he realized that his ankles were also chained to the wall. Other than his head, which throbbed where it had hit the tool cabinet, he seemed to have suffered no additional injury.

As he went systematically down a mental checklist, he noticed that the space he was in was not just dark but completely black. This was also unusual: in most cells or holding areas, especially improvised ones, there was a little light—from under a door, a crack in the ceiling, a ventilation shaft. Here there was none. It was silent, too—utterly so.

As he continued the inventory, he noted his clothing had been exchanged for sweatpants and a light, loose, sleeveless top that felt like a hospital gown. His shoulder holster was, of course, gone.

He tried to assess how much time had passed. He felt no strong desire to urinate; then again, it was possible he'd pissed himself and his captor had rinsed him off before dressing him again. But he felt roughly the amount of hunger he normally would when returning home from a job, which reinforced a growing conviction he'd been out only a few hours.

Returning home from a job. Was this fallout, or collateral damage, from Foreman's warning? It seemed likely—Proctor did not believe in coincidence. Should he, then, have been more on the alert during the moment he stepped back into his garage? Where, exactly, was his point of failure? He'd been preoccupied with securing his holster and adjusting his jacket, but those were feeble excuses.

One thing was obvious: the sleepy suburban neighborhood had taken the edge off his alertness. He reminded himself bitterly that he should never have overlooked his sidearm. More important, he should never have allowed his mind to slip into a state of preoccupation. The things he'd done in his past life meant that now he could never fully drop his guard—and yet here he'd done just that.

The attack and abduction was meant to remove him from what was going to happen during the transport. Nothing else made sense.

As his mind cleared further, he thought about how, specifically, he'd been taken down. He recalled nothing in the attacker's eyes, expression, or posture that would set off his instinctive alarms. The only notable thing about the man was his size—six foot four—and his high fitness level. The man had a cut-down cattle prod clearly capable of delivering over a million volts. During training, Proctor had had the unpleasant experience of feeling the bite of a similar prod, and he knew one this powerful couldn't be purchased in a local farm supply store. The man's uniform had looked authentic, and he'd known enough not to park too near Proctor's driveway. He'd calmly waited for his chance, slipped into the garage, taken Proctor by surprise, neutralized him, then no doubt backed his van up to the garage door and placed Proctor in the back.

The shotgun and payload master—Foreman referred to his men by their assignments rather than names—wouldn't have needed to don an elaborate disguise: he knew them already, there'd be no need for deception. As he considered the elements at length—Foreman, the job, the woman in the box—he realized the pieces might not be falling into place as neatly as he'd just assumed.

Proctor moved his head this way and that, ignoring the pain in the upper right quadrant of his skull. If it had to do with the job, that would be over with by now, one way or another. In any case, there was nothing he could do but wait—and Proctor was good at that.

In the blackness, he gently leaned his head against the wall, took in a deep breath, closed his eyes, then exhaled slowly. Within five minutes he was asleep.

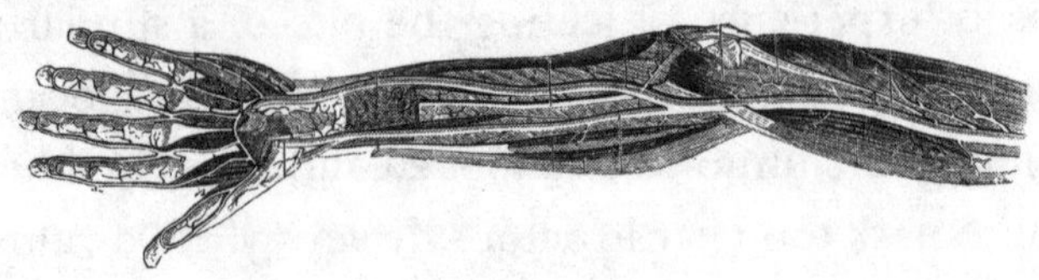

5

Proctor was dozing when a soft noise near the far wall brought him instantly to his senses. He remained motionless except for his eyes, which he slowly opened. Now there came another sound: the whisper of a door opening over a soft surface.

Still motionless, Proctor scanned the far wall with half-lidded eyes. It remained utterly black, as it had since he first woke.

The sound stopped. Had it been his imagination? No—Proctor prided himself on having little to no imagination.

"Good," a voice sounded out of the dark. "You're awake."

The voice belonged to the utility man with the metal binder.

There was the noise of a door shutting, then the room was bathed in brilliant light. Instinctively, Proctor shut his eyes and turned away, but not before he caught a glimpse of the man, standing against the far wall, observing him.

The man remained there, waiting, while Proctor's eyes adjusted to the light. In one hand he held a flashlight with a blue-purple lens. Ultraviolet: used to detect certain minerals, dyes, and bodily fluids. Why?

Now that the room was illuminated, Proctor took a quick opportunity to observe it. He was in a padded cell. There were no windows, furniture, ventilation ducts—nothing save for a high ceiling of fluorescent bulbs behind a thick wire grille, and a small round hole in the corner of the floor. The door was padded as well, no knob, only a keyhole. The padding that covered everything save the ceiling was of a coarse, tough material, well bolted into the frame of the structure.

Next, Proctor examined the man's face. He was in his early thirties, fit, tall, and powerful, more or less like Proctor in age, build, and height. Blue-eyed, blond, wearing a zipped and buttoned black jumpsuit, along with slip-on rubber loafers, also black, and nitrile gloves.

Keeping well out of range, the man opened a director's chair he'd been holding in his other hand, placed it on the floor, then sat down as if to enjoy a show.

He remained silent, looking Proctor over with a curious intensity. Proctor, also silent, took several calming breaths and resisted speculation. All would be made clear soon enough.

"You're awfully quiet," the man said.

Proctor did not respond.

"You'll be here for a little while," the man continued. "A few days, at least. I'm no sadist, and I want you to be comfortable. You must be hungry—I'll bring you food. Over there—" he nodded over one shoulder— "in the corner, you'll find a drain for your toilet needs. It's plastic, glued five feet around and ten feet into the ground with a cyanoacrylate adhesive, so if you try to pry it free, you'll just end up breaking your fingernails."

He paused, as if to examine what effect his words were having on Proctor. "As long as you behave, I'll unchain your feet from the wall, but you'll remain hobbled. Your hands are tied loosely, so your arms should be comfortable. I imagine you'll spend some time looking for a way out—or, perhaps, some weapon you can use. Go ahead—I won't try to stop you. You'll realize soon enough it's a waste of time. The food will come through that opening at the bottom of the door. Once I've brought it, I'll keep the lights on for fifteen minutes—that should be sufficient for you to eat and empty your bladder. Be sure you do both, because the darkness will return and you may be left alone for a long time. Any questions?"

Proctor said nothing.

"Like I said, I won't stop you from seeking a way to escape. But I'm going to lay down a few ground rules. First, you must not injure yourself in any way. Second, I expect you to eat and drink everything I bring you—no hunger strikes. The food will be good. Those are the only two rules—no self-harm, and eat well. I'd advise against breaking either. As I said, I'm no sadist...but my discipline is extremely harsh."

Once again, the man ran his eyes lingeringly over Proctor's form. Proctor merely stared back. Given the calm, unmodulated voice in which these instructions were recited, he initially suspected his captor presented with symptoms of blunted affect. But by the time he was finished speaking, Proctor revised that presumption: flat affect.

"You might wonder why, among the rules, I didn't warn you against trying to harm me. That's because I don't need to. I'm in full control. When I leave, the lock on your ankle chain will disengage, allowing you to move around. Feel free to do so. You're a fit man—you might find exercise a good way to pass the time.

"I'll bring your dinner now. It will come through beneath the door. Remember—eat everything. Don't try to starve yourself." He stood, picked up the chair, folded it, and turned toward the door.

Proctor had planned on saying nothing at all. But now he changed his mind. "So—I assume the op was a success? You got what you wanted from the crocodile attaché case?"

The man stopped. "What was that?"

"Or was the woman your main object, and the case just a decoy?"

The man looked at him quizzically. "You must have hit your head harder than I realized," he said.

He let himself out; the door shut with a clang of steel, and Proctor heard the bolts shoot. A moment later, the lock on his ankle chain clicked off. He stood up, glad to be on his feet, and shuffled around the padded room, ankles loosely hobbled together with a steel cable and cuffs, but no longer attached to the wall. A few minutes later, dinner was slid in through a slightly raised section along the bottom edge of the door, on a cut-down cardboard tray with fold-out sleeves. It held a liter of water in a bottle on its side, a turkey sandwich, and Jell-O. There was no cutlery of any sort.

Proctor exhaled, staring at the food. He had little appetite and wondered at the emphasis the man had put on eating. But still more curious was genuine puzzlement the man had shown when reacting to his question. His abduction, it seemed, had nothing to do with EMT. Was it, perhaps, connected somehow to his past life?

But this seemed too odd, too complicated, too random. Any old enemies of Proctor would know better than to engage him like this—a double tap to the head would have sufficed. He went back over the interaction with his jailer, keeping this new understanding in mind. And as he did so, something began to dawn: the friendly, dead-looking eyes, the flat affect, the strange emphasis on food...

The person who had captured him was clinically insane.

PART TWO

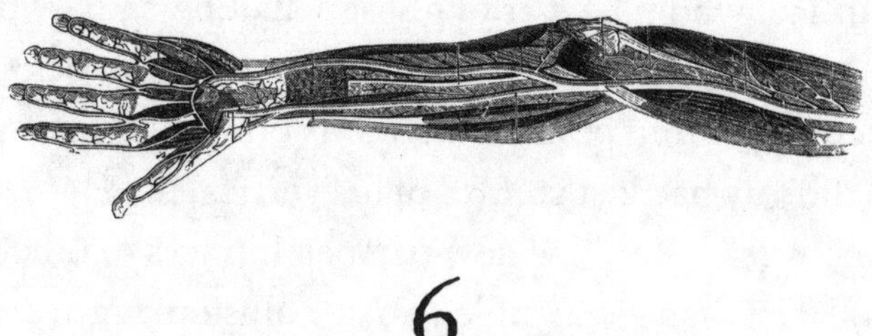

6

August 10, 1994

DWIGHT D. CHAMBERS PULLED his Impala SS into a free spot, put the vehicle in park, and sat for a moment staring at the building in front of him: a monolithic slab a dozen floors high, like a giant checkerboard stood on end. A quarter century earlier, this skinny piece of concrete—unvexed by architectural flourishes—had looked like the future. Now it just looked like a prison. A new building had broken ground across Pontchartrain Park, but chances were good he wouldn't be around to see it completed.

He unbuckled his seat belt as the news continued its background drone on the radio. He turned it up, hoping the blare would help drown his thoughts.

Strange how six months ago—a time when he'd been happy, when he'd enjoyed his work—now felt so far away. He'd never taken a supervisory path, being content to remain a field agent. New Orleans was low-key as far as FOs went. He had eighteen years under his belt and didn't mind the idea of another two, until he made his twenty.

Then his longtime partner and buddy, Fenton, got badly winged trying to stop a restaurant holdup while off duty. In return for his bravery, he'd been reassigned to a desk job in the Fed Building on Maestri Street. Chambers, who loved his partner like a brother, had been looking forward to a final two years of bad jokes and bourbon chicken wings. Now he was abruptly in line for a new partner, fast-tracked out of Quantico, whom he was to ghost. Chambers knew the FBI had relaxed some of its standards, but he'd met the new jack and wasn't sure he liked either him or his pretentions one bit. In fact, he was half convinced the guy had lost control of his vertical hold.

Then, one week before the new partnership was to officially begin, Chambers's wife had been killed in a collision with an eighteen-wheeler driven by a methed-up son of a bitch on I-610. And that had pretty much given him a fresh perspective on the entire fucking world.

He didn't remember much of the days that immediately followed. He had no kids or siblings, and his parents were dead. Only after she was gone and the numbness started to fade did he realize just how much of his life was invested in two things: Janice and his job. After losing her and reporting back to the office two weeks later to mentor his new partner, he learned that the second didn't matter much to him, either. Years of complex cases; the occasional close call; commendations—she'd been there with him every step of the way. They'd finally put the money together for the down payment on the Miramar Beach condo they planned for their retirement.

Now the thought of sitting in the surf alone, with broken dreams for company . . . no way.

He'd basically sleepwalked through the last two months. Instead of pulling his weight as senior agent and doing the mentoring thing, he gave his peculiar new partner his pick of cases to cull through on his own—he'd seemed particularly interested in a stale, six-years-cold case involving a freighter washing up in Bayou Grove with the entire crew dead—while the stack of paperwork on Chambers's own desk had grown higher and higher.

". . . meanwhile, the fallout from the genocide in the Central African nation of Rwanda continues to grow. President Clinton has stated—"

Chambers cut off the radio announcer in mid-sentence and forced himself out of the car and toward the checkerboard monstrosity, practically swimming through the heat. It was quarter to ten. He'd been an early riser all his life, but not anymore. Now, instead of sleeping, he sat in bed wide awake, service piece on one bedstand and a bottle of

Tanqueray on the other, trying to decide which way to go. So far, he'd chosen neither.

At first, a lot of his colleagues at the Bureau had been sympathetic. They told him it would get easier with time—which was, clearly, bullshit. But over the last several weeks, as his apathy showed no signs of dwindling, they'd started dropping by his office less and less often. He couldn't blame them; he was exhibiting all the signs of being—in FBI parlance—a "broke-dick."

Nothing had made this clearer than his reaction to the new assistant special agent in charge, installed just a month before Janice's accident: Gerald G. Urbanski. Chambers had seen his share of petty tyrants, but Urbanski took the cake. Estevez, the special agent in charge of the office, was a decent enough guy, but within a few years he was in line to be kicked upstairs to Washington. It was already clear Urbanski was gunning for his job. Urbanski was a tin Hitler, constantly issuing edicts for agents and administrative staff alike, usually concerning things that were glaringly obvious.

Estevez was no dummy; he had to realize what was going on, how morale was suffering, and what a dick the ASAC was. Chambers guessed he was simply unwilling to rock the boat so close to the shores of his own promotion. There was an old Bureau saying: *Better a prick on the most wanted than a prick with seniority.* But while the rest of the agents muttered around the watercooler, pining for the good old days, or gathered for gripe sessions after hours, Chambers just couldn't bring himself to give a shit. Just like he couldn't decide between the Glock or the gin.

He entered the building, passed through the sleepy security screening, and got on the elevator. He reached his floor, stepped out, and stopped. A fresh notice had been tacked to the Agony Board.

The "Agony Board," as it had quickly become known, was Urbanski's brilliant idea. He'd had it installed right outside the main investigative office a week after arriving, and he used it to post scoldings, mini-manifestos, or edicts for the edification of his subordinates.

Chambers stepped closer, idly squinting at the laser printing. He realized it was the same one Urbanski had put up the week before: the ASAC must really like his own prose, or perhaps he felt it hadn't been given the consideration it deserved, because he'd reprinted it on different-colored paper and stuck it up in place of the old one.

> The main FO of the NO division is looked up to by our six resident agencies, and the city of New Orleans itself, to maintain discipline and enforce its own strict codes of conduct. There are twelve separate parishes under our jurisdiction, and if we are not seen to act professionally, whether in the office or in the field, whether on duty or off, we will not command—or deserve—the respect necessary to do our jobs. Toward that end, internal assessments are authorized and in fact encouraged, as long as they do not compromise security or interfere with day-to-day operations of the field office. In short: all rules for conduct, security, and professionalism in its many aspects are to be strictly followed. This includes the stated guidelines for grooming...

Chambers stopped reading. It was, indeed, the same rant as the week before, except Urbanski had added the sentence about "internal assessments"—in other words, encouraging people to rat each other out.

He made his way into the crowded central office, desks lined with folders, the air thrumming to countless fingers hammering away at word processors. His own semi-private office was near the front entrance—good because it meant a short walk, bad because it put him near Urbanski and the man's loud, endless bullshit. Estevez, as SAC, had his own office down the hall and thus was spared.

Chambers was halfway through his office doorway, jacket already off, when he stopped. His new partner was not there—and by the looks of things, he hadn't clocked in yet. His desk was as neat as Chambers's was messy. He glanced at his watch: almost ten. Was he sick?

"Hey," sounded a voice behind him. "Where's your junior?"

Chambers glanced over. It was Win Malone, office wit and scourge of newly whelped agents.

"Good question," Chambers replied.

"Well, make sure he gets this." Malone dropped a sealed envelope on the chair by the empty desk. "It's for his scrapbook." And he chuckled cynically.

His laugh was cut short by the sounds of Urbanski's boisterous chatter coming from the direction of the elevators. Malone immediately made himself scarce. A minute later, the conquering hero appeared in person, accompanied by two gentlemen. Chambers recognized one immediately: T. J. Fulsom, president of New Orleans's second-largest bank and a big wheel around town, supposedly harboring mayoral aspirations. The other was a stranger: a plump man in a dark-blue Baracuta with prematurely graying hair, glasses thick as Coke bottles, and a straw hat so blue it would have made Bing Crosby envious. Chambers guessed he was a lawyer. The three stepped from the elevators into the lobby, accompanied by much camaraderie and backslapping.

"Fascinating, fascinating," the bank president was saying. "Clearly, our great city is in capable hands."

"Thank you, T. J.," Urbanski said as he gestured down the corridor. "If you'll please make yourself and your associate comfortable in my office. I'll be along in a moment." And as the banker headed down the hall in one direction, Urbanski went in the opposite direction, toward the evidence room, the armory, and most important, the john—where, no doubt, he planned to drain the main vein.

Chambers felt his lip curl. Urbanski had already made a practice of sucking up to bigwigs. He showered civic leaders, commissioners, and wealthy donors with FBI merchandise, courtesy cards, and especially private tours.

A couple of minutes later he came back into view, headed toward his office while simultaneously smoothing down the front of his jacket. As he passed the central workplace, he gazed over at the researchers and stenographers, his expression assuming a martial sternness. Chambers rolled around the doorframe and into his office to escape it.

Like all petty dictators, Urbanski was also a hypocrite. He knew tours of headquarters had to be vetted weeks in advance—and they were not supposed to include sensitive work areas.

Chambers hung up his jacket, sat down at his desk, turned on his Gateway 2000, and unlocked the drawers of his desk. He'd reached the GS-13 salary cap, netted a nice set of commendations over his years with the Criminal Investigative Division—but now that meant fuck-all. He pulled a three-and-a-half-inch floppy from a drawer and stuck it into the computer's empty drive. Since his wife's death, he'd been going through the motions of cleaning up the Shattered Shield case involving a dozen corrupt cops running a protection racket. The case had been so big, and generated so much paperwork, that it was easy to look busy. Staring at the amber letters on the dark screen was better than what awaited him later: a silent house full of memories, a frozen dinner—and then another night spent trying to decide between the Glock and the gin. The lady, he thought bitterly, or the tiger.

These musings were interrupted by a flurry of raised voices, so loud that all other conversation in the central office ceased. Chambers rose from his desk, leaving the floppy grinding away in its drive, and stuck his head out the door.

The same three men were again standing near the exit to the elevator bank: Urbanski, Fulsom, and the guy in the hat. But instead of engaging in courtly farewells, the ASAC seemed to be angry—very angry—with the man in the hat, gesticulating and making accusations while the man was busily taking photos with a Polaroid camera. It made no sense: Urbanski had invited these two into HQ to curry favor—not piss them off.

It didn't take long for Estevez, roused out of his office by the commotion, to appear. He stepped between the men. "What's going on here?" he shouted at Urbanski. Then he glanced around the office and its staring crowd. "All of you, get back to work."

Chambers had never heard Estevez raise his voice before. Neither had anyone else, it seemed, because the vast room went silent. But nobody went back to work.

"Sir, this, this *man*—" Urbanski, red-faced, gestured at the man in the blue hat— "has just made the most outrageous accusation..."

"Allow me," the man said in a strangely familiar voice, "to introduce a certain item of evidence into the conversation." With a movement so quick Chambers wasn't sure he'd seen it, the man darted his fingers into the suit jacket of T. J. Fulsom and whipped out a manila packet that had been tucked in an inside breast pocket.

"What the devil—!" Fulsom cried furiously, but fell silent as the blue-hatted man handed the packet to the SAC.

Estevez took it, his face a mixture of confusion and suspicion. "What's this?"

"Now that's in your possession," the blue-hatted man said, "I shall remove these thalian trappings and explain."

The man then proceeded, in his own sweet time, to remove first the hat, then the thick spectacles, and then a wig. He removed the windbreaker—which had been artificially padded—subtracting at least thirty pounds from his frame and revealing a black suit underneath. He then plucked a tissue from a box on a nearby desk and gave his face a quick swipe, revealing remarkably pale skin.

Chambers, recognizing the man, was stunned. This was not some mucky-muck New Orleans citizen after all...but his own partner. The man stood there, smiling faintly, his silvery eyes glittering in marked contrast to his somber black suit.

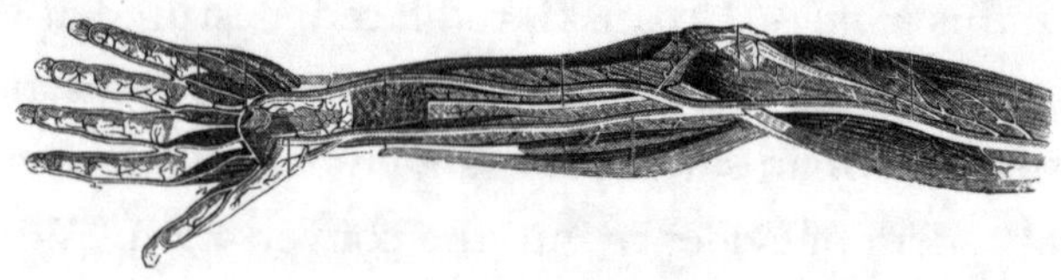

7

WHAT THE *HELL*?" URBANSKI raged, as surprised as anyone else. "That belongs to Mr. Fulsom!"

"Mr. Estevez, sir," came the honeyed drawl of Chambers's junior partner, "I would suggest examining the contents of that envelope in private."

"This is outrageous!" Urbanski cried, reaching for the envelope.

Estevez pulled it back and gave everyone a hard stare, which seemed to shut them all up. "All of you, in my office." And then, while the shocked silence still held, Estevez turned and looked at Chambers. "You too, Agent Chambers."

Then he walked briskly down the hallway.

"I protest this in the most vehement terms!" said Fulsom. Nevertheless, he and the others followed Estevez down the hall. Chambers threaded the maze of desks and followed in their wake, aware that all eyes were turned in their direction.

Estevez opened the door and ushered everyone in. He strode past his secretary to his inner office, the others following, and shut that door hard. Then he moved behind his desk and sat down. The rest remained standing, and he made no effort to invite them to sit.

"All right, Agent *Pendergast*," he said. "Mike Decker's a personal friend of mine, and he strongly recommended you—and with FBI star power like that, I'm going to give you a little slack here. But just a little. So before I apologize to one of our leading citizens, from whom you just snatched what looks like personal property, I'd like to hear your explanation."

"No explanation necessary," said Fulsom hastily. "I demand that it be returned to me."

"I wouldn't dream of denying Mr. Fulsom the opportunity to hear why I picked his pocket," said Pendergast. And with that he put his camera—a Polaroid 600 Impulse—on a nearby desk, along with its still-developing pictures.

Chambers had known from the jump his new partner played by his own rule book. He'd also heard rumors he had a guardian angel high up in the Bureau. But coming into the office in disguise like that, creating a bizarre spectacle in front of the entire CID—it made absolutely no sense, unless Pendergast was not just eccentric but crazy, and...

Pendergast turned to Estevez. "May I continue?"

"Just hurry up."

"Gladly. Agent Urbanski here," Pendergast resumed in a honeyed voice, "has made the vital point that security in this building is to be maintained at the highest level. In his latest posting he states, and I quote: *Internal assessments are authorized and in fact encouraged.* Or, to put it colloquially: snitch on your fellow workers if they stray."

"Get to it," Estevez said.

"In my admittedly short time here, I've noticed one particularly egregious lapse: Urbanski's penchant for bringing men and women of wealth or authority into this secure area for private tours. A clear violation of protocol."

"You little prick!" Urbanski began. "I have every right to bring important city officials in here—!"

"Quiet," Estevez said, eyes still on Pendergast. "Continue."

"Several evenings ago, while I was in the parking garage beneath the building, I happened to see a figure—whom I recognized as the distinguished Mr. Fulsom now standing before us—approach Agent Urbanski as he was getting into his car. From the body language, I gathered that our banker wanted something, perhaps a favor—and not necessarily an altruistic one. I managed to hear only the tail end of the hushed conversation, but enough to understand they would discuss the issue more fully at a restaurant in LaPlace at lunch the next day."

Urbanski stared at Pendergast, eyes narrowed, face the color of day-old liver.

"I was troubled by this conspiratorial exchange. And so, with Agent Urbanski's own admonitions regarding 'internal assessments' ringing in my head, I, too, went to LaPlace the next day, arriving at the rendezvous point a few minutes early—in the guise you saw just now—in order to have a few private words with Mr. Fulsom. I mentioned I'd overheard the discussion in the garage the night before. I told him that Urbanski was not a man to be trusted in such dealings; that I myself was an agent on the take and in disguise; and that if he let me pretend to be a shady lawyer employed in his service, I would see that—for a small cut—he got what he wanted. I hinted that repulsing my offer would not result in a good outcome for him. He accepted.

"Soon afterward, Urbanski joined us. Naturally, he did not recognize me, and he swallowed Fulsom's explanation that I was his attorney and must be part of the discussion. And then, over lunch, I learned of Mr. Fulsom's concern about Operation Pink Champagne."

This, Chambers knew, had been a sting operation the FBI had recently conducted in a French Quarter mansion involving sex traffickers, wealthy patrons, and underage prostitutes. Cameras had been installed, and female agents had impersonated ladies of the night.

"Sir!" Urbanski cried. "Are we really going to listen to this rookie talk such—!"

"Urbanski!" Estevez said sharply. "You'll get your turn. Now *stay quiet*."

Chambers could see Fulsom was white-faced, but at least he was smart enough to keep his mouth shut.

"Regarding Operation Pink Champagne, it seems Mr. Fulsom was on the premises the night before the raid. It was only after the raid that he learned about the cameras—and, according to rumor, one of the videotapes incriminated him. That videotape was duly deposited in our secure evidence room. For a consideration of fifty thousand dollars, Fulsom proposed to Special Agent Urbanski that, under the guise of a tour, he might retrieve said videotape and put the original into Fulsom's hands."

This is crazy, Chambers thought—*more than crazy.*

"You will find the videotape in that envelope," Pendergast said. "You will also find, among the pictures I took, the envelope being handed from Urbanski to Fulsom—I intentionally used a Polaroid so that the photos would develop in real time, and I could not be accused of doctoring them."

He fell silent. Urbanski and Fulsom were themselves mute, as stricken as statues.

Estevez, still holding the envelope, stared at Pendergast. "Let me get this straight. You undertook, on your own, without any authorization whatsoever, to set up a sting operation—right here, in my field office? Without letting me know? And then you *pickpocketed* this man?"

Pendergast said nothing.

"I'm not even sure I have the legal right to open this envelope. We don't have a warrant to search his person—and it was improperly obtained."

"Not so, sir," Pendergast said coolly. "We are in a high-security area on federal property, and I had direct evidence that a crime had been committed. If you check with legal, you will find that this evidence *was* properly obtained and will stand up in court. And of course, when you open that envelope you will find it is not his property, but the property of the FBI."

Estevez turned red. "You have some nerve, Pendergast. Pulling a stunt like this is bad enough—but not informing your superiors makes your actions unprecedented in all my experience."

Suddenly—without even realizing he was doing it—Chambers heard himself speak up. "Sir, before you say anything else, I think it's important to get the facts straight here."

Slowly, with the precision of a machine, Estevez's eyes swiveled toward him.

"You know my record, sir—and you know my service."

"Go on," said Estevez, his voice with a menacing undertone.

"Agent Pendergast and I discussed this sting operation. And I—I approved it."

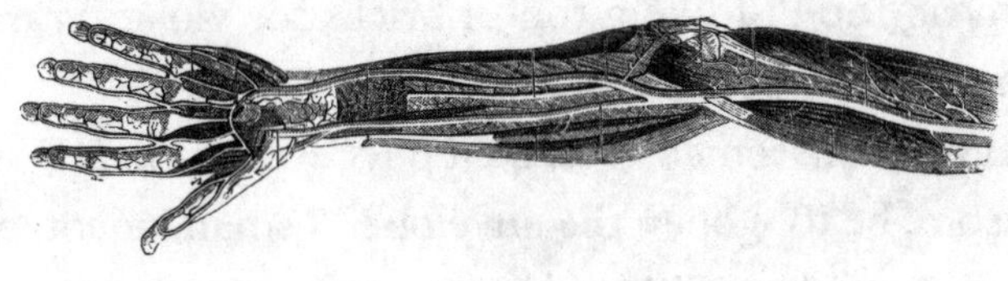

8

FROM THE CORNER OF his eye, Chambers saw Pendergast turn toward him and raise an eyebrow.

"Approved it?" Estevez asked. "Without my knowledge?"

"Sir, it's been pretty clear to all of us in the office that morale has been declining under ASAC Urbanski."

"You, of all people—talking to me of *morale*?"

Chambers felt his cheeks flame. "That's . . . exactly why I was afraid you'd veto it. Respectfully, sir, I do indeed have the authority as senior agent to authorize an operation like this."

Estevez stared at Chambers a long time. Chambers looked down, then up, then down again. It was impossible to read the FO head's expression.

Chambers hadn't intended to speak out or jump to Pendergast's defense like that. Half an hour ago, he hadn't given a shit about anything except whether he'd make it until tomorrow without offing himself. He hardly understood what he'd done, or why.

Pendergast spoke into the silence. "Perhaps it's time to open that envelope?"

Estevez looked at Pendergast, then Chambers, then at Urbanski and Fulsom.

"If you open that," Fulsom said, "I promise you, my attorneys will come down on the FBI like a ton of bricks for violating my privacy rights, assaulting my person, and taking my property."

That, perversely, seemed to make up Estevez's mind. With a nasty look at Fulsom, he tore open the envelope. A small videotape fell out, sealed in plastic, with an FBI evidence tag affixed to it.

In the freezing silence, Estevez calmly pressed a button, then spoke to his secretary in the outer office. "Would you send two agents in here, please—each with a set of handcuffs? There are two individuals to be taken into custody." He hung up and, in a low monotone, recited Miranda warnings to each man in turn. The two agents arrived just as he'd finished, and under his supervision—hardly able to restrain their own surprise—they put Fulsom and Urbanski in handcuffs and led them out.

Now Estevez turned his eyes back on Chambers and Pendergast.

"I'm senior partner, sir," Chambers said, doing his best not to babble. "I'm ghosting Agent Pendergast. Although I've admittedly been doing a piss-poor job of it, his actions are still my responsibility, and if there's any blame to go around here, it should fall on me. That's... well, that's all I wanted to say, sir."

Estevez looked at him with hooded eyes. Then he turned to Pendergast, almost as if Chambers had never spoken. "Decker's the reason I took you on. He's also the reason I assigned you to Chambers here. You don't fit the FBI mold—that's putting it politely—and Chambers is more open-minded than most around here. And he was a good agent... *once*."

There was an excruciating silence before Estevez continued.

"Maybe he can be one again." He took a breath; pondered a minute; took another. "Here's the deal. I know you have friends in high places. Decker told me that. He also told me you have a problem with authority. Well, as it turns out, *I* have a problem with insubordination. You ran this sting operation in *my* FO, under *my* nose, without *my* authorization. So what we now have on our hands is a *big—fucking—problem*."

Estevez pierced them each in turn with his eyes. "Pendergast, I don't care who your guardian angel is—this is *my* crib. Try another stunt like this and I'm not only pulling your badge and gun, but writing up a report even Mike Decker can't wipe clean. As for you, Chambers, I'd hate to see your illustrious career end in early termination—with prejudice. *Questions?*"

This closing word echoed loudly through the room with no response.

"In that case, both of you get the hell out."

Pendergast and Chambers began to turn.

"Shall I put Agent Pendergast on the Shattered Shield case with me, sir?" Chambers asked, thinking it better late than never to show some responsibility.

"I don't mean out of this office. I mean out of this *building*. Grab some rat-shit investigation that will take you both far out of town. I don't want to see either of your sorry asses in here for at least seven days. Take the time to get your attitudes straight. *Or! Else!*"

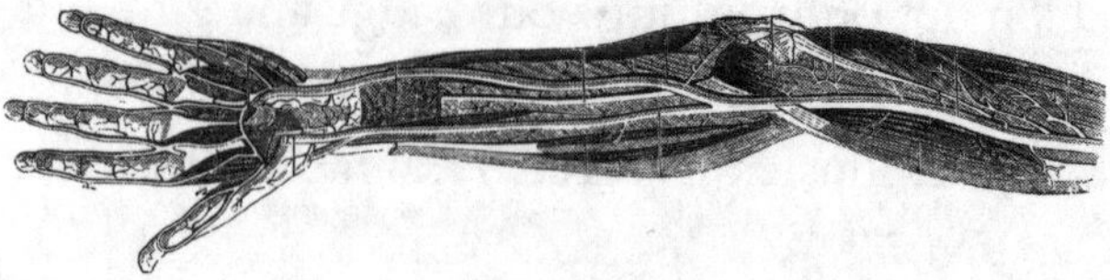

9

TEN MINUTES LATER, CHAMBERS found himself out on the street. He'd taken nothing with him except his jacket and briefcase. Pendergast, on the other hand, had spent several minutes sorting through items hidden in drawers beneath his spotless desk. Now they stood side by side outside the field office HQ.

"Where's your car?" Chambers asked.

"I, ah, have myself driven."

"What—you mean, taxi?" He was under the impression Pendergast lived way out somewhere in St. Charles Parish.

"No."

"O—kay." Chambers was struggling with what had just happened, and why he had done what he did, when he didn't particularly like Pendergast. It didn't take long for the stifling heat to render this struggle a secondary consideration. "Well, hell. Do you want to get a coffee somewhere?"

"I'd prefer tea."

"Fine. I know a breakfast joint that serves the best sweet tea in—"

"I'm sorry, Agent Chambers. I meant green tea."

Chambers, defeated, fell silent.

"I, too, know an excellent place—where both green tea and coffee can be served. If you wouldn't mind driving, I'll direct you."

Chambers didn't mind. As they approached his car, Pendergast slowed. "What an unusual shade of robin's-egg blue. It reminds me of a certain Magritte painting."

"*The Empire of Light*?" Chambers asked.

Now Pendergast stopped altogether. "That's correct," he said.

"Well, get in and I'll turn on the A/C. You must be melting in that black suit."

"Actually, the climate rather agrees with me."

"This is turning into a day of firsts." Chambers unlocked the car, threw his case in the back, slid into the seat with a grunt, and started the ignition.

They didn't speak much, Pendergast giving terse directions when needed. Merging onto I-90, they crossed the river, then ramped off into the Warehouse District. From there, they took local roads southwest through residential neighborhoods. During the drive, Chambers had a chance to sort out what had gone down that morning... and not just as it concerned his new partner. *Chambers, I'd hate to see your illustrious career end in early termination—with prejudice.* That was the last thing he'd expected to hear when he pulled into the parking lot that morning, moping as usual.

Moping. That label, or at least its self-administration, was unexpected, too.

"Pull in over here, if you please." Pendergast motioned to a free spot near the corner of Carondelet and Sixth Street in the Faubourg Delassize neighborhood.

Chambers slid the Impala into the parking space, then followed Pendergast half a block down Carondelet to what at first glance looked like a dry cleaner. The window facing the street was papered over with posters, the overhead sign was written in Chinese or maybe Japanese, and the storefront itself was so narrow, Chambers could almost gauge its width by stretching out his arms. But the place turned out to be a tea shop. There were several small tables arranged along one wall, and across was a counter behind which a dozen gleaming tin containers with lids were arranged, with slates above each on which were scribbled more characters. Nothing was written in English.

An Asian woman approached them, order pad in hand, and gave them a polite little bow. Pendergast nodded his head in return, then replied in some rapid-fire tongue. The woman smiled, wrote something on her pad, then turned to Chambers. "*Dozo?*" she said to him.

Pendergast regained her attention and spoke again, this time at greater length. The woman nodded, bowed again, and walked away.

"I had no idea you speak Chinese," Chambers said. "Were you stationed in Hong Kong or something?"

"Actually, that was Japanese," Pendergast replied. He'd brought his own briefcase with him when they left the car. "The Chinese population here is still rebounding from the Exclusion Act. To get better tea, you'd need to go to Chinatown in New York."

Chambers digested this as they sat down. The woman brought Pendergast's tea in an exquisite little teapot and cup.

"Um, and where's my coffee?" Chambers said, after the woman left.

"They're not quite as used to making coffee."

A brief pause.

"You're from around here, right?" Chambers asked. "Originally, I mean."

"My family had a house on Dauphine Street."

"No kidding. You're an honest-to-God local, then."

"I left New Orleans when I was sent off to boarding school, and the house no longer exists. However, I'm pleased to be back."

For some reason, Chambers felt himself wince. His numb disbelief was fading, but a strange discomfort was taking its place. "Look," he said, trying to push the feeling aside. "I've got to tell you: that was the craziest experience I've ever had as an FBI agent."

"I must admit to seeing things far crazier in my prior career."

Chambers figured this was true, given Pendergast's classified past in some esoteric military unit.

"I do, however, owe you an apology," Pendergast went on. "For being the instrument of that imbroglio, I mean. I also thank you most sincerely for your intervention on my behalf—which I did not expect."

Chambers nodded. Of course Pendergast hadn't expected him to lift a finger. Probably the same reason he'd taken on the assignment without guidance or assistance in the first place.

His coffee arrived and he took a hesitant sip. It tasted freshly ground, with a touch of cream and, he guessed, two sugars.

"This isn't bad at all—just the way I like it," he said, surprised.

Pendergast nodded. "I noted your preference in beverages. At the office, at least."

Chambers put down his cup. "The office..." He hesitated. "As long as we're on the subject, I think I'm the one who owes the bigger apology. Instead of mentoring you, I've basically thrown you into the deep end."

"The water's been pleasant enough. And you have my sympathies regarding the loss of your wife."

Chambers knew that as the supervising agent, he should maintain a certain reserve and keep his personal life to himself. But having just been thrown out of the office with his junior partner, there no longer seemed any point in keeping up appearances. Chambers wondered if Pendergast knew other agents were calling his mentor a broke-dick.

He drew in a ragged breath. Christ, here he was, drinking coffee in this hole-in-the-wall, having maybe just wrecked his career. And here, right on schedule, he could sense the return of that fog of depression through which he'd moved, zombie-like, for months.

"I hope you won't take offense," Pendergast said, "when I say that I saw you as a good agent who had suffered an insupportable tragedy in his life and couldn't cope—leaving me to operate on my own. Not a role that displeased me, to be honest. But I do have a personal question."

This candor was surprising enough to stave off—for now—the returning fog of depression. "Sure, what's the question?"

"I reviewed your record with Agent Decker when we were selecting the most agreeable posting for me. You're well educated in criminalistics, mathematics, and deviant psychology—but as far as I can tell, you displayed little interest in cultural disciplines."

"Go on."

"And yet just now, you rather offhandedly mentioned a painting by Magritte."

"That's thanks to my wife," Chambers said. "She taught art history and comparative lit at a private high school, and her father was the most well-read man I've ever met. I never saw her without a book or a palette and a brush in her hand." He shrugged. "I absorbed more from her than I realized... until she was gone."

Pendergast remained silent.

"That Impala outside—it was to be hers. Magritte was her favorite artist, and *The Empire of Light* her favorite set of paintings. That's why I bought the car to surprise her. I'd taken possession, driven it home, and was waiting for her—when I got a call from the hospital."

Pendergast said nothing—for which Chambers was grateful. He took in another shallow, shuddering breath, then let it out slowly. His head ached, and he felt drained of emotion. Despite this, he forced himself to lean into the silence. "How did you know to target Urbanski like that?"

"A most unpleasant fellow. Those edicts, posted in the lobby like stone tablets from God, urging us to inform on our own, were a disgrace."

"I don't mean that. I know he's an asshole—but how did you sense he was crooked?"

After a long silence, Pendergast said, "There are some things I just *know*. There's no simple way to put it. I'm... still learning to act properly on them, rather than question their source." And he took another sip of tea.

Chambers sat back. He knew Pendergast wasn't going to give him any more. At least not now.

He took one more breath—tentative, but deep this time. There was no denying it: the fog of melancholy and grief that usually hung over him was, for the moment anyway, keeping its distance. Still, here he was: set adrift for his sins, with this strange new agent he was supposed to mentor—although it felt more like he was the mentee and this ivory-skinned man his mentor.

Pendergast, meanwhile, had picked up his briefcase and removed an envelope.

"What's that?" Chambers asked.

"This," said Pendergast, "is what Agent Malone left on my chair. He said it was for my scrapbook. Shall we see what it is?" A small knife suddenly appeared in his hand, and he slit the envelope open.

"Thoughtful of him," Pendergast murmured as he drew out the contents: a recent newspaper article, folded up.

Every agent had some kind of hobby during off hours. Some collected firearms. Another kept bees. Chambers wondered if Pendergast really did keep a scrapbook full of juicy clippings, like Malone had told him, or if the guy was just having fun with a new jack.

"Unsolved murder in Diamondhead, Mississippi," Pendergast said, perusing the article. "Brutal, bizarre. Victim from Louisiana—"

"Pendergast?" Chambers interrupted.

The pale figure looked up.

"I hate to interrupt, but what the hell are we going to do now? I don't exactly feel like going home. Any suggestions?"

Silently, Pendergast raised the article, letting it dangle between his fingers. "What was it Estevez told us to do? *Grab some rat-shit investigation*, is how I believe he phrased it." He gave the article a little shake.

After a moment, Chambers cleared his throat. "Diamondhead?"

"The body was discovered there early yesterday morning."

"That's only sixty miles away."

A nod.

"And the cross-border issues allow us to claim it's federal."

Pendergast nodded again.

"And you have no problem with my being in charge."

"I should insist upon it."

"Then let's go." Chambers stood up. "You can tell me what's in the article on the way."

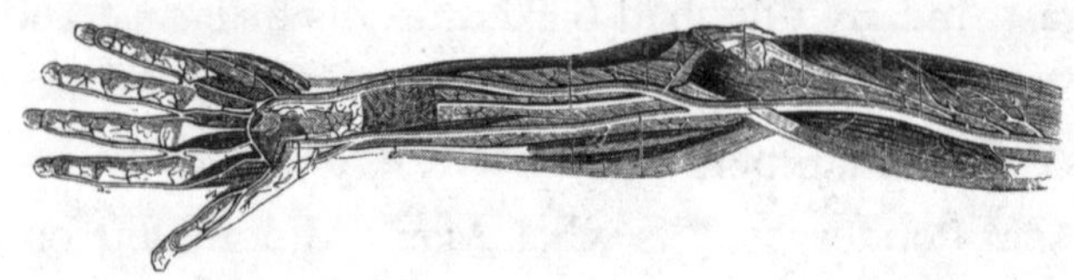

10

THEY HEADED EAST OUT of town, past Bayou Sauvage and over the Twin Span Bridge, making for the Mississippi line. Chambers concentrated on driving while Pendergast silently read the clipping. Finally, he stirred.

"The body was found in a storage facility," he said in his lazy drawl. "About three o'clock yesterday morning. The place employed a watchman during the overnight hours, and during his patrols he noticed one of the steel doors wasn't closed properly—and seemed to be emitting an unpleasant odor."

"I've seen people rent those places for everything from practicing their drums to balling the neighbor's wife. Keep going."

"A man was found dead and mutilated within that storage room—possibly vivisected."

"You mean, cut up while still alive?"

"Perimortem—at the time of death, either right before or after. One arm was amputated."

"Nice." Chambers focused once again on his driving. Had this been a day earlier, he'd have been tempted to drive the car over the embankment and into the Mississippi. But driving to a crime scene like this, he was beginning to feel like a human being again instead of a walking corpse.

"That is an impressive swamp, even for Mississippi," Pendergast said. They'd just crossed the river, and below them spread an apparently endless swamp filled with water lettuce and alligator weed, punctuated by enormous, ancient cypress and mangrove trees. Spanish moss hanging from the spreading canopy formed a kind of eternal twilight beneath the massive trunks.

"You never heard of the Grand-Morte Swamp?"

"Ah. The famous Ghost Swamp," Pendergast said, using its local name.

"So you do know it."

"I know *of* it. My family didn't spend much time east of the Pontchartrain... as a rule."

East of the Pontchartrain. Sounded like typical old-money family, to go with his upper-class accent. "Then you at least know it's the most haunted swamp in the state—and that's saying something. Used to be a little town down there called Frenier. Nothing special, just a bunch of pirogue-paddling, crawfish-eating huckleberries... and a Creole priestess by the name of Julie Brown. She cursed the town back in 1921, in the midst of a hurricane. She went down with the rest of the place, cursing and chanting voodoo songs. And her body glowed as yellow as the moon, people say, before she sank beneath the wind and waves."

"Fascinating. Or perhaps she simply chose to end her own life, rather than let nature's violence do it for her."

"What are you talking about?"

"Ingesting match heads laden with phosphorus was a common form of suicide in the 1920s. It tended to give the victim's intestines a rather ghostly glow—along with 'smoking-stool syndrome,' which—"

"I get the picture, thanks."

A pause. "Have you ever been in there?"

"Me? Hell, no."

"But you believe in the curse."

"I didn't say that."

"No—you didn't. So perhaps you're more like Edith Wharton."

"Who?"

"A novelist known for her depictions of America's gilded age. She once said: *I don't believe in ghosts . . . but I'm afraid of them.*" And, settling back in his seat, Pendergast took his gaze away from the window.

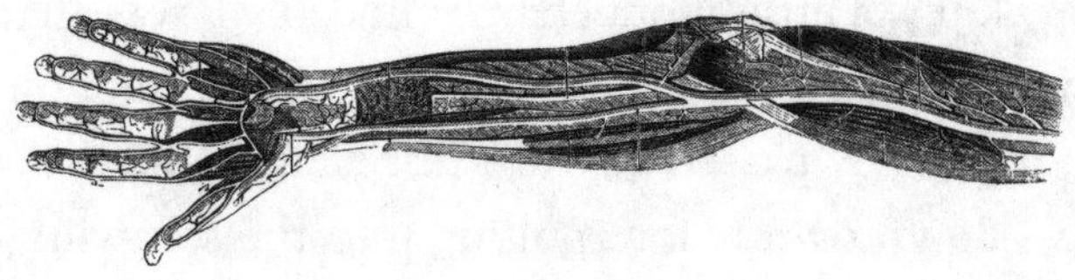

11

WHILE CHAMBERS DROVE, PENDERGAST radioed ahead to local Diamondhead law enforcement, informing them the two were inbound to find out more about the murder. The body was in the sheriff's morgue at Diamondhead, and Pendergast arranged to examine the body with the officer of record present.

As they crossed from Louisiana into Mississippi, the land grew increasingly lonesome and swampy. This, Chambers knew, was an area that flooded after any decent downpour. He'd seen water moccasins and even saltwater crocodiles crossing vacant swaths of land like this—if you could call a place that seemed in fragile balance between solid and liquid "land." What always surprised him was the number of abandoned buildings that littered old, rarely traveled roads like this—ancient gas stations with glass bulbs atop their pumps; small warehouses, their signage too old and faded to see, collapsing in on themselves; and most commonly, ancient tiny houses or cabins. These were often set back from the road and barely visible. Others, however, were right up near the shoulder: stinking of goofer dust and other hoodoo wards that kept off the evil eye, their entire facades covered in green masks of tree-of-heaven, Chinese wisteria, or other invasive vines. Locally, they were known as "shantybellum" houses. People had lived here, albeit sparsely, at one time—but that time was long past, and with the Gulf fast encroaching, they never would again.

Chambers knew a little about Diamondhead—it was an unincorporated town overlooking Rotten Bayou, the highest point on Mississippi's Gulf Coast. They passed a NASA test facility and drove through an attractive downtown before pulling into the sprawling lot of the sheriff's department of southern Hancock County. A deputy named Willis—a tall, rangy African American with an infectious smile—met them in the waiting area and escorted them into a conference room.

They all took seats. Willis looked at them in turn. "How can I help you gentlemen, exactly?" he asked: polite police code for *Why the hell is the FBI interested in this?*

Chambers glanced at Pendergast. In the car, they'd agreed on proceeding in the traditional FBI mentor-ghosting relationship. Pendergast would take the lead; Chambers would, for the most part, only intervene if something was overlooked or he saw Pendergast going off the rails.

"It's in the manner of a routine inquiry," Pendergast said, laying his New Orleans accent on thick. "Our SAC told us to look into this case—"

At this, Chambers had to smile inwardly.

"—and here we are."

Willis laughed and shook his head. "Yeah. I get it. So let me know how I can fill you in before I show you the body."

Pendergast got out a small pad of paper and a gold pen. "The newspaper mentioned the deceased was taken hostage in Louisiana and brought here. How do you know that?"

At the mention of newspapers, Willis made a face. "The body was discovered at the storage place around three AM the night before last. Nude. Recovered at the scene was some torn and bloody clothing and a hospital gown. Basically, we got lucky: three nights earlier, two girls had been driving along Chef Menteur Highway, near where it crosses the Old Pearl River. They were in a late-model Civic, 1992. It was a dark night. The only thing within miles of there is an airboat rental or two. Anyway, around eleven PM on the night of August 5 they see a white van pulled over on the shoulder, angled sharply, as if it had stopped in a hurry. Rear doors ajar. They were slowing down to pass when, out of nowhere, this guy runs out of the swamp and crosses the road. He was wearing a green hospital gown, and their description matches the one found by the body. A moment later, another guy comes out of the dark, chasing the first guy down. He was wearing black pants with a black sweatshirt, hood pulled up. He caught the guy at the far shoulder, then manhandled him up and into the back of the van. Then he turned toward the Civic and started pulling something from the pocket of his hoodie. At that point, the girls put the hammer down and hauled ass out of there."

"And then they reported this to the police?"

"Let me go pull the file." Willis was gone only a few minutes. "Not until they got home to Pearlington. Hardly any pay phones, gas stations, or anything along that stretch. First thing the next morning, I went down and interviewed them at the Pearlington station."

"Did they provide a description of the men or the vehicle?"

"Even after they'd had time to calm down, they remained too freaked out to remember much. It was a white panel van, dinged up. The kind you see everywhere. No rear windows. Like I said, it was dark, and the license plate was obscured by mud, but one of the girls thought it was a Louisiana plate."

"And the men?"

"The pursuer was big and fast. That's all they could say. From the description of how he tackled and dragged the gowned guy into the van, we think he was probably pretty young and in decent shape. They got a better glimpse of the victim who'd escaped the van—cropped hair, seven-day beard, dirty, ass shining in their headlights as he was manhandled across the road, hospital gown flapping." Willis paused. "You can listen to the 911 call, and I've got a tape of the next morning's interview here." He patted a VHS cassette.

"I assume you have an APB on any white van matching the description?"

"We've already stopped a dozen since then. No joy."

"Have you identified the person renting that storage unit?"

"We're working on it. It appears to have been rented under a false name and address, paid in cash."

"Which way was the man running?" Chambers asked.

"North. Toward Bayou Malheur."

When there were no more questions, Willis played the 911 call and showed them the taped interview. It was pretty much as the deputy had described: two pale-looking girls with trembling voices repeating, "I dunno," "It was dark," "Out the rear of the van," and "Can't remember."

Willis passed the folder across the table: the case file of the murder. It was thin—not surprising for a case only a few days old. That would change, Chambers thought. He'd seen cases that had metastasized from thin folders like this to stacks requiring a bookcase to accommodate them.

The photos of the scene were typical CSI shots, well framed and lit. The storage unit was small and relatively bare, save for a metal table in its center. The nude body of a man was sprawled across it, eyes and mouth wide. The right arm had been severed and was lying on the ground next to the table, badly slashed. There was surprisingly little blood . . . until, looking closer, Chambers noticed a tourniquet tied off just above the amputation.

"Killed by asphyxiation," Willis said. "The cord is buried in the flesh of his neck; you can get a better view in the coroner's photos."

"Got an ID?" Chambers asked.

"Kenneth Drakos, thirty-two, hotel manager from Bogalusa. Reported missing by his wife just over a week ago." Willis paused. "I can save you a little time here: no enemies, no debts, no drugs, no record. Two young kids."

A brief silence settled over the conference room. Then Chambers pushed his chair back. "I guess it's time to meet him. Thank you, Deputy, for such a professional and thorough backgrounder."

* * *

All morgues stank in more or less the same way; the one in Diamondhead was no exception. The coroner was waiting for them, and he opened the locker containing Drakos, pulled it out to full extension, then unwrapped the body with fussy precision.

"With the autopsy complete and death certificate expedited, the family is picking up the remains tomorrow morning," the coroner said. "If you want to gawk, now's the time."

Chambers gave the corpse a thorough look, running through the mental punch list he'd assembled over years of examining stiffs, both fresh and otherwise. The head, with its bulging eyeballs and black tongue—the latter protruding, like an unsmoked Montecristo, straight up from the throat—was typical of strangled victims. The coroner had placed the severed arm next to the body, and for whatever reason the killer seemed to have paid it the most attention—it was sliced, stabbed, and chopped like a fencing dummy. The coroner believed it had been amputated perimortem. Aside from innumerable scratches—from the chase, probably—the rest of the body was in good condition, considering it had probably been ripening in the heat of the storage facility for about four days.

This was enough for Chambers. Not, it seemed, for Pendergast. To the senior agent's surprise, the man asked for a pair of nitrile gloves. Then he whipped a magnifying glass from a pocket of his black suit and spent a quarter of an hour examining the body, paying minute attention to the severed portion of the amputated arm, particularly the site of the incision itself. This went on so long that Deputy Willis grew visibly restless. Chambers himself began to grow irritated at what increasingly felt more like a Sherlockian performative stunt than an actual examination.

He cleared his throat. "Thank you, gentlemen, for your assistance and patience. Deputy, if you'd be so kind as to get us copies of the photographs and the CSI reports, we'll get out of your hair."

Pendergast halted his examination. "Forgive me," he said smoothly, "for detaining you inconveniently."

By the time they were out of Diamondhead and headed back toward NOLA, it was quarter to four. The relief Chambers had felt from the series of distractions began to give way to dread over the night ahead. Trying to shake this away, he turned toward Pendergast, who had said little since seeing the body.

"Nice work back there questioning Willis, covering the bases," Chambers said, trying to assume the mentor role. "Feels like you've done that before."

"I have."

"I was under the impression you'd never worked in law enforcement."

"I haven't." A pause. "It was field experience."

"What kind of field experience?" Chambers couldn't help asking.

For a moment, Pendergast—seemingly lost in thought—did not respond. Then he looked over, the ice-blue quality of his eyes startling no matter how many times Chambers saw them. "In a past life," he said simply.

"Right," said Chambers. "Anyway, now that we've heard about the crime and examined the body, I'd like to hear your conclusions—if any."

"I'm still a child in these matters," came the reply. "So if my conclusions are rather humble, I hope you'll understand."

"I won't laugh—scout's honor."

"Very well. This person has killed before, probably many times. He has some money. He may have been in the armed forces, where he worked as a medic and had surgical experience. He has a safe house or similar refuge for his work. He is certainly psychotic, yet he derives little pleasure from the act of killing itself—the usual motives, such as the need to dominate or control, or impulsivity, are absent here."

Chambers was astonished at the conviction with which this litany was delivered. "Mind explaining to me how you arrived at all those conclusions?"

"Not at all. The main point, however, is they all lead back to a fundamental mystery."

"Which is?"

There was a bump as they joined the causeway that rose in a graceful curve over the Mississippi.

"What would motivate a person to amputate a limb with great skill and care—and then use the same surgical tools to slash that limb to shreds? That is something—to invoke Shakespeare—not dreamt of in my philosophy."

Chambers pondered this. "And your other conclusions?"

"He killed by garroting and tied off the arm—in both cases, presumably to prevent exsanguination. That implies he had a reason to keep the victim alive until the last moment. Considerable microsurgical expertise was displayed in the amputation, especially in the way the major arteries and nerves were dissected out and tied off. Our killer has performed this operation a number of times before; hence my conclusion he has killed many times before. He is therefore psychotic *res ipsa loquitor.* This killer has money enough to conduct his business, which is expensive and time consuming. Again, a safe house or other refuge would be a necessary adjunct. My guess that he was in the military is based on his high fitness level, self-confidence, and size. The killing was quick, efficient, and humane—if you will forgive that word—and there were no signs of torture. Hence my conclusion that the killer derived little or no pleasure from the act of murder. The killing was, rather, a means to end; a furtherance of his business."

"You talk about the killer's 'business.' What business is this?"

A cold smile gathered on the pale man's face. "*That*, Agent Chambers, is the fundamental mystery."

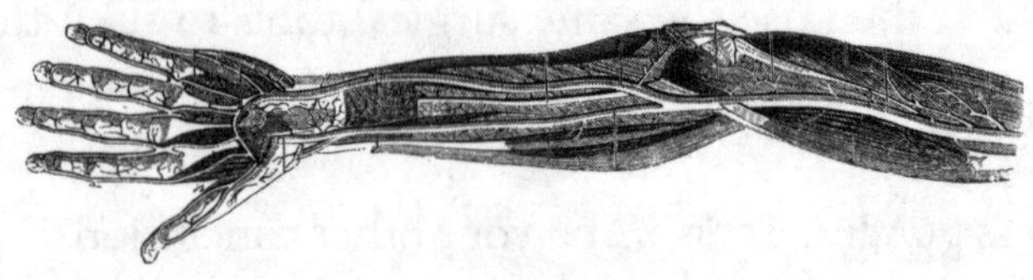

12

Before the lights snapped off and the room was once more plunged into darkness, Proctor had finished his meal. He had no intention of starving himself; on the contrary, he knew that now, of all times, he needed to keep up his strength.

Proctor did not feel afraid. He had witnessed things over the last decade to render fear in a situation like this both superfluous and counterproductive. The central problem now was the identity of his captor—and why he'd been kidnapped.

He used the brief period of light to give his surroundings exceedingly precise scrutiny. His captor was not just insane, but insanely cautious: he could see no flaw in the room's security, nothing that might be useful as a weapon.

When the room fell again into sudden blackness, he put the food tray back into the slot, retaining the water bottle for later use. He closed his eyes, clearing his mind with a series of mental exercises. And then he stood up—mindful of limbs that ached from lack of movement; careful not to let the blackness, or his cuffed hands, confuse his sense of balance.

He walked back and forth for a while on his hobbled feet. He squatted down, testing his cuffs once again. No possibilities there. Then he spent an hour on his hands and knees, familiarizing himself with the cell: crawling along one wall, then another, to the piss-drain—which he used—then completing the circuit of the room. He did this several more times. Then he tried crossing the middle of the room diagonally, aiming for the opposite corner in the dark: first slowly, then more quickly, until he had gained a proprioceptive sense of the dimensions of the room and his place in it. He'd used the light to estimate the room's size, and now he used the blackness to practice crossing it at speed, low to the ground and from various angles. It seemed unlikely he'd be given a chance, but this was his best shot at catching his enemy in the dark.

His enemy. Funny how quickly the old mindset returned to him.

He went back to his original position. He did a vigorous round of push-ups, sit-ups, and calisthenics, then leaned against the wall. He estimated three hours had passed since the lights went off, but keeping track of time wasn't a concern—his captor had made it clear he'd be fed at regular intervals, and for now that was enough.

He moved on to considering the situation from a larger perspective. He was clearly in a basement room—many things, including the musty, humid smell, made this evident. This argued for him having been moved inland, above sea level, or perhaps on a geological ridge such as where the French Quarter had been built. He was not the first to have been imprisoned here—the smell of stale urine and other, faint human scents made that obvious. More revealing was his abductor's evident prior experience with captives. The man's efficiency and the advice not to starve himself—everything argued that a former tenant, or tenants, of this padded hellhole had refused to eat, made noise, tried to escape, perhaps pissed and shit themselves. His foe had learned from them, and Proctor was now the unfortunate beneficiary of that experience.

He briefly considered the fate of those former tenants, and the conclusion was not pretty.

The man was clearly a sociopath—the way he'd come into the garage in his uniform, smiling, completely at ease: Proctor would have detected any scent of deception. But there had been none. And the quick, efficient way he'd incapacitated Proctor, of all people, implied experience with kidnapping—perhaps a lot of experience.

Beyond that, though, Proctor could not determine a precise motive. If his captor was a serial killer, which seemed increasingly likely, he did not fit the MO of any Proctor had heard of. Also disquieting was how intently the man had looked him over during their interaction—not his face so much as the rest of him, particularly his right arm, bared as it was by the hospital smock. It was as if the man was sizing him up for something.

He had neither the information nor sufficient observations to make a more informed judgment. He'd done all he could for the present, and he should probably rest. He shifted into a prone position, twisted his hands to a spot where the zip ties felt least bothersome—and then, after taking a deep breath, began relaxing the muscles of his face, followed by those of his shoulders, biceps, forearms, thighs, and calves: first the left side, then the right.

He was asleep before the next step—clearing his mind—was even necessary.

⋆ ⋆ ⋆

He was woken by the ceiling lights, turning night into day. He sat up, muscles tense, ready to take advantage of any opening. He heard the voice of his captor through the small slot at the bottom of the door.

"You ate everything," he said. "Good. And you've rested. I'm glad you're intelligent enough to accept your situation and not waste energy screaming or attempting to harm yourself. As a result, I think you'll find today's meal a lot more appetizing."

There'll be little reason to speak again—so he'd said when he entered the room. Nevertheless, he was speaking now, and Proctor saw no reason to interrupt. The smell of roasted meat reached his nostrils.

"Please put the tray and your trash back beneath the door once you've finished your meal."

A tray of food appeared. "See?" came the voice. "I promised you would eat well."

Wrapped in thin waxed paper was a pound of filet, cubed and grilled. In the other cardboard compartments were boiled carrots, folded pancakes, and more Jell-O. There was significantly more food this time, with another bottle of water.

"Since you ate everything and haven't made a nuisance, what I've brought you today is not only more palatable but more ample," he said.

Proctor thought to himself that the man liked to talk. That was one weakness.

"You'll also find a multivitamin and a couple of amoxicillin tablets in the food container," the man said. "After eating, you will swallow the pills with some water. They aren't really necessary—the antibiotic is just a precautionary measure—but if you don't take them, I will have to punish you."

Proctor did not respond. He simply looked at the food—which was indeed ample and prepared with care. Unusual care. And now a grim thought entered his head. The way the man had looked him over with an almost slavering expression; this insistence on eating well and staying healthy—these hinted to Proctor at the fate his abductor had in mind for him.

"You're a strange fellow," his captor said. "Other than that nonsense about the crocodile attaché case, you've remained quiet. You don't plead. You haven't offered me the PIN code for your ATM card. You don't even ask questions."

Proctor didn't reply.

"Fifteen minutes," the man said. "Enjoy your dinner!"

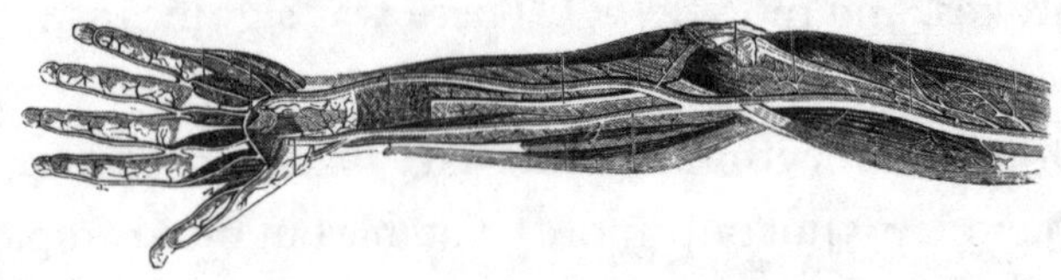

13

Chambers spent a miserable night. He found the silence and memories that greeted him when he got home almost overwhelming. The day had been... unique in his experience. His impulsive "confession" to Estevez, imaginative but false; getting reamed out and banished from the office; taking on a crappy case that, on closer look, turned out to be slightly less crappy than expected. But the fact was there had been periods when he'd almost forgotten his fierce anguish. Although he kept the bottle of gin uncracked on one bedside table, this night his sidearm had slept locked away in the drawer.

He lay awake as the world brightened outside his bedroom windows, the sun rising at last. He showered, dressed, and shaved, wondering what this day would bring. *Dreading* was probably a better word. His mind wandered over to the man with the amputated arm, and Pendergast's seemingly extrasensory deductions. What a strange guy he was.

He heard the doorbell. Hastily washing the foam from his face, he trotted downstairs and opened the front door—to find a uniformed man standing there, cap in hand.

"Agent Chambers?" the man asked.

For a brief moment, Chambers wondered if the OPR—the Bureau's version of Internal Affairs—had sent over a flying squad to bring him in. But the cut of the man's uniform and his deferential attitude made this obviously paranoid. He glanced out at his driveway and saw the gleaming outline of a vintage Rolls-Royce.

The man was a chauffeur.

"What do you want?" Chambers asked.

"Begging your pardon, sir, but Mr. Pendergast sent me."

"He what?"

"He sent me to bring you to his residence. He asked me to tell—to *suggest* to you that it might be a convenient location to continue the work you began yesterday."

"He sent a Rolls?"

"Yes, sir."

Chambers did his best to conceal his surprise. This was strange. But hell, it beat sitting at home with his demons.

"Give me a moment, please," he told the man.

Ten minutes later, the long, gleaming machine was turning heads as it glided through the suburban sprawl north of New Orleans. Chambers, practically drowning in the soft rich leather of the rear seat, was taken aback by the opulence of the interior: the retractable drinks setup in book-matched burlwood, the crystal decanters of expensive liquor, the ashtray, the hinges and trim plated in gold.

The car soon emerged from the crowded streets and entered the sleepy byways of St. Charles Parish, where the trees hung thick with Spanish moss and ancient mansions could be glimpsed past ancient tree trunks, set among dark bayous and old, private family cemeteries, where the stones lay at angles and moss hid forgotten names. Then the Rolls made a turn into a long, white-graveled lane—lined with black oaks—that led to a pillared plantation house. Two trucks, with blue IBM logos and the words GLOBAL RESOURCES AND SOLUTIONS on their sides, were parked before the covered porch: one had a huge dish antenna on its roof, and several thick black cables snaked from the other, up the front steps and into the house. They looked anachronistic in this placid antebellum setting.

The chauffeur parked, got out, and opened the door for Chambers. He had barely made it up the steps before the entrance opened. The slender figure of Pendergast—pale as a ghost and dressed, as always, in a tailored black suit—greeted him.

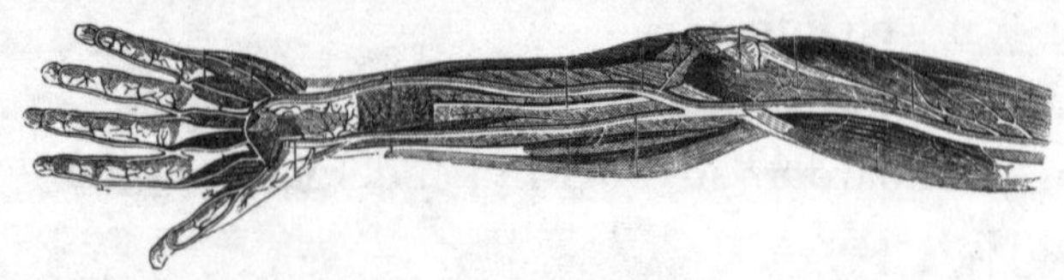

14

WELCOME TO PENUMBRA PLANTATION," Pendergast said. "And thank you for coming."

Chambers tried to tamp down his mingled confusion and astonishment. So his hunch had been true: the guy was old-money rich. Unusual for an FBI agent, but no big deal—beyond the inevitable black suit and other personal eccentricities.

"I wasn't sure I had a choice," Chambers said, mustering a grin. "Besides, how could I resist taking a ride in *that*?" And he jerked a thumb toward the Rolls.

"Ah, yes. My 1959 Silver Wraith. Some consider it ostentatious, but frankly I don't give a damn—I find its capaciousness most agreeable."

"Pardon my asking," Chambers said as Pendergast ushered him into a reception area redolent of furniture polish and cedarwood, "but are we really going to take on that case? I thought we went there on a lark, more or less."

"Indeed we did. But the body we examined yesterday—and the circumstances surrounding it—piqued my curiosity."

"Okay."

Pendergast paused. "Do you feel my interest to be misplaced?"

"No."

"Were you at all intrigued?"

"Yes. Sort of." The fact was, Chambers felt grateful for anything that got him out of the house. And he reminded himself he was supposed to be mentoring a new agent, and this was a fine opportunity to do that.

"Nice place you got here," he added, trying hard not to sound sarcastic.

"It's been in the family a long time."

"So if we do take on the case, where's our base going to be? We can't go back to the office, and we don't have access to the central archives."

"Right here." Pendergast pointed to the thick cabling at their feet. "Follow me."

Chambers followed the agent through a dazzling drawing room and into a large den, where he was astonished to see three technicians—IBM identification cards dangling from lanyards around their necks—laboring over several personal computers set up at temporary workstations.

"My old colleague Mike Decker happened to call last night, and we got to chatting about that body in the storage unit. I won't bore you with the details, but the upshot was he considered it worth pursuing—for a week, at least—and said that, if I paid for the necessary T-1 line and computing equipment, he would arrange access to the FBI databases from my private saloon here. I hope you agree, Agent Chambers, that we will be comfortable?"

"No doubt."

This was an eye-opener, and no mistake. Chambers remembered what Pendergast had said yesterday: *I reviewed your record with Agent Decker when we were selecting the most agreeable posting for me.* At the time, the sentence construction had struck him as odd, as if Pendergast was doing the picking instead of the other way around. He again wondered about Pendergast's background and just what kind of pull he had with the Bureau. During Chambers's long fog of mourning, Pendergast had done nothing to demonstrate he was a favored son. He went about his work with initiative, it was true, even in the absence of direction. And Estevez *had* been uncharacteristically evasive when he'd briefed Chambers on his new partner...

The voice of a technician roused him. "We're all finished here, Mr. Pendergast, sir."

"Excellent, most excellent. Let us just make sure." Pendergast made a tour around the table, examining the screens of the three computers whose hulking CPU towers were sitting beside them on the table, humming loudly. Chambers noticed all three screens currently displayed the sign-on screen used by the FBI's investigative staff.

Finishing his circuit, Pendergast nodded to the men. "Thank you. Will I be able to reach you if there's any problem?"

"These Server 85s are top-flight, and your T-1 data stream is holding steady at one megabit per second, plus," said the person who seemed the lead tech.

"I take it that is a good thing."

The tech dipped a hand into his jacket and pulled out a card. "I'll stop by in the afternoon to see if any troubleshooting needs to be done. Meanwhile, if you experience any difficulty, call the number on that card—they'll be able to get in touch with me immediately."

"Thank you kindly."

As if summoned by magic, a figure dressed in an old-fashioned but natty suit—apparently a butler or other manservant—appeared to usher the three out. A minute later, the man returned. He was thin and elegant and ageless. "Anything to drink, gentlemen?" he asked.

"Lemonade, if you please, Maurice," said Pendergast.

"I'll have the same," said Chambers.

As Maurice left, Pendergast beckoned Chambers to a seat. "Shall we try this out? Those technicians told me the computers are running OS/2 Warp—which puts me in mind of a certain vulgarism in ancient Greek—but as you heard, they assured me we should encounter no problems."

Chambers sat down at the proffered seat, then entered his credentials and password at the log-in screen. It came up with the menu he was intimately familiar with. He entered a few commands.

"Seems responsive enough."

Pendergast took a seat beside him. "The murder we examined

yesterday was, as I said, not the killer's first. I hoped that combing our databases of unsolved homicides might turn up some leads to confirm this speculation."

Chambers nodded slowly. In all honesty, he hadn't given the case much thought since the night before. But now his brain began to churn. "If this is a serial killer, we don't have enough information to understand his MO. Is garroting people his bag? Or is it hacking off limbs? Leaving bodies in storage units? We'll need to cast a wide net here."

Pendergast nodded—after waiting just long enough to make Chambers curious. "How shall we proceed?"

"You tell me, Agent Pendergast," Chambers said as Maurice returned with their lemonades. "I'm mentoring you. Tell me what you think the next steps are."

"Very well, then." Pendergast, it seemed, already had an idea in mind. "Such predators usually strike in territory they know, where they feel comfortable—usually a radius of five to thirty miles. I'd suggest we cast our net over such a range, with its center at the place the two girls witnessed the victim. Where Chef Menteur Highway crosses the Old Pearl River. Or perhaps the storage unit should be the center point?"

Chambers smiled. "You choose."

"Let's do both."

"And what filters will you be using?" Chambers asked. He was starting to enjoy this.

"Any unsolved homicides involving cutting, mutilation, or amputation."

"Going back how far?"

"On that point, Agent Chambers, I really must defer to you."

"Let's try five years. If this is a wild goose chase, no point in beating ourselves up."

"An inspired suggestion."

Chambers sat down at one computer and Pendergast took another. The room fell into silence as they accessed the FBI databases and began searching. Chambers was familiar with this process and had grown to dislike it intensely. Part of him longed for the old days of index cards and giant binders filled with paper. But this was 1994, and that ship had sailed. The problem was, the Bureau was still finalizing its changeover to digital recordkeeping, and the search tools remained crude and uneven. With index cards you could get a feel for things, but looking at endless computer screens seemed to dull his sixth sense. Maybe in twenty or thirty years he could type in a command—*compile a list of all unsolved killings involving amputation or mutilation within such-and-such radius over the last five years*—and it would be delivered to him on a silver platter. As it was, he couldn't shake the feeling these screens and their fixed categories might cause him to miss an important clue—if only because that clue had not been scanned or had been indexed improperly.

He applied various filters to his search—age, location, type of injury, manner of death—and ran each of these against the numerous sub-databases at his disposal. Once, Maurice came in and silently refilled their lemonades. Chambers had the sense that Pendergast—unfamiliar as he must be with the system—was having his own difficulties: there would be long stretches of silence from his keyboard, punctuated by staccato bursts of typing before another protracted silence.

An hour passed, then two. Chambers came across several promising items, only to have them fail to pan out on further examination. Nevertheless, he made a note of each.

Silent as a ghost, Maurice appeared to announce that lunch was ready. Pendergast raised his hands from the keyboard and—to Chambers's surprise—dug into his jacket, fished out a gold pocket watch on a chain, flipped open the cover, and consulted it.

"Half past twelve," he said. "Shall we take some refreshment, Agent Chambers?"

They adjourned to a rear veranda overlooking cypress groves, where Maurice served them an excellent lunch of cold chicken breast, hush puppies, and fried green tomatoes with rémoulade sauce. They ate quietly, preoccupied with what they had or had not found.

"Food to your liking?" Pendergast asked, dabbing a linen napkin at the corners of his mouth in what seemed a very proper fashion before allowing Maurice to take their dishes away.

Maurice, Chambers thought, would make an excellent chef. "Slap-your-momma-down good."

There was a puzzled silence.

"It was first-rate," Chambers said. For a guy supposedly from New Orleans, Pendergast seemed to have lived a remarkably sheltered existence. He prepared to stand up—until he noticed that his host showed no inclination to move.

"It's interesting," he said instead.

"What is?"

"That those two girls saw Mr. Drakos running across the road."

Chambers didn't know Pendergast well, but he could nevertheless sense there was something behind what seemed a blindingly clear observation.

"If I'd seen something like that, I would have found it interesting, too." That seemed like the proper answer to draw out his host.

For a moment, Pendergast looked like a poker player whose bluff had just been called. Then he assumed his normal air again and continued.

"I should clarify. Why do you think Drakos was running around at that precise spot when the young women were driving by?"

"Because he was trying to get the hell away."

"No, no, Agent Chambers. Why *there*, exactly?"

"Because that's the point where he managed to escape out the back of the van. There's that curve in the road right before, after the bridge over the Pearl River, and it was slow enough for him to bust out without breaking half the bones in his body."

Something sparked in Pendergast's pale eyes, and he raised one slender figure. Evidently, this was the response he'd been looking for.

"Good. That's been the implication all along. But if you were Mr. Drakos, frightened and improperly dressed—and you'd managed to free yourself from any restraints holding you, then timed your leap out the back of the van to a moment when the vehicle had slowed—what would be your next move?"

"*Run, run, as fast as I can,*" Chambers replied, in singsong repetition of the nursery tale. He wished Pendergast would get to the point.

"But *where* would you run? Back down along the road?"

"Hell, no."

"Where, then?"

Now Chambers realized: Pendergast was not stringing him along—he was working something out... or he had already worked it out and wanted to see if it made sense to his partner.

"I'd go into the swamp, as far as I could go, and then hide in the darkness—probably up some tree so a snake wouldn't get me."

Pendergast nodded. "I'd do the same. Drakos undoubtedly had the same survival instincts we have—it seems likely he ran off into the swamp."

"Yes."

"Why did he go north?"

Chambers was momentarily confused. "I'm sorry?"

"Say he'd escaped the van, done what you or I would do—run deep into the swamp and hid. He wouldn't even have had to go that far before locating a place where his pursuer—and killer—would never find him. So why did he then rise out of his place of concealment and run back the way he'd come—to the van, from which he'd escaped—crossing the road in the process?"

Chambers considered this. "From what the eyewitnesses said, the other guy was hot on his heels."

"Which could mean one of three things. First, he was out of his head with fear, not thinking straight, and just running back and forth like the proverbial chicken, rather than finding a place to hide. Second, he'd found a place to hide, but it wasn't good enough—maybe he'd been crouching in a lagoon, say, and felt something just a little too big nudge him from underwater, causing him to betray his position to the searcher."

At this point, Pendergast sat back and arched one eyebrow.

"And the third?" Chambers asked.

"That the man was running in more or less a beeline, trying to get away from something or somewhere in the swamp, and was *intercepted* near the road."

"But that's not possible."

"Why not?"

"Because—well, because the eyewitnesses saw he'd escaped from the van."

"Did they? All they saw was that the van's rear doors were ajar. They *assumed* he'd escaped from the van. And everyone else—from Deputy Willis on, including us—have been working from that same assumption."

"What other assumption is there?"

"That Drakos had escaped, not from the van, but from some place of confinement to the south. A building, a trailer, a cave, whatever. Remember: he was seen *crossing* the road. He'd run north, toward the highway, doing his best to escape. He'd be heading in the direction of freedom, as best he could calculate it. But his captor, learning of his escape, got into his van, drove quickly to the highway, and parked there—perhaps waiting in the bracken near the shoulder—where he could nab his quarry."

Chambers digested this, along with his meal, for a moment. "That's not possible."

"Why?"

"Because there's nothing down there. The hurricane of 1921 buried that little jerkwater community I told you about under a dozen feet of water—and that's where it stayed. There's precious little 'land' down there now, it's more water than solid earth, and the most you'd find is a few more of those endless shacks we passed, crumbling along the highway. And there certainly isn't any road that van could take from down there to outflank Drakos."

There was a silence.

"Maybe he'd run off and was doubling back," Chambers suggested. "To throw the guy off the scent."

"If you'd found a good place to hide, or a blind where nobody could find you in the dark—would you abandon it?"

"No." Chambers ran over this third scenario of Pendergast's again. "No, I wouldn't. But I'm telling you—there's no good land down that way anymore, it's all bayou, poisonous snakes, gators, and katynippers."

"Katynippers?"

"Mosquitoes."

"Ah." And with this, Pendergast rose from the table. Chambers did the same, almost eager at this point to stop hypothesizing and get back to work.

But Pendergast paused. "I wonder: would it be out of line for the junior special agent to suggest to the senior special agent that we attempt to get our hands on some plats, or maps, of that area? Aerial photographs, if they're available. And ideally covering various periods of time—pre-hurricane, post-hurricane, modern day."

Christ. Pendergast was like a dog who'd just dug up a nasty old bone and now refused to part with it.

"No," Chambers replied, trying not to sound like he was humoring his mentee. "It's not out of line—necessarily. We can't go back to the office, of course, but I'll make a few calls."

"Thank you for your patience, Agent Chambers." And with that he led the way back into the saloon.

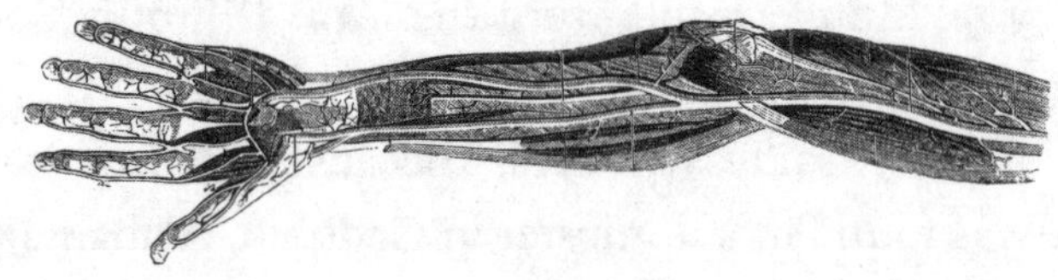

15

After lunch they returned to their computers. Chambers discovered that, in their absence, his had crashed, so he moved over to the spare computer and logged in. As he was waiting for the menu to load, he had the idea of cross-checking his list of near-misses against each other, using in-state as well as out-of-state files.

Ten minutes later, he got a bite.

"Pendergast," he said, "come take a look."

The pale man rose and leaned over his shoulder to stare at the screen. Chambers scrolled with his mouse, pointing out specifics. Earlier, he had come across an unsolved homicide in which a badly decomposed body had been found—minus an arm and both legs—in Bayou Gauche. It was identified by dental records as a small-time gangster named Jimmy Socks, and numerous bite marks made it obvious that alligators had been feasting on the remains. It had been marked down as a gangland hit—a turf war flared up late the previous year—and was now sitting in the cold case file. But when Chambers had pulled up organized crime files from surrounding states, he discovered that a decomposing arm had been found in Alabama several days earlier than the body in the swamp.

"So nobody investigated whether this arm belonged to Jimmy Socks?" Pendergast asked.

"Apparently not."

"Did they take fingerprints from the arm? If Jimmy Socks was a gangster, surely they'd have those on file."

"They couldn't," said Chambers, "because the arm was missing its hand. It was found in a dumpster in Gadsden, Alabama—a place I wouldn't drive through with a tank. Lots of drug activity."

"Can you find pictures of the body and the arm, and compare them side by side?"

This sounded like an easy request, but it turned out to be a major hassle that took almost half an hour. Finally, Chambers had two official photographs up on his screen, appropriately sized: a shot of the severed arm from Alabama's Drug Enforcement Division, and a disgusting photograph of the corpse, courtesy of the NOPD Organized Crime Unit.

They contemplated the two photos, side by side, for several minutes. "May I?" Pendergast finally asked.

"Be my guest."

Pendergast sat at the computer screen and began fussing with the images. After a few false starts, he managed to zoom in on both, focusing on the amputated areas on the shoulder and the arm.

"Same size, same musculature, same approximate build," he said, peering closer. "Note the spot on the Gadsden arm where it was severed from the body. Even after it suppurated for a few days, you can see it looks like a clean cut. And those bluish edges of the skin appear to be freezer burn." He pointed toward the enlarged photo from Bayou Gauche. "The missing limbs have been lacerated by alligators—but if you look closely at the spot where the right arm was severed from the body, you can see the same precise cut."

Chambers leaned in, squinting at the screen. What was left of Jimmy Socks resembled a giant, half-chewed plug of tobacco. He couldn't be sure if Pendergast was right or wrong: the screen resolution was not fine enough to show the necessary detail.

He sat back. For a moment, both men were silent.

"Do we know what happened to the body and the arm?" Pendergast asked.

"Most of Mr. Socks was returned to his family and cremated. As for the arm... well, who knows? It's gone one way or another. Evidence like that wouldn't be kept around for more than a week. They might have kept some tissue samples under glass, but when the case went cold—sayonara."

"And I presume neither NOPD nor the Gadsden police would have evidence other than what we have here?"

"I think you're looking at it." Chambers shook his head. "Even though this particular connection was mine, I'm not sure it's worth pursuing. The Diamondhead arm was found with the body. It was slashed to pieces. Except for the missing hand, this one wasn't slashed. And the distance between the body parts violates your thirty-mile rule."

Pendergast said nothing.

"What are you thinking?" Chambers asked at last.

"I was thinking there are a great many swamps and bayous around here, in which a great many body parts—including arms—could have disappeared into the bellies of carnivorous reptiles."

"Tell me about it." The swamp was a favorite excuse for local law enforcement when a body was missing. They would say it had turned into "gator guano."

"I'd be curious," Pendergast said, "to see the storage facility where Mr. Drakos's body was found. Shall that be tomorrow morning's assignment?"

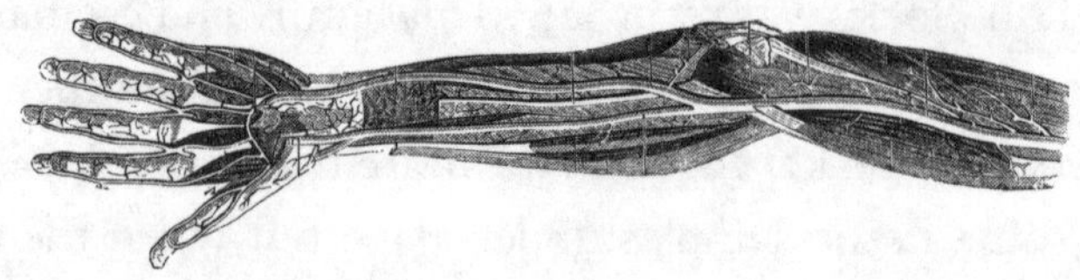

16

THE NEXT MORNING FOUND Dwight Chambers behind the wheel of his Impala once again, driving himself and his junior partner east. Pendergast had volunteered his Rolls-Royce, but Chambers thought this a bad look for two FBI agents on a case, and instead suggested they meet outside his usual breakfast joint a few blocks from work. Chambers was just mopping up the last of his grillades and grits when he saw the polished bulk of the Rolls glide to a stop beyond the window. He met Pendergast in the parking lot, and together they headed for the Mississippi line.

As they drove, Pendergast once again looked through the morgue and CSI photos of Kenneth Drakos. It creeped Chambers out, especially when Pendergast pulled out a magnifying glass for closer inspection. What the hell he was looking at, or for, Chambers couldn't guess. He figured he'd probably find out soon enough.

They reached Haul-U-All Self Storage around half past ten. It was surrounded by a chain-link fence on a property that ran alongside a stagnant bayou full of abandoned shopping carts. The lower part of the fence was overgrown with weeds. Passing through an entrance of chain-link gates, they rolled onto blacktop that was cracked and pockmarked. Dark clouds scudded across the sky, giving the place a menacing look. Chambers pulled up to a shed with a lean-to tin roof that was evidently the office.

Nobody came out to meet them, so the two got out and went in. The office consisted of a battered green chair, a desk with built-in file drawers, a locked key cabinet, and a toilet with no door. A skinny, withered-looking man of at least sixty sat at the desk, rolling a cigarette. His thinning black hair was slicked down against his scalp, and as they entered he rolled a bugged-out pair of eyes their way. Chambers was reminded of Peter Lorre in one of his later roles.

"Help you boys?" he asked in a distinctly unhelpful tone.

Chambers took a meaningful step back, and Pendergast got the cue. He took out his badge. "Agents Pendergast and Chambers, FBI. And your name is—?"

"Rockelton."

"Mr. Rockelton, we're here to have a look at the unit in which Kenneth Drakos was found three nights ago."

"Again? The police been here already—two different teams for hours—looking the place over with a fine-tooth comb. Told me they were done."

"I am sorry to tell you, Squire Rockelton, that *we* are not done," said Pendergast. "Among other things, we would like to interview the gentleman who found the body."

"That would be me," the man said, rolling his eyes from one agent to the other.

"I see," said Pendergast. "And your position in this fine enterprise?"

"Owner."

"Ah. So you're owner *and* night watchman."

"No night watchman. Place is open eight AM to two AM."

"But the body was found at three on the morning of August ninth."

"Sounds about right."

"By you."

"Yessirree."

"Then is this shack your domicile as well as office?"

"Nope. But I come by after closing now and then. Making sure there's no tomfoolery going on. Live half a mile down the far side of that river."

As Chambers followed the man's gesture, he saw that the clouds had parted briefly and the sun was coaxing a chemical sheen to the water's surface.

"And you found the body after noticing the storage door had not been properly locked."

The man paused to lick one edge of the cigarette paper. "The door wasn't all the way down. Some of them doors are ornery, and if you don't give 'em a good hard pull, they hike back up an inch or two. Well, I was driving past, and I saw this one was closed and locked—except the lock wasn't tight in the hasp, and that killer or whoever didn't close the door properly, and sure enough it had hiked up a couple inches, pulling the shackle of the lock with it." He lit the cigarette. "I got out to check... and that's when I noticed the stink."

It wasn't hard to see the operation this old geezer was running, Chambers thought. After closing time he'd come by now and then, test the locks, see if any could be opened. If he found one, maybe he'd help himself to a little of what was inside. Storage units—at least, the ones that didn't contain dead bodies—were usually so full of crap it wasn't likely anybody would notice something missing.

"And the name of the person who rents out that unit, please?"

"I gave that to the cops. Go ask them."

"If you wouldn't mind looking it up again?" Pendergast asked. "We would hate to feel left out."

With a muttered curse, the man rolled his chair over to the file cabinet, unlocked it, and rummaged through its contents. Then he pulled out a card.

"The cops kept the original, gave me this copy," he said, handing it over.

Pendergast took the card, and he and Chambers read over the scrawled writing: Mr. Jack Daniel, PO Box 8949, West Gulfport.

Chambers snorted when he read the name. "You didn't think this was fake?"

"I don't pay no mind to people's names."

"What did this Mr. Daniel look like?" Pendergast asked.

"Don't know."

"Didn't you see him?"

"People come and go. How'm I supposed to remember? All I can tell you is, he didn't stand out noways. Although I seem to recall he was a big guy."

"And his payments?"

"In cash, dropped through there, regular as clockwork." The man pointed to a mail slot in the door. "Paid by the year. Got the 10 percent discount."

"So he'd rented that space for a long time?"

"I already told the cops all that."

Chambers sighed. Naturally, the rental card had no date on it. He decided he'd had just about enough of this vinegar-pussed old bastard. Pendergast, he thought, was being too deferential. He'd mention it to him later.

"Do you remember seeing a rather dilapidated white van passing in and out of here—especially in recent days or weeks?" Pendergast went on.

"Mister, everybody who brings their stuff in here uses a van. It's a storage facility, not a safe-deposit box. If I had a dollar for every white van I've seen, I'd have retired years ago."

"Then it seems you can be of no further use to us." Pendergast's tone was starting to change. "Take us to the unit, if you please."

A truculent look came over the wizened features, and the man sucked in half an inch of hand-rolled cigarette, then streamed the smoke out his nostrils. "It's number thirty-two. It's locked up. You gents go find it yourself, 'if you please.' "

"You'll lead us to it," said Chambers, breaking in, "and you'll bring the key and open it for us, to boot."

"I run an honest place here," Rockelton said, his voice rising in complaint. "It don't look good, having you fellers here questioning me. The cops have been here again and again. I'm just waiting for the word so I can hose the place out and rent it again."

Just waiting to hose it out and rent it again. Putting a light hand on

Pendergast's arm, Chambers stepped forward. "If we have to get a court order, we will."

"It's a free country. Do what you want. Sure, bring me a court order... and then I'll open her up. I know my rights. Otherwise, forget it."

"Getting a court order is a pain in the butt," Chambers said.

"Ain't no pain in my butt."

"But here's a pain in your butt, Rockelton—losing your customers and getting shut down."

Rockelton snorted.

"How do you think your customers will feel when they learn just *where* they're storing their belongings? I'm talking about the history of this property."

"What history?"

"You mean you didn't do a title search of this shithole when you bought the land?"

The truculent look remained, but now there was a glimmer of concern in Rockelton's eyes. "What are you talking about?"

Chambers snorted. "Well, four of your lovely acres were once a cemetery for children who died of tuberculosis. The rest was owned by a factory that made munitions during the Second World War. They used arsenic and lead and all kinds of poisonous chemicals in the manufacture of shells and primers."

"I... I don't give a damn about that."

"I know a journalist in town who does give a damn, and he'd just love to break a story about a potential new Superfund site—and get your peckerwood operation shut down in the process. Now: *If. You. Please.*"

* * *

Within five minutes they were back in the Impala, following an ancient 1950s Dodge Power Wagon driving past row after row of storage units. It was a bigger place than Chambers had realized.

"Prickly old geezer," he said as he drove.

"I'm curious. What made you decide to research this site? We didn't anticipate this uncooperative reception."

"Research? Never did any."

"How did you know those details about the old munitions factory? And the TB cemetery?"

"There was no factory or cemetery."

A silence. "In other words, that was a fabrication."

Chambers nodded.

"So you blackmailed that man into giving us access."

Chambers chuckled. "Criminals blackmail. FBI agents insinuate. I wasn't interested in twiddling my thumbs waiting for a court order." He looked over at him. "To be honest, Pendergast, if you want a bit of advice, you seemed a little too obliging to that uncooperative old fucker. I hope you didn't object to my butting in like that."

"Certainly not. It was most entertaining. Good Lord, a TB cemetery *and* a munitions factory? What a delightfully noxious combination."

"Thank you."

"Agent Decker told me to pay close attention to your methods. Now I see why."

Chambers scoffed. "You're not bullshitting me, are you, Pendergast?"

"I do not, as you so colorfully put it, engage in *bullshitting*. Especially to my respected senior partner."

As Pendergast turned his eyes once more to the front, Chambers could have sworn he saw the faintest of smiles play along the edges of his patrician mouth.

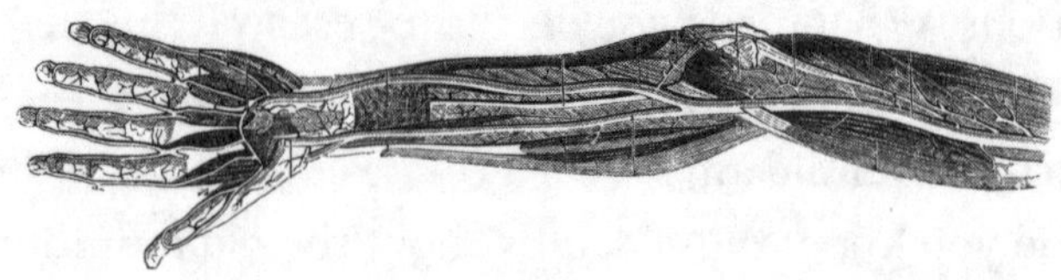

17

ROCKELTON STOPPED AT THE VERY LAST row of containers. He got out of his vehicle, and Pendergast and Chambers followed suit. Walking over to the first container, the old man knelt to unlock the padlock, removed it, and stepped back.

"We'll take it from here," Chambers said, opening the door, evidence folder in one hand. "Leave the padlock with us. We'll lock up when we're done and meet you back at the office."

Without a word, Rockelton got back into his car and left. Pendergast, Chambers noticed, had already plucked a flashlight from somewhere in his suit and was standing on the concrete lip of the storage unit, playing the light around the interior. A foul smell emanated from the unit. Inside, Chambers could see it had been fully processed by the police. There were no remaining signs of CSI activity, save for scatterings of fingerprint dust. The stainless-steel table that had held the body, and the concrete floor around it, were still stained with dried blood. There was no light switch, but after looking around for a minute Chambers located a pull string, and the small space became bathed in fluorescent light.

"Last row of storage units," Chambers said as he looked around. "First bay, so he could keep a lookout. Tell me that's a coincidence."

"Only one way in, but no security cameras," Pendergast murmured. "Back here, he could work with minimum interference. It seems odd, however, he would be so careless as to not completely secure the unit when he left."

"Okay, Pendergast," said Chambers. "I'm gonna step back into my mentor role and let you go to town."

"Thank you."

Chambers watched as Pendergast looked around critically. The hospital gown the victim wore was not visible, nor were the surgical tools that—in the photographs—he'd seen on the small wheeled equipment cart and the nearby floor. They had obviously been taken away as evidence. However, although the storage unit was for the most part bare, he could see other hospital gowns hanging on hooks, as well as a metal rack against the far wall holding sheets, towels, gauze, and a box of what appeared to be scalpel blades—all new and in the original packaging.

Pendergast remained in place for so long, just looking around, that Chambers wondered if he was at a loss. He decided to give a helpful nudge. "So: You're an FBI agent. You're looking at a crime scene already worked over by CSI, which means the most important evidence has been removed. How do you proceed?"

The question hung in the air for a moment. Then Pendergast turned toward the senior agent. "May I suggest an alternative? It strikes me this is an ideal opportunity to observe a veteran agent 'work the scene,' to use the vernacular."

If Pendergast wanted to observe instead of taking the lead, that was all right, too. "Okay," he said. "I go first, you second. Fair enough?"

"Excellent."

Chambers began stepping thoughtfully around the small enclosure, careful to breathe through his mouth. He'd seen so many similar crime scenes it was easy to picture in his mind what had happened here. There were signs an experienced eye could read: the initial discovery; the first cops on the scene; the arrival of detectives; and, lastly, the CSI team, who had combed through everything and handled the most items, yet left the fewest signs of their intrusion.

"The site was thoroughly processed by CSI," he said with a trace of finality. "Quite a lot of evidence was removed—especially items stained with blood. The hospital gown, surgical tools, tapes and bandages, all gone. You can see that the bloodstains on the table and floor were swabbed for testing. The place was carefully dusted, but no fingerprints were lifted. Very unusual. The guy was using this place for a while—some of those bloodstains on the floor look old. As you'd pointed out, this whole place gives me the impression of someone who's been trained in surgery—maybe a surgical nurse. He's a careful, methodical killer—look how neat everything is. But there's a recent overlay of disorder, indicating a hasty retreat. And look at the amount of unused surgical supplies, gowns, tape, stockpiled in the rear—this guy's in it for the long haul. My conclusion: this case ain't the garbage case I thought it was."

"I'm sorry—'garbage case'?"

"A low-profile murder that isn't likely to be solved. We're almost certainly dealing with a serial killer."

The storage space fell silent. Chambers looked at his partner. "Those are my thoughts. Now—what are yours?"

"From my inexperienced perspective, all of your observations—as far as they go—appear correct."

"As *far* as they go?" Chambers felt a little annoyed.

"Forgive me. The last thing I meant was to cause offense."

"I'm not offended. But what stands out to you that I didn't mention?"

Pendergast hesitated, then said: "I wonder if you could give me some time to make my observations. As a beginner, you know."

"Of course. Take all the time you need."

Once again, as in the Diamondhead morgue, Chambers was treated to a remarkable display of observational fanaticism, as Pendergast drew a magnifying glass out of a pocket and proceeded to examine every square inch of the storage unit—front-to-back, top-to-bottom, lifting one item off a shelf and minutely examining it, then replacing it and peering at the next one in turn.

After fifteen minutes, Chambers began to get impatient. After half an hour, he was ready to call a halt to the proceedings. But at the very moment he was about to say something, Pendergast turned to him.

"Just one last thing," he said, motioning to the table. "Would you mind climbing onto this table and assuming the position of the victim, as best you can re-create it?" He pulled one of the photos out of his black suit jacket and examined it at arm's length. "The head goes here, feet there."

He held the photo out to Chambers. Instead of taking it, Chambers merely looked at it for a moment, then turned toward the table, with its splatters and runnels of blood leading into a sticky pool, the entire thing encased in fingerprint dust.

"Hell, no," Chambers said. "Are you kidding me?"

"I withdraw the request," Pendergast said quickly. "Forgive the thoughtlessness; I will do it myself."

And to Chambers's astonishment, Pendergast immediately climbed onto the table, still holding the photograph, and arranged himself accordingly, making fussy adjustments here and there to position himself at the precise attitude in which the corpse had been found.

"Pendergast, what the hell are you doing?" Chambers asked.

"It's an exercise that helps me concentrate and visualize a mass of complex information. It won't take long."

"How long?"

"Thirty to forty-five minutes. I appreciate how strange it must seem, and I beg your indulgence."

"Jesus Christ. Really? I'll wait for you in the vehicle."

Chambers stomped off to his car, got in, and slammed the door. It was damn hot, so he turned on the engine, then flipped through the radio dial, at last settling back to listen to Nirvana and cool himself off.

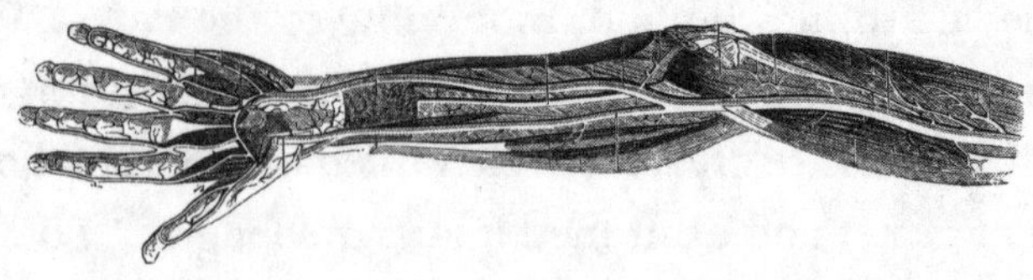

18

Chambers waited. From where he was parked, he had a partial view of the storage unit—enough to see that Pendergast was lying on the bloody table. Once he'd gotten into a position that seemed to satisfy him, he remained entirely motionless.

Chambers wasn't exactly sure how to feel. He'd tried on impatient, angry, stupefied, disgusted, aggravated—but none of the emotions quite fit. His gut told him he wasn't being made fun of—whatever Pendergast was doing must make some kind of sense, at least to him. But this bizarre behavior once again raised his initial doubts about the guy. And there was a lot to worry about—from him running a rogue sting operation and jamming up Urbanski, to investigating this case out of his mansion—and now this. Maybe he should just drive off and leave Pendergast in his near-necrophilic state. But even as this ran through his mind, his lack of sleep finally caught up with him and he ended up nodding off.

He was awoken by the rolling slam of the shed door as Pendergast closed and locked it. He spent several minutes wiping his suit free of powder and dried blood. Then at last he slipped into the passenger's seat.

Chambers looked at his watch. "You were in there almost an hour."

"My apologies."

Without replying, Chambers drove back to the shack, shouted out the window that they were done, then peeled out onto the highway. The sun was now sinking toward the horizon, breaking through a layer of storm clouds.

"Pendergast, we need to talk," he said.

Pendergast looked at him. "Of course."

"First, I owe you an apology for being a shitty mentor. Somehow, I don't know how, you managed to pull me out of a nightmare—you have my gratitude for that. But I have questions."

"Very well."

"Not to put too fine a point on it, but you're a weird guy. Your fancy car, your fancy house, your black suit, your connection with this Decker."

He stopped, breathing hard. Pendergast looked back at him, an unreadable expression on his face.

Chambers said, "So what's your game? With all that money, why do you even bother to work? How did you get so buddy-buddy with the FBI brass?"

When Pendergast continued to fix him with those silvery eyes, Chambers saw the questions were unwelcome and wouldn't be answered.

"Okay, then. If you won't talk about that, tell me what the fuck you were doing lying on that table for an hour. As your partner, I've got a right to know that—assuming you want us to keep working together."

"I see." Pendergast took a moment, as if to gather his thoughts. "Before joining the FBI, I was involved in a highly classified military unit. Agent Decker was also part of that unit, as were several others who now occupy governmental positions. That explains my connection. That work led me to an interest in justice, and from there to law enforcement."

"Okay, thanks for that. But the table?"

"My training, and areas of expertise, extend beyond the military. Some of it was learned at Oxford; a great deal more was picked up on my own initiative. In part, it consisted of mastering a form of meditation—known as Chongg Ran—that was developed in an isolated monastery in Tibet. In addition to esoteric mental focus, the meditator's physical location plays a vital role. Hence my action in the storage unit. I realized I had the opportunity to place myself in the victim's location of death to conduct a Chongg Ran session."

"Wow. That's some crazy shit."

"Allowing you to see me undertake this ritual was a display of trust on my part. I would ask that you keep it to yourself."

"Okay." Chambers chewed on this for a minute. "So what *did* you figure out about the murder from that... session—if anything?"

"From that, and from all the other evidence we've reviewed, I have drawn some additional conclusions."

"Let's have them."

"The victim's body was a revelation—he was a healthy and powerful man in the prime of life. He was being held prisoner and managed to escape. He fled through the swamp in terror. By the time he reached the road where the two girls spotted him, he was so exhausted that he could be chased down and recaptured by the killer. Given his level of fitness, I estimate the victim would have run at least five miles, but no more than ten, before reaching the road—running through a swamp is not at all like running along a jogging path. It also suggests the killer is a man of similar health and fitness level. Although it stands to reason that, tracking his quarry down while driving a van, he would not be nearly as winded."

"Go on."

"The killer obviously knew he was seen by the girls. After recapturing his prisoner and presumably driving straight to the storage unit—which may or may not have been his original intention—he becomes increasingly agitated. Had they seen his face? Did they get his license plate? Were the police already looking for him? Whatever he had in mind for his victim, the timetable was now accelerated. So he brings the victim, drugged and unconscious, into the unit; lays him out on the table; and performs microsurgery to remove his arm. He is now working in haste. The man is strangled either before or after the surgery."

"How do you know all this?"

"My examination of the amputation indicated skill *and* haste. There were also some fresh scalpel nicks on the operating table that I'm confident were caused by excessive downward cutting force. The condition of the unit also showed the disorder of recent haste—as you noted."

"Okay."

"After the arm is amputated, something crucial occurs. Or the killer realizes something significant—there is no way yet to know exactly what happened. But he flies into a rage, slashes up the arm, discards his surgical tools—and flees in such a panic that he neglects to properly secure the door."

"Maybe he was interrupted. Someone arrived."

"Quite possible. It could have been our friend Rockelton. At any rate, he abandons the storage room, knowing that in this heat the body will be found in a few days."

"But without having time to hack off any more limbs before the cavalry arrived."

Pendergast was silent for a moment before continuing. "You used that same expression once before, back at Penumbra: *hacking off limbs*. In my opinion, he'd accomplished his task—at least, most of it—*before* leaving the storage unit."

"What are you saying?"

"I'm saying that—based on how carefully the amputation was done, and, as far as we can tell from the photographs on Mr. Socks as well—our quarry wasn't interested in vivisecting the rest of the body. He was interested in one thing: an arm. Specifically, the right arm."

"Why just an arm? And the right arm, at that?"

"I don't know. The evidence as I interpret it is that he was more or less finished. That is why the orderly state of the container showed recent disarray: he was always prepared to abandon it at short notice. Hence his exceeding care never to leave incriminating evidence such as fingerprints, hair, or fibers. I have no doubt that when the CSI analyses are done, and the local police trace all the supplies, equipment, and clothing back to their purchase points, they will find nothing."

He blinked slowly, like a camera shutter closing and reopening. "You yourself made a vital observation: the container was well stocked, indicating he had used it before and planned to use it again. As we speculated earlier, we are certainly dealing with a serial killer."

"Who likes chopping off right arms."

"Carefully *excising* right arms."

"That kind of MO isn't like any serial killer I've studied."

"Perhaps because the killing itself is not his motive." Pendergast held up a finger. "In fact, I would hazard to say he does not enjoy killing. It disturbs and even disgusts him. These are not sexual crimes; nor is the killer acting out a need for power and control."

"He enjoys chopping—I mean, surgically removing—people's arms."

"Without further evidence, that is my assumption."

"Then why leave it with the body?"

"Agent Chambers, I do not have all the answers. Speculation is what I can offer. All I sensed on this subject during my meditation was this: he is a seeker. These things he's doing, the motivation behind them . . . he's searching for something and can't find it."

"How do you know he's searching for something?"

"Process of elimination. As you just said, these murders—we've only seen one, but there are undoubtedly others—are unlike the normal serial killer's. They display a yearning—even, perhaps, a great longing. Look at how carefully, how elaborately, he set up that container. Yet when the crisis arrived, he abandoned it without a second thought. That implies he has other safe houses in which to work."

"If he's so careful, how can you explain the fact his victim got away from him?"

"That is another mystery. Also significant is the physical condition of the victim. Our killer picked an individual who would be exceedingly difficult to capture and control. Most serial killers go after the weak and defenseless. What we do know is that escape set in motion a cascade of failures, ending with the killer leaving the body behind and abandoning his, ah, operating theater."

Pendergast fell silent. Chambers glanced over in time to see the man slowly lean his white-blond hair against the headrest. "I wonder, Agent Chambers, if you would mind dropping me off at Penumbra? Given the current state and odor of my suit, I find myself rather eager to get out of it."

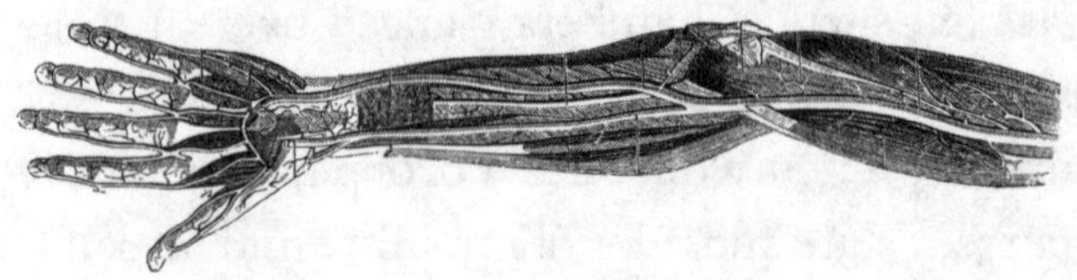

19

PROCTOR SAT IN THE DARKNESS, breathing slowly and regularly. He had now, he felt, familiarized himself with his surroundings to the greatest degree possible—a painstaking, but necessary, first step. He had meticulously paced, again and again in the dark, the transit from front wall to back; between the side walls; and from various angles afforded by the corners. He was now able to picture the room in his mind almost as clearly as he could have with his eyes, and was able to run—or at least, move as quickly as his hobbled legs allowed—between the various points, always stopping a handbreadth before reaching them. He practiced moving from his usual sitting position to leaping up and running toward the door, again and again and again. All this accomplished, he went on to practice calisthenics, push-ups, and sit-ups, increasing the number each day. This would be a routine he would continue for as long as was necessary.

But this was not all he occupied himself with. Roughly twelve hours before, while making use of the rudimentary toilet facilities, he'd managed to pry off a strip of the bonding cement surrounding the drain. The adhesive that had been used was very hard, but—as Proctor knew and his captor apparently did not—it also dried in a stratified way that allowed someone with the proper skills to prize off a semicircular slice. Proctor's piece was thin—almost as thin as mica—but it fit nicely along the underside of his index finger, curved like the talon of an eagle. He could conceal it easily between his fingers, and even if his jailer were to take the unlikely step of examining the drain, Proctor had permanently camouflaged the missing strip. He had spent much of the night painstakingly rubbing this strip against the rough edge of a bolt in the many padding restraints, shaping it and sharpening the inner edge. He had stopped before developing a callus. But within another twenty-four hours, the business edge would be sharper than any scalpel. It was short—perhaps two inches, extended to its maximum—but Proctor could easily inflict lethal damage with even that length of blade. All he'd need was that one brief moment of distraction, and it would be lights-out... figuratively as well as literally.

Now he lay with his back against the wall, eyes closed. Judging by his meal schedule, it was around noon. He did not feel any particular degree of apprehension. The training he'd undergone years before, extensive and rigorous, enabled him to put anxiety aside without dulling his hypersensitivity to the surrounding environment. He'd grown more adept at gauging the passage of time, and there was no need for him to sleep for eight or ten hours yet. So he amused himself with a mental exercise. Starting with the standard parametric equation for bullet trajectory—$x(t) = (v_0\cos\theta)t$, $y(t) = (v_0\sin\theta)t - \frac{1}{2}gt^2$—he then used the variables for initial velocity, launch angle, time, and gravitational acceleration in a series of scenarios of his devising: different weapons, ammunition, bores, wind drifts, temperatures, and altitudes, all with an eye toward zeroing in on a target, having taken all ballistic and environmental factors into account.

As he was occupied with this—having progressed through a series of simulations utilizing a Barrett M82A1 rifle with .50 BMG cartridges—he was considering which weapon to choose next when—suddenly—his instincts came to full alert.

His body remained frozen in position, but all his senses came to attention, seeking a change in the environment. What had set off his hair-trigger instincts? Mentally reviewing the last fifteen seconds, he realized it was a quiet sound—a slow, almost stealthy scraping—overhead. He looked up in the darkness, but of course he could not see the heavy wire grille of the ceiling, which in any case was too high for him to reach.

Yet he was certain the sound—and, though the cell was now quiet, it was definitely a sound that had interrupted his calculations—had come from above.

He remained still, all senses at hypersensitivity. Now, he thought, another sound came from above—this one even quieter. It was unusual, and it lasted only a second or two before the cell lapsed into silence again. Proctor went over possibilities in his head: a tiny peephole being opened for spying with active near-infrared or even military-grade image-intensifying NVGs; some adjustment or enhancement to the security systems his captor assured him were hidden all around; or perhaps—

Suddenly, Proctor realized that—even in the darkness, with nothing to focus on—he was experiencing a peculiar dizziness, almost a sense—in the deep black—of twirling around and around a drain, about to plunge into an unknown abyss. He shook his head to clear it and began to stand, but his legs felt like rubber and he collapsed. One additional attempt to rise—and then he sank prone onto the floor, the external darkness now matched by the internal darkness of unconsciousness.

★ ★ ★

...He was aware of a sensation of straining—ineffectual straining. After a moment, he realized that his body was, instinctively, trying to return to a sitting position. He stopped, falling back to the padded floor, and let his body relax as full consciousness slowly returned.

His head throbbed, but it was not the pain of blunt trauma: rather, it was more like the hollow ache of a hangover. As control returned to his limbs, he quickly checked himself for injuries or other changes of any kind. Finding nothing, he tried again—successfully this time—to push himself back to a sitting position.

Now it was time to determine what had happened.

He let his mind go back to his last conscious memory: sudden light-headedness, dizziness, and disequilibrium. After that, blackness. And yet he could sense teasing phantoms of what had happened *within* that blackness: shadow memories of an interrupted dream, or the anterograde amnesia of drugs like midazolam, where the user experiences blank periods of memory, with only filaments of sight and sound remaining as brief, half-remembered events.

Proctor knew that trying to force these fragments of memory to the surface was the surest way of eradicating them. Instead he consciously shifted his train of thought, considering what might have just happened to him while giving the subconscious memories time to reassemble themselves.

He was certain of one thing—he'd been drugged. Now the faint sounds from overhead made sense: the scraping noise had been the opening of a small hatch or vent; and the second, even fainter sound, the opening of a gas cock. Both had been done stealthily, with the aim of keeping him off guard until it was too late and he'd lapsed into unconsciousness.

But, quiet as the noises had been, now that he felt sure of what they were, he would be constantly on the alert should they ever recur.

And now, very gently, he turned back to the vestiges of memory left behind by the anesthetic. As if through a haze of grogginess, he recalled bright lights—and then a blurry image of his captor, Taser in one hand, his head oddly out of proportion. Perhaps he'd been wearing a gas mask. In any case, the man must have taken it off, because after this there was more blackness and, then, only one more memory, seconds or minutes later—of the man kneeling over him. Proctor seemed to remember he'd been palpating or even stroking his arm—his right arm—and making low, cooing noises of approval. That was all.

That was all... but it was enough. The gas had been very fast acting, but it also seemed to have dissipated quickly enough for the man to remove his mask at some point; otherwise, Proctor would not have heard the unpleasant noises the man had made while touching his arm...almost like a mother fussing over her baby.

Except that wasn't the image that came most sharply to Proctor's mind—not at all. The mental image that lingered most strongly was that of a butcher, patting the haunch of a prized pig.

He had not forgotten the salacious, almost hungry look in the man's eyes when he looked over Proctor's bare arms, lingering on the right, during their first and only face-to-face encounter. Nor had he forgotten his captor's obsessive interest in his health, the insistence that he eat everything given to him—or else.

He recalled reading somewhere that, in order to produce the tastiest foie gras, workers would shove tubes down the gullets of geese and pump up to four pounds of grain and fat into their bellies every day. The practice was known as "gavage." Such a soft, French-infused word for such a barbaric act.

He, too, was being force-fed—the method was more subtle, but the result, Proctor now felt sure, would be the same. His captor was not only a psychopath—he was a cannibal.

Naturally, the thought had occurred to him already—but so had other possibilities: that he was to be stuffed and mounted, perhaps. But now, Proctor put those other possibilities aside.

He'd been gassed to make it easier for his captor to check on him. The man had no doubt turned on the gas, stuffing a towel quietly under the door until he could safely enter the cell. He wouldn't have gone to this trouble unless he was satisfying himself—up close—that his special repast was nearly ready.

The next time Proctor heard those two stealthy sounds, he knew, would be the last. While he could not see into the madness of his tormentor, the vestigial memory of cooing approval assured Proctor that, as a meal, he was just about ripe. When next the gas cock opened, it would be to remove him from the cell, kill him, and—

But Proctor did not need to imagine how such a scenario would play out. Earlier, while sitting in the dark amusing himself with bullet trajectories, he'd still been speculating about the man's unhealthy appetite—and when, or how, he would be harvested.

Now he knew a great deal more. And in addition to keeping himself fit, sane, and prepared, he would begin assembling something else to occupy his time:

A plan.

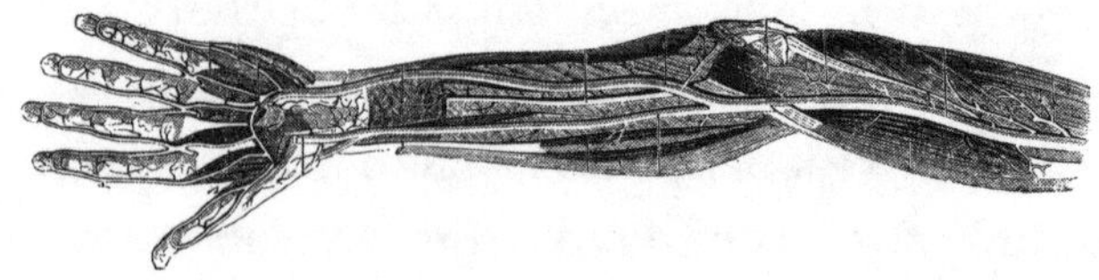

20

TRUE TO HIS WORD, Chambers had made some calls, and when he next arrived at Penumbra a bulky package—sent on by a buddy of his from the DHL facility a few blocks from FBI headquarters—was waiting. He opened it and, together with Pendergast, went through a series of aerial photographs, most of them from the 1970s, as well as plats and maps from several different eras, all covering the area where the hurricane of 1921 had swallowed up the town of Frenier and everything around it.

The aerial photographs were not much help—almost everything was covered in a screen of trees and swampy canopies. But Chambers lined up two maps, one from 1901, the other from 1951. The latter had been made by the Department of Defense at a time when it was looking for ideal spots to construct military bases or dig missile silos.

"Take a look at this," Chambers said. He pointed to the old map, which clearly showed a small but intact community on the bank of the river, maybe five miles south of Chef Menteur Highway—at the time rather less than a highway and dubbed "Diamondhead Pike." Several larger structures, all labeled, sat back from the town on a bluff, and a narrow road followed the course of the river south from the pike until it reached the town. Then he pointed to the 1951 map, which showed no existing road, and only river where the town had once been. Topographical lines were indicated, but—although one or two structures remained on the bluff—they were not named. However, by comparing the two maps, Chambers was able to recognize them.

"These two structures—the Rabineau Plantation and the Wichman House—were spared the storm surge of the hurricane, due to their being on higher ground," he told Pendergast. "I say 'spared,' but I notice the other half a dozen buildings on that ridge no longer existed in 1951. If those are still standing, they must be in ruins by now. And this map makes clear there was no road in or out, even forty years ago. The swamp's only going to be thicker now. If you're right about our perp having a series of safe houses, seems to me that easy access to them—and *away* from them—would be a priority."

"Yes," Pendergast murmured. After a moment, he added: "So it would seem." Then he straightened up and glanced at Chambers. "Don't you find it rather stuffy in here?"

Chambers didn't find it stuffy; it was more like a steam bath. The interior of the Pendergast mansion had never seen a whiff of air conditioning. Even with Maurice throwing open the French doors and windows in the mornings to aid a flow of air, when it was a hundred degrees outside it was a hundred degrees inside—no two ways about it. His friends at the agency called this month in Louisiana "the depths of hell"—and for good reason.

"Yeah," he said. "It's hot."

"Shall we take a stroll around the grounds to refresh our mental faculties before resuming our search?"

"Hell, yes."

Chambers was relieved when they stepped out on the veranda—but not by much: it was still damn hot. Even so, Pendergast had not even bothered to remove his black suit jacket of worsted wool. In fact, Chambers couldn't recall Pendergast ever taking his jacket off—even when he'd lain down on that butcher's gurney for that weird meditation, or whatever it was. Yet no matter how hot, he always looked cool and immaculate. How did the guy do it?

After descending from the veranda, Pendergast set off at an unexpectedly fast pace down a walkway and across the lawn, toward a parallel line of ancient oaks draped in Spanish moss. Chambers hustled to keep up with the man's long strides, wondering where they were going now. They entered the oak grove, following the path paved in brick and overspread with moss. It ended at a hedge with a gate, which Pendergast threw open, leading into an arboretum of ancient specimen trees, unkempt and overgrown.

Here Pendergast paused and cast him a mischievous glance. "It's only fair to warn you, my dear Chambers, that we may encounter a ghost."

"What sort of ghost?"

"One of my felonious ancestors who managed to get himself hanged. Poor fellow—his grave is just beyond."

Glancing in that direction, Chambers could see a wrought iron fence enclosing a small burial plot.

"Shall we enter?"

Do I have a choice? Chambers thought as he followed Pendergast in. A scattering of slate and marble headstones, crooked and leaning, could be seen peeking up from the tangle of grass.

"This is the family plot?" Chambers asked as he looked around. The giant trees enveloped the graveyard in welcome shade, and he could feel a cooling mist drifting in from somewhere.

"Indeed it is. For me it is a place of meditation: a reminder of our common fate. More than that—I am required by my grandfather's last will and testament to visit his grave at least once every three years, such visit to be recorded by a notary public. And here it is." Pendergast moved aside the grass with his shoe to expose a gravestone. "Louis de Frontenac Diogenes Pendergast. We called him Pépère."

"*Tempus edax rerum,*" Chambers read from the inscription. "What does that mean?"

"Time, devourer of all things," said Pendergast.

Somehow, this reminded Chambers of his wife—and how brief, in retrospect, their time together had seemed. The pang caused him to fall silent.

"Time is our deadliest enemy," Pendergast said in a quieter tone.

Chambers bowed his head. "True."

"But also our fast friend."

"How's that?"

"The past is immutable and the future unknown. This moment—now—is the only reality. It is our challenge to accept the rule of time—which is to say that we accept the past for what it is, and cease worrying about the future and what it might bring."

"You mean, enjoy the present."

"Not 'enjoy.' *Live.* There lies the difference."

This philosophical side of Pendergast was something new, especially delivered as it was in a honeyed accent that seemed to have become more pronounced than ever now that he was in his native element. As the minutes passed, the pang of Chambers's loss ebbed, and somehow the peaceful stillness of the graveyard gave him a sensation of acceptance he hadn't experienced since his wife died. He wondered if, perhaps, that was why Pendergast had brought him here.

"But now," said Pendergast, his voice more brisk but still quiet, "let us return to the case—because I believe I've come to an unexpected realization. You may recall from the behavioral science curriculum at the Academy that serial killers fall into categories or, as they say, *types.*"

Chambers nodded.

"In this case, however, I believe we are dealing with a serial killer who is sui generis."

"Sui—what?" For a moment, a scene from the movie *Deliverance* came to Chambers's mind.

"He is unique. Reluctantly, I'm coming to the conclusion that there has never been another killer like him. He does not fall into those neat categories that behavioral science—which, in my opinion, is a science still in its infancy—has laid out. Which means the parameters of our search to date have been little more than useless. In other words, he may be living within the radius ascribed to serial killers; he may live without. He may cut off the arms of his victims; he may merely slash them, if that. His motives are personal and idiosyncratic to himself, and we cannot hope to understand them by studying his *type*—since he belongs to none."

"So what do we do?"

"We discard—or at least revise—the parameters of our search. We drop the majority of our assumptions and stick with only what we *know* to be true. And what are those things we know?"

"We know he seeks out strong, healthy men. Until we get contrary evidence, you think his interest is focused for whatever reason on their right arms. He seems to have had some surgical experience."

"Correct on all counts. And I would add, given the incident on the highway where he was chasing Drakos, it's reasonable to believe one of his numerous safe houses is fairly near that location: probably within a ten-mile radius. However, at *this* moment he may be operating far from that location—we can no longer count on the usual serial-killer radius rule."

"I'd go along with that," said Chambers. "But I have one question."

Pendergast arched his eyebrows in response.

"Those serial-killer categories you just disrespected—they aren't exactly useless. They've been carefully curated based on *all* serial killers, and their motives, that we know of to date. Why—how—can this person be different?"

"An excellent question. All I can say is that we'll have our answer—but only when we find the killer."

Pendergast then turned and headed out of the graveyard, holding open the gate for Chambers and walking with that same fast stride back to the mansion. Chambers considered that their roles had slowly, almost unnoticeably, been reversing; now he was more the mentee, and Pendergast the mentor.

Oddly enough, it didn't bother him.

* * *

An hour later, back in the stifling room, sitting in front of a computer, Chambers found himself—having widened his net across three states—now paging through dozens of open homicide files. He began to wonder if this wasn't just turning into a wild goose chase of a different sort. He'd had no idea so many killings remained unsolved. They were mostly banal killings of people involved in petty crimes, to which investigators had given only cursory attention before moving on.

But there was one case that gave him pause, though he wasn't sure why. On the surface, it seemed like yet another mob or gang killing—a guy hog-tied to a chair, face beaten to a pulp, stabbed in the heart. Unlike the others, he was not missing an arm. But the body showed signs of torture—cuts, bruises, cigarette burns. His left arm had been broken and the fingernails pulled. The right arm, the coroner had noted in passing, was unblemished except for some needle marks on the right shoulder, indicative of drug use.

Right shoulder? That didn't sound to Chambers like drug use—who injected themselves in the shoulder instead of the arm? And why was one arm brutalized while the other was relatively undisturbed?

"Hey, Pendergast? Check this case out."

Pendergast came over and peered over at the screen as Chambers paged through the slim covering file. "Nicholas Mabley, Husser, Louisiana. Murdered two years ago. Death investigated by the Tangipahoa Sheriff's Office. Rather briefly, it seems." Pendergast straightened up. "If we take the Rolls, we can be there in about an hour," he said, more to himself than to Chambers. "Of course, the Spyder would be faster. And more entertaining, as well."

"Spyder?"

A twitch of the lips came and went on Pendergast's face. "To the garage, mortal—where you shall look upon my works, and despair."

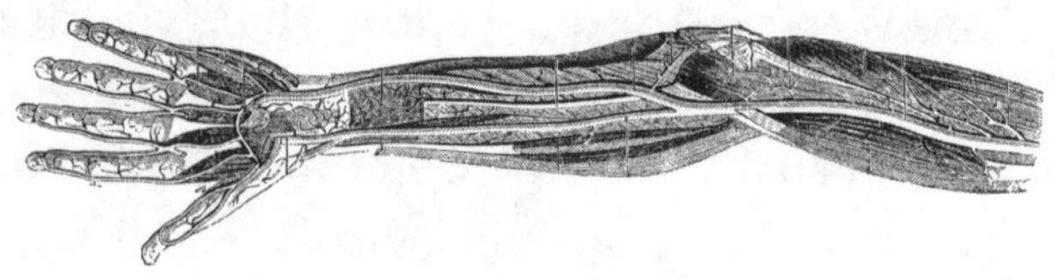

21

WICKMAN MOVED QUIETLY UP the felt-covered steps. There were a lot of them—the basement of the rambling old building was set deep—and there was a landing halfway up where they took a ninety-degree turn. This had become useful for him: when he opened the door at the top, the light from the first floor was attenuated by the right angle and did not reach the bottom landing.

In any case, that was not much of a concern today, the afternoon skies having grown overcast, a brief but savage thunderstorm brewing—common in this humid, semitropical region of the United States. Closing the top door, he paused to sit on a nearby bench, where he removed his felt slippers and hung his night-vision goggles on a hook in a nearby recess built specifically for that purpose. Next, he rose and went back, back, toward the rear of the dilapidated mansion until he reached what had originally been the servants' area, now converted to a commercial kitchen. He took off his rubber gloves and washed them carefully, then did the same with his hands. Then he spent a moment in an adjoining suite of connected annexes—all retrofitted to manage the resource currently installed below—checking to make sure the apparatus was fully disengaged.

The fact that he'd now perfected his technique was a source of both pride and frustration. Pride, because of the many breakthroughs necessary to come this far; frustration simply because it *had* taken so long, with so many wrong choices and near-misses.

He shook his thoughts away by glancing again over the apparatus that sent the anesthetic into the room below. It was just one of his many achievements. To be both effective and safe—safe for him, at least—the inhalation agent had to have high potency and rapid onset, ideally without a pungent scent...or any scent at all, which would only alert the resource. In the end, he'd developed a racemic of several gases, including halothane and enflurane. This latter was a particularly inspired choice because it had fallen out of favor in the '80s as an inhalational anesthesia, subsequently becoming much cheaper and easier to purchase on the underground pirate servers he dealt with. He made use of the World Wide Web for this: a brand-new content-sharing protocol that was mostly the domain of programmers and hackers—an unregulated, unmapped Wild West where, at least for now, anything and everything was available...to those who knew how to find it.

He checked the array of tanks to make sure there was a sufficient reserve of gases, then stepped back with something close to regret. Such an ingenious design—it seemed almost a shame that, having been perfected, it would be put to use only once more.

But that was the burden he bore, he mused as he walked out of the annex, through the kitchen, down the corridor, and up to the windowless, soundproofed room he used as a command post. He felt more confident than ever that, at last, his time had come. The escape of the Drakos resource had shown the necessity of hardening the holding area to an even greater degree; he'd never gotten far enough along to test the gas induction on him, but it had worked perfectly with this new and final resource, including the slow offset period that had given him plenty of time—and would once again. With the holding area now escape-proof, there was no reason to wait any longer.

He picked up his phone, dialed a number.

"Microbiology department, Dr. Telligren's office."

"Let me speak to Dr. Telligren, please."

"He's in with somebody at the moment, can I—"

"Tell him Dr. Moreau is calling."

There was a pause on the other end of the line.

"*Tell* him, please."

"One moment." There was a series of clicks; about twenty seconds of silence; and then a familiar voice came on the line. "What is it?"

"It's time."

"Time?" The voice had more than a touch of irritation. "That's what you told me a week ago."

"Something unexpected came up. I couldn't avoid that delay. But now it's time."

A faint sigh of what might have been exasperation. "After your last call, I rearranged my entire schedule, pushed everything back. Now it's going to be harder to—"

"Dr. Telligren?" Wickman interrupted.

The voice went silent. Wickman thought about the irritation he'd heard in that voice; the frustrated sigh. "Do we need to have this conversation again?" he asked.

"No."

"I think we do. Perhaps you've forgotten that it's in your interest, even more than mine, that this...process be brought to fruition. You've got *so* much more to lose—you know all the necessary steps I've taken to ruin you should you back out now or try anything—how should I put it?—*funny*."

Although Wickman tried to keep his anger confined to dead bodies, he could feel a righteous indignation rising strongly. "With so much at stake, is it wise to show impatience, Doctor? Don't forget how all this started. And don't forget, either: I can take my business elsewhere. You can't. I could crush you like a bug anytime I wanted to."

More silence on the other end of the line, and Wickman felt his anger quickly abating. It would not do to beat this dog too hard—best to put the club away and offer a bone.

"I realize this unexpected delay is inconvenient for you," he said. "But then again, every day of my life, for the last decade, has felt a lot *more* than inconvenient. We're so close now; let's see it through. Six hours of work, three days of direct observation, six more via remote monitoring—and it's done. You won't hear from me again... and this chapter in both our lives will be closed. To the betterment of all. Wouldn't you agree, Doctor?"

A brief pause, then: "Yes."

"Very good. Thank you."

"When do you want to... that is, what day are we talking about?"

"Night, actually. Two nights from now. That will give you time to finish any critical appointments—and cancel anything scheduled for next week."

When the voice sounded again, it was tight, carefully controlled. "Will everything be ready on your end? All preparations made, all necessary items at hand?"

"It's ready now. If I were you, I'd worry about stocking my own bag of tricks. And be sure to bring enough units—four, five—to cover anything unexpected."

"Friday night..." There was the sound of pages being flipped. "I could meet you at the ramp at six. Six thirty, at the latest."

"That's acceptable. You won't hear from me again unless something unexpected comes up—but I guarantee that will not happen again."

"I'm relieved to hear that guarantee."

Wickman noted a faint emphasis on the final word but decided to let it go. The doctor had no choice in the matter; if a little passive-aggressive pushback gave him some satisfaction, however subtle, Wickman had no objection. "In that case," he said, "I'll see you Friday—the day after tomorrow."

"Friday." There was a click as the connection was broken.

Wickman replaced the handset into its cradle with a slow smile.

It was, he imagined, the kind of smile that might have come over George Washington's face after Cornwallis's surrender—a long campaign, carefully planned...not without setbacks or delays, but nevertheless concluding in complete and utter victory on that long-ago afternoon atop the earthworks, the setting sun gilding the York River.

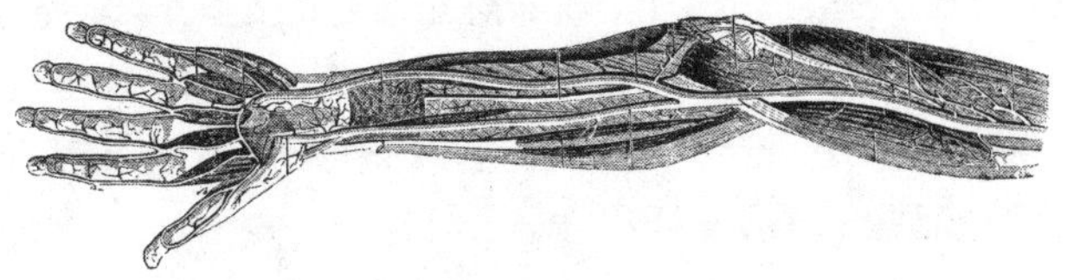

22

Forty minutes later, Pendergast pulled his two-seat, absurdly loud vintage Porsche into the modest parking lot in front of the Tangipahoa sheriff's office in Hammond, Louisiana. It was a modest, one-story brick building surrounded by flowering myrtle trees, with cicadas droning in the heat and enveloped in an almost somnolent air.

Chambers got out and smoothed down his hair, which felt like it had been permanently blown back—if not clean off—by the ride. Pendergast emerged from the vehicle still in black, unruffled save for his blond hair, now ludicrously wild. A tiny comb came out of a pocket somewhere in his suit jacket, however, and with a few quick sweeps all was once more perfectly in place.

"Invigorating ride, wouldn't you say?"

"That's one word for it. Invigorating. Jesus."

They walked into the lobby, where a sour-faced receptionist eyed them from behind a glass partition. Chambers took the lead and held out his lanyard. "Special Agent Chambers, Special Agent Pendergast, Louisiana Field Office. Here to see the sheriff."

"Do you have an appointment?" asked the man.

"Apologies, we do not. It's a matter of some urgency."

The man pressed a button, murmured into his mouthpiece, then turned back to them. "Door at the end of the hall," he said, buzzing them through.

The door at the end of the hall was shut. Chambers gave a polite rap and a moment later it was opened by the sheriff himself, in full uniform, pressed and immaculate, a trim man in his forties with close-cropped hair and very pink skin around his neck.

"Come in, gentlemen," he said.

They entered a modest office, passing a secretary on their way to the sheriff's inner sanctum. Here, the sheriff took a seat behind his desk—backed by a wall of framed commendations and citations—and gestured for them to sit.

"What can I do for you folks?" he asked.

Chambers leaned forward to read the nameplate. "Sheriff Ledbetter, thank you for seeing us on such short notice. My partner and I are looking into a homicide that took place in your jurisdiction two years ago." He briefly described it, then gave Ledbetter the case number.

"That's some time ago," Ledbetter said, adding, "I thought you told my man at the desk it was a pressing matter."

"It is," said Chambers. "It may be connected to an active serial killer we're tracking."

Sheriff Ledbetter punched the intercom, read the case number into it, asked for the file, then sat back and gazed at Chambers impassively. "As I recall, it was an open-and-shut mob killing."

"My partner and I just need to put ourselves at ease on that point. You know: glance over the file, talk to the investigating detective and the ME who did the autopsy."

"*I* was the investigating detective," said Ledbetter.

"Good, good. Can you give us a quick briefing?"

"Like I said, it was a mob-style killing. In some locations, it might have been gang-related—the body was brutalized, obviously to send a message—but we don't have gang problems anywhere near here."

Yet, Chambers thought cynically.

The intercom buzzed. The sheriff picked up, listened, hung up. "The file was transferred to long-term storage."

"Would it be possible to retrieve that file?"

"Of course. It might take a few weeks—we're a bit short-staffed."

"Then perhaps we could talk to the ME who did the autopsy?"

"There's no point in troubling him when his entire report is with the case file."

There was a brief silence.

"Sheriff Ledbetter, we're really hoping for a quicker turnaround on that file if at all possible—or at least, to speak with someone who can fill us in on the case details." Chambers tried mightily to keep the irritation out of his voice.

"If you'll leave your card, I'll see what I can do." The sheriff rose. "I'm sorry I can't help you folks further, but that's such a cold case I couldn't provide any additional details without seeing the file myself." He stepped around the desk to see them out.

Chambers was about to protest when Pendergast spoke up, voice once again smooth as honey. "One moment, Sheriff. I was trying to place your name—I knew it rang a bell. Weren't you the one who took down that active shooter at the Woodhaven School a couple of years ago?"

At this, the sheriff hesitated. "That was me, yes."

"Well, that was some piece of work! You're a brave son of a bitch, I'll say that."

Chambers was astounded at this previously unseen side of his partner: the breathless appreciation, the cursing, the fawning manner.

"Only doing my duty," Ledbetter said.

"Hell, no! As I recall, you went in there when the others were hanging back, scared and confused. You saved lives." He extended his hand. "It's a real pleasure to meet you—after all, it's not every day you get a chance to meet a true hero."

"Well, now," said Ledbetter, coloring, "as I said, just doing my duty."

"You did a lot more than your duty, Sheriff. Imagine—some crazy bastard bent on shooting up a school full of innocents. I'm proud to know you, sir, proud to know you." He shook the sheriff's hand. "Well, we'll get out of your hair and let you get back to work. Sorry to break in on you like this."

"Glad to be of help."

"And... well, we'd love to see that file when you can find time to pull it."

At this, the sheriff hesitated. "Let me just check with Dolly to see if we can't rustle that up for you now." He opened the door to the outer office and spoke to the secretary, who got up and left.

"It'll take about ten minutes. Long-term file storage is in the basement."

"That's damn good of you, Sheriff," said Pendergast. "Now, about this case—do you recall what made you think it was mob-related?"

"The guy was tied to a chair, gagged, tortured, and beaten up before being shanked in the heart. Classic MO."

"Shanked in the heart." Pendergast shook his head. "With what sort of knife?"

"That I can't recall. You'd have to ask the ME."

"And who might that be, again?"

"Dr. Franklin Brantley. The coroner's office is on North Cherry. If you're heading over there now, I'll call ahead and let him know you're coming."

"You're a good man, Sheriff," said Pendergast.

The secretary returned, carrying an expanding file. She handed it to the sheriff along with a piece of paper, which he in turn gave to Pendergast. "If you could just sign out the file, I'd appreciate it."

"Many thanks." Pendergast signed his name with a flourish, handing back the paper and tucking the file under his left arm. He seized Ledbetter's hand with his right. "All I can say is, wait until my kids hear that I met the man who took down the Woodhaven shooter."

* * *

Five minutes later, they were out of the parking lot and headed toward North Cherry.

"Excuse me," said Chambers, "while I vomit. Forgive my saying so, but your lips stink from being jammed so far into the sheriff's ass. How the hell did you know all that stuff about the Woodhaven shooting?"

"Vomit if you must—but only on the condition that you stop wearing that cheap aftershave: Drakkar Noir, is it? As for the 'stuff,' it was all there on the wall behind the sheriff. Framed plaques, citations, anything and everything you needed to know. Fortunately, *I* have keen eyesight."

"You laid it on pretty thick. I thought he might sense you were buttering him up."

"My dear Chambers, I can assure you the butter of flattery can be laid on—even as thickly as my grand-mère used to slather over our grits—with no fear of suspicion or exposure." He paused. "And I imagine it leaves the subject in a better humor than a bolus of lies about one's property having been a toxic waste dump."

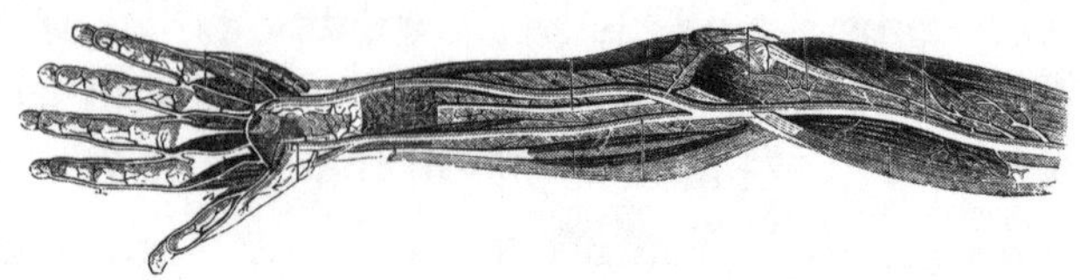

23

PENDERGAST LOOKED VERY BRIEFLY through the autopsy report, then handed it to Chambers for review while he drove to the coroner's office. It did, in fact, look like a mob killing on the surface—but if you drilled down, things got weird.

Dr. Frank Brantley couldn't have been more different from the unhelpful sheriff—excited, even boisterous, and eager to assist any way he could. "Come in, gentlemen!" he said as they entered his office. He, too, had a wall of framed diplomas and citations behind him, and he was dressed in an immaculate white lab coat over a seersucker jacket. "Please have a seat." He sat down and clasped his hands on his desk, an inquiring look on his face.

"Thank you for seeing us on short notice," Chambers said.

"Of course, of course. Nothing's going on here, anyway. Things slow down in the heat—people are too sleepy to kill each other."

Chambers put the file on his desk. "Do you recall this case? Please feel free to refresh your memory."

"I do. It was, let's see, about two years ago." He flipped through the file. "Ah, yes. Body tied to a chair, badly beaten, signs of torture. Didn't catch the perps, but in these cases you so rarely do. The wiseguys in New Orleans like to drive a good way out of town, sometimes, to conduct business of this nature. Less headaches for the city police—and little towns like ours are left with a modicum of clues. And the mob gets its message across nevertheless." He closed the folder. "What's the FBI's interest?"

"We think this might possibly be connected to an active serial killer."

"What makes you think that?"

Chambers tapped the report. "You say here that the body showed signs of torture—cigarette burns, cuts, bruises. But the right arm seems untouched. Why's that?"

Brantley shrugged. "Fellow died before they got around to messing it up."

"The serial killer we're after seems to have an interest in the right arm of his victims."

"What for?"

"We don't know."

Now Pendergast picked up the line of questioning. "In looking over your report, we noted the right shoulder of the victim had a cluster of pinpricks in it, done perimortem. Do you recall that?"

"I do. My guess is it was due to drug use."

"Have you ever seen drug use involving the shoulder?"

Brantley thought a moment. "Come to think of it, I haven't. It's an odd choice. But sometimes they run out of veins and inject themselves in strange places, between their toes and such."

"Did you section or take any samples of those prickings or markings?"

"No. It didn't seem relevant."

"Was the victim a drug addict?"

Brantley glanced through the report. "There was no obvious evidence of that."

"So he wasn't likely to have been a 'hard stick,' or to have run out of veins. Did the autopsy identify any drugs in the cadaver?"

"Yes it did—flunitrazepam."

"Known by the brand name Rohypnol." He paused. "Any thoughts on why he was given flunitrazepam?"

"I would assume as a sedative to control the victim."

"Injected or ingested?" Pendergast continued in his smooth manner.

"Ingested. We found traces in the stomach."

"Seems rather thoughtful to administer a sedative to your victim while simultaneously torturing him," Pendergast observed.

When there was no reply, he continued. "The victim was stabbed in the heart after being tortured—correct?"

"That's correct. And that, of course, was the proximate cause of death."

"With what sort of implement?"

"Examination of the wound led us to believe it was probably a forty-eight-millimeter scalpel blade."

"Which is not a particularly common murder implement for mob killings—at least, to my knowledge."

"Never seen it before, actually."

"And after the autopsy, what was the disposition of the body?"

"It was returned to the family and, I believe, cremated."

"Pity." Pendergast leaned forward. "Doctor, could you take a look at the photograph, here, that shows the markings in the shoulder? A dozen or so, shaped roughly like an inverted V?"

The doctor looked.

"Think back, if you will. Is it possible that those pricks—rather than being traces of earlier needle marks—were in fact made at the time of the killing by the *point* of that forty-eight-millimeter scalpel?"

The doctor looked at the top of the folder for a moment. Then he said: "Now that I think back, I believe you might be correct."

"And *that*," Pendergast said as he turned to Chambers, a suppressed note of triumph in his voice, "is the signature we've been looking for."

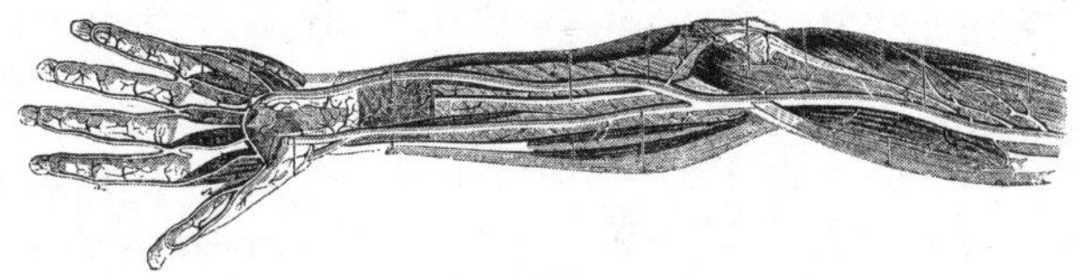

24

In the dark of his improvised cell, Proctor finished his meal, slid it through the narrow grate below the door, then returned to his favored position against the rear wall. He had now sharpened the talon-shaped blade to a maximal edge. He no longer practiced pacing or running from wall to wall; he knew the room's dimensions as well as or better than a blind person knew his own home. There was something else occupying his time now—but before he returned to it, he knew it was important to both rest and digest.

He decided to take a one-hour break.

He was certain he was being held by a cannibal: one who could barely wait to sink his teeth into Proctor's flesh—his bare arms first, it would seem, starting with the right—and who believed his repast was ready. This last meal Proctor had eaten was smaller than the others, low in protein and prepared in a slapdash fashion. That alone started an emergency siren sounding in his head: the next time the gas came, the man planned to kill him... Proctor did not know exactly when, but it would be soon.

Although the gas was odorless, he was now aware of the noises that would herald its approach: the scrape of the retracting ceiling panel, and the low hiss of the gas cock being opened. That would be the signal for him to slip the talon between his fingers, take a deep, deep breath—and hold it long enough for his captor to believe he'd passed out and enter the room, guard at least partially down. He'd be eager by now, very eager, and might well drop some of the earlier precautions.

There was one problem with this plan. His captor might be insane, but he was no fool. Proctor wasn't sure if the man guessed he knew about the gassing—the chances were probably fifty-fifty—but he would certainly have some idea of human lung capacity.

The average person, Proctor knew, could hold his or her breath between thirty and ninety seconds. Factors like fitness, cigarette smoking, age, even genetics could affect this to some degree. Even if the man guessed Proctor knew about the gas—or assumed he was holding his breath—he'd reason that three minutes, three and a half at most, was the longest his captive could hold out.

This was why Proctor had returned, in earnest, to the breathing exercises he'd first been drilled in almost fifteen years before.

In 1981, after joining the navy, he soon became part of the special boat detachment UDT-11, redesignated two years later as SEAL Team Five. The harsh and rigorous training he'd endured—much of it in and under water—remained with him even today. CO_2 tolerance exercises, hypoxic workouts, apnea training—all the grueling methods used by SEALs to maximize breath-holding skills and lung capacity were so deeply ingrained in him, they were almost part of his nervous system. Completing the underwater knot test, enduring "Dark Angel" ambush challenges: all these were part of building mental and physical toughness at a school where passing out from hypoxia became a common occurrence.

After several years of distinguished service, much of it in combat, Proctor was taken aside by an enigmatic senior officer named Howard Longstreet. A major shift in detachments and designations was taking place due to the formation of Special Operations Command, Longstreet told him, and as a result Proctor and his exemplary service had come to his attention. He asked Proctor if he'd like to step out from under the umbrella of SOCOM and join the Ghost Company: a shadowy, all-volunteer descendant of the whispered "Blue Light" detachment and the Vietnam-era MACV-SOG Hatchet Force, combining not only different military branches but various intelligence services as well. The "Company," as it was known to its members, was based out of what during World War II had been the Amphibious Scout and Raider School in Fort Pierce, Florida, and never numbered more than its name implied: one company, made up of three platoons tasked with classified and dangerous missions, frequently "wet work," often in unsanctioned theaters of engagement.

Proctor had spent half a dozen years in the Company, working under Longstreet's right-hand man, Michael Decker, and more immediately under another senior operative, Aloysius Pendergast. But then—for reasons never fully explained, most likely the need to maintain deniability—the Ghost Company was disbanded, then deprecated. What few whispers of it that were drifting around military camps and bases began to dissipate. Longstreet had offered the survi vors their pick of assignments—but Proctor knew any other position, line or staff, would be anticlimactic. So he'd left the service five years before . . . and, for better or worse, remained a pilgrim ever since. His unique skills, honed and perfected over a decade, were suited for one job in particular—a job that no longer existed.

"Fidelitas usque ad mortem," he murmured to himself. Loyalty unto death.

Now Proctor shook these memories away. His musings, he calculated, had taken up the better part of an hour. It was time to get on with his training.

Even though most SEAL workouts took place in the water, there were numerous "dryland training" exercises he could practice in his cell. If the cannibal was watching him with NVGs from above, he wouldn't even notice many of them. Pursed-lip breathing; rib stretches; static apnea workouts; diaphragmatic breathing—these techniques, and others, would increase Proctor's tolerance for oxygen deprivation, as well as his lung capacity. Thanks to his years in the Company and with the SEALs, Proctor could already hold his breath much longer than most men—now he was working, under pressure, to push himself to the limit.

Although he of course had no watch, he could use his fingers or toes as a chronometer, tapping out the minutes one second at a time. The longest any SEAL trainee in his team had held their breath, he recalled, was seven minutes.

Proctor would try for eight.

He had to be careful, of course. Too much of any exercise, done too quickly, would be counterproductive. But Proctor had vast experience in how to toughen himself in the shortest period of time.

And at the moment, he had the strongest possible motive to do so.

He sat back in the dark, preparing to begin his next training session.

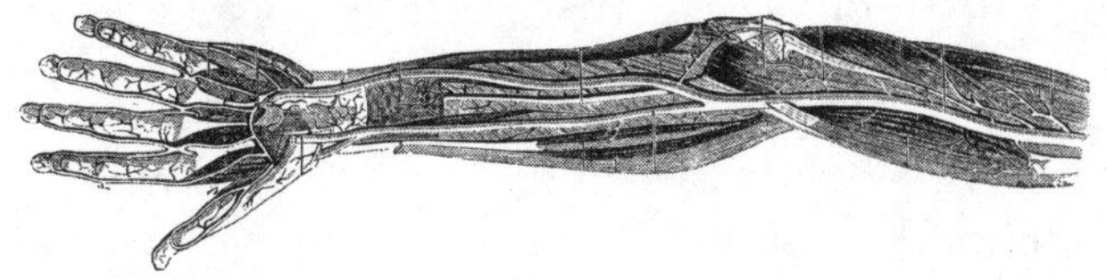

25

"And now, my dear Chambers, let us revisit the database—now that we have concrete evidence to look for."

"Concrete?" Chambers echoed. Another afternoon, and he was back at Penumbra Plantation, in the sweltering computer room.

"I believe," said Pendergast, taking a turn around the room, "that these tiny injuries to the top of the right shoulder may well be the key we've been searching for."

"If so, it makes no sense," said Chambers. "Given the mauling, the slashing, even the amputations—what's the purpose of those tiny marks?"

"It may be..." said Pendergast slowly, "... a sort of test."

"What kind? To see if the meat's tender enough?"

Pendergast fixed him with his silvery eyes, and the laugh that was rising in Chambers's throat quickly died away.

"Precisely."

"You think the man's one of those serial-killer cannibals, then?"

Pendergast did not answer. He simply sat down at the large desk and turned his attention to the nearest PC.

Chambers looked at his own computer, trying to think of a correct search term. If pinpricks had been noted—which might have been rarely—it would have likely been by the coroner or medical examiner.

What would a doctor have called pricks to the skin? MEs always had a fancy name for something.

He tried "pinprick" and got no hits. "Incisions" came up with too many. "Tiny puncture wounds" brought up another sea of hits.

He heard an exclamation from Pendergast. "Remarkable," he said. "Truly remarkable."

Chambers got up and went over to stare at Pendergast's screen.

"I asked for the association of 'petechiae' with 'puncture' and 'cluster' as noted in the ME's report, for all criminal incidents within a one-hundred-mile radius. Here are the, ah, ripostes."

"Ripostes? You mean, hits?"

"Yes, thank you. Hits."

Chambers stared at the list. "Pendergast, some of these aren't homicides. You've got car accidents, falls, drug overdoses, and the Lord knows what else."

"As we determined earlier, our man is sui generis, which means we must avoid assumptions—including the assumption his activities inevitably resulted in a homicide."

This sounded like gibberish, but Chambers said nothing.

"Now," said Pendergast, "you take half these hits, and I'll take the other half, and let us see what we come up with."

Chambers downloaded his portion of the list onto a three-and-a-half-inch floppy disk and once again sat at his computer. He sighed deeply, then began paging through a mass of autopsy reports, medical records, and criminal incidents. He'd never heard the word *petechiae* before, but he quickly learned it referred to a tiny spot of bleeding under the skin—in this case, due to pricking or shallow jabbing. It was easy to dismiss most of the hits, but there were a number consistent with the kind of cluster they were looking for. In each case, the ME had noted an anomalous cluster of shallow pricks made with what appeared to be the tip of a scalpel. In a few cases the arm had been cut off beneath the shoulder, but in other cases the arm was still intact—slashed or not. And when an especially alert ME had actually bothered to note the number of pinpricks, they always amounted to eleven—and the shapes of these clusters were always the same.

"It seems," Pendergast said, as if reading his thoughts, "that we can in fact rule out accidents, falls, and overdoses unless the precise signature shows up."

This was fine with Chambers—so far, the only signatures he'd found had shown up on obvious homicides.

He continued winnowing down the files. As he was wrapping up, he came across one that he was about to dismiss—a criminal complaint against a funeral home for abuse of a corpse—when he was stopped by a photo that showed the corpse missing an arm, with an unmistakable cluster of pinpricks on its shoulder. He enlarged the photo, counted the marks—eleven. But for the first time, this was not a homicide—the file included a death certificate indicating the individual had died from accidental trauma.

"How are you doing, Chambers?" Pendergast asked.

"Just finished."

"Excellent! Let us print out our results and compare them in the drawing room."

Chambers followed Pendergast across the central hall into another section of the mansion. The drawing room was very grand, with polished oak floors covered in Persian rugs, tall windows with velvet drapes, an elaborate marble fireplace, a sideboard brimming with crystal and silver decanters, and numerous portraits in gilded frames adorning the walls. Pendergast took a seat at a small mahogany side table with four chairs, placed his files upon the table, and motioned for Chambers to take the seat opposite.

Almost instantly the butler—what was his name, Maurice?—came floating in like a ghost. "May I offer the gentlemen a refreshment?"

"Yes, indeed, Maurice. A sherry, if you please." He turned to Chambers. "And you?"

"Um," said Chambers. He needed something cold—very cold. "An Abita beer, if you have one on ice?"

Maurice bowed and left, returning almost immediately with a silver tray on which stood a glass of sherry—along with an Abita beer, still weeping chips of ice.

Now, this is service, thought Chambers. It was the first drink he'd had in a week and, damn, it was good.

"I received six 'hits,'" said Pendergast, laying out his files. "In each case, the medical examiner noted a cluster of tiny pricks, always numbering eleven, always in the same spot above the acromioclavicular ligament, and always of a similar shape or design. It appears our man has been busy longer than we supposed."

"And I've got five. Plus a weird incident at a graveyard." When Pendergast looked at him inquiringly, he said, "It's the only one I found in which marks were evident on someone who died of natural causes."

"Most interesting. Let us exchange files." Pendergast downed his sherry and turned to Maurice, hovering in the background. "Another Abita for Agent Chambers and another sherry for me, if you please."

Chambers went through Pendergast's files, astonished at how similar each set of pricks was to the ones he'd found—in the same place, always numbering eleven. There were ten murders in total, plus the death by apparently natural causes, stretching back five years. Pendergast was right: their killer had been very busy. In some instances, he had severed the right arm; in some he'd merely slashed it; in others he simply left it alone. In several cases it appeared he'd tried to disguise his MO by dressing up the killing to look like the work of gangsters. But there were always those eleven tiny pricks.

"Our man is clever," said Pendergast. "He's been careful to vary the killings just enough to cloud the modi operandi, to prevent connections from being made—unlikely in any case, as we've learned with difficulty. But always—always—he 'tests' the shoulder in that exact spot." He paused. "Pity the Drakos body was too torn up for those marks to be evident."

"Jesus Christ," said Chambers. "It feels like we've just discovered Louisiana's own Jack the Ripper. If you count the ones we started with, there are at least twelve or thirteen killings here—and I'll bet there are a lot more that passed under the radar." He shook his head. "It feels like we're starting all over again. Where in hell do we begin?"

"Tomorrow, we shall begin at the beginning."

"Which is?"

Pendergast held up a slender file. "Your incident in a graveyard."

"That wasn't even a murder. The guy died a natural death—I mean, it's all there on the death certificate. He fell off a girder and bashed his head in."

"Yes. But it is the first, and a great deal can be deduced by studying a serial killer's initial victim—even a serial killer as unique as this." He drained his glass. "And it would appear he began his spree with a corpse, victimized postmortem."

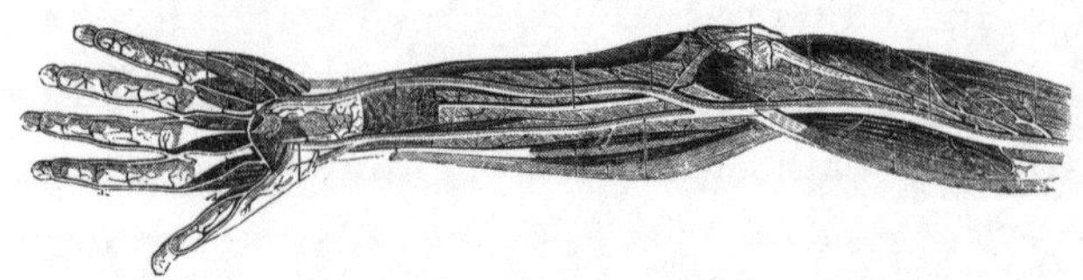

26

Proctor's warm-up for another round of breathing exercises was interrupted by the faint noise he'd been waiting for: the scrape of the hatch sliding open.

This was it, then. Good—Proctor had been getting impatient.

He knew he had only seconds to prepare before the gas cock opened. But that was enough. Almost without thinking, he dropped into survival mode. Quickly, he emptied his lungs; took a shallow breath, let it out; repeated this; gulped several deep breaths in succession—and then at last began, from the belly up, to fill his lungs to their uttermost, and even beyond, with as much air as possible. Then he let himself sag to the floor, slipping his shank out of hiding and nestling it between his fingers as he did so. He heard the gas cock opening as his head came to rest on the rough canvas.

Almost imperceptibly, the index finger of his free hand began tapping out the seconds: one per beat of his heart.

Eight minutes: that was his goal. He figured his captor would not wait nearly that long—once psychotic killers had begun to act, the desire to bring that act to completion became almost overpowering—but he would try for eight, anyway. He imagined boasting of the feat to his old SEAL buds—without context, of course—and knew none of them would believe him. Still, it would be a feat he could always be proud of.

If he lived through the next half hour.

The first minute passed while, essentially, he completed preparing himself, mentally and physically. The second and third minute passed with situational awareness, running again and again through the steps he'd take once the man entered, working through the various ways it might play out.

At three minutes, the lights snapped on.

Now, for the first time, Proctor took stock. The urge to breathe was faint but growing. This, he knew from experience, was natural... already, he felt on course to make eight minutes. Although that wouldn't be necessary: the lights coming on meant the guy was directly outside the room, probably watching him via some hidden means.

The lights meant business. The lights meant he was coming in. Three minutes and a half had now passed—the longest his jailer could expect Proctor to hold out. But the man had proven himself to be very careful, to take no unnecessary chances. Weighing this against the sick urges he felt sure the insane man was feeling, Proctor guessed he'd wait four minutes—four and a half, max—before removing the cloth from beneath the door, opening it, and entering carefully.

As the need to breathe began to slowly intensify, Proctor turned his thoughts to what would happen after the man stepped in. His fragmentary memories indicated that, the first time, his captor had worn a gas mask—but they also indicated he'd almost immediately taken it off. That meant the anesthetizing agent, whatever it was, neutralized very quickly. Proctor would need to resupply himself with oxygen before initiating his attack; he couldn't very well overcome the psycho while still gasping for breath. So when he heard the door open, he'd initiate the second stage of his plan. He would continue holding his breath while the man approached him—no doubt with gas mask on and an incapacitating device of some type, probably that murderous Taser, at the ready. The removal of the gas mask would be his signal to act.

Four and a half minutes had come and gone—five minutes was approaching. His need for air was beginning to grow past the point where it could be ignored. He knew that the record for holding one's breath was over ten minutes... maybe over eleven. But that was almost unnatural... anyway, he wouldn't need to make it nearly that far. Five minutes had passed; surely any moment the door would open and the man would come in. If he waited so long that Proctor began to feel faint, he could grab the assailant's gas mask and briefly use it himself while he neutralized his opponent...

Five and a half minutes. He remembered from his SEAL training that, by this point, several trainees would have passed out and been pulled from the water. He focused on the things that had been drilled into him: visualization techniques; using mental toughness to embrace discomfort; keeping one's mindset fixated on the goal at hand; drawing on one's team members to find additional strength in a shared ordeal... except here, he had no teammates.

Belay that—he had one: the cruel, talon-shaped blade hidden between his fingers, ready to deal death at a moment's notice. When it came to close-quarters fighting, Proctor had learned to be equally lethal with either hand, and he'd chosen to put the weapon in his left. The freak's gaze so obviously drifted to his right arm that—if Proctor timed things right—he'd never see it coming.

But now he'd passed the six-minute mark, and despite his best efforts, the need to breathe was growing extreme...

It was at that moment he thought he heard—from beyond the door—a chuckle.

He froze, lack of breath momentarily forgotten. It must have been his imagination: a trick of his increasingly oxygen-starved brain.

But then it came again, and this time there could be no question.

"I know you're holding your breath, my friend," laughed the all-too-familiar voice from beyond the door. "Six minutes—very impressive. But unlike you, I have all the time in the world. You, on the other hand, will have to breathe sooner or later... sooner, I'd imagine... and then you'll go under."

Proctor's mind, even as it grew groggy from lack of oxygen, began to race. This had to be a joke—or, rather, a test. The man was guessing, making sure. Proctor could have been wrong about the dispersal period of the gas—maybe it was longer than he'd anticipated. Or the psycho was being even more cautious than he expected. Either way, it couldn't be much longer. Any second now, the door would open. And half a minute later, he'd be free. He forced his mind to focus on this outcome as his lungs began to scream for air...

Then the voice came again. "Oh," it sounded through the door, mocking, self-confident. "By the way, I know about that shank you have hidden. Palmed in your left hand—correct? You won't have a chance to use it, I'm afraid. Because sooner or later you'll have to breathe, and then it's lights-out for you, my friend."

Shock coursed through Proctor. How could the man know about that? Had he been watching, via some night-vision peephole, as he honed the edge of the blade? No, that couldn't be—Proctor had taken too much care to keep his movements stealthy, slow, obscured from any possible angle of view. He was just guessing again; a final test before entering.

...But then, how could he know about the left hand? Even if by some miracle he'd seen Proctor shape the weapon, it was impossible he'd seen him slip it into position as he mimed sinking to the ground. Guessing he had a weapon—maybe. But...

Another laugh. "Surrender to the inevitable. I know everything. All you're doing is wasting time—and it would annoy me to have to pump a fresh load of gas in there."

Proctor had been struggling with a combination of disbelief and lightheadedness, while meanwhile every cell in his body now cried out for oxygen. But—for a few seconds—clarity returned, and he realized that, whatever unexpected way this situation was playing out, he had run out of options.

As a member of the Ghost Company, though, he also knew that even when you were out of options, one final option was still open to you.

He gasped in a single deep breath, pushing himself into a sitting position at the same time. The relief was immediate...but so was the peculiar twirling sensation, swiftly stealing over him already.

"You know everything?" he cried, coughing. "Bet you didn't know about *this*, motherfucker!"

And, raising his left arm, weapon extended and at the ready, he brought it down across his right arm.

"Your trophy is spoiled, you bastard! Can you see? I'm slicing up your meal *myself*!" And Proctor slashed at his arm a second time.

There was a howl of rage from the far side of the door. It seemed to go on for a long time, but—with each breath he took—the noise grew fainter to Proctor. The blade slipped from his hand as he felt the warm blood start flowing into the crook of his elbow.

"I'm going to leave you to bleed out!" came the faraway voice, trembling with fury. "You can die alone—in the dark!"

But Proctor didn't hear him.

A few seconds later, the lights went off as well, plunging the room once again into utter darkness. But Proctor—already in a deep darkness of his own—did not notice.

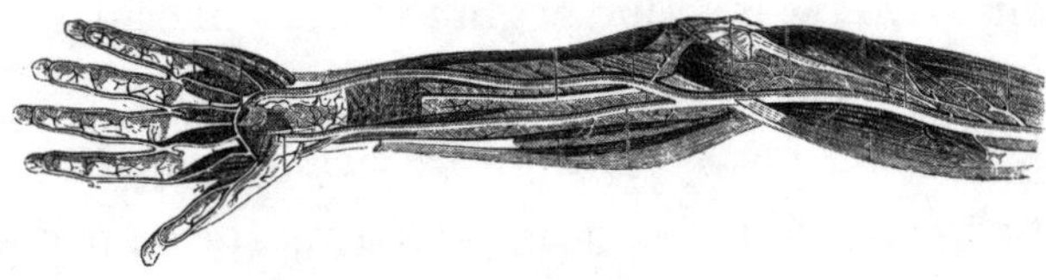

27

WICKMAN DROVE ALONG THE rutted path at fifty miles an hour, the vehicle jouncing and rocking violently, the brush that pushed in on both sides whipping against its flanks. He forced himself to slow down—he'd kept the road, if you could call it a road, intentionally overgrown and crude, more a trail than anything else. It wouldn't do to break an axle or lose a tire. Not now, of all times.

He pounded the steering wheel again and again, cursing. It wasn't fair. After so many years, so much planning—risking danger or even capture dozens of times, only to find the resource he'd just taken wasn't suitable and it had been for naught... now, he'd finally been able to relax, certain he'd succeeded. This last resource had been perfect in every way. Except he'd been more clever than even Wickman, comfortable by now with expecting the unexpected, had imagined. Even though ultimately Wickman had seen through his sham unconsciousness, who could have ever anticipated the man would then—before succumbing to the gas—do what he'd done?

I'm slicing up your meal myself. What the hell did that even mean?

He couldn't stop to think about that now. He'd put off Dr. Telligren and the operation once already—doing so a second time would make things much more difficult. And with the evil stirring ever more aggressively in that limb, he couldn't wait any longer. It had remained in his arm, almost dormant, longer than he could have hoped—he knew that any day now it would begin to spread like an infection... at which point, he'd be done for.

No. Telligren and his assistant were arriving that evening, and Wickman hadn't called to postpone. That meant he had only a few hours to find a new, perfect resource.

He was approaching the camouflaged barrier, close to where the old dirt track met the highway. He eased to a stop, got out of the van, and approached the steel cattle gate—on the far side of which he'd attached the base of a fallen tree trunk, blending it carefully with the other roadside vegetation. This was a stretch of Chef Menteur Highway, like so many surrounding areas, where not only was the road terrible, but the primary landscape was swamp; as a result, the drivers who infrequently sped down this straight stretch of blacktop were intent on getting somewhere rather than gazing out at the endless creepy foliage.

Assuring himself the coast was clear, Wickman swung the gate inward, careful not to disrupt the camouflage wired to its outer side. Then he got back into the van and crept the last hundred feet out onto the highway. As he did so, a lash of rain sprayed over his windshield. He craned forward and glanced up at the dark, bruise-colored sky. His route from the manse to this road had been so densely covered by a canopy of trees and sagging bamboo that he hadn't even realized it was drizzling.

The road was still empty. He paused one last moment, checking the rearview mirror, ensuring the gate of his fallen-tree contrivance had swung closed behind the van. Then he turned the vehicle to the left and pressed hard on the accelerator.

He wondered why he'd instinctively turned westward. Normally he would have gone east; most recently, his hunting ground had been a carefully mapped scattering of towns fifty or more miles into Mississippi. But then he smiled to himself. *Of course.* In his dismay and sudden trauma, he'd almost forgotten how—lolling around his manse first with Drakos, and later the security guard or whoever he was, safely locked in the basement—he'd whiled away part of the waiting period by considering quicker and safer ways to obtain a resource. He'd never need to act on them, of course—after nabbing the security guard, he thought that part of his life was done—but with his years of practice, and his own "radar" mature, it seemed almost second nature to keep dreaming up new and better scenarios to collect resources.

Now he would put one of those scenarios—the one that seemed quickest and most certain—to the test.

Less than half an hour later, he was cruising down the boulevards of Slidell, Louisiana. Not only did Slidell have advantages of proximity and demographics, but the manner in which its sprawl had overtaken the neighboring towns meant game would be more plentiful.

He continued until he reached the fringes of town, where a no-man's-land of sorts—part commercial, part residential—overlapped. More slowly, he passed a lonely landscape of gas stations, bars, Blockbuster Video outlets, and gyms, for the most part all scattered widely apart.

He pulled over across from one gym and stared at it with a critical eye. He'd used the place himself once, years ago, when he was first preparing. He had disliked the atmosphere—the flexing; the masculine preening and primping; the furtive looks, checking out how much weight the guy on the next bench was lifting—and so he instead had assembled a gym of his own in the basement of his grandmother's old mansion.

The gym was well separated from other buildings, and the rain was now pouring harder, with occasional tongues of lightning licking through the clouds. This spot was not ideal for his scenario—and besides, the gym wasn't the kind he was looking for. It was old-fashioned, without a lot of the newer machines that added aerobics to the mix. Younger men would be turned off. Putting the van into drive, he pulled back onto the road and continued.

Half a mile farther on, he saw what looked like an ideal spot: Diamond Gym. The signage was new, and through the gaudy neon-adorned front window he could see it was enjoying heavy use. He glanced at his watch: quarter past one. Guys using their lunch hours to pump iron. Like Tantalus, they'd keep struggling at it but—he thought with disdain—never be satisfied.

Next to the gym was a tavern, with an alleyway between that was empty except for trash cans. As he watched, two men in their late twenties walked out of the gym and headed into the tavern. It was Friday, after all: why not follow a workout with a burger and a beer—or maybe five—and get the weekend off to an early start?

Twisting the wheel hard, he turned the van around and parked in front of the gym, just back from the large front window. It was raining cats and dogs, but so much the better: the rain had washed all the mud from the wheel wells of his van; the downpour kept traffic to a minimum; and any passersby would be intent on getting from point A to point B without looking around at the scenery.

In his scenario, he hadn't accounted for rain—but he realized it only made the odds of success more favorable.

He took a quick look around the interior, making sure he hadn't forgotten anything and that all was prepped. He scowled as he did so. After ditching the white van in a swamp and buying this gray utility van from a retired Alabama electrician for cash, he figured that—once he'd taken the security guard—he wouldn't need a vehicle for any further harvesting. As it was, in his haste he'd almost driven off without some critical elements of his tool kit. The scowl faded as he saw all was in readiness. Then he hopped lightly down from the driver's seat, closed and locked the door, and jogged toward the tavern, keeping as much as possible out of the rain.

Stepping in, he glanced around. It was just as he'd hoped: most of the patrons were exercise freaks in various sizes. A few heads swiveled toward him at the noise of the opening door, but they all looked away again disinterestedly: he was wearing a technician's short-sleeved blue polo shirt, the name of a fake machine parts store stitched on it, and his chest and arm muscles stretched the fabric admirably. Just another well-ripped blue-collar worker bee with close-cropped blond hair.

He quickly sized up the scattering of tables, and particularly the long bar that took up the entire rear wall of the place. A lot of the patrons seemed to prefer sitting on its stools and having their lunches there. He walked along the nearest wall, and then—when he got to the bar—he turned and strolled along it at a leisurely pace, as if deciding which stool was most suitable. In truth, he was using the inner power he'd been given—refined and developed, now, to the point where it was instinctual, not to be doubted—to discern if any of the patrons seated at the bar would make a good resource.

Wickman's radar—as he'd come to call it—suddenly went off, and he glanced over at the seated man he was passing. Well built, under forty, check, check, check... but then Wickman noted the ugly tattoo on the man's right arm. *Shit.* He continued almost to the end of the bar, then took a stool and ordered what everyone else seemed to be having: Bud Light.

He sat there, nursing the beer and doing his best to be patient. Glancing around stealthily, he reassured himself he fit in well and was, essentially, unnoticed. The place was full of fit young men, drinking and laughing. His scenario was proving to be as perfect as he'd imagined, save for one thing: not just any one of these fine specimens would work. To fit his needs—to put a stop to the crawling evil that even now threatened to spread to the rest of his body—the resource had to be *ideal.* He'd learned how to channel his inner power to check for that; he'd perfected various ways to procure a target... the one thing he could not control was when an acceptable resource would appear.

Half an hour went by. Two o'clock. He ordered another Bud as the sounds of Pearl Jam, Green Day, and Nirvana abused the jukebox again and again. The stools to his left emptied as a big group left, heading back to work.

Jesus, what could he do? Was it possible, after all, that he could settle for *any* resource, not solely a perfect one? No—that was desperation talking. He'd learned painfully, over many years of false positives and near-misses, exactly what he needed. Another four hours, and Dr. Telligren would be arriving at the boat launch. He required time to not only harvest the resource but also make the necessary preparations to...

At that moment, the door of the pub opened and three youngish men came in: boisterous, jovial, with that faintly smug look one often wore after a strenuous workout—muscles engorged with plasma, veins coursing with endorphins. It seemed they were regulars, because they greeted the bartender as they took the three stools next to Wickman. He was certain they'd come from the gym: their hair was wet beyond the power of any rainstorm; they had obviously just showered and come here for lunch.

...More important, Wickman's inner radar had begun going off, three-alarm. And now, he felt the affirmation in his gut—an ideal resource had just arrived.

He casually took a sip of beer as he glanced over at the three. Visual cues, in addition to the selective inner power bestowed on him, helped narrow down the resource. It was the man sitting between the other two. He was the most cut of all, a magnificent specimen. Wickman pretended to look over his shoulder, toward the door, before returning to his beer—but not before taking another, lingering look at the man's right arm.

Perfect.

He finished his beer, keeping a low profile while listening to the loud, joke-laden conversation going on beside him. Within minutes, he'd learned all he had to learn, and a lot more besides: the target's name was Jake, and he had a relatively new girlfriend named Stacey—a real looker, apparently, but the jury was still out whether she was too much of a flake, running hot or cold at a moment's notice. Still, it was worth waiting to see if she might work out long-term because, drama queen or not, she could suck the chrome off...

Wickman dropped a twenty on the bar, slipped off his stool, and strolled out, attracting no notice.

As soon as the pub door had closed behind him, he looked in both directions. Satisfied the coast was clear, he began to move much more quickly. Running past the alley and into the fitness club, he quickly bought a white T-shirt, with a Diamond Gym logo splashed across it, from the woman behind the front counter. Then he walked out again and got back into the driver's seat of his van. Just before Wickman left the pub, Jake had ordered a bacon cheeseburger, rare, and it wouldn't arrive for a few more minutes. Time was no longer an issue. Wickman took a moment to slow his heart. He felt no fear, only excitement. His worry had been the lack of resources; bagging a suitable resource was an art he'd perfected.

Now he pulled off his polo shirt and shrugged into the T-shirt with the gym logo on its front. He rubbed a little grease from the steering column onto one side, rolled up each sleeve to the shoulder, then—reaching into one of his toolboxes—removed a pack of cigarettes and stuffed it into the left-hand roll. He didn't bother changing jeans—too generic—and besides, he was certain nobody would remember the ordinary-looking guy who'd come in an hour earlier.

If they remembered anybody, it would be the patron about to enter the bar.

He fitted a wig of ear-length curly black hair onto his head, then secured it with a baseball cap. Last came a pair of aviator glasses with lenses of clear glass. Starting the engine, he drove the van forward and into the alley. Slipping the final necessaries into the pocket of his jeans, he got out, leaving the engine running; made his way back out the narrow alley, opening the rear doors of the van and leaving them ajar; then, arranging his expression into a look of distress, ran into the adjoining tavern.

He stepped through the first rows of tables, stopped to look hurriedly around. "Jake?" he asked. Then, a little louder: "Is there a Jake here?"

A moment of silence. Then the resource at the bar turned toward him. "What's up?"

"Your name's Jake? You just come from the gym?"

Jake frowned, puzzled. "Yeah?"

Wickman exhaled, making sure to look relieved. "You've got a call."

"What?" the resource echoed.

Clearly, most of the meat was in his biceps, not his cranium. "Yeah. Someone named Stacey."

At this, Jake's two buddies leaned in toward him, muttering in concerned whispers.

"Says she needs to talk to you. Right away."

"What about?" By now, the entire tavern was listening... to the dark-haired, glasses-wearing man in a gym T-shirt. Wickman liked that.

"*I* didn't talk to her, man. All I know is she says she needs to talk to you. Like, *now*. They say she sounded frantic."

Jake slipped off his stool. His buddies did the same.

"They were calling your name all over the gym," Wickman went on. "I just volunteered to see if you were in the parking lot... or someplace nearby."

The three began to approach him.

"She said it's a personal matter," Wickman added immediately. "*Real* personal."

The three hesitated.

"She said—" Wickman paused for dramatic effect— "she said you'd understand."

It was the perfect psych-out. The resource turned to his buddies, told them to order him another beer, warned them not to touch his burger when it arrived, then headed to the door after Wickman.

They stepped outside, and Wickman made the briefest of recons—

nobody in sight, no cars passing, rain falling harder than ever—then they turned left, toward the gym, the alley looming directly ahead. Wickman made sure he stayed to the man's right side.

"Didn't you hear anything about why she was calling?" the resource asked, his mind obviously already ticking through the possible unpleasant reasons the bitch might be so bent out of shape.

"No," Wickman said as he pulled a small leather case from his jeans pocket. "The one thing she said was—" As he said this, he pulled a small, steel-jacketed syringe from the case, shoved the man violently against the back of the van, and plunged the needle into his neck. The movement, and the injection, were performed so quickly that by the time the resource reacted he was already beginning to stagger. Wickman opened the rear doors wide, hoisted him inside, closed the doors, picked the leather case off the ground, slipped the empty syringe back into it, and looked around a final time.

Still nobody.

He rolled the side door open and clambered in. The resource was already out—no surprise, given the ninety micrograms of flunitrazepam he'd just been dosed with. This, Wickman knew, was three times the normal amount used to induce anesthesia—but that was nowhere near LD_{50}, and besides, Jake weighed at least two hundred pounds. A quick check with a stethoscope confirmed his heart was strong. Moving quickly from long practice, Wickman checked a few more vitals, examined the inside of the man's elbows to make sure there were none of the telltale needle marks of a junkie, then bound him well enough for the journey home. Once back there, he could make the final preparations at his leisure.

Before taking his place in the driver's seat, he paused a moment. It had all gone so well, he deserved a reward. He reached into the back, his fingers palpating the resource's right arm. Sure enough, there it was—that spiritual connection; that ineffable link.

He backed the van carefully out of the alley, then started back down the street in the direction he'd come from, pulling off the cap, wig, and glasses as he did so. By now, the burger had probably arrived.

But it would be at least five or ten more minutes before Jake's friends thought to check on him.

Wickman smiled to himself. Talk about snatching victory from the jaws of defeat. Best of all, Dr. Telligren wasn't arriving for several more hours.

He had all the time in the world.

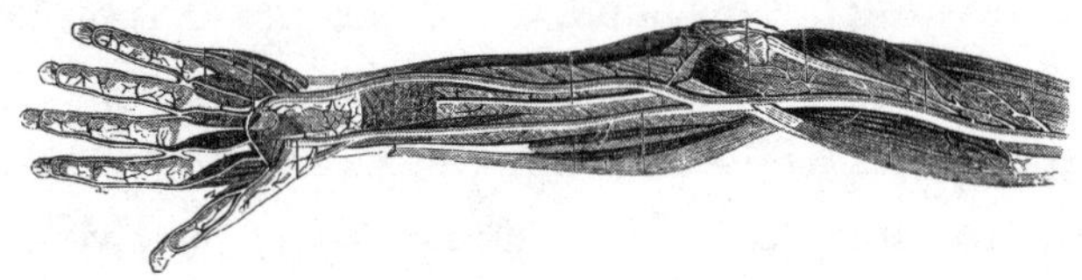

28

IF I EVER OPENED a funeral home," said Chambers, "I'd sure as hell change my last name first."

"Is there something wrong with the name?" Pendergast asked, as he eased the Spyder into one of the last free parking spaces in front of the funeral home né Victorian mansion.

"*Kroker* Brothers Funeral Home?" said Chambers, pointing at the sign with a laugh.

"Is *croaker* a term of the vernacular? I'm not familiar with it."

Pendergast, Chambers mused, was a man out of time, strangely oblivious to the modern world of 1994.

They had driven straight from Penumbra, not wasting time by calling ahead and possibly being put off. Their week's break was drawing to a close, and Chambers felt confident it would be nice to stride triumphantly into the office with a big, fat closed case—rather than simply slink back to his desk.

He led the way, Pendergast following. Entering the foyer, he could see there was a viewing in progress in an elegantly appointed room to one side. Standing in the doorway was a short man in a black suit, hands clasped in front of a large, smooth belly, his glossy black hair slicked back. A pencil mustache completed the picture.

He turned as they approached, holding out both hands as if preparing to clasp theirs in a sympathetic embrace. "I am so sorry for your loss."

Instead of holding out his hand, Chambers grasped his lanyard and held it up. "Mr. Albert Kroker?"

Kroker stared at the ID. "FBI? What's this about?"

"I'm sorry to interrupt," said Chambers, in a low voice, "but we have some questions of an urgent nature. Is there a quiet place we can talk?"

"Can't you see we're in the middle of a funeral?" Kroker hissed, his face screwing up with annoyance, all signs of phony sympathy vanishing.

"I do apologize," said Chambers in a low voice, "but this can't wait."

"It certainly *can* wait," Kroker whispered. "You have no right to barge in here like this, with no notice whatsoever. Do you have a warrant?"

"We're not here to search the place," said Chambers. "Just looking for a little friendly cooperation."

"And I will be glad to cooperate when my *own* schedule allows. Good day, gentlemen. The door is over there."

Now Pendergast stepped forward. Chambers wondered how he was going to handle this one. He'd been astonished at the sugary ooze of charm in which Pendergast had smothered the sheriff; he wondered if the manager would get the same treatment.

"Special Agent A. X. L. Pendergast," he said in a loud voice, holding out his hand. "Federal Bureau of Investigation, New Orleans Field Office." He seized Kroker's hand before the man could move it away and gave it a vigorous, seemingly endless shake. "We're investigating an unfortunate—a very unfortunate—incident that occurred *here* five years ago, and we'd like to ask you a few questions. Voluntarily, of course."

Pendergast's curiously penetrating voice had reached every corner of the next room, and the entire audience of bereaved people had turned and were staring. Even those shuffling past the coffin had stopped in their tracks.

"For God's sake, man, your *voice*—!" Kroker began, in a furious undertone.

"Now, Mr. Kroker," Pendergast went on, speaking over him even more loudly, "I ask again: is there a private place where we can speak about this unhappy occurrence, or shall we talk here?"

Kroker moved swiftly from the doorway. "This way," he said, walking fast on stubby legs. "Follow me, and for heaven's sake keep your voice down!"

They followed him down a long hallway and into a small room. Once they were all inside, Kroker shut the door and turned on them, face furiously red, practically spitting as he talked. "What the devil do you mean by bursting in here and interrupting a funeral? I will register a complaint with your superior!"

At this, Pendergast turned to Chambers. "He would like to register a complaint with you, Agent Chambers."

Chambers turned to the man. "Look, Mr. Kroker, I do apologize for the intrusion, but we're investigating a serial killer who may have murdered scores of people over the last decade. We need some questions answered. We will either get them answered here and now, or we'll subpoena you and get those answers down in New Orleans. Your choice."

"I'm outraged at this conduct!"

"So I can see," said Chambers calmly, taking out his pocket tape recorder and placing it on a table. "Now, shall we sit?"

Kroker sat down and they did likewise.

Chambers went through the preliminaries, then asked: "Mr. Kroker, five years ago you handled the funeral of a man named Bernard Montcalm, thirty-five years old, a construction worker who died in a fall. Do you recall it?"

Silence.

"There was an incident in the graveyard," said Chambers, "that generated a criminal complaint against your funeral home for abuse of a corpse. Perhaps that will help jar your memory."

"It was a ridiculous complaint, and it was immediately dropped. The family's attempt to weasel their way out of paying—that's what it was!"

Chambers nodded. "I can't speak to that. But it appears the corpse was missing an arm, which was discovered when the coffin fell into the open grave and broke apart."

"Dropped by the drunken trash I hired as pallbearers!"

"Let's focus on the missing arm. It was never recovered, is that correct?"

"Never."

"The body was embalmed and prepared in your mortuary, which is in the basement of this building—correct?"

"Yes."

"But you can attest to the fact the body arrived with both arms, and somehow during the embalming process the right arm disappeared—correct?"

"Look here. If you're trying to imply that my mortuary business—"

"Mr. Kroker," said Chambers, "we're not implying anything or casting aspersions on your business. We're simply looking for answers. I can assure you, none of this will be used to revive the complaint against you."

Kroker adjusted himself angrily in his chair. "I have no idea what happened to the arm."

"But something *did* happen between the time the body arrived and the time it reappeared for burial."

"I can't say that for sure. No one can. All I can say for sure is that, when the body fell out of the casket, it was missing an arm."

There was a brief silence. Then Pendergast began again. "At that time, how many people did you employ in the mortuary?"

"I fired them all after that. Cleaned house."

"Very well. Who were they?"

"I had an embalmer, two mortuary science technicians, and a crematory technician. And the pallbearers, of course, who worked on a standby basis."

"You fired them all?"

"The crematory technician wasn't on the premises, so I kept him, fired the rest. It was outrageous—no one could tell me what happened to that arm. I was as shocked as everyone."

"And may we have their personnel files? If you need a minute, we can wait."

A brief silence.

"You can leave out the pallbearers for now, if your memory isn't clear," Pendergast went on.

"I remember their names. All of them. It was a horrific incident, and I'll never forget it. There was Marc Bloomquist, the embalmer, along with Parker Wickman and Carlos Medina Michelson, who were the mortuary science technicians. Fired the whole lot of them. Pallbearers, too." He had risen and was pawing through a file cabinet in the rear of the small room.

"If asked, could you single out a potential suspect among the three who had possible access to the corpse?"

"No. They all came with good references, and I'd never had problems with their work before. I had no idea one of them could have done something like this... that is, *if* one of them did it. There'd been some grumbling about pay—that was the only thing I could think of. I thought it might be a way to get back at me." He handed them a few battered files, then stared at them with tiny, hostile red eyes as they leafed through them. "Are we finished?"

Chambers looked at Pendergast.

"I'm finished," said Pendergast cheerfully.

"Thank you. I *will* be making that complaint. You know where the door is—please leave without making any further disturbance. I will now rejoin the viewing you so grossly interrupted." He got up and left.

In the room, Chambers turned to Pendergast—who had shown no inclination to rise from his chair. "Wickman... the name rings a bell." The photo in the personnel file had shown a man with an unusually long face, like that of an Irish setter.

"According to this, he was only employed a few months at the funeral home before being let go." Pendergast paused. "If you recall, while looking at those antique maps of the Grand-Morte Swamp, you noted an old mansion labeled *Wichman House*. I believe it was roughly seven miles as the vulture flies from where the two women saw Drakos being recaptured."

Chambers stared. "Jesus. You think Wickman's the killer... and that old place in the swamp is his safe house?"

"I certainly do," said Pendergast.

"Many of those maps are fifty years old. The hurricane wasted the nearby town, and it never recovered. Hell, I don't think there's even a road leading into that area."

"Shall we find out?" Pendergast pulled out his pocket watch and glanced at it. "We have four hours of daylight left—just time enough for a lovely miasmic excursion."

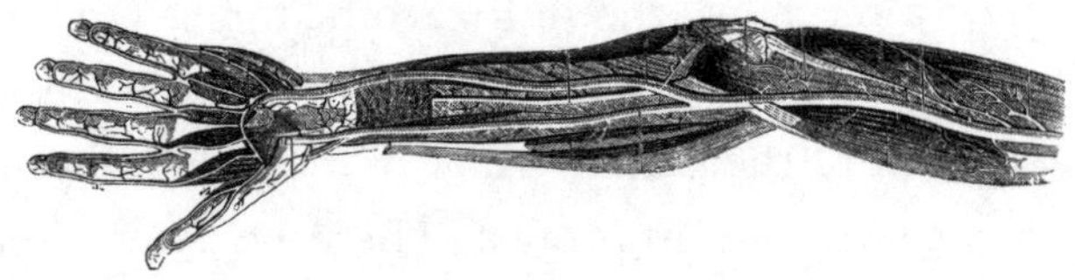

29

WICKMAN GUIDED THE CENTER-HULL console, its hull just battered and dirty enough to blend in with the other craft that plied this particular bend in the river, toward a dock that had seen its share of bad weather. It was just after 6:00 PM. The rain had finally let up, but so far he'd made his way along the river mostly by feel, all navigation lights off—long experience serving as a mental map to shoals and sandbars. Now he turned on the masthead light. The dock was listing, the auger posts leaning at odd angles, the wooden planks slippery with moss and mildew, its mooring end barely protruding from the wall of mangroves that lined the wild bank. The boat did not stop at the dock, however; it merely idled there a moment while Wickman followed the narrow pool of light along the shore for a moment, then shut it off again, along with the motor. He waited for a minute, bobbing lazily in the darkness. Finally, satisfied no observer was anywhere near—which would have been unusual indeed, especially at this late hour—he fired up the outboard, turned the masthead light on again, and coaxed the motor ahead at a dead-slow pace, past the dock, and then sharply to port, heading directly toward the screen of swamp trees.

One of the two men seated on the rear cushions drew in his breath sharply. "What are you planning to do—beach us?"

"Take it easy, Doc," Wickman replied. Still moving at just over idle speed, he maneuvered the narrow boat into a gap between two of the mangroves. For a moment, the hull caromed gently between, then slid past, the bizarre root-tendrils of two mangrove trees, twisting like huge veins out of the water, while branches overhead bent and scraped against the Bimini in protest. Then they were free, inside a minuscule bayou where the foliage parted and the lone light revealed a watery glade completely covered by the green canopy. Ahead lay the dim shape of a stone boathouse, its regular lines at odds with the surrounding vegetation. Its doors were spread wide in welcome. Wickman maneuvered inside, killed the engine, and let the craft slide into its berth. He jumped out, secured the lines, pulled the boathouse doors closed, took his guests' single large suitcase in hand, then helped the doctor and his assistant out onto the improved jetty. With the doors to the outside world closed, the boathouse interior was black as pitch; Wickman pulled the string of an overhead light, then fished in his pocket for the key to the padlock that led into the basement.

"Welcome to my humble abode!" he said with mock gravitas, ushering the two in.

He'd barely been able to keep a shit-eating grin off his face the entire trip to the public boat launch and back. The last twenty-four hours had been as desperate and hectic as all his years of preparation and adaptation had been gradual—but that was behind him now. He'd succeeded in finding a new and perfect resource just hours ago, with no need to delay Telligren yet again. Both he and the resource had been unharmed during the taking. The only witnesses had been in the bar, and they'd remember his disguise, not how he'd looked during his initial recon. One couldn't ask for a fresher harvest. And now, the last step—the arrival of the doctor and his assisting surgeon—was complete.

He could well see that Dr. Telligren was not at all in such high spirits. He did not want to be here, and the lengths he'd taken to disguise himself had only added to Wickman's mirth. This man was a physician at the top of his field, a leading researcher in some of the most important work being done in his subspecialty, perhaps even ultimately a candidate for a Nobel... and yet here he was, sneaking in via water to the basement of a rambling old mansion so decrepit it looked almost abandoned. He'd been a ridiculous sight, arriving early and waiting at the launch site, disguised in sunglasses, a Panama hat, a floral shirt, and a big Tommy Bahama bag stuffed full of necessaries—all despite the fact the sun would soon be setting.

The other man, dark, silent, and poker-faced, made Wickman uneasy. He had known Magnus from the old days, but the man was very different now, having become a celebrated young surgeon. Unlike Telligren, it was impossible to know what he was thinking.

Wickman pushed aside his anxiety and briefly anticipated the happy results of the surgery, waking up afterward, his body finally fixed, his life transformed.

Entertaining himself with these thoughts, he led the two men down the stone hall toward what had once been, more than a century ago, storerooms for crops and canned goods. Years earlier, when he realized that what he needed had to be performed here, he'd begun the lengthy, expensive process of transforming those rooms into a surgical suite. And now—as he held the double doors to the sterile area open—he was gratified to see even Dr. Telligren's eyes widen in surprise.

"Impressive!" said Magnus, an edge to his voice, placing the large medical cooler he'd been carrying with him on the floor. "Dr. Frankenstein would be envious."

Telligren had always been something of a prude and a tight-ass. But Magnus, who had been an excellent fellow student, serious, high-minded, and ambitious, seemed ominously different now. Wickman felt reassured knowing the man was a superb surgeon—at least, that was now his reputation.

Dr. Telligren began to open his mouth, but Wickman guessed what he was likely to say and beat him to it. "I know you're eager to get started. So am I. Let me quickly show you to your rooms and give you both a brief tour of the house. I think you'll find everything you need... to keep yourselves comfortable, I mean, in addition to medical supplies to cover any unexpected complications. After all, you'll be here the better part of a week—and for at least several hours, I'll be either sedated or coming out, and you'll have to fend for yourselves. This way, if you please."

Wickman took them up to the second floor, showed them their wing—which, unlike the rest of the manse, was in excellent shape, well furnished and clean—followed by the kitchen, the backup generator, and the storage areas for food, equipment, and medical supplies. As they moved through the house, he wondered idly if the damn fool in the basement who'd slashed his arm so badly was still alive. Not that it mattered; no noise could escape from the soundproofed room.

At last they returned to the surgical suite, where another quick tour familiarized the two men with the layout. Wickman had the bags of saline ready, along with scalpels, retractors, cauterizers, and everything else—after all, he'd done the initial steps often enough himself now that he could probably teach a class in the procedure—and he watched as Dr. Magnus took the units of blood from the cooler, admiring the brisk, professional way he hung them on a nearby rack, ready for use.

Then Magnus turned toward Wickman. "Where is your better half?" he asked. "Or should I say, better quarter?" And he laughed again. It was the bark of a hyena, sharp but restrained, as if recalling he was in polite society rather than the swamp. Wickman wasn't sure he liked the implication of this quip, but he quickly brushed his doubts away as misguided pride.

"He's in there—" Wickman nodded with his chin toward a metal-handled drawer set into a far wall, like a coroner's corpse tray, only substantially larger.

"Wrapped in the arms of Morpheus, no doubt?" Dr. Magnus asked as he set out the other contents of the cooler—certain anesthetics that Wickman himself had been unable to procure—on a rolling metal table.

"Probably. I sedated him before leaving to pick you up, but—" he checked his watch— "I imagine he'll be coming to shortly. Don't worry, however—he has plenty of oxygen and is too well restrained to harm himself. Too well restrained, in fact, to move—you'll have no trouble with the needle... when the time comes."

Telligren looked around once more; exchanged glances with his fellow doctor; took a deep breath, then exhaled. "Shall we proceed?"

"In a moment." Wickman moved to an equipment rack in the far corner of the improvised surgical bay, where he picked up a clipboard with several papers attached. He walked back toward the two, raising the clipboard as he did so. "I'd like you to both sign this, please."

Dr. Telligren frowned. "What is it?"

Wickman held the clipboard out at arm's length, miming an old man looking through a pair of spectacles at the end of his nose. "Merely a short document that restates points we've already discussed. First, this evil presence in my arm grew out of medical experiments you conducted on me. Second, you understand that should anything happen to me, I possess evidence that would thoroughly incriminate you. This evidence is secured in diverse locations unknown to you. Third, you will not only perform the procedure but remain here until it is clear I am free of infection and well on the way to recovery. Once the healing process is complete, I will turn over all original copies of my evidence to you and agree never to speak of the matter or to approach you again."

"You've waved these threats and promises in my face before," Telligren said. "Why do you think I'm here? Since you have so much damning evidence locked away already, why ask us to sign this ridiculous paper?"

"Because—before I go under the knife—I wanted it on the record. One last time."

"With any operation, there are risks," the older surgeon said. "How can I possibly guarantee the outcome 100 percent?"

"Those pesky little scalpels," Dr. Magnus said. "Always slipping."

"You can't," Wickman told Dr. Telligren. "But this will, at least, make sure you are *extra* careful. Now—would you both please sign?"

He handed the clipboard, along with a pen, to each physician in turn. "Thank you." Then he detached the pages, glanced at the signatures... and, turning to a paper shredder sitting next to the equipment rack, fed the sheets into its feeder slot.

"What—what perversity is this?" Dr. Telligren asked.

"Calm yourself, Doctor. It's no perversity at all. Shredding that was merely my way of demonstrating my trust... just as signing it was your acknowledgment of what awaits you should anything go wrong." He had already begun shedding his clothes as he spoke these words and ended by flinging them into a corner with a flourish. Then he donned a nearby surgical gown. "And now, Doctors, time to put me under and perform the operation."

With that he slid onto the gurney, set beneath a large, bowl-shaped operating lamp, and lay back. As he closed his eyes, he heard the snap of rubber gloves being fitted; the sound of a well-oiled drawer opening, along with the faintest of muffled moans. "I think we're ready," said the voice of Dr. Telligren—it was some distance away, no doubt from where he was examining the resource. Then Wickman felt a blood pressure cuff being fitted around his left arm, followed by a pulse-ox clamped lightly to his middle finger and a nasal cannula inserted beneath his nostrils. He breathed in the heady, humid mixture—a pharyngeal concentration, he guessed, of 40 percent oxygen.

A rubber hose was deftly wrapped and tied around his upper left arm—always his left—then came the cool swab of alcohol on the inner edge of the elbow, followed by the sting of a needle.

"Pleasant dreams, Parker," came the masked voice of Magnus. "See you on the far side."

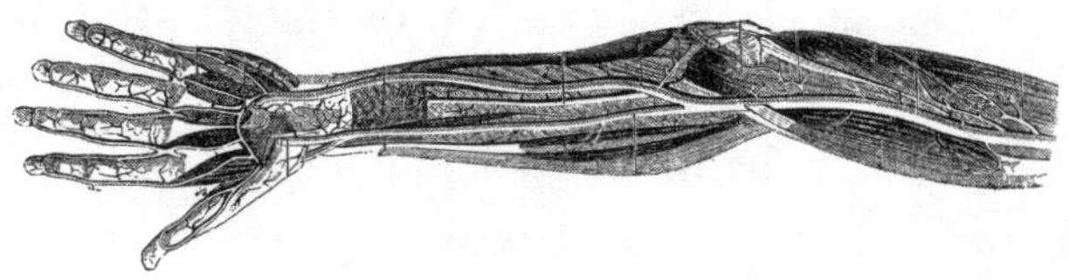

30

"The turnoff's here on the left," said Chambers, old map in hand, as Pendergast maneuvered the Spyder down the rutted road. The car they were in was the worst possible to negotiate the dirt path that now faced them. They had already been down some pretty awful roads. It was crazy, Chambers thought, for Pendergast to risk damaging such a valuable vehicle, but the man seemed unconcerned about the scrapes, bumps, and bangs they would endure if they continued.

Pendergast pulled over to the side of the road at the turnoff. "May I see the maps?" he asked.

Chambers handed him the two maps—one was old, showing the roads as they were in the 1920s before the disastrous hurricane wiped out Bayou Sauvage, and the other a contemporary map of the same area.

While Pendergast studied the maps, Chambers took stock of where they were. The afterglow of sunset was already shining between the mossy trunks of bald cypresses and casting a golden sheen across the winding waterways of the swamp. Even though it was dusk, the air was dead and the heat stifling. There was a faint whine of insects.

Chambers next turned his attention to the old Wichman road. It was a badly eroded dirt track—clearly impassable to the Spyder—that wound away into the swamp, barely above the level of the water. Even though it was washed out and potholed, it looked suspiciously free of weeds and grass. There did not appear to be any fresh tire tracks on it, however, and a fallen tree a hundred feet down the road blocked further progress.

"Let us do a closer inspection," said Pendergast, laying the maps aside. He got out of the car, and Chambers followed.

Pendergast walked over to the margin of the dirt road where it turned into the old track, at one point kneeling in his black suit, minutely inspecting the ground. Then he straightened up. "Our man is likely in there now."

"You mean Wickman? How do you know?"

"I see evidence that a vehicle passed along this track quite recently. There has been a rather meticulous effort made to cover up its tracks to maintain a look of desuetude and abandonment."

Chambers stared down the road. "Okay, Tonto—but what about that tree?"

"Ah, the conveniently fallen tree! Let us examine it."

They walked down the road to where an uprooted, medium-size bald cypress had blown down over the road.

"I don't see how someone could have used this road recently," said Chambers doubtfully.

Pendergast smiled and pushed his hand among the dead branches, deftly moving it about. There was the rattle and click of a latch, and he then gave the tree a gentle push. It swung back on well-oiled hinges.

"Holy shit!" said Chambers.

"Indeed."

Chambers eyed the road. "Maybe we should come back tomorrow in the Tahoe."

Pendergast shook his head. "We must not use the road at all. It will surely be monitored."

"So how do we get in?"

Pendergast said, "Pirogue."

"Pirogue? You mean one of those Cajun boats? Are you serious?"

"I am quite serious. They're the ideal mode of transportation in these swamps, being flat-bottomed, silent, and stable."

"I'd much rather rent an airboat."

"Airboats are noisy and would ruin the element of surprise."

"So where are we going to rent a pirogue? There isn't a rental place around here for miles."

At this, Pendergast smiled. "On the way in, did you note the fishing camp we passed?"

"Yeah, I saw it. Looked pretty ramshackle, and I didn't notice any pirogues."

"There was a boat shed on the water, padlocked, which probably contains at least one, as they are essential watercraft for any fisherman in these parts."

"So we're going to steal it?"

"*Expropriate* it, Agent Chambers. Let us go."

At this Chambers didn't move, gazing steadily at Pendergast. After a moment of uncomfortable silence, the only sound the whining of insects, Chambers said, "Pendergast, I think you're forgetting something. I've given you an awful lot of leeway—you know the reasons, and no more need be said about it—but I'm still the mentor here, and you the mentee. Going in there at dusk, dressed as we are, out of radio contact, with no backup, is not only dangerous—it's dumb-ass stupid."

"I apologize. You are right—in the heat of the moment, I forgot my place. But may I be given the opportunity to change your mind?"

"Give it your best shot. But we're not stealing a pirogue and rowing into that swamp at night, hoping to catch a serial killer hiding in some ruined mansion." He punctuated this by slapping a mosquito on his cheek. "No way."

"The problem," said Pendergast, "is that our man will not be there tomorrow. He will be gone. One top of that, all the evidence of his killings—and possibly even an imprisoned victim—will also be gone. We must go in now, or we will miss our chance."

"And how in hell do you know all this?"

Pendergast merely pointed in the direction of the Wichman House. Chambers looked. Against the evening sky he could see a thread of smoke beginning to rise.

Pendergast said, "It appears he—or *someone*—has fired the mansion."

★ ★ ★

They drove back to the old fishing camp. And—naturally—Pendergast, who seemed able to conjure up tools and other bric-a-brac like a magician, pulled a bolt cutter from the trunk of the Spyder. When they cut the lock on the shack, there, as Pendergast had predicted, sat a nice clean pirogue, painted in camo, with paddles.

They dragged the boat quietly down to the water and got in.

"Do you know how to paddle this sucker?" said Chambers.

"You may recall I'm New Orleans born and bred," said Pendergast. "May I ask the same of you?"

"You take the bow and navigate. I'll take the stern."

They pushed off and began paddling. A pencil light appeared in Pendergast's hand—again, as if by magic—and he perused one of the maps as Chambers paddled. Pendergast finally rolled up the map and pointed at their heading, then picked up his paddle and added his powerful stroke to their forward motion. "If we are not hindered, we will be there in ten minutes."

Now they were gliding swiftly along, passing among the trunks of cypresses, branches heavy with Spanish moss. They soon came to an old drainage channel choked with water lettuce, alligator weed, and lily pads. Chambers could see the thread of smoke was getting denser, turning into a black, twisting spire against the dying sky.

They passed an alligator, only the snout and eyes above water, motionless as it watched them slide by. At the speed they were now moving, they were leaving behind the clouds of mosquitoes. Pendergast had apparently memorized the map, since he no longer checked it but simply pointed from time to time in the direction they should go. In the breaks of the tree cover, Chambers could see the pillar of smoke getting heavier, and he wondered if they were going to make it before the old place burned up. Fortunately, the houses in these parts were so damp and moldy that they sometimes refused to burn—they just steamed.

The channel now silted up completely, and Chambers could hear the soft sound of mud sliding along the bottom. They used the paddles to pole their way into deeper water and resumed their forward momentum. But half a mile farther, the open water once again shoaled up into mud.

"I'm afraid we must disembark and wade," said Pendergast.

With distaste and misgiving—keeping a keen eye out for cottonmouths and water moccasins in the failing light, and recalling just how fast alligators could move even in shallow water—Chambers got out, feeling the warm mud sucking up to his knees as his feet sank in the mire, squeezing out a flurry of swamp bubbles that rose in a sulfuric miasma. *Son of a bitch*—he was ruining not only a good pair of shoes but also a decent suit. It gave him only scant comfort to see Pendergast ruining his own clothes, far more expensive than his own.

They managed to drag and slide the boat across the muddy stretch. Where the channel resumed, they got back in. They were closing in now. Chambers could see, rising above the trees, the dark gables of the old Wichman mansion, draped with vines. A dull-orange glow could be seen at the base of the right wing.

As they came around a bend, an arm of the bayou opened into a broad expanse of water, and an old boathouse came into view, its concealing shroud of vegetation backlit by flames, leaning perilously in the twilight. The mansion stood behind it on a rise of dry land, the cypresses giving way to sweet gum, live oaks, and a rank, overgrown lawn. Chambers could clearly see the fire that was consuming the right side of the ramshackle manse, the flames starting to climb up the sides and out the roof, the windows glowing orange against the dusky twilight.

Chambers aimed the pirogue for the embankment to the right of the boathouse and gave a strong, deep stroke.

"Belay that!" Pendergast cried suddenly, reversing his own paddle and thrusting the pirogue sideways. There, in the murky water, floated a naked arm, white as ivory in the dusk. Before Chambers could say anything, Pendergast had slipped his paddle over the thing and drew it to the side of the boat.

"No, wait—"

Pendergast reached over and grabbed it with his hand, drawing it upward and examining it closely, paying particular attention to the severed area. He gave a loud sniff and then released it back into the water.

"Remarkably fresh. We'll collect it later—no doubt the conflagration will keep any carnivores at bay."

He dug his paddle into the water, and they once again stroked toward the embankment—but before they could get very far, the pirogue nudged something soft, floating just under the surface. A body.

"And here's the rest of it—I believe," said Pendergast, pulling out his light and shining it on the body—missing an arm. There was a strange uncertainty in his voice. He used the paddle to turn it over, then played the light over a ghastly white face.

"Good God, it's Wickman!" Pendergast said in astonishment.

"What the hell?" Chambers stared. It was unmistakably Wickman: the same Irish setter face and long nose as in the photograph Kroker had shown them at the funeral home.

Pendergast pushed the body roughly away with his paddle. "Someone got to him before us. We must get into the house before it goes up in flames—and all the precious evidence with it."

A few more strokes brought them to the embankment, the bow of the pirogue sliding up on the grass.

"Oh heavens; what stuff is here?" Pendergast cried abruptly, his light now shining on something in the shallows.

Chambers turned to look—and saw yet another body, naked, also missing an arm, which bobbed gently in the water a few yards away.

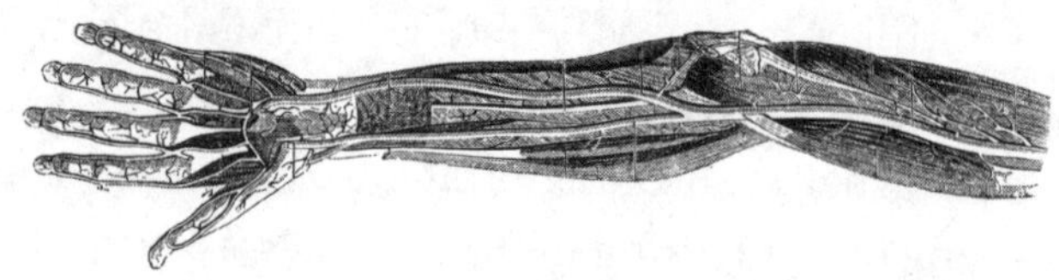

31

PENDERGAST RACED UP THE HILL toward the house, leaping up a set of brick steps, Chambers huffing up behind him. A pillared portico led to the front door, wide open and swinging slightly on its hinges. Chambers had the odd feeling that whoever got here first had just departed.

They entered a grand foyer with a central curving staircase, parlor to the left and dining room to the right. Smoke was boiling out of the dining room entryway with a loud crackling noise.

"We need to get down to the basement," Pendergast said as he passed through streams of smoke toward a closed door on the right. The wooden door was locked, but with a single kick Pendergast smashed it open. It led into what looked like servants' quarters. The fire hadn't reached that part of the house yet, but acrid smoke was beginning to drift in from the other direction. The muffled roar of the fire seemed to be vibrating the entire frame of the house.

Darting this way and that, they made their way through a warren of small, shabby rooms, stripped of furniture, the plaster on the walls falling from the rotting lathe.

They came to the end. No basement.

They retraced their steps into the foyer. "It would be through the kitchen," shouted Pendergast over the din. "Which means this way."

"But that's right into—"

Pendergast wasn't waiting to discuss. He threw himself onto his hands and knees and crawled into the smoke, keeping his head down and the rear of his suit jacket over his face. Chambers hesitated, then followed. The smoke was surging over their heads and licking down at them, and he could feel the heat buffeting the walls. No light was needed; the glow of the fire from down the corridor was enough to cast an orange illumination over everything.

They crawled through the dining room and into a kitchen. Now the fire was closer, and when they were halfway across, a sudden crackling sounded and the wall burst, scattering kitchen tiles everywhere as a huge ball of flame burst through. The ceiling was sagging and threatening to collapse.

Chambers blindly followed Pendergast, trying to breathe through the cloth of his jacket, his eyes burning and streaming.

They reached another wooden door, unlocked. They piled through it, suddenly in fresh air once again. Chambers stood, gasping and inhaling, while Pendergast slammed open the door and stuck a chair under the handle.

It was dark and Pendergast flicked on his penlight. They were in a pantry-like corridor, lined with shelves of ancient canned goods and sacks of flour and sugar torn apart by rats.

They came to a steel door at the far end of the pantry.

"Son of a bitch," said Chambers, trying the handle and finding it locked. "This must be the door to the basement."

Pendergast paused, breathing hard. They had very little time. Smoke was creeping up through cracks everywhere.

Pendergast bent over the keyhole and extracted a small tool from his pocket.

"You're . . . not going to pick that lock, are you?"

"I shall attempt to, yes."

Christ, thought Chambers, this was a guy with a lot of surprises up his sleeve.

"Et voilà!" Pendergast pushed the door open on silent hinges. A staircase led downward.

"Booya," said Chambers with considerably less enthusiasm.

They started down the stone steps, beaded with moisture. The sound of the fire was now muffled. The staircase ended at another door, locked, which Pendergast also picked, more rapidly this time. He pushed it open and probed the darkness with his light. Chambers was astonished: a long, gleaming hospital-like corridor stretched ahead, doors on either side. There was a light switch nearby, and Chambers hit it. Bingo—the lights went on, brilliant white. There must be a generator still operating somewhere on the premises, he thought.

"What have we here?" Pendergast asked, staring at a trail of what appeared to be blood along the linoleum floor, leading to a set of double doors at the end of the hall. He knelt and touched his finger to the trail, examined it, then rose. "Not more than thirty minutes old."

"Jesus," Chambers breathed. "What the hell happened here?"

"Let us follow the crimson trail and see where it leads."

Feeling a rising sense of dread, Chambers followed Pendergast down the hall and through the doors. Pendergast turned on a light, revealing an operating table draped in bloody sheets. A nearby tray was covered with gory surgical instruments, bandages, bloody sponges, and suturing material. Blood was splattered on the floor, tracked around by footprints. The trail of blood led from the operating table.

"I'm afraid," said Pendergast, "the procedure was not a success."

"Is anyone here?" Chambers called out. His voice died in silence.

"We are running out of time," said Pendergast. He took a brief but careful look around. "Let us split up and search these rooms."

They returned to the hall. Pendergast took one side and Chambers the other, slapping open doors and turning on lights. There were several storage rooms, labs, a bathroom, and sleeping quarters.

Chambers entered one lab that showed evidence of recent use, with microscopes, worktables, and a medical freezer. A titration had been set up on a table, and it looked like it had just been done, the liquids still remaining in the beakers and burettes. He went over and examined the freezer: the door was padlocked. He grabbed the padlock, but it was a big case-hardened one made out of steel.

A moment later Pendergast came up behind him. "I would expect," he said, "there is something quite interesting in there, judging from the size of that padlock."

Chambers stepped aside as Pendergast took the lock in his hands. With a quick fiddle it released and he opened the freezer door. It contained only one thing: a gleaming, stainless-steel case—again locked. Pendergast set upon the lock with his tools.

"Done," he said, stepping back. "You do the honors."

With another feeling of dread, Chambers raised the lid—to reveal a rack of frozen tissue samples, as thin as paper and stained with various colors, mounted on large glass plates.

"That crazy motherfucker," said Chambers. "Looks like we found his trophy case."

Pendergast reached in and slid one glass plate out, staring at it with glittering eyes. "These are not trophies," he said.

"What do you mean? Most serial killers collect trophies from their victims—and this is Wickman's stash."

"These tissue samples have been microtomed and histologically prepared by an expert biotechnician, stained with hematoxylin, eosin, and trichrome. No, my dear Chambers, these are not the grisly trophies of a serial killer. These are biological specimens, prepared by our killer for scientific testing."

"Testing? For what?"

Pendergast turned his silvery eyes on Chambers. "That, my friend, is an excellent question."

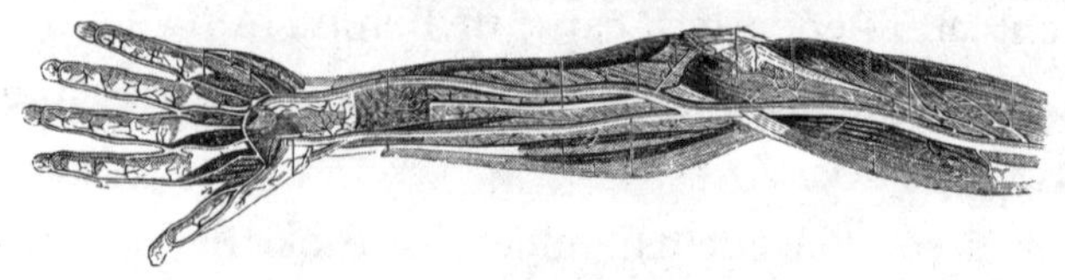

32

Chambers began to speak, but Pendergast stopped him. "But presently, we are almost out of time. There's a possibility there may be another victim imprisoned in the subcellar—which I believe lies beyond that steel door at the end of the hall—who will have a most unhappy time of it if we don't rescue him."

"Yeah."

Leaving the lab, Chambers followed Pendergast out into the hall. The fire above them was louder now; it, along with Pendergast's penlight, provided the only illumination. Chambers took a breath and another. He felt lightheaded. "We might be running out of oxygen," he said.

"All the more reason to hurry."

Pendergast had to work on the next door's lock a bit longer than the others. It led to yet another stone staircase, descending into what Chambers guessed must once have been some sort of root cellar. It ended at another blank steel door, which Pendergast once again focused his attention on. This lock resisted even longer, but finally it swung open.

Beyond was a padded cell. A tall, muscular man lay unconscious on the floor, loosely shackled by his ankles, bleeding from two deep slashes in his right arm.

"What the hell?" Chambers said, staring.

Pendergast drew in his breath sharply. Chambers turned to see the agent staring at the figure. He had never seen the junior agent so completely dumbfounded.

"*Proctor!*" Pendergast murmured.

"You know this man?"

Pendergast rushed over to the unconscious figure and grasped him in his arms, lifting him into a sitting position. Chambers came over and helped get him upright. He was heavy as hell.

Pendergast looked the man over quickly, examining the wounds in the arm and the blood still seeping from them, ascertaining the man's condition. "Proctor. *Proctor!*" He shook the man and slapped his face gently.

The man groaned, and Pendergast smacked him again, harder. The man's eyes fluttered open.

"Water," came the faint voice.

Chambers rose and ran up the stairs. He could now feel the air in the subcellar being drawn past him in the updraft of the fire. It occurred to him they wouldn't burn up down there—they'd suffocate.

In the operating room he filled a bowl with water and carried it back down. Pendergast had already gotten the shackles off the prisoner's ankles. The man fumbled with the bowl and drank the water down, spilling half of it.

"Stand up," said Pendergast sternly, still holding the man, guiding him to his feet. "Move."

The man staggered forward and nearly fell.

Pendergast held him upright. "Straighten up, soldier. Forward, on the double."

They led the man out of the padded room. The man was slow, confused, and wobbly, but able to move up the staircase to the regular basement.

"Stay here with him," said Pendergast to Chambers. "Keep him upright. I need to find another way out."

Pendergast disappeared down the corridor. The air, vibrating strongly now, was thin and hot, and Chambers could feel the lightheadedness growing. The sound of the fire thundered through the walls.

A minute later, Pendergast returned, carrying his muddy suit coat, which he had evidently cut into strips and soaked in water. The man was breathing hard and Chambers, too, felt a thickness in his head and lungs. He followed Pendergast and the big man down the hall and into a small storage room to the back, where a half-hidden door was open to a steep, narrow staircase. They climbed up, stopping to gasp several times for air.

At the top was a landing and a small door, smoke creeping through the cracks.

"That door," said Chambers, "is just going to put us into the fire."

"It's our only choice." He handed Chambers a wet strip of his jacket and prepared another for the big man—who was still moving like an automaton.

"Breathe through it," said Pendergast. "Stay low, move fast, and *never stop*. Ready?"

He threw the door open.

There was a sudden roar and surge of heat so violent it temporarily pushed them back. Chambers recovered his balance and plunged into the swirling smoke and flame, following the dark form of Pendergast and the big man. The heat was unbearable, and Chambers could hear his hair crisping. He ran, staying low, holding his breath and then breathing through the wet cloth. It felt like his entire body was on fire.

And then, suddenly, they were out of it. He stumbled forward, gasping and coughing. The flames and smoke roared above them, but there was now a layer of fresher air below.

"Don't stop!" Pendergast cried.

They continued running forward at a crouch. Pendergast kicked open another door; they passed through it and he slammed it shut.

They were finally free of the smoke and flames. They halted: coughing, bent over, gasping for air. When Chambers had recovered, he saw they had entered some sort of ancient, decaying library. The whole house was shaking from the fire, and one wall of books was smoking, the light of the fire peeking through widening cracks.

"No time," said Pendergast. "Follow me."

Again they ran. The big man seemed to be rousing himself and moving at a less shambolic rate. They passed through another door at the far end of the library and unexpectedly found themselves in a rude kind of chapel, with hard benches for pews and a cross and podium at the front for sermons. Behind the podium, on a kind of improvised altar, stood an elaborate votive candle stand, arranged in an upside-down V, with five candleholders on each side and one at the top center, containing the guttered and dribbling remains of ancient candles. Above all was an amateurishly painted scroll with the words THE SLUGGARD CRAVES AND GETS NOTHING, BUT THE DESIRES OF THE DILIGENT ARE FULLY SATISFIED.

Chambers stared: there was something strikingly familiar in the V formation, now outlined by the fierce backlighting of the fire through chinks in the decrepit rear wall. And then the epiphany hit: that formation was the same pattern of the eleven pricks the killer had made in the shoulders of his victims.

He turned and pointed, but Pendergast was already nodding. "Indeed. The source of the killer's signature."

A moment later they exited the side door of the chapel, which finally led them outside, into a graveyard behind the house. Stumbling downhill among the overgrown tombstones, illuminated only by the mounting flames, Chambers finally collapsed in the rank grass, gasping air into his seared lungs, eyes weeping from smoke. As his vision cleared, he watched as the roof beam of the great mansion broke with a crack like a rifle shot and, with a terrible groan that followed the echoes, surrendered itself to immolation by the whirlwind of fire.

PART THREE

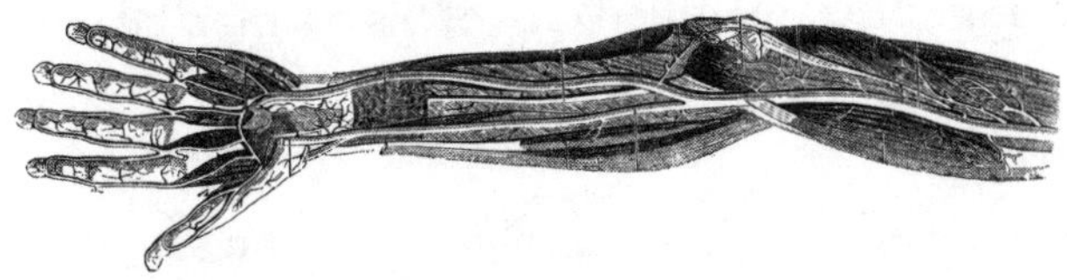

33

CHAMBERS—EXHAUSTED, ACHING, THROAT RAW—STOOD and watched mutely as the firemen finished hosing down the smoking ruins from multiple sides. Pendergast stood silently beside him. The great mansion had collapsed, leaving only four tall chimney stacks, which now stood like blackened sentinels amid the charred timbers and cracked bricks that were all that was left of the mansion.

The ambulances had come and picked up the victim they'd found in the subcellar, the man named Proctor. Another ambulance was taking the two bodies and their severed arms, fished out of the swamp, to the morgue adjacent to the field office. The fire departments of every town in the vicinity had turned their hoses on the conflagration, sucking the water up from the swamp itself, but too late: the great house had burned to the ground, taking with it—Chambers thought—many secrets.

And now, after the long night, dawn was breaking through the bald cypresses, casting an orange glow over the ghastly scene. The firemen were almost finished. Chambers knew that Estevez was on his way with a large Evidence Response Team. But it was a long drive from the New Orleans FO, and Estevez and his people were still perhaps thirty minutes away. Chambers didn't know what was going to happen when he arrived. The ATF were also on their way, and it was never easy when the FBI and ATF had to cooperate at a major crime scene. Glancing at the unruffled face of his partner, he wondered if he was ignorant of the shitshow that was coming, or if he was just maintaining his cool.

The firemen were now rolling their hoses and starting to pack up. He felt Pendergast stir next to him.

"Shall we?" Pendergast asked.

Chambers stared at him. "Shall we what?"

The man gestured with an open palm. "Investigate."

"Hold on," said Chambers. "You don't get it. The cavalry is on its way. You've got a massive FBI ERT coming, you've got an ATF Certified Fire Investigator team, you've got photographers and forensic technicians up the wazoo, you've got the local sheriff and his deputies—and you've got Estevez, which is the cherry on top. A lot of them are already arriving."

"Which is why we must hurry," said Pendergast, "before they ruin the crime scene."

Chambers couldn't believe what he was hearing. "Ruin it? These guys are the experts. We're the ones who're going to ruin it. And if they see us poking around in there, they're going to be pissed."

"I can't help that." Pendergast started walking toward the inner perimeter that was already being set up by the county sheriff and his deputies.

Chambers followed. "You know this is against protocol, right? We're supposed to wait."

"I've waited long enough." He turned to Chambers. "I do hope you'll accompany me."

"I will, but—"

Pendergast ducked under the perimeter.

"Hey!" said a deputy. "You can't go in there!"

Pendergast took out his shield and held it in the man's direction. "FBI," he said in that honeyed voice of his.

"Oh. Sorry."

Chambers likewise ducked under the tape and followed Pendergast toward the brick steps leading up to where the porch and front door had been the night before. *In for a penny, in for a pound,* he rationalized. Beyond was a wilderness of broken and charred timbers, heat-shattered bricks, melted metal and glass and misshapen, skeletonized objects transformed by fire.

Pendergast entered the ruin and then, with a delicacy that surprised Chambers, began picking his way through the sodden mess, casting his silvery eyes every which way. Chambers had taken courses in evidence gathering back at the Academy, but looking over the scorched wasteland, he wondered how any evidence could possibly have survived. And even if it had, he was clueless as what to look for.

"Pendergast," he said, hesitating at the edge, "I'm telling you this is not a good idea."

Ignoring him, Pendergast continued moving slowly. Suddenly, he gave a little exclamation, bent down, examined his find, and then—to Chambers's great surprise—pulled a tiny test tube and tweezers out of his black jacket, picked up something, placed it in the tube, and sealed it. The tube disappeared back into his jacket. He worked his way along, more test tubes and small evidence envelopes appearing, each in turn filled with crumbly pieces of ash and odd things tweezed out of the wasteland. Chambers following, having no idea what he was picking up or why. The rising sun finally broke through the trees, striping the ruins with golden light and illuminating the coils of rising smoke and steam.

"Hey, you two!"

Chambers turned and his heart sank. There was Estevez, gesturing. Behind him, two big evidence teams were gowning up. One was the FBI Evidence Recovery Team, getting dressed in monkey suits. The other must be the ATF Certified Fire Investigation team. Behind Estevez, Chambers could see FBI and ATF agents already arguing.

"What the *hell*?" Estevez yelled. "Get out of there!"

"Pretend you don't hear him," Pendergast murmured.

"Jesus Christ, Pendergast," Chambers said through gritted teeth.

Now Pendergast dropped to his knees in the gummy mess and began pulling aside some broken slate shingles to reveal a metal filing cabinet, lying on its side, partially melted.

"Ah, look at this," he said, pulling away the sides, exposing a mess of scorched and carbonized files. Peering and poking at them intently, he eased several out with exquisite care. They were burned around the edges, but the interiors were only partially carbonized. These files he slipped into a thin Mylar sleeve, which disappeared as quickly and mysteriously as it had appeared.

Now he stood up, looked over at Estevez, and waved. "Hello, Director Estevez! Glad you could come!"

"Get your asses out of there!" Estevez yelled back. "Now!"

They waded through the mess and were soon standing in front of a sweating, red-faced director. Before Chambers could begin apologizing and explaining, Pendergast said, speaking rapidly: "Sir, Agent Chambers and I have put our little sabbatical to good use. And I hope we've been a credit to the New Orleans FO and your excellent leadership. A pity that Mississippi's FO seems to have so sadly fallen short. I imagine the press will be quite interested to know how efficiently your office operated in cracking this case. Ah, and speaking of the press, here they come now."

Estevez turned and groaned. Several vans were arriving, emblazoned with television call signs. They were pulling up haphazardly on the overgrown lawn, beyond the outer ring of tape. The doors were flung open and reporters and technicians spilled like termites out of a kicked nest, carrying cameras, mics, and booms.

Estevez turned back to Pendergast and Chambers. "Okay, I see where you're going with this. Congratulations are in order." He spoke with an edge of sarcasm. "And I've no doubt commendations will be forthcoming. Now: thank you, Agents Pendergast and Chambers. I'll take it from here."

"That's your prerogative," Pendergast said. "Meanwhile, we shall continue our sabbatical working out of our, ah, temporary offices, glad to assist in every way, until we are reinstated. Because, sir, to be frank, I wouldn't feel right returning to the office—before I've served my just punishment and period of exile, that is."

"You'll do no such thing," said Estevez, lowering his voice. "You're coming back into the office now, and nothing more need be said about this so-called sabbatical. Understood? I'm putting Agents Mears and DuBois on the case. They're two of our best, and it'll be in good hands. You'll be debriefed in full later today."

Chambers felt a rising sense of injustice. A couple of mutts like Mears and DuBois? This was wrong. "Sir, I protest."

"Yes?" said Estevez, turning on him, frowning.

"Sir, we took up a case everyone had missed. For years. And it wasn't just any case, but a big one involving multiple homicides. We developed the case and we cracked it wide open. We not only ended a serial-killing spree, but we saved the life of one of his victims—and exposed a new killer in the process. It's only fair to let us finish this."

"Excuse me, Chambers, but I've said what I've said."

"Don't worry, partner," said Pendergast breezily, clapping Chambers on the back. "If we can't work the case, we can at least use the rest of our banishment to deal with what will undoubtably be a monstrous level of national press. Look at them over there, ravenous as wild boars. And what a story it is: two FBI agents sent into the wilderness as punishment—only to crack the case of the Pinprick Killer!" He turned to Chambers. "Did you bring a comb for the cameras? Your hair is mussed up. If not, I have one."

"You will *not* talk to the press," said Estevez.

Pendergast turned and locked a pair of ice-chip eyes on Estevez. "Oh, sir, but we will. We most *assuredly* will—if the case is expropriated from us."

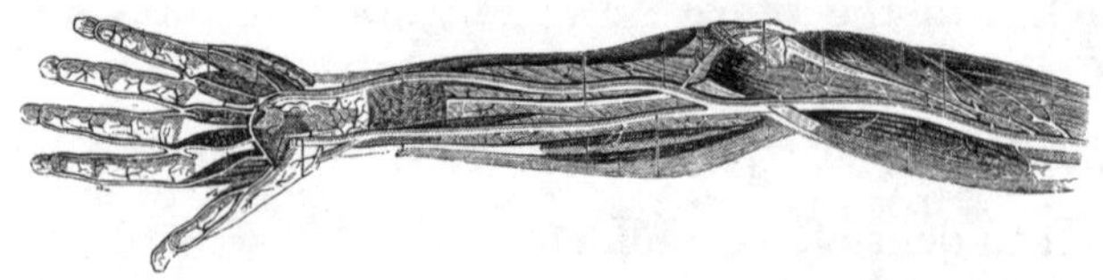

34

THEY SPENT THE ENTIRE MORNING at the scene of the fire, and as they drove away, Chambers felt exhausted, his lungs still aching from breathing in the smoke of the burning mansion. Pendergast, on the other hand, somehow looked as composed as ever, not a hair out of place, his black suit appearing as if it had just come back from the cleaners. It was like magic—black magic, probably, he thought as he recalled childhood stories about the wealthy old antebellum families of New Orleans and their strange ways.

On cue, Pendergast spoke up. "We have much to talk about."

"I just want to go home and crash."

"We have a double autopsy to attend later this afternoon. But in any case, the first order of business is to discuss the way forward."

"Now?"

"Certainly now, while the information is fresh in our minds."

"Nothing is fresh in my mind."

"Perhaps some food and drink would revive you?"

As Chambers thought about it, a drink might be just what the doctor ordered. And as the surrounding bayous slowly began giving way to bits and pieces of civilization, he saw, up ahead by the side of Chef Menteur Highway, what looked to be his kind of place: a rib joint busily serving lunch, with a smoker as massive as a boiler from the *Titanic* set out front, gushing gray clouds. A sign with blinking light bulbs read LOW & SLOW CAJUN BBQ.

"Slow down," he said.

"What, you don't mean to stop *here*, do you?" There was something close to alarm in Pendergast's voice.

"This looks like just the place for some ass-kicking baby backs and a frosty brew."

They parked and got out. Chambers tucked away his FBI badge and glanced over at Pendergast. "Might want to put that away," he said.

"In a place like this," replied Pendergast, "an FBI badge seems like an excellent way to ward off impertinence."

Chambers reflected that Pendergast appeared to enjoy stomping out impertinence, but maybe he just felt like flashing the badge. He was a new jack, after all—and Chambers doubted the man's classified military career had involved wearing uniforms. "Suit yourself," he said.

A busty woman met them at the open front door and ushered them to a table outside, on an elevated deck overlooking the swamp. A southern rock band was just putting down their instruments for a break as the two sat.

"Will you look at that?" said Chambers, gazing out over the bayou at an enormously fat alligator lying half in, half out of the water. "Man, that's a big mother, and it looks like it's just waiting to be fed."

"That's Sir Chompers," said the waitress, coming over. "We throw him all the roadkill. He's especially fond of possum. Oh, *and* rowdy drunks."

"In that case, we promise to remain sober," said Chambers.

"Honey, I didn't say sober. I said rowdy."

Chambers laughed. "I'll have a pint of Abita Amber." He had decided to stick to beer for the indefinite future.

"And you, sugar?" She turned to Pendergast, giving him the once-over with an eye that had, no doubt, seen everything.

"Do you offer the Sazerac cocktail?"

"Sure thing, sugar. That's our specialty, made with Vieux Carré absinthe."

"Excellent! I shall have it."

She went off and Pendergast turned to Chambers. "Perhaps this establishment isn't as bad as it appeared at first glance."

Their drinks arrived and they ordered food. The cold beer did wonders for Chambers's raw throat. As his mood improved, he considered his partner's proposal—discussing how they should proceed. He felt a little hammered down by the man's astonishing deductions earlier, and—now that he was feeling up to it—decided he should assert his authority and, if only subtly, reestablish the mentor-mentee relationship.

"Speaking as your mentor," he said, "I'd like to hear *your* thoughts on how we should proceed now."

"We need to search back in time," said Pendergast, without hesitation, "and examine the life of Mr. Parker C. Wickman in minute detail. It is important to further elucidate his motive—given what we just learned."

Chambers felt a certain satisfaction in hearing how off track this was. Typical of a green agent, actually. The man was smart, but he was still a babe in the woods when it came to FBI protocol and best practices.

"Trying to understand Wickman's motives is a worthy goal," said Chambers, "but given that he's dead and isn't going to trial, there are now higher priorities."

"Such as?"

"For one thing, we've just seen that there is a fresh homicide to investigate—not committed by Wickman, but *of* Wickman. We need to identify and apprehend the perpetrators."

"Undoubtably."

"Any thoughts on why Wickman might have been murdered?"

"I do."

Chambers waited, but Pendergast seemed disinclined to share

them. "Well," he finally said, "it seems pretty obvious to me it was a revenge killing of some sort. A family or friend of someone Wickman killed tracked him down and did the same to him—killed him and then cut off his arm as a way to declare that justice was done. An eye for an eye—literally."

"That is a viable hypothesis."

A viable hypothesis. Sounded like what his wife would have called *damning with faint praise.*

"This is a lesson for you, Pendergast. Now that he's dead, we can let the profilers at Quantico explore Wickman's bizarre psychological motives—his state of mind isn't our business anymore."

"In my view," said Pendergast coolly, "his state of mind is of vital importance."

Chambers cocked his head. "And why is that?"

"For one thing, there are surely more victims of his to identify and various informational lacunae to fill in. More important, the answer to the *mystery* of Wickman, why he killed and who killed him, will be found in the deep past, just as we noted how the V-pattern of pinpricks mimicked the arrangement of candles in the chapel."

"And I *just* explained to you," said Chambers, annoyed, "why his crazy motives are not a priority. Sure, if the guy were alive and we were building a case, the jury would want to know his motives, crazy as they undoubtedly were. But he's *dead*. The Wickman case is more or less solved—beyond the question of who killed the killer."

Pendergast had finished his Sazerac and now poked his finger politely into the air. The waitress came over. "I shall have another, with compliments to the mixologist," he said.

Chambers ordered another beer.

"The case is *not* more or less solved," said Pendergast. "The persons who killed Wickman—there were at least two—may well have been involved in Wickman's earlier killings. What revenge plan would involve killing not only Wickman but somebody else, as well?"

"We won't know that until we get an ID on the guy," Chambers said, beginning to feel defensive.

"And we have not yet heard from the victim found in Wickman's basement—a man named Proctor, whom I know well."

Chambers stared. "So you did know him. I thought I was just seeing things."

"You were not. And when he is able to speak, he may be able to provide valuable information about possible accomplices. But the answer to Wickman's life and death does not lie in dutifully cataloging the other murders he might have committed—that can be accomplished by such homunculi as Mears and DuBois. The answer lies in the *whys*. The *motive*. And that means delving into Wickman's past—where the origin of that triangular pinprick pattern will be found, along with the genesis of his other grotesque psychopathologies."

Chambers listened to this pushback with a surge of exasperation. Pendergast was impossible. He took a moment to bury his face in the beer that had just arrived. Finally, making an effort to moderate his tone, he said: "Pendergast, you're going to have to trust me on this. I've worked hundreds of cases. Rule one is don't complicate a straightforward homicide with the stuff of murder mysteries." He took a breath. "Somebody killed Wickman in revenge. Who, we don't know. But you know what? He did a public service. The FBI will of course look into it, but as I see it, the case is now in the wrapping-up phase."

After a long silence, Pendergast spoke quietly. "On the contrary, this case has entered a most urgent and dangerous phase. Naturally, I bow to your greatly superior experience. But let us take a moment to look at the two people involved in the killing of Wickman. These were not lowlifes bent on revenge. These are prominent members of the community."

"And how would you know that?"

"From evidence I observed at the scene, as well as a glance into the files, my observations of the medical supplies and surgical setup, I have concluded that at least one is an MD—a surgeon, likely still in practice. The second is probably a surgeon as well and is a man who smokes hundred-dollar cigars. They knew Wickman well. Wickman appears to have welcomed them into his house. Wickman evidently allowed them free use of his state-of-the-art operating room—installed at a cost of hundreds of thousands of dollars—for a *particular* purpose. What was that purpose? We do not know. Surely it was not to kill him, cut off his arm, and dump his body in the muck. So: if they were not actual accomplices, they were involved with Wickman in some deep and important way. And, I might add, this doesn't even plumb what might be the strangest depths of this crime—the copycat murder of another young man at essentially the same time Wickman was killed. And so it is my hope, Agent Chambers, you can take a step back from the FBI book and revisit your assumptions. There is a dangerous and complex conspiracy behind the murder of Wickman—and it *lives on*."

Pendergast had not raised his voice, but his tone carried a peculiar urgency that increasingly brought Chambers up short. His irritation moved up a notch, but even as it did so he had to admit Pendergast had made some inarguably valid points.

"And from a purely self-interested point of view," Pendergast added, "if another Wickman-connected killing occurs on our watch, the case would almost certainly be taken from us. Estevez is looking for any excuse to put us in our place."

Chambers said nothing for a long time, thinking. The beer had cleared his head and he began to realize that Pendergast was, in his own way, not wrong. Except what he was saying didn't quite hang together. "Okay, I see your point. But what kind of complex conspiracy would get itself involved with a deranged psychopathic serial killer? Why not just report Wickman to the police?"

Pendergast raised his eyebrows inquiringly at Chambers. "A good question."

"Because he knew something," said Chambers, answering his own question. "They're not accomplices. Wickman *knew* something about them—something very damaging. They needed to kill him *because* he's crazy, and was killing people, and would eventually get caught—and then the singing would start."

"Bravo!" said Pendergast. "That is an excellent deduction, and one even I hadn't yet considered. But that's all the more reason to look into Wickman's history. Because those men, you can be sure, will be woven, one way or another, into his life's thread... and one is forced to wonder: if they were implicated somehow—why did they wait so long to do something about Wickman?"

The band was on stage and tuning up again. Chambers shook his head. "I don't know how you manage it, Pendergast—but all right. I'll give you—us—three days to pursue this line of investigation. If it doesn't pan out, we'll do it my way."

"Done," said Pendergast extending his hand.

They shook.

At that moment, a chef in a bloody rubber apron, carrying an overflowing bucket of meat scraps and offal, passed by their table. The other diners apparently knew what was about to happen, and many of them rose from their tables and gathered at the railing to watch. The chef reached the edge of the elevated deck, leaned over it, and dumped the scraps into the bayou. Sir Chompers exploded into action, propelling his enormous body off the mud bar. Thrashing and snapping, he went to work gobbling up the scraps while the diners *ooohed* and *aaahed* and applauded.

"Good heavens, it's straight out of *Moby-Dick*—Stubb orders his supper, and then the cook tosses the leavings overboard for the sharks!" Pendergast finished his Sazerac and dabbing. "But then, we're not much further advanced a species, are we?" He waved around at the entranced onlookers. "Even I find this spectacle of ferocity and gore to be strangely compelling."

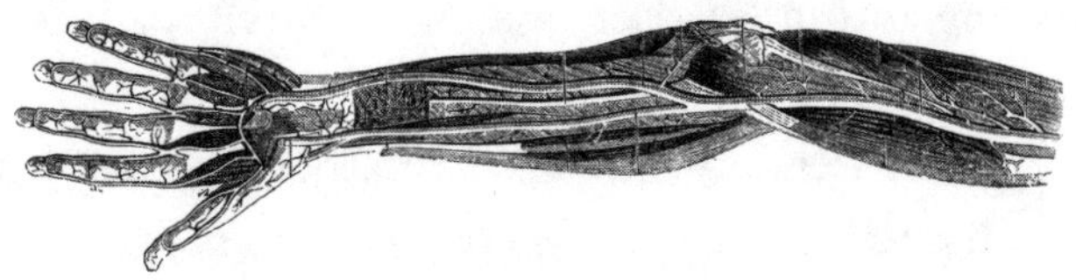

35

Mix and match," said the medical examiner, drolly holding up an arm. "Mix and match—am I right, Molly?"

"Yes, Dr. Bloom," said the assistant.

It was midafternoon, and both cadavers lay on gurneys in New Orleans's FBI morgue. The ME and his assistant were now fussing with the two arms, shifting them back and forth, examining the incisions and matching them up with the bodies they came from.

Chambers, gowned up with Pendergast at his side, stood back in the viewing area behind a glass window. "Somebody fucked up," he murmured, shaking his head. "They should have kept the arms with the bodies from the beginning."

"Indeed," Pendergast agreed. "The churning mass of investigators at the crime scene did not inspire confidence." He leaned forward and pressed the intercom button. "Dr. Bloom?"

The doctor looked up, irritation creasing his face. "What?"

"I wish to direct your attention specifically to the small punctures or prickings on the right shoulder of one of the victims. Make a careful note of those. And also, if you please, examine the surgical incisions with great care and copious macrophotography."

"Certainly, certainly," said the ME, annoyed at the advice.

Now that they had finally matched up the arms, the doctor began describing the first cadaver for the video camera, walking around it and murmuring into a headset, his comments broadcast into their viewing room on an intercom.

"I must say," said Pendergast, "this is a rather inconvenient arrangement. I'd much prefer to be in close contact with the cadaver, visually, tangibly, and olfactorily."

Chambers did not agree at all, but he said nothing.

The preliminary examination complete, the doctor began his Y incision on the first corpse.

"It's the god-damnedest thing," murmured Chambers, "how Wickman, the serial killer, is killed by someone else—using his very same MO."

"Not exactly the same. You will note that one of the severed arms—undoubtedly Wickman's—did not present those telltale pinpricks."

"But... why? Who did it?"

"Who did it is a mystery. Why Wickman's arm was dismembered is less of a mystery."

"It's a message. Like I said, revenge."

"Message? I would rather say it was a morbid joke. And perhaps an effort to confound the investigators, as well."

Chambers grunted. A morbid joke? It made no sense, but then, Pendergast seemed to relish things that were nonsensical. "Tell me, Pendergast: what in the world did you discover in the ruins this morning? I couldn't make rhyme or reason out of what you were doing."

"I was trying to reconstruct the events and individuals on the scene immediately preceding the fire."

"Did you?"

"Not nearly to my satisfaction."

"So what *did* you find out, if anything?"

"The fire was not set for our benefit."

"How do you know?"

"Because of the timing. It was set before they could have known we were coming."

"Makes sense. And then?"

"It was set with an accelerant—ethanol."

"And how do you know *that*?"

"Smell. Pure ethanol, my dear Chambers, is usually only obtainable with a license, and it is used liberally in surgery."

"Right."

"The person who set the fire was an MD. A surgeon, in fact."

"Good Christ, how could you know that?"

"A charred surgical mask and the intact finger of a melted nitrile glove were both associated with the placing of the accelerant. One might conclude the fire was set by the very man who surgically removed Wickman's arm and that of the other victim—or the surgeon assisting him."

"And how could you know that?"

"Fresh blood on the nitrile glove tip."

"You're a regular Sherlock Holmes."

"Further evidence, which I hope our good Dr. Bloom will note, is that both arms were removed by a true surgeon, not a first-year medical student or other dabbler in the surgical arts. There was nothing amateur about the incisions—they were done with self-assurance and reflexive skill. The unidentified victim was alive when his arm was removed; Wickman, however, was dead. In the latter case there was no need for precision—and yet the habits of a fine surgeon die hard. He couldn't help making incisions that were instinctually expert."

"And what did he look like?" Chambers asked sarcastically.

"He's short, possibly pusillanimous, and over fifty years of age."

Chambers had to laugh. "Okay, so you found a hair, I suppose?"

"Indeed I did. Gray."

"How do you know he's short?"

"That I noted in the OR before the fire—the operating table height was set for a diminutive man."

"And that other thing?"

"Pusillanimous. One man, submissive, did most of the surgical work. Another man, arrogant, observed and possibly gave instructions."

"I suppose you're going to tell me how you could possibly know that."

"I noted another pair of discarded nitrile gloves on the far side of the operating room, flecked with blood. Next to them, on the floor, was a fine, dense fragment of a cigar ash, which, when picked up, gave off the faintest scent of Montecristo. This gentleman's assistance in the procedure seemed to take place only at the start. Then he stood back, smoking a cigar—in an operating room!—and as I said, perhaps gave instructions. Any man who lights up a cigar in an operating room while a surgery is in progress is surely arrogant. Not only arrogant—but whimsical."

"What are you talking about?"

"And I would hazard to guess it was that same sense of whimsy that prompted him to have both arms removed. This is what I mean by it being a morbid joke."

"Anything else? You seem awfully sure."

"The arms of both victims were amputated by the same surgeon. Wickman normally performed the operations himself, but he certainly did not remove his own arm. Instead, he brought his victim to the house alive and had the surgeon remove his arm—*while* the man was still living, but likely under anesthesia."

"Strange."

"Strange indeed. Clearly, this operation was planned ahead of time. Wickman must have been in contact with the surgeon before he himself arrived with the victim. We know this because the operating room was set up and ready to go at the time of his arrival, when he delivered the victim to them."

"And then?"

"Then they removed the unknown victim's arm while he was alive… and killed him. At around the same time, Wickman was killed on the operating table, his arm removed postmortem. In other words, both were conveniently murdered on the operating table. And then they threw the bodies into the swamp, where they would surely be discovered."

While he'd been answering Chambers's questions, Pendergast had been watching Bloom proceed, apparently now with little interest. Suddenly, he turned to Chambers.

"Why make no effort to get rid of the bodies—why not leave them to burn in the mansion, fully destroying the evidence? Because those responsible did not care if they were found. It might even have suited their purposes. Why did Wickman call for a surgeon and then, apparently, submit to anesthesia himself? Because he wanted them to perform a surgical procedure *he could not perform on his own*. And what might that procedure have been?" Pendergast paused, then finished with great relish: "To amputate his right arm and surgically replace it with the arm of his victim!"

"That's some crazy shit. So why the hell did he cut off so many arms before doing this?"

"He was searching for the perfect replacement, of course."

"Jesus. And... who the hell are his accomplices?"

"Agent Chambers, *that* answer lies in his past, a journey we must now undertake."

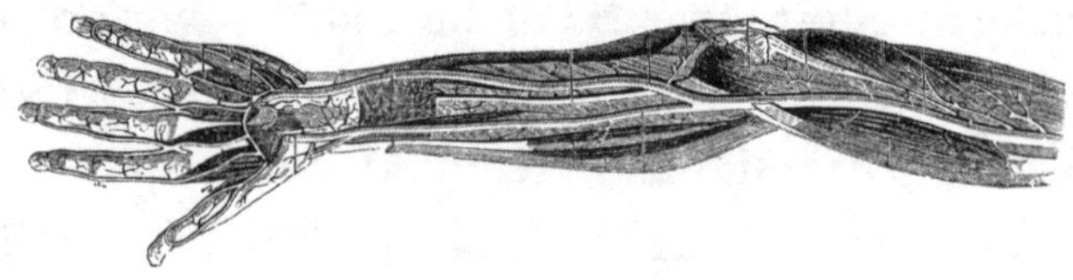

36

As THEY STOPPED BEFORE an unnumbered door on the unnamed hospital floor, Pendergast put a restraining hand on Chambers's arm. "It would probably be best if I went in alone."

Chambers thought a moment, then nodded. "Okay."

Pendergast looked away, glancing in turn at the armed men in military uniform flanking the door. No words were exchanged, but one opened the door to the room, closing it again when Pendergast had disappeared inside.

* * *

The hospital room was sterile, consisting of a bed, table, two chairs, and various nursing and medical apparatuses. Proctor lay asleep in the bed, a hanging cart holding a unit of blood and another of saline beside him. He looked like a pale simulacrum of the last time they'd met. Pendergast glanced around for a minute, inspecting the room more carefully. He took the vitals chart hanging from the end of the bed and leafed through it quickly. Then he turned on the desk radio, spun the dial until he found a dreadful country station, cranked it, and moved one of the chairs around the bed until he was beside the fluids cart.

He leaned in closely, watching Proctor. The man's rest was disturbed by the noise—quite understandably.

"Sergeant Major?" he said quietly, his lips close to the patient's ear.

Proctor moved again.

"Sergeant Major. *I debere societatum solam.*"

Proctor's eyes opened as Pendergast sat down. *"Fidelitas usque ad mortem."* He glanced toward the chair. *"Colonel!"*

Pendergast quickly silenced him. "I can only stay a few minutes; there will be time, more time, to speak later. Right now, I need to know everything you can tell me about your assailant."

Proctor was quiet for about a minute. "He was good."

"No doubt."

"He caught me off guard, dressed as a utility lineman, sauntering into my garage. My reflexes were down." His words were slow at first, then they came more quickly. "I woke up in a padded cell. It was… exceptionally well hardened."

"I saw it when we rescued you from the burning mansion."

"Mansion?"

"Go on."

"He demonstrated the impossibility of escape, and the punishment that would take place if one was attempted."

"And?"

"That was it. I was given freedom of movement around the cell at intervals, and he brought me food twice a day. He insisted that I eat it. He was most solicitous of my health."

"Interesting. Keep going."

Another brief pause. "I was not the first captive to be in there. The man had practice. There were redundant surveillance systems, and he was exceedingly cautious."

"But what did he want?"

"My arm."

When Pendergast did not laugh or scoff, he continued. "He was always looking at it. He used some kind of nerve gas to anesthetize me. When I was under I believe he felt it thoroughly, pinched and probed at it."

"Your right arm."

Proctor nodded.

"And is that why you scarred it? You did that yourself?"

"It was a last resort. I knew he wanted the arm, so I decided to… well, to frustrate him in that regard."

"And did it?"

"Yes. He became unhinged."

Pendergast also paused. "Where were you living when this happened?"

"A suburb of New Orleans."

"Working?"

"Nothing professional. A sort of armored car delivery service."

"Armored *car*?" For a second, Pendergast showed surprise.

"It's not only your reflexes that slow down if enough time passes."

Pendergast nodded slowly. He asked a few more quick questions, then rose. "Your recovery from blood loss and smoke inhalation is coming along." He laid a hand on the man's arm. "You'll be out of here in days. Let me talk to Decker."

"Thank you, sir."

"*Vale.*" Pendergast turned off the radio before he left the room.

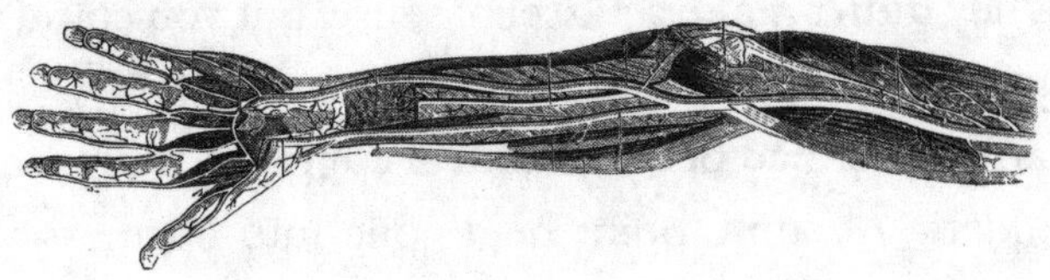

37

He was a sensitive child," the old woman said, with a fond sigh of remembrance. "Oh, he liked to play, the way any young boy did—especially back then, when all the bleeding hearts weren't so afraid of cap guns and plastic bowie knives—but his favorite activities were reading. And drawing. Oh, how he loved to draw."

Chambers took a sip of weak lemonade—his third—and tried to pay attention. The old woman, who'd been Wickman's nanny when he was young, had a lot of colorful stories about the young man, but he'd heard them all twice now and it seemed she was starting in on the third rotation. But Pendergast kept encouraging her—perhaps trying to get his psychological theories to bear fruit by sheer force of will.

They were in the town of Winter Park, Florida, where Wickman's parents had owned a large house. The town was a surprise to Chambers—it wasn't full of date palms and shotgun bungalows, but closer to what he imagined an Ivy League community would be, with avenues of stately trees and old, well-manicured houses of the kind they built up north.

"What kind of things did he draw?" Pendergast asked.

The old lady thought again. "Not the usual things boys drew—cowboys and Indians or battleships. They were boats. Or rather, plans for boats. They didn't make a passel of sense, but you could tell he was trying to do a little boy's version of his father's work."

Wickman's father had been a nautical engineer, designing hulls for big shipbuilders. At some point he'd gone into business for himself and begun crafting what was then a unique design: small vessels with inline jet drive engines fabricated into the stern, driven by impellers, allowing for not only very shallow draft but also power and convenience. It was an inspired idea, and it allowed the budding family of three to purchase a large house here in Winter Park.

"What were your last memories of the boy after—after the accident?" Chambers said, trying to forestall the third go-round.

But it seemed the old lady had focused only on the word "accident," and started in again. "It was sad. The saddest thing you could imagine. Dr. Wickman might have been a brilliant engineer, but he didn't have a nose for character. That Randall Fortnum he hired as a bookkeeper was a slippery one, all smiles and doff-your-hat-for-you-ma'am, always eager to put in a few extra hours of work—but it was all a bunch of hooey. That piece of trash really went to work. By the time Wickman realized the truth, Fortnum had already stolen or sold off everything but the silverware. And then it was too late. The man had had plenty of time to mess with the books, sell off assets—he even sold the company's industrial secrets to competitors before Dr. Wickman could apply for patents, which would have set the family up for good."

"Did he have Fortnum arrested?" Pendergast asked.

"He lit out a day or two before Dr. Wickman called the authorities." The old lady shook her head.

"And was he never caught?"

She shook her head again. "Never. For all I know, he's sitting on a beach in Panama somewhere this very minute."

"What happened next?"

"The couple were devastated, of course. They'd have to start all over again. But Dr. Wickman seemed to take it pretty well. His wife was a doctor, you know, and had a good practice. Anyway, he and the missus decided to take a weekend down to Key West to plan their next move, leaving the boy with me." She paused. "Of course, you know what happened next."

Chambers knew. The small Cessna pontoon plane Wickman's father owned had crashed into the Gulf of Mexico about thirty miles off the Dry Tortugas.

"And then," the woman said, her voice rising, "all that talk—that he'd done it for the insurance. There *was* no insurance—Fortnum had made sure of that. And a man like Dr. Wickman would never have taken his life and his wife's, leaving behind a young boy—an orphan." And she wiped away a tear. In the momentary silence, Chambers could hear the buzzing of flies outside the half-open windows, and the curtains fluttered listlessly in a humid breeze.

"He was a good man," she said, her gaze going past the two agents. "He deeded this house to me. That was something even Fortnum couldn't take away."

Then she seemed to brighten up. "May I freshen your lemonades, gentlemen?"

★ ★ ★

The White Kitchen Preparatory School was located on a low bluff near the Louisiana line. It appeared to have once been surrounded by stands of live oaks, but as they pulled in Chambers could see that the entire area had been recently clear-cut. There were only two cars in the parking lot. It gave Chambers the impression the school was strapped for funds and selling off what property it could.

James Aiken, high school English teacher at White Kitchen, received them in his cramped, messy classroom at the appointed time of three thirty. He'd jovially shaken their hands, offered them cups of coffee, then arranged three school desks in a semicircle so they could talk.

"So!" he said, rubbing his hands together. "What do you think of our educational institution?"

"It is most picturesque," Pendergast said, as if he hadn't noticed all the stumps in the fields outside.

This clearly pleased Aiken, who seemed proud of the tiny facility. "I've always thought so! You know, given the—ah—financial demographics in this neck of the woods, not to mention the declining population, White Kitchen functions as not only a high school but a middle school as well—for a number of the surrounding communities: Tammany, Honey Island, half a dozen others. Some kids need to be bussed as far as thirty miles to get here—but we pride ourselves on making sure every youngster in our district gets a good education." He paused. "But you gentleman—I do apologize but I need to ask: may I see your badges?"

This seemed a spontaneous question born of curiosity, and both complied.

"Thank you! As I was saying, you gentlemen must have a lot on your plate, and I don't want to keep you here while I jawbone."

"You were very kind to agree to meet with us on a Sunday."

"Not at all, happy to help. You said you had some questions about one of my students?"

"Parker Wickman," Chambers said. They had not previously provided a name.

Aiken's eyes visibly went slightly glassy as he thought back. "Parker Wickman... there's a name I haven't heard in years."

You will, Chambers thought grimly, *very soon*.

"If you could tell us what you recall of him," Pendergast said. "How he came to the school, what he was like, any anecdotes that come to mind—it would be most helpful."

Aiken's eyes sharpened again. "Of course. He came here in—oh, it must have been '75 or thereabouts. Some tragedy had taken his parents, and he came to live at Pearl View Estates, which was being run by his grandmother at the time. Esther Wickman. A kinder lady you'll never meet—though she was rather strict in her religious views."

Chambers noticed he'd pronounced the name *Wishman*. That corresponded to the spelling of *Wichman* he'd seen on the older maps.

"Pearl View Estates," Pendergast repeated.

Aiken nodded. "The family had always been pretty well off, even after that hurricane in 1921. But wealth, like everything else, has a tendency to pass away, and she began taking in elderly boarders, converting the mansion into a rest home. She'd been a nurse, and living alone in a place like that—it was still quite grand back then, I understand—she could afford to charge substantial fees for care. The fact it was so remote made it even more attractive to some..." Chambers thought the man was about to say *of their younger relations*, but he ended the observation there.

"How was Wickman?" Pendergast asked. "As a student, I mean—and as a person?"

"He wasn't in my class his first two years here, so I can't really say a great deal about how he acclimated himself. But by the time he was in my ninth-grade English class, the tragedy seemed to have left no visible scars."

"Can you elaborate?"

"He was intelligent and well adjusted. He didn't get into trouble—I recall his eighth-grade biology teacher, Mrs. Beecher, particularly doted on him. It was obvious that he was well loved and cared for at home—even if that home was rather unusual, it probably gave his active imagination free rein. The other children liked him, as well. They even had a nickname for him, I believe. Let's see, there were so many..." Another pause, another glassing of the eyes. "Ah, yes. Atlas."

"Atlas?" the two agents said in unison.

Aiken nodded. "Apparently—this was before my time, when he first came to the school—he was small for his age and a bit shy. That, perhaps combined with his intellect, made him an obvious target for some minor bullying. But after a growth spurt in high school, he cut a formidable figure—if he hadn't been so gentle and kind by nature, of course. Do you know, violence distressed him so much that he couldn't bear to see animals teased or hurt? Even insects."

Chambers saw out of the corner of his eye a mystifying look pass over Pendergast's usually neutral face. "Not even insects?"

"He was a little Buddhist, that one," said Aiken with a laugh.

"You said his grandmother had strict religious views. Could you elaborate on that?"

Aiken shrugged. "I don't know much. She'd built a chapel at the rest home, and Parker had to attend services every morning. It was all he could do to catch the bus in time for school."

Hearing this, Chambers flashed back on an image—of a V-shaped candelabra in the burning mansion, set before rows of benches, aglow with fire.

"Anything else of importance?" he asked. "Habits, anecdotes, anything?"

Aiken shook his head. "You know how some kids go through dramatic changes in adolescence? Not Parker. He was the same thoughtful, intellectually curious, sensitive person on the day he graduated as he was when he first entered my class. He went to Tulane on a full scholarship, you know."

★ ★ ★

As they drove away from the school, Chambers felt secretly vindicated. Pendergast clearly had been hunting up an abused, twisted childhood for Wickman and was puzzled at finding none. Chambers, too, was surprised, but in his mind it only reinforced his assertion that looking into Wickman's childhood was a waste of time. Perhaps this experience was teaching his junior partner an important lesson. These mundane, almost bucolic stories gave the lie to any hint that Wickman might have had a troubled childhood.

He stretched, then glanced at Pendergast. The man had schooled him so many times over the last week, he felt a little good-humored maliciousness might be in order.

"So, Agent Pendergast," he said. "I'm curious about where your theory will take us next. It's not too late to hunt up the school janitor, you know."

Instead of responding, Pendergast merely tightened his lips—but whether he was deliberating or stewing in his own juices, Chambers had no way of knowing.

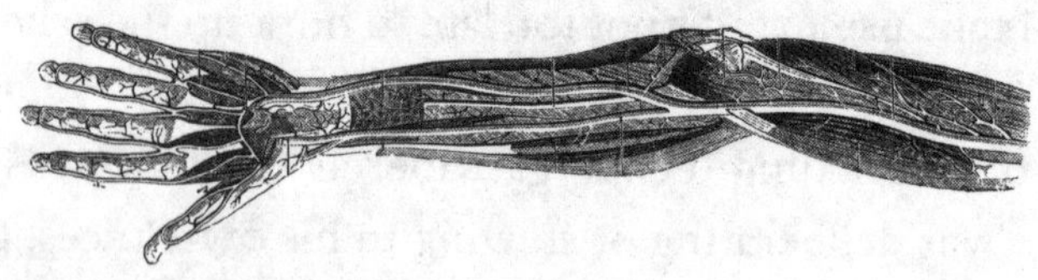

38

Wow," said Chambers, getting out of the rental car and looking out beyond the motel parking lot. "You ever been here before, Pendergast? These views are sublime."

They had flown into Flagstaff and driven to Sedona, Arizona, to interview what their research indicated might have been Wickman's last girlfriend, Sophie Petruska. They had extended their interviews—at Pendergast's insistence—to Wickman's undergraduate years at Tulane, speaking to a dorm RA and a roommate. But as before, their probing into Wickman's background confounded all their assumptions and yielded nothing—young Wickman had been a delightful child, an earnest and highly intelligent teenager, and an industrious, straight-A college student.

Following Chambers's gaze, Pendergast also glanced up and around at the landscape of surrounding mountains and sharp ledges of a peculiar red color that was Sedona's claim to fame. "There is only one step from the sublime to the ridiculous," he said.

Chambers had to laugh. Pendergast was clearly annoyed, in a sour mood ever since that interview with the English teacher. His method wasn't panning out, and he was being provocative and contrary just for the sake of it. "You don't see the glory of nature here?"

"What I see are a great many dangerous precipices and rocks. I will say this, however: the climate is not unattractive."

At this, Chambers shook his head. It was over a hundred degrees and Pendergast, as usual, was dressed in one of his black suits. At least it was a dry heat and not New Orleans soup. He took out a card on which he'd jotted an address. "Sophie Petruska, Petruska Jewelry, Capitol Butte Road. We can walk there from here."

"Excellent."

This was the last clue left to follow up on—the girlfriend Wickman's roommate said the serial killer had in college.

They found the jewelry store, a small but prosperous-looking establishment with a plate-glass window featuring an array of glittering gold jewelry pieces, many encrusted with gems.

Chambers paused to look. "There's some incredible work in there."

Pendergast stopped as well, uncharacteristically showing some interest. "Lovely," he said. "And all in crown gold—unusual."

Chambers didn't know what crown gold was but didn't ask. Nothing good came of asking Pendergast to explain something.

They entered the store, the door announcing their arrival with a tinkling of bells. A woman behind the counter greeted them.

"We're here to see Miss Sophie Petruska," said Chambers, holding up the ID on the lanyard. "FBI. We called earlier."

"She's in the workshop," said the woman behind the counter. "Um, she's in the middle of casting—I'll take you back there, but you might have to wait a few minutes."

They followed her into a rear workshop that was considerably larger than the store. A woman wearing a heavy apron, gloves, and Plexiglas face cover was in the process of removing a yellow-hot crucible from a furnace and, with great focus, using tongs to pour a stream of molten metal into a mold. Chambers watched with interest.

Petruska finished pouring the metal and put the crucible aside to cool off, then shut off the furnace and arranged her tools. Finally, she turned and came over, removing her gloves and face mask. An enormous quantity of mahogany-colored hair tumbled down, which she shook out.

Chambers realized he was looking at a very attractive woman, with fine high cheekbones, full lips, jade-colored eyes, and smooth white skin. Recovering, he said: "Miss Petruska? I'm Agent Chambers and this is Agent Pendergast, FBI. We spoke on the phone."

"Of course. Follow me into my office."

They settled down in a tiny office behind the furnace, Petruska behind a small desk while the agents wedged themselves into uncomfortable wooden chairs on either side.

"Apologies for the tight quarters," she said. "I keep all the space I can out there for the workshop."

"I find it intriguing," Pendergast began, "that you work in twenty-two-karat gold only."

Chambers had suggested Pendergast take the lead in the interview, but that was before he'd seen her. Now he was annoyed at himself. The man was so damn honey-tongued.

"I see you have an eye for gold. I would never work in lower karat—the color just doesn't have the richness. Even eighteen karat is a pale imitation of real gold. Those cultures that truly value gold, such as in India and Arabia, only settle for twenty-two or twenty-four karat."

"Indeed," said Pendergast. "I share their love of the one true color. I also note that you seem to be using the Dutch technique of delft clay casting. I had thought that rather rare."

She looked at him curiously. "For an FBI agent, you seem to know a great deal about working gold."

"The ancient art of gold-working is an interest of mine. *Ars longa, vita brevis.*"

Christ, thought Chambers, disgusted, Pendergast was really laying it on thick.

Petruska's face brightened. "A Hippocrates-quoting FBI agent! However, I hope you won't handcuff me if I point out that the original was written in Greek, not Latin—*Ὁ βίος βραχύς, ἡ δὲ τέχνη μακρή.*"

Pendergast bowed his head slightly. "And I thus stand corrected."

"My father taught ancient languages at Princeton. You just happened upon one quote I remember."

Chambers could see that, apparently for reasons of his own,

Pendergast was charming the hell out of this jeweler, and now he'd finally had enough. He cleared his throat. "Can we, ah, ask you a few questions, Miss Petruska?"

"Of course. You were quite mysterious on the phone. I'm curious to know what this is all about."

Chambers seized the lead. "Miss Petruska, we're here to ask you about a former boyfriend of yours, Parker Wickman."

At this her face seemed to go very still and watchful. "Yes?"

"Could you share with us how you met him, when, your relationship to him—the basic details?"

A short silence. "And this is in reference to what?"

"We're working on a homicide case. I wish I could share specifics with you, but I can't. We need your help. Of course, this interview is totally voluntary."

"I don't see any reason not to answer your questions," she said. "I'd like to help. Is Wickman in trouble?"

A silence. "I'm sorry to tell you he was the victim of a homicide."

"Oh." She drew her hand to her mouth. "Oh my."

"So, can we start from the beginning?"

She smoothed down her hair with a long hand and tried to collect herself. Nevertheless, Chambers could see she was badly shaken up by the news.

"We met in college."

"Tulane?"

She nodded. "It was the beginning of our junior years. Class of '85, so this would have been . . . the fall of '83."

Chambers nodded, taking notes. He often avoided using a microcassette recorder, finding it could prove a hindrance. "Go on, please."

"He was one of the most interesting men in the class. A brilliant student, but not a grind. Lots of fun, lively, with a good sense of humor. Nerdy in a lovable way. He liked playing dumb practical jokes."

"Jokes?"

She managed a laugh while recollecting. "Once he got a bunch of guys together and they hauled the dean's VW Bug up into the main dining hall. Another time, he borrowed a tray from the kitchen and made the usual Jell-O dessert, only he put giant garden slugs in it instead of bananas. He put it out there and thought it was hilarious when everyone tucked into it—before realizing."

Chambers shuddered. "So he had friends?"

"Tons. Everyone loved him."

More of the same wonderfulness. What the hell had happened—and when? "How did you meet?" he continued.

"We were both in the chess club. I whipped his ass a couple of times and he apparently liked that, said getting whupped in chess was sexy. We began dating." She paused. "I fell for him pretty hard."

"What was his major?"

"Psychology, on a med school track. I majored in chemistry. At the time I was fascinated with PSI."

"Sigh?" Chambers repeated, confused.

"PSI. You know, the parapsychology discipline that covers ways that human beings can perceive things outside the five traditional senses, like ESP. It comes from the Greek letter *psi*. I was trying to find chemical factors in the brain that could explain it, or at least identify it. He thought it was hogwash at first, but eventually he became fascinated. He even wrote his senior thesis on precognition in dreams."

"And the relationship continued with no issues?"

"We went out for a year, but over that following summer—well, we sort of drifted apart and ultimately broke up. But we remained friends, good friends, for the rest of senior year. He went on to graduate school in parapsychology at Tulane, while I moved to Arizona and apprenticed to a jeweler."

"No more chemistry?" Pendergast asked.

She smiled almost shyly. "Metallurgy and its chemical qualities began to interest me more."

"Why did you break up?" Chambers resumed.

"No reason in particular." She hesitated. "I think we were meant to be more friends than lovers. These things happen."

"Did he date any other women?"

"Not that I know of."

"And you?"

"I had boyfriends after that."

"And he didn't mind?"

There was an uneasy pause. "Not at first."

"But then later?"

Another awkward pause. "We lost touch after graduation. I sometimes wondered how he was doing, whether he went to medical school or pursued a career in PSI research. But then..." She hesitated. "I was back home in New Orleans visiting family, and I ran into him. At a car wash, of all crazy places."

"When was this?"

"Let's see. A few years after we graduated—1988 or thereabouts." She hesitated again and a troubled look crossed her face.

"And then?"

"It was a shock. He looked different—all buttoned up like a '50s Madison Avenue advertising exec. He told me he had a job fixing up cadavers. I couldn't believe what I was hearing. He'd dropped out of the graduate program at Tulane. He looked good—if kind of weird—it was the way he talked that had changed the most. Flat, kind of. Not at all like his previous funny and easy manner. He was...kind of all wound up."

"Do you have any idea what might have caused the change?"

"No. I probed, asked him if everything was okay, you know... But he wasn't forthcoming. I thought maybe he'd been in a car accident and gotten a traumatic brain injury. But as we talked, I realized he was still just as smart as ever—maybe even more so. But almost... Machiavellian. No longer an open book. Nobody else would have noticed it, and he seemed to be at pains to act like his old self. But I'd been his girlfriend. I could see it. Later, I wondered if it was my imagination. But instinct told me no." She shuddered. "Instinct also told me I shouldn't see him again—and I never did."

At this, Pendergast spoke again. "Machiavellian?"

"For want of a better word. Devious. Calculating. Careful."

Pendergast gave a slow nod. "You said you'd remained friends through your senior year. So this change must have occurred during his time in Tulane graduate school?"

"I... think so."

"He was there two years, you say?"

"Yes. Then he dropped out."

"Do you know if, during that time, he took a human anatomy class? Dissected cadavers?"

"Funny you should ask. He mentioned that he'd gotten the job at the funeral home because he'd taken just such a class, and right after dropping out he'd worked as a kind of diener for the medical school classes on human anatomy. Seemed really proud of how he knew his way around a corpse."

"Did you, by chance, read his thesis on dream precognition?"

"I did. It explored the fact that dreams often seem to predict future events in a person's life. He had a theory about that."

"And that theory?"

"It was a variant of the Jungian idea of the universal subconsciousness. Not only was the unconscious a source of wisdom, but it could potentially be used or cultivated to see into your future—in a misty sort of way, of course, especially in dreams."

"Do you believe that?"

"As a matter of fact, I do."

"Who was his thesis advisor in graduate school?"

"I don't know. He didn't want to talk about it."

"Do you think he had a falling-out with a graduate school professor, or something else that might have soured him, causing him to drop out?"

"It's possible. I really don't know."

"You implied there might have been some friction between you two about your later boyfriends."

"Not friction so much as a... well, a kind of morbid curiosity. Wanting to know details."

"Such as?"

"Like what I did with them."

"I see." Pendergast paused. "When you were in a relationship with him, did he evince any unusual proclivities?"

At this she reddened a little. "Well, nothing outside what, ah, people usually do."

"Was he a skillful lover?"

Chambers wondered where the hell Pendergast was going with this. If he pushed her too far, they might lose the interview.

"Yes," was all she said.

"What was the subject of his dissertation?"

"I don't know. We never talked about the details of his graduate work—beyond the anatomy class, anyway."

"One final question. What kind of car was he driving at the car wash?"

She thought for a moment. "It was a large white panel truck."

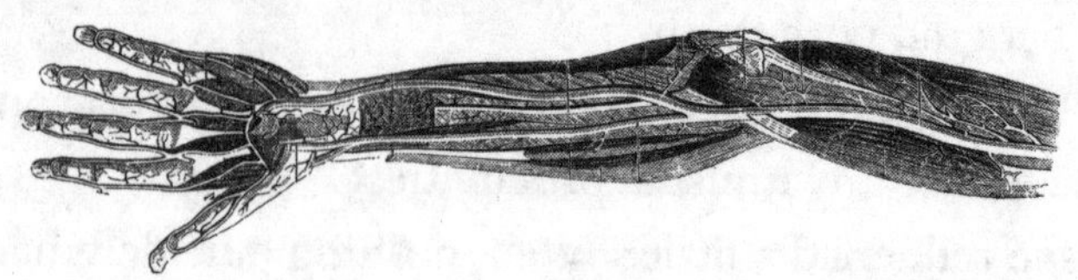

39

CHAMBERS HAD DRIVEN PAST Tulane University countless times—heading down Audubon or Calhoun Street on a case or a personal errand—but he'd never actually set foot on campus. That was about to change. He'd decided to let Pendergast and his chauffeur drive them around, Rolls or no. He didn't give a fuck anymore how it looked, especially since this was Pendergast's wild goose chase. Speaking of that, this was day three of three... and so far they'd come up with nothing. Chambers wondered how Pendergast would take it when this day ended with, once again, zip to show for it.

The Rolls drove slowly down Freret Street—getting the usual number of stares—until Pendergast murmured to the driver to pull over at the intersection of West Road. They got out and Chambers looked around. It was a pleasant Tuesday morning for late summer, not unbearably hot, and although a few students were walking here and there the campus was obviously quiet, gearing up for the fall term, and there was a drowsy haze over the ornate buildings of rusticated stone.

Pendergast noted Chambers's curiosity. "All—or most—of these structures were built after the school of H. H. Richardson. Hard to believe he was the architectural darling of the late nineteenth century."

Chambers nodded, wondering if his wife would have known that. She probably would, he decided.

They walked across a grassy quad, heading toward a massive building that stood out from the others for its modernist appearance.

"Graduate library for the sciences," Pendergast informed him as they climbed the steps.

"For the sciences? How many libraries are there?"

"Two. The reason I've chosen this one, however, is because it houses the graduate school's reference department."

Chambers fell silent. Pendergast hadn't told him exactly what the game plan was for today, and he was damned if he was going to ask. It was much more enjoyable thinking about what tomorrow would bring—back in the FBI offices, poring over new homicide files, with Estevez no doubt looking on approvingly. Estevez had left a voice message on his home number the night before, asking for an update and pointedly wondering why he had not seen them the last couple of days. Thank God tomorrow would be his turn, per their bargain.

He followed Pendergast into the cool shelter of the library, then followed a winding path upstairs and down corridors until they came to the reference section. Pendergast led the way in, approached an information desk, and asked where the course catalogs were kept. Getting the necessary directions, he made his way to a bookcase sandwiched between massive chemical and medical encyclopedias.

He stopped before the bookcase and slowly moved his head from top to bottom. "All colleges and universities print course catalogs for each semester," he said. "With course descriptions, professors' names, and class schedules—to help students choose the classes they are interested in or required to take."

Big of you to explain. "And how does that affect us, exactly?"

"We know from his girlfriend that Wickman switched from psychology as an undergrad to parapsychology for his graduate studies—and that she'd stoked his interest in PSI. Beyond that, we know nothing about what he did here before dropping out... except we can assume that, for those two years, he'd have been actively taking courses. That would have been 1985 and 1986." He paused, examining the shelves. He walked down one line of bound catalogs, then back up again. He began shaking his head. "Shame."

"What?"

"It would appear all the catalogs for those two years are missing—as are the catalogs for the preceding years."

"They've probably been misfiled."

Pendergast offered to let Chambers check for himself. With a sigh, he came forward. The top shelves held ancient, foxed catalogs with cloth bindings. As his eye traveled down the shelves, the colors, fonts, and spines changed with the years—a microcosm of changing fashions in typography and design—but Pendergast was right: he could find no catalogs for 1985 or 1986.

"Shall we have a word with the reference librarian?" Pendergast said.

The woman behind the desk expressed surprise; went to take a look for herself; disappeared into a private room for about ten minutes, then returned to say she was sorry, but there was no sign of them. "And there are no syllabi for those years, either," she added. "How odd. You'll have to go to the humanities library—I believe they have backup copies."

"Where can we find more general information on Tulane's PSI program?" Pendergast asked. "It was rather famous in its day."

The woman thought for a moment. She picked up a phone and made a call. This produced another reference librarian, who knew nothing and who in time produced yet another librarian. This person finally seemed to know something. He was younger than the others and dressed casually. "They threw out a lot of that stuff, departmental memos, catalogs, and the like, in a purge a couple of years ago," he said. "There's only so much space . . . decisions had to be made." He lowered his voice. "And as I understand it, this was one of the easier ones to make. The whole PSI program eventually embarrassed the university, fell under a cloud. The catalogs should have been retained, but who knows, maybe they tossed them as well."

"Is there anyone remaining," Pendergast asked, "on the faculty from that department?"

"That would be Dr. Telligren," said the librarian. "He survived the purge—brilliant man and a good professor."

★ ★ ★

The graduate library of the humanities was three blocks away. As they threaded their way between dormitories along narrow streets, Chambers shook his head. "Correct me if I'm wrong, but you can't check books out from a reference library—right?"

"That is correct. You can access them, but they don't leave the library."

"Then they must have been stolen."

"So it would appear. There were entries for them in the master catalog."

"But who the hell would steal shit like that? It's crazier than collecting phone books."

Pendergast said nothing.

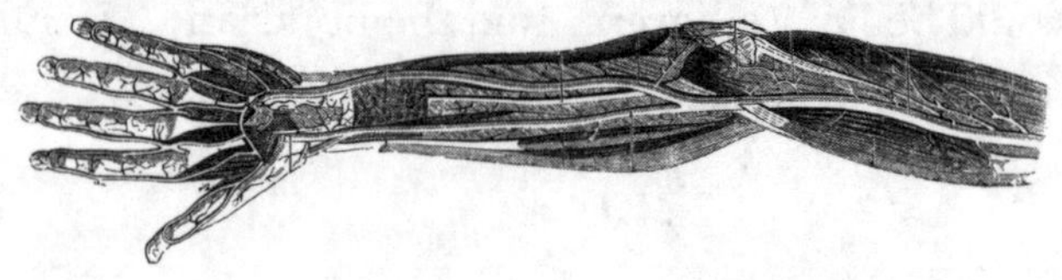

40

THERE WAS NO JOY at the humanities library, either—the same course catalogs were missing.

"The university must've been embarrassed," Chambers said, "if they really tossed away everything about that department."

"I do not think it was the university."

"Then who? What was so incriminating? I think it's just messed-up shelving."

Pendergast did not answer.

"So where are we going now? Back to the Rolls?" he asked hopefully. The day was almost half over.

"Not yet. There are a few more stops I'd like to make."

Chambers glanced at his watch: ten thirty. "You're the boss." *For exactly another six and a half hours*, he thought.

* * *

The next stop turned out to be the Cassat-Watson Center, a hulking building of the usual weathered stone that held, among other things, the registrar's office. Chambers followed Pendergast into the main office, where he looked around for a moment—standing still as marble—then indicated a row of chairs where students were waiting their turn to register for classes.

"Shall we have a seat?" he asked.

"Hell no. We're FBI, we can jump the line."

"Humor me," Pendergast said, taking out his pocket watch and checking it. "Let us wait."

"Jesus." Grumbling, Chambers sat down in the uncomfortable wooden chair and watched as his partner tucked the antique away.

Pendergast and his damn affectations. "Want me to get you a pair of pince-nez to go with that thing?" Chambers asked sarcastically.

"With what?"

"That museum piece you tell time with. I'm surprised the Bureau even allows it."

Pendergast eyed him for a moment. "If you are referring to my pocket watch, then—seeing as we have a moment—I'll acquaint you with its pedigree. If it's a 'museum piece,' that's only because of rarity—Patek Philippe made fewer than two hundred pocket watch *rattrapantes*."

"Two hundred what?"

"Split-second chronographs." Pendergast took out the timepiece again, opened the case, and turned the face toward Chambers. It was the first time he'd looked at it up close, and Chambers was shocked at how beautiful—and, especially, how complex—it was. In addition to the main, hand-painted enamel dial, there were sub-dials, a total of five hands of varying sizes, along with what seemed a tiny porthole into the actual components of the watch that displayed the elegantly carved, fantastically detailed metal workings within.

"Don't all those hands make you dizzy?" Chambers asked, trying very hard not to be impressed by what he'd always considered an anachronistic affectation.

"They do not. Most have specialized applications—horse racing, for example." He pressed the pendant and the largest of the blued hands started ticking, like a stopwatch. "Let's say you're timing two horses. You can record when the first passes the finish line... and still time the other one." He pressed a button on the case, and what Chambers had thought was a single moving hand now split into two—the top one remaining stationary, and the one previously hidden beneath it continuing to move—until, with another press of the button, Pendergast stopped it as well, simulating the finishing time of a second horse. With a few more presses of the pendant, both hands returned to their original position.

"I admit, the timepiece is not new. It was assembled in 1916 and given to my great-grandfather by the Swiss government in return for services rendered. It has been passed on from son to son, ultimately to me. It is one of perhaps three such watches the Swiss had adjusted to not five, or even six, but *seven* positions—the last being used as an anti-shock safeguard for the others in the event of, ah, unexpected gravitational pressure." He closed the lid gently and returned the watch to his jacket. "Can that ridiculous piece of black rubber strapped to your wrist time two events simultaneously?"

Chambers glanced down at his Casio, all knobby edges, minuscule print, and tiny, slippery buttons. Of course it could. Probably. He'd just need to read the manual.

"You said your ancestor was given that in 1916 for services rendered?" he asked, changing the subject. "Services to Switzerland?"

"I said the watch was *assembled*—with great care, craftsmanship, and taste, with the dual complications of a *foudroyante* and a *rattrapante* included, in addition to the chronograph I just demonstrated for you—in 1916. He was not given it until after the Armistice."

"You mean, that ended the First World War? Switzerland was neutral."

Pendergast smiled grimly. "More blood and treasure was lost—more secretly—to keep things that way than you could ever imagine, Agent Chambers. During *both* world wars. Read up on Operation Tannenbaum when you have some spare time."

As he sat back in his chair, Chambers thought of what Pendergast said: the watch—delicate as it looked—having been designed to withstand "unexpected gravitational pressure." It wasn't much of a stretch to imagine such shock and pressure being the result of incoming bombs and trench warfare.

Then, abruptly, Pendergast jumped to his feet. Taken by surprise,

Chambers realized the man had not just been giving him a lecture in antique watches: all the time, he'd been observing the three registration workers as they handled the students coming through—waiting for a certain pink-faced, elderly woman at the far end of the counter to become free.

She looked at them with raised eyebrows as they approached. Chambers saw a title card pinned to her blouse that read LOUISE FERRAGAMO, HEAD REGISTRATION CLERK.

"Hello, gentlemen," she said. "Interested in some senior education courses?"

A wiseass. Chambers could only guess how many thousands of clueless students she'd had to deal with over the years.

"No, Miss Ferragamo," said Pendergast in his buttery tone. "Not today, at least."

"Good. Because personal-enrichment classes are offered by an establishment about a mile and a half down Calhoun Street."

"Actually, we're not interested in our own educations at all—sadly lacking though they may be. We're interested in a graduate student who left Tulane in 1986. Parker Wickman."

She stared at them. "Surely you know our records are strictly confidential? Or is one of you Wickman?"

"I'm afraid not. Our interest is professional." He slipped a hand into his jacket and pulled out his FBI shield. Not satisfied with looking at it, the woman actually took it.

Chambers did the same, but the woman paid no attention to his. She was peering closely at Pendergast's gold badge, turning it over and over and looking as if she might bite it as proof of authenticity.

"You see," Pendergast continued, "Mr. Wickman—he never finished his doctoral degree—has gotten himself into trouble. Rather scandalous trouble, I'm afraid."

The woman's jaunty attitude slipped somewhat. "Trouble, you say?"

Pendergast nodded a little sadly. "The kind that might reflect badly on Tulane."

"And why are you coming to me about this?"

"We'd like to see the transcripts of his graduate years."

"For an investigation."

"Yes."

"I believe that requires a warrant."

"That is more or less true." Pendergast added a little honey to the butter. "Naturally, we could get a court order. But that would likely become public. You see, the kind of trouble Mr. Wickman's landed himself in is deeply unsavory—and would reflect badly, *very* badly, on Tulane itself."

The woman pulled herself up. "Tulane is in no way responsible for the bad behavior of its students," she said. "We're a respectable institution, founded as a medical university one hundred and fifty years ago."

Pendergast leaned forward and whispered something in her ear.

The woman blanched. "He did what? To *what*?"

Pendergast leaned forward and whispered again, more briefly this time.

The woman reached into a drawer beneath her side of the stand, pulled out a tissue, dabbed at her forehead and temples, then blew her nose. "Mercy sakes," she murmured, pulling herself together.

"And that's not only why we're here today—but why I chose you in particular to speak with. As the head clerk, Miss Ferragamo, you lived through Tulane's recent history. Not many people realize it, but it's remarkable how much one can learn, being a registrar: listening to the idle chatter, tabulating the courses that students sign up for. Seeing what grades, honors, and I presume disciplinary actions are meted out. Am I correct?"

She gave a pert nod.

"So you see, if you could provide us with copies of Mr. Wickman's graduate transcripts, that will give us the information we need to maneuver him into a . . . well, confession isn't exactly the right word. Let's just say that when confronted by the information they contain—which in many cases will probably give the lie to his sworn testimony—we'll be able to quickly wrap up this whole sordid mess, and he will no longer be in a position to do Tulane's reputation any harm. We'll make sure of that."

"And the copies?"

"They will be sealed deep within the FBI's evidence storage, where no one will see them. The alternative is stories in the newspaper, a public trial and conviction, bringing shame upon Tulane."

The head clerk stood for a moment at her station, considering. Then she walked away. Five minutes later, she came back with a white legal-size envelope, which she handed to Pendergast. He thanked her with a little bow, then turned and left the office so quickly that Chambers practically had to run to keep up.

"What's the sudden hurry?" he panted. It had been a pretty masterful performance, but he was damned if he was going to puff up Pendergast's ego more than it already was by admitting that.

"Miss Ferragamo is excellent at her job: a stickler for protocol, but also experienced enough to employ pragmatism when it comes to dealing with problems. However, she is also perspicacious. I think it prudent that we make ourselves scarce before she comes up with additional questions—or, worse, ponders things through a little more thoroughly and sees the holes in my, ah, little story."

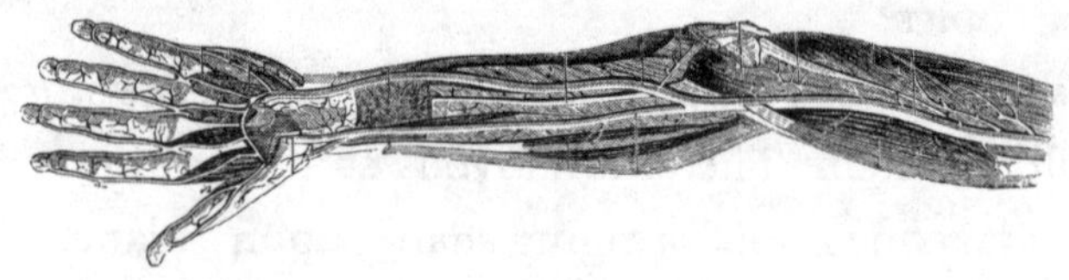

41

IT WAS ALMOST NINETY minutes later, and Chambers was once again sitting next to Pendergast—this time in the lobby of the university's Roscommon Center for Biotechnology and Biomedical Engineering. Using the only name that had been dropped that day—Dr. Telligren, the one professor still around who'd taught some of the courses Wickman might have taken—Pendergast had used a combination of lies, threats, and brandishments of their FBI badges to break down two unusually stubborn secretaries plus an obdurate research assistant and secure a half-hour appointment with Dr. Telligren during the professor's usual lunch break.

Chambers looked around. Situated on St. Charles Avenue, the Roscommon Center was much more modern and high-tech, inside and out, than most of the places they'd been that morning. It was less a lecture hall than a hospital or research lab—and Chambers figured that this was most likely exactly what it was.

"What the hell is biomedical engineering?" he said out loud. "Sounds like a course in how to build suspension bridges out of elephant bones."

"Scientific disciplines are, for better or worse, undergoing mitosis into ever-greater subcategories faster than the humanities can ever keep up with. You can thank the march of technology for that."

He was leafing through Wickman's transcripts as he spoke. The way he said "technology," Chambers wasn't sure if he approved, disapproved, or was indifferent. Maybe the vintage Rolls was a clue.

"This is most peculiar," Pendergast said.

"What is?"

Pendergast pointed to a transcript. "This list of courses that Wickman took. Several make sense for someone interested in a career involving psychology and medicine—these pathology courses, for example: Gross Anatomy, Pathology Techniques. Same with Molecular Biology. But I can't find any mention of PSI courses in here. Where are the parascience, psychical history, and like courses? Where are the reports from his thesis advisor on his progress? Who *was* his thesis advisor? Instead, these transcripts are salted with eccentricities." He held up the page. "Public Health Grant Writing? Interracial Themes in American Art? Fundamentals of Industrial Hygiene?" He gathered the pages and let them drop into Chambers's lap. "This is too eccentric to be plausible. The choice of courses is almost... whimsical."

"You yourself said he went crazy during grad school," Chambers replied, stuffing the pages back into their envelope.

"That is true. But this..." He gestured at the envelope. "I sense a devious, even perverse hand at work here."

Cue the sinister organ chord, Chambers thought to himself, managing not to roll his eyes.

At that moment, the door leading to the faculty offices opened and a young man, clearly a research student, appeared. "Dr. Telligren will see you."

They rose and followed him through the open doorway, down a corridor that managed to look sterile and high-tech at the same time, until the student stopped at a door about halfway along the passage. He knocked.

"Come in," came a cultivated voice from the far side.

The student opened the door and Chambers followed Pendergast into a large, wood-paneled room, a brace of windows in the far wall rising to the ceiling, bathing the spotless furniture and bookshelves in mellow, warm light. The contrast between the corridor and this room could not have been greater—Chambers was imagining a lab of some kind, with Telligren hunched over a beaker and holding a pipette in one rubber-gloved hand. But instead the man sat behind an elegant desk, a row of windows behind him, leaving his face partially obscured in shadow. As they approached, Chambers made out the face: steady blue eyes; patrician features; a full head of gray hair, carefully combed. He was wearing a suit—not a lab coat—and he rose as they came closer.

"I'm Dr. Telligren," he said in a voice with a trace of old New Orleans in it. "Which of you is Special Agent Pendergast?"

"I am, sir, and it's an honor to meet you." Pendergast offered his hand, and they shook. "This is my partner, Agent Chambers."

Chambers shook hands as well, and then took a proffered seat from one of the three that sat arranged in a semicircle before the desk. Countless rows of books, arranged on shelves, rose on both sides of the room—and though many of them looked valuable, with leather spines, they also bore the obvious marks of reading.

"It's a very close thing, actually—your getting the chance for a meeting on such short notice, I mean," Telligren said. "I always have a weekly luncheon with my colleagues, which I wouldn't miss on pain of excommunication, but today's was canceled because two are out of town. And so I have—" he consulted his watch— "thirty-five minutes to hear what, exactly, is so urgent that it could not wait."

"We appreciate your sacrificing your time like this," Pendergast said. His voice was still smooth, although less buttery than it had been with the registrar. "And given how precious it is, we'll get straight to the point. We're here about one of your students—Parker Wickman."

For a moment, Chambers thought he saw Telligren's face go blank. But when he glanced again, he saw the same look of sharp intellect and half-concealed impatience he'd noticed before. "I'm sorry. Could you repeat the name?"

"Wickman. He was your student in 1985 and 1986. Involved with your research studies into PSI and parapsychology."

"Parapsychology," Telligren said as if tasting the word. "I had little to do with that field—should you wish to call it that."

"Odd. I thought you had been one of the professors spearheading the initiative... before it was debunked as a pseudoscience, I mean."

If this was an attempt to rile Telligren, it didn't work. "That's why I hesitated to call it a 'field.' I didn't know if you were a believer or not—there are quite a few zealots out there, and one must be careful." He paused as if recollecting. "It is true that we made a few attempts to conduct research into certain aspects of parapsychology, but they were brief—nothing like Duke University, which for a time jumped in with both feet. But then we realized no legitimate discipline could be fashioned from it. It's our duty as scientists to examine any potentially promising avenue, no matter how risible it may seem initially. Gravity, evolution, *Helicobacter pylori*, the earth orbiting the sun, they were all ridiculed at first—why, when Edward Jenner tried to spread the news about the vaccine he'd created to eradicate smallpox, a portion of the population threatened him... thinking the 'cowpox' vaccine would turn them into cows!"

"You said you made 'a few attempts to conduct research on certain aspects of parapsychology,'" Pendergast replied, ignoring this burst of historic trivia. "What sort of research, may I ask?"

"Precisely what you'd expect. Looking into whether the pioneering Zener and Ganzfeld experiments could be duplicated in double-blind tests. Establishing the historical context, and a scientific baseline, for testing the validity of such phenomena as out-of-body experiences, dream telepathy, precognition, psychokinesis." He shrugged dismissively.

"And this despite knowing that—for example—psychokinesis violates certain fundamental laws of physics."

"Such as?"

"Conservation of momentum. The second law of thermodynamics."

Dr. Telligren raised his hands. "Please—far be it from me to defend PSI research! On the contrary. As I said, our work was confined to seeing if it was possible to establish scientific criteria. After a few years, we decided further research would be a waste of time, that there was no scientific basis for PSI hypotheses, and that was that. We canceled the program."

"Then let's get back to Parker Wickman, your graduate student in 1985 and 1986," Pendergast said.

Dr. Telligren went silent for almost a minute. "That's a decade back. You can't expect me to remember all of my students."

"*Do* try, Professor Telligren."

Pendergast's tone had become aggressive and skeptical.

Another pause. "I do remember him now—faintly. He'd majored in psychology as an undergraduate, I believe... but the rigorousness required for the doctoral program was not to his taste. As I recall, he dropped out."

"Would you happen to have course catalogs or syllabi from the years when Wickman was your student?"

"I would not. If I had need of them, I'd ask a research librarian."

"You would be disappointed, Professor. The course catalogs and all other relevant information are missing from both graduate libraries. It appears they were stolen."

Chambers wondered exactly what Pendergast was trying to get out of this guy, especially with the sudden, challenging tone. They'd done what little background research on Telligren they could while setting up this appointment, and it looked to Chambers like the man was a highly respected researcher and winner of several prestigious awards. If Wickman had been his student—if he'd really gone crazy during his graduate years, which was what Pendergast's investigation seemed to be whittling it down to—the guy would remember him.

Dr. Telligren sighed, looked at his watch. "Let me ask you, Agents Pendergast and—I'm sorry, was it Chambers? Did you *really* make such an effort to secure a few precious minutes of my time only to pepper me with questions about an abandoned and disgraced project and a long-forgotten student? You come in here like Don Quixote and Rocinante—full of misdirected virtue. All you've done is waste my time."

Chambers couldn't have summed it up better himself. Pendergast was starting to embarrass him.

"I would my horse had the speed of your tongue," Pendergast said, sounding a little provoked.

"God send you, sir, a speedy infirmity, for the better increasing your folly."

This was spoken not by Telligren, but someone behind them. Chambers looked around to see a man standing in a far corner. He couldn't be sure if the guy had been there when they came in, or whether he'd quietly entered during the conversation—he suspected the former, because he knew Pendergast's ears could detect even a fly farting. What surprised him more than the man's presence was his appearance. He was dressed in a beautifully cut chalk-stripe suit, black horse-bit loafers, with a diamond stickpin and gaudy vintage tie. His features interested Chambers even more than the attire. He looked to be in his early thirties, eyes fairly sparkling with an impish yet discerning intelligence. He laughed at this exchange of quotations: a brief, barking laugh, like the yelp of some night creature. With tight blond curls framing his forehead and ears, he reminded Chambers of some Roman emperor or, perhaps, the Caravaggio masterpiece of Bacchus brandishing a bunch of grapes—a painting his wife particularly admired.

Now the man came forward and took the empty seat, which happened to be between Pendergast and Chambers. "Forgive me for not introducing myself earlier. I'm Dr. Dorion Magnus, a colleague of Dr. Telligren's. When I heard that the FBI were here, I was intrigued! In fact, I was the one who persuaded him to see you."

Pendergast was looking at the man intently. "A pleasure to make your acquaintance. Are you a professor of Shakespeare, Dr. Magnus?"

Another perverse, barking laugh. "Please call me Dorion."

"Dorion, then." He did not offer to reciprocate.

"Nothing so straightforward, I'm afraid. I specialize in bioengineering—biomechanics and biotransport. Rather recondite subjects, and they keep me more in the research lab than the lecture hall or a surgical bay—but they're proving quite promising in terms of new pharmacology and diagnosis tools." He waved a hand with a dismissive, effeminate gesture. "But let me not distract you. By all means, continue the Inquisition."

"The fact is, Dorion, we're investigating a serial-murder case."

"Serial murder," Magnus repeated. "Oh my! Has somebody shot up a box of Frosted Flakes?"

It took Chambers a moment to get the joke. This man Magnus was amazingly obnoxious.

"My time available to you, gentlemen, is almost gone," Dr. Telligren said, an edge to his voice. He seemed to have been given new backbone by the presence of this cherubic-looking fellow. "What murders are you talking about?"

"The murder of your ex-student Parker Wickman, for one," Chambers broke in, tired of all this beating around the bush. "He died on the grounds of his house on the Pearl River, which burned to the ground just a few nights ago. It's been confirmed as arson."

"Ah, yes, I saw a news report about the fire. *Man is born to trouble as the sparks fly upward*," Magnus intoned. "I always knew Parker Wickman would be a loser. Pardon me: I should phrase that as 'one whose post-college life might prove difficult.' "

"So you knew him," said Chambers.

"We were classmates," said Magnus.

"As I've been telling them," Telligren broke in hastily. "I've confirmed he was a student here—briefly, before dropping out. Now, gentlemen: do you have what you need? Your time is up."

As he was speaking, Dr. Magnus slipped a gold cigar case out of his suit pocket and opened it. "Cigar, anyone?" he asked as he showed it to Chambers, Telligren, and last of all Pendergast.

Nobody took him up on the offer. Pendergast peered into the box, complimented Magnus on his taste in cigars, and turned back to Telligren: "Why did Wickman drop out?"

Dr. Telligren shook his head. "It's exactly like I said. Some students can't handle the graduate workload. Or the long hours of lab work. I really have no idea."

"Did you notice a change in him—more specifically, a change in personality—between the time he first became your student and the time he left Tulane?"

"As I've said *repeatedly*—" Telligren's voice was now impatient— "I barely recall the fellow!" He rose from his chair with a finality that added special gravitas to his short stature. "And now we've run out of time, and I'll have to bring this interview to a close."

Chambers quickly rose. High time to get the hell out of here. Even though the Rolls had a decanter of brandy in a rear compartment, he thought he could manage to keep away from it—as long as they got their asses back to the office. Pendergast had made a hash of it. It was embarrassing.

As they got up to leave, Magnus said cheerfully, "But, gentlemen, no need to stay at arm's length." He placed a comradely hand on Pendergast's shoulder as he steered them firmly to the door. "We're always delighted to help—*perfectly* delighted, anytime!"

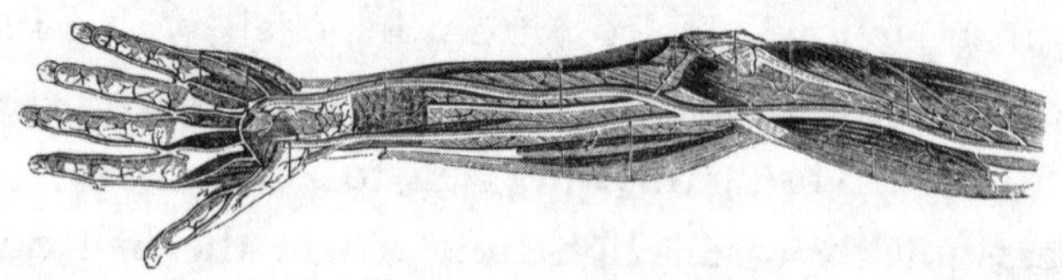

42

THEY HEADED BACK DOWNTOWN in silence, which suited Chambers just fine. He snuck a look at his watch—just a few minutes before two. It was the afternoon of Pendergast's third day of investigation, per their agreement. It had been a grueling morning—two research libraries canvassed, a registrar wheedled out of information, and a useless interview with Telligren—but now the clock was ticking down. Chambers glanced sidelong at Pendergast. The man, although looking crisp and cool as ever, seemed to be in deep thought—or maybe it was just a deep funk. Privately, Chambers thought that, since this last meeting had been a total bust, his partner might finally be mulling over the recent events and concluding they'd proved pointless. Now at least they could get back to the real work at hand—and not a moment too soon.

The Rolls pulled up at Chambers's usual breakfast hangout, as before; he got into his Impala, and—before Pendergast could suggest some way to waste the afternoon—left a trail of rubber on his way back to the field office. Twenty minutes later, he was at his desk, suit coat on the rack, cup of coffee steaming in front of him, when Pendergast glided in. He too sat down, remained silent for a few more minutes, then finally spoke.

"I confess to being very dissatisfied."

Not an unusual way to feel after seventy-two hours of fruitless digging. But despite everything, Chambers felt almost magnanimous and decided not to rub it in.

"Why's that?" he asked.

"I am convinced that an elaborate scheme of deception, including the counterfeiting of files and removal of documents, has taken place."

Chambers raised his eyebrows. "Really?" was all he allowed himself.

Pendergast, perhaps hearing a faint trace of gloating, looked over at him for a minute. "I see you think this entire line of inquiry profitless."

"You said it—not me."

"This scheme of erasure has been done with great care—in most respects. This was not a hasty or spontaneous effort. There was plenty of time to see it done, and done well. I'm convinced Telligren and Magnus are not what they seem."

Alarms rang in Chambers's head. This didn't sound like a partner ready to concede his failure and turn the reins back to him. The man was impossible. He was like a terrier unable to let go of a bone. His mood changed from magnanimous to mulish. "Now look, Pendergast. I don't know what's going on in that strange mind of yours, but it's obvious to me everything we've done over the past few days—interviewing nannies, teachers, professors, and librarians, and getting Wickman's damn transcript—has been a dead end."

"Ah, the transcript," Pendergast said. "That was what I was referring to when I said this cover-up has been extremely thorough *in most respects.*"

"Meaning what, exactly?"

Pendergast took the white envelope and placed it on his desk. "This transcript has as much in common with a serious graduate student's work as a 'pig-picking' has with luncheon at Galatoire's. Courses in grant writing? Art history? Industrial hygiene? These are fake, my dear Chambers."

There it was again, that *my dear Chambers* bullshit. He took a deep breath. "Pendergast, you've been gripping a wild goose by the neck for too long. Look, I get it. I've done it myself. The more you look into something that you can't quite nail down, the easier it is to think, *Just one more interview, one more bit of research, and it'll all become clear.* Take it from me—that's not how it works. Now your three days are up, as agreed upon. Okay? So, please—learn a few tricks from this old dog and let me do the case my way."

"The rogues we're searching for were right in front of us...and practically laughing at our impotence."

Chambers sighed angrily. "What... who are you talking about?"

"Magnus, for one. Did you notice that, shortly after we mentioned Wickman's residence had burned down, he offered us cigars?"

"So?"

"We found fine ash from an expensive cigar in that surgical bay."

"Don't tell me you know it was the same brand?"

A hesitation. "I can't say."

"Christ, Pendergast!"

"I believe the man was taunting us."

Chambers was about to unload a piece of his mind when a shadow crossed his peripheral vision. He looked over to see Estevez's secretary leaning in at the open door. "Agent Chambers?"

"Yeah?"

"SOC Estevez would like a word with you and Agent Pendergast. Immediately."

⋆ ⋆ ⋆

Roughly three minutes later, they were in the chief's office. Estevez was standing behind his desk, pacing, not offering either of them a chair. Chambers waited a few minutes, watching his boss go back and forth, back and forth. He'd never seen the man as restless as this. He didn't know what it portended—except it couldn't be good.

Abruptly, Estevez stopped and wheeled toward Pendergast. "What the *hell* have you been doing for the last three days?"

"Sir," Chambers broke in, "we—"

"I'm not speaking to you. I'd like to hear your junior agent explain this clusterfuck."

"Sir," Pendergast began, "we have not spoken with the press."

"That wasn't my question. What *have* you been doing? Where's my debriefing? Christ, as far as I can tell you've never even been in the office since I last saw you at the site of the fire."

Pendergast said nothing.

"Pendergast? Could you grace us with your answer to my question?"

"We've been attempting to solve the case, sir."

"How?"

"By taking a deep look into Wickman's past, trying to ascertain his motives, his state of mind, what made him—"

"Agent Pendergast!" Estevez said, bringing him up short. "The man is dead. *Dead*. The fucking case is the other corpse face down in the mud. Remember *him*? Have you ID'd him?"

Amen to that, Chambers couldn't help but think.

"No, sir."

Estevez turned toward Chambers. "Chambers—you're the one who fell down on the job here."

"Sir?" Chambers said.

"You're the senior agent here. It's your job to teach new jacks, no matter how arrogant or insolent, to toe the line and learn from your own example. I knew I was taking a chance when I assigned Pendergast to you—and from where I'm standing, it looks like you've failed to control your junior partner. Utterly."

Chambers could only move his jaw. No sound came out. *I knew I was taking a chance when I assigned Pendergast to you . . .*

"What were my last words to you?" Estevez continued. "*You're coming back into the office now.* I even agreed to let you continue the case, because what you said at the time made a modicum of sense. You'd solved a case—*solved*, past tense—everyone had missed. You'd exposed a new killer and wanted to finish the case. What, exactly, did 'finishing' the case entail?"

As Estevez yelled at him in drill-sergeant fashion, Chambers felt a strange boiling deep in his gut. He knew his face was aflame. "It meant identifying other homicides Wickman might have perpetrated.

It meant looking into who killed Wickman. It meant IDing the other victim and following up on that homicide."

"Spoken like the Chambers I used to know!" Estevez yelled. "So what happened to you the last three days? Your balls drop off or something?"

Even in his shock and dismay, Chambers sensed that despite everything he'd done, Estevez still thought he looked like a broke-dick.

"That was how I intended to prosecute the case, sir," he said. His chest felt tight, and it was hard to find the air to speak. "But my junior partner advocated a completely different approach: looking into Wickman's past, attempting to find—"

"So you let your junior partner's infantile theories take precedence. You allowed yourself to be led by the nose. Jesus! I've got to believe—"

"*Sir!*" Chambers couldn't help but interrupt. "I am now fully aware that Agent Pendergast's assumptions about the origins of Wickman's mental illness have not been borne out. Nothing in his past is relevant to the current case."

Estevez turned to Pendergast. "What do you have to say to that?"

"I have nothing to add, sir."

This—spoken in a mild tone—further drove Chambers crazy.

Estevez looked back at him. "What now, *senior* partner?"

"Sir, we should be investigating who killed Wickman. We need to examine the crime scene not just for clues to the fire, but to the one who set the fire and killed two people. We should even be dragging the swamp for this motherfucker. We need to learn more about the other dead man—because those two homicides are the case, as I see it."

"Correction, Agent Chambers—you needed to be doing this shit three days ago. Now: are you going to get your ass all over this, pronto?"

"Eagerly, sir."

Once again, Estevez turned to Pendergast. "And you're a real piece of work. I have to hand it to you: I've never seen a greenhorn climb on top of his senior partner like that. Hope you enjoyed the view while it lasted. Because if you don't listen to Agent Chambers here, you're going to find yourself in a world of shit—Decker or no Decker. Now, both of you—get the fuck out of my office. And I want daily reports of your progress. Daily."

⋆ ⋆ ⋆

As they walked away from Estevez's office, Chambers felt lightheaded. He'd blown off some of his steam. He may have been reamed out, but he'd also ratted out his partner. Not that he didn't deserve it—but it just wasn't done, and deserving had nothing to do with anything. He felt overcome with remorse.

Pendergast stopped abruptly. He adjusted his tie, glanced at his pocket watch.

"There is a black-tie party that I need to attend tonight," he said. "Until tomorrow." And he gave a small bow.

As Chambers stopped dead in his tracks in disbelief, Pendergast continued down the hall, eventually disappearing in the direction of the elevator bank.

"Motherf—" Chambers muttered. Just when he thought he'd heard it all. He took another deep, shuddering breath, feeling his chest loosen as he made a decision—or, rather, as Pendergast made it for him. He didn't know if Pendergast was an ungrateful junior partner touched in the head, or if he was just touched—but he did know one thing: he was done covering for the guy.

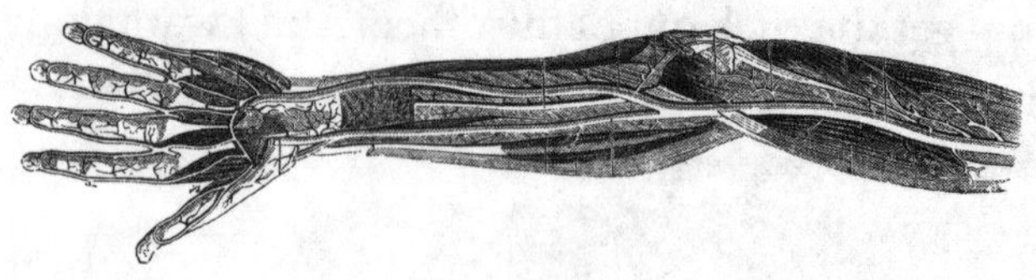

43

HAND ME THAT FILE," Chambers said, flapping his hand at Ron Fleury, the junior agent he had dragged into the case. "Not that one, for Chrissakes, the other one."

He took the file from the proffered hand and slapped it down on the grubby Formica table the three of them were working around. The table, located in a cheerless, windowless room in the basement of the Louisiana FO, was strewn with documents, files, and photographs. Chambers had corralled Fleury, along with an archivist, to help him pull files and sort through boxes, while a tech guy hammered away at an IBM computer, looking for more potential Wickman homicides.

Chambers knew he was acting like a dick, but he didn't care. Pendergast had put him in a foul mood. He'd ignored the fact that Chambers was the mentor and senior partner; he had a penchant for going off on wild goose chases at the drop of a hat—and worst of all, he'd landed the both of them in hot water with Estevez. It was almost impossible to have Pendergast's back when the guy operated with no regard for protocols or even common sense. And now he'd effectively left Chambers to do all the grunt work in this cinder-block prison, digging up leads on who might have killed Wickman, while he was out tilting at windmills. It was obvious Wickman had been murdered in a revenge killing by a family member or friend of one of his victims:

the cutting off of Wickman's arm was proof of that, a clear message of vengeance—and that was Chambers's focus now.

Pendergast had, effectively, walked off the premises at 3:00 PM—but Chambers was going to make damn sure he put in some good old-fashioned policework before the day was out.

He'd decided to first comb through the cases they'd already pinned on Wickman, looking for likely suspects. If that didn't yield some leads, he intended to follow through by chasing down more Wickman murders and looking at those cases—which promised to be a long and tedious process. He needed to find someone who knew, or at least suspected, Wickman to have ghosted a friend or relative—but one who'd rather handle it himself than report his suspicions to the authorities.

He flipped open the file he'd just been handed. The man in the black-and-white photograph paper-clipped to the folder stared back at him: Nicholas Mabley, Husser, Louisiana. This was the case they'd picked up from the Tangipahoa Parish Sheriff's Office—one of the first cases they'd linked to Wickman. Mabley was ripped, with sandy-colored hair, a big square jawline, pale killer eyes, a brutal face. And a scar on his cheek that looked like it had been made with a knife. The guy was supposed to be mobbed up. Wickman had killed him and made it look like a mob killing to fool law enforcement. And it had—until he and Pendergast had come along.

He flipped through the details. The guy had been tied to a chair, gagged, tortured, beaten up, then shanked in the heart. Drugged with flunitrazepam. Only the right arm, it seemed, had been left untouched. And those weird pinpricks—Wickman's signature. Christ, it was so crazy, so senseless. Why Pendergast thought there was any use in figuring out Wickman's motivations for killing people and messing with their arms was beyond him.

He paged through the file. This was a real possibility. If Mabley had been a wiseguy, a revenge killing would be the likely outcome. These were the kind of people to retaliate in their own way—and send a message in the process. He turned to the autopsy report, flipping through it, recalling the specific details they had noted earlier.

No wife or widow. The body had been released to the family, a brother, for cremation.

He moved on to Mabley's biography. The guy was in the vending machine business—cigarettes. A mobbed-up trade if there ever was one: all cash, territories to defend, threats to be made, arms and legs to break. Mabley had a criminal record, although he'd managed to avoid prison time. Criminal tax evasion, assault, a firearm misdemeanor... and each time, an expensive lawyer had gotten him off.

He felt his heart accelerate as he went through the file. This was a strong lead, for sure. He paused, checking dates, building a timeline in his head. They had linked the Mabley killing to a serial killer five days ago. The next day, the sheriff's department had sent a bereavement messenger to the next of kin telling him his brother was not a victim of a gangland slaying, as previously thought, but of a serial killer. That killing had taken place two years ago. At the time, a younger brother, Lucius Mabley, lived in Natchez. Chambers jotted down the date. Just a day after the family had been notified, Wickman had been murdered, his arm cut off, and his house burned down.

Quick work.

He dove back into the file, fished out the document labeled FAMILY. There wasn't much on Lucius Mabley: the investigation had been thin. There was an old photo of Lucius, and if anything he looked even meaner, tougher, and bigger than his older brother. Just the kind of guy who would take things into his own hands.

Damn, this was looking better and better.

"Hey," he called to the guy on the personal computer, "see if there's a Mabley still living on Clifton Avenue in Natchez, Mississippi."

A moment later, the tech guy said, "Yup, still there, Lucius Mabley, 346 Clifton."

"Agent Fleury?" Chambers said, turning.

The junior agent turned toward him. "Yes, sir?"

It was now after six. Chambers pushed the document on Lucius Mabley toward Fleury. "We need to question this guy—tomorrow. Give him a call and see if he'll agree to meet with us voluntarily. Tell him it's a routine follow-up on his brother's murder, that we've got some new information for him."

"Yes, sir," said Fleury. "Will you need me to come along?" There was a hopeful, even eager, tone in the agent's voice that Chambers liked.

"Sure, why not—if my partner Pendergast can't make it."

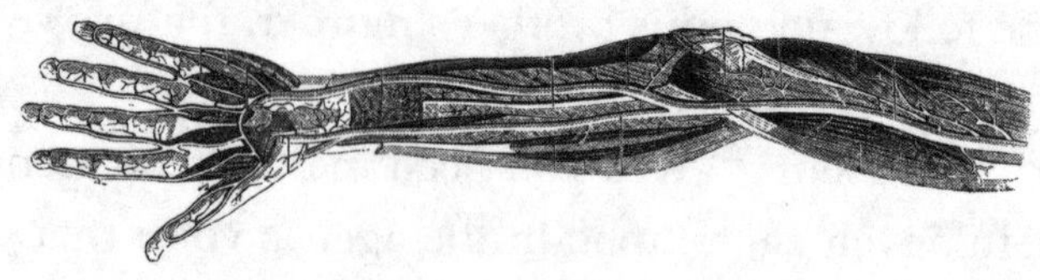

44

As agent A. X. L. Pendergast stepped out of his Rolls-Royce in front of the Elms Mansion in the Garden District of New Orleans, he gave his tuxedo jacket a little tug to straighten the shawl collar, making it lie flat and sleek on his chest. A red carpet had been laid out leading up to the pillared portico, and the arriving guests were lined up and walking into a chorus of popping flashbulbs. As he emerged from the Rolls, many of them turned and stared at him in curiosity. Pendergast knew he cut a striking figure. He intended to cut such a figure; it was part of his plan.

Several photographers from the local press converged on him, flashes going off. Of course they had no idea who he was; all they knew was he looked important—they would try to figure him out later.

Pendergast was not on the guest list: he was quite certain Dr. Dorion Magnus would not want an FBI agent at the reception and ceremony in which he was to receive Louisiana's highest honor, the Huey P. Long Medal. And it seemed the guardians at the gate meant business.

At the short line that had formed to check invitations, Pendergast paused to turn and help an elderly lady directly behind him, whose corgi had gotten its leash tangled in her sleeve. He then proceeded past the invitation checkers, showing them his with a distracted air. He paused once again. The dowager behind him was fishing in her handbag for her own invitation.

"I believe you dropped this," he said to her, handing her the invitation he'd relieved her of just a moment earlier. Accepting her effusive thanks with a gracious bow, he entered the sumptuous foyer of the grand old mansion, glowing with stained glass, gilded sconces, and intricately carved dark oak paneling, and paused to take in the splendor of it. It had been built in 1869 by Watson Van Benthuysen II, a wealthy wine and tobacco merchant, who had clearly spared no expense. As he strolled contemplatively down the central hall, he glimpsed to his left a drawing room in white with gilded accents, featuring a grand marble fireplace. Straight ahead, a dark oak staircase swept in a curve to a landing above. To his right was a dining room in the grand style, with a green marble fireplace, gilded moldings, Persian rugs, and rich brocaded wall coverings. Next to it was an extravagant room decorated in the high style of the Napoleonic Empire: neoclassical pillars, heavy mahogany furniture, bronze accents, and a magnificent onyx Sphinx.

He felt, deep down, the faintest of twinges. The mansion unexpectedly reminded him of his childhood home, Rochenoire, not far away on Dauphine Street, which had burned in a fire set by a mob, taking both his parents with it. He unexpectedly felt the haunting weight of his family history on his shoulders, his strange and unhappy upbringing, before recoiling from those feelings and focusing his mind on the matter at hand.

He stepped out the back portico and paused to survey the reception and dinner for Magnus, now in full swing, taking place in the mansion's famous patio and garden. His eye was drawn to an octagonal temple in the center of the patio with Corinthian columns, modeled after the ancient Athenian Tower of the Winds. An orchestra was playing Mozart to one side, while on another side tables sufficient to seat several hundred had been set for a sit-down dinner. A generous bar, heaped with flowers and attended by numerous bartenders, dominated the middle. The temple, he noticed, had been hung with enormous garlands of fresh flowers. This, he assumed, was where Magnus would receive his medal from the mayor of New Orleans.

He glanced at the time. Seven thirty. Dinner would be served at eight, and at eight forty-five the awards ceremony would begin. Magnus hadn't arrived yet—he was apparently planning to stage a grand entrance once everyone had gathered.

There was time for a cocktail—or perhaps two.

He descended the marble stairs to the garden and headed toward the long, sumptuous bar. He was aware that a number of eyes had turned to him, all wondering who he was. Of course, there were some who would recognize the venerable Pendergast name, which among certain of the ancient, decaying society of New Orleans was now looked upon with abhorrence.

Amused by this thought, Pendergast stepped up to the bar—guests opening a lane for him.

"What may I get you, sir?" asked a young bartender, hurrying over.

"A Sazerac, if you please, strong, made with that absinthe I see on the top shelf—the Vieux Carré."

"I'm so sorry sir, that's the mayor's private reserve."

Pendergast's silvery eyes remained on the young man's face and he said nothing, waiting, as the seconds ticked by.

"But I'm sure he won't mind," the young man said. "With all the big doings going on here, I mean," he added, flushing as he removed the bottle and, preparing the cocktail, placed it in front of Pendergast. There was no tip jar—that would be déclassé—so Pendergast extracted a hundred-dollar bill and, with an almost invisible movement, slid it over the bar.

He took up the cocktail and sipped it. Most excellent. "I thank you," he said.

Carrying the drink, he took a turn around the gathering. He recognized a few relics from the old New Orleans families: various decrepit dowagers draped in diamonds and pearls, clinging to desiccated old men sporting black tie or wearing military uniforms emblazoned with medals. The wearing of uniforms seemed to be coming back into vogue these days, Pendergast noticed with approval. He wondered, idly, how many of them were members of the Round Table, the most prestigious and secretive gentleman's club in the city. His own father, of course, had never received an invitation—not with the Pendergasts' history.

More curious eyes turned his way. Pendergast scanned the crowd again and found what he was looking for. He strolled over. "Why, Madame Pontalba, how lovely to see you!" He held out his white-gloved hand.

"Oh, yes, delightful to see you too, Mr.—" the large dowager said with a faint hesitation, which Pendergast immediately filled.

"Pendergast," he said. "Aloysius Pendergast." And he bowed, bringing her silk-gloved hand to within two inches of his lips.

"Mr. Pendergast, how delightful."

"What a happy occasion," said Pendergast, taking a goodly sip of his cocktail. "Dr. Magnus has done so much for the community—*so* much."

"Oh yes. Have you seen the riverboat? I can't wait until the renovations are complete—I'm *dying* for the invitation to its christening."

The dowager seemed not only ignorant of the Pendergast family but quite taken with him, as well. This was as he had hoped. But Pendergast knew nothing of a riverboat. "Ah! Please tell me about it," he asked, deeply interested eyes gazing into hers.

"Well, it's called the *Fantôme*—a larger cousin, they say, of the one mentioned by Mark Twain in *Life on the Mississippi*. He's restoring it to absolute perfection. It's a tremendous undertaking, and I can't begin to imagine the expense, but when it's complete it will be one of the treasures of the city."

"Madame, if you don't mind my asking, how is it that you're so sure you will receive what must be a coveted invitation to its ceremonial launch?"

She waved a gloved hand deprecatingly. "You know, the old family thing and all."

Pendergast did know. Pontalba was one of the oldest and most distinguished names in New Orleans—descendants of the Baroness de Pontalba, who back in the 1840s funded the construction of several now-historic buildings.

"You may find this strange," said Pendergast, "but I'd not heard of Dr. Magnus until just a week ago. I've been away, you see, and only recently returned."

"Oh yes—he's a quiet, modest fellow, doesn't like the limelight," said the woman. "But so charming and generous. And handsome. Doing *such* good work at the university and the hospital. They say he's one of the top pharmaceutical biologists in the country—and, you know, those pharmacological patents of his practically mint money." She tittered. "He oh-so-quietly gave a million dollars to Tulane University Hospital just last year. He's a major philanthropist—and still short of forty. *And* single. Quite the catch!"

Pendergast followed her glance to see Magnus himself striding in, wearing an understated tux. He was in fact a remarkably handsome man, his yellow hair curling about his face, deep-green and almost feminine eyes, a jaw cut as if from granite, and a high smooth forehead. His manner was charming and animated.

"There he is now!" said Madame Pontalba, clasping her hands together. "The man of the hour."

A hush fell over the crowd, then a susurrus of applause rose as Magnus paused at the top of the stairs, flanked by a small entourage. He smiled and waved, then descended, and walked through, working the crowd, shaking hands, dropping bons mots, laughing and nodding, kissing ladies on both cheeks. He was trailed by the mayor, who was taking the opportunity to do his own glad-handing, and on the other side of him was Dr. Telligren, gray-haired and distinguished, wearing not a tux but a Marine Corps uniform sporting silver eagles with spread wings—he'd been a full-bird colonel—and a rack of campaign decorations. From a quick scan of the breast bar, Pendergast could see the man had served in Vietnam as a medical officer.

This was a side of Dr. Telligren that pleaded for further exploration. He turned to Madame Pontalba. "And I see he's with Dr. Telligren."

"Oh yes. They're the greatest of friends at the university hospital."

"Of course," said Pendergast. He then bowed. "It was a pleasure seeing you again, madame." Having gotten what he wanted, he excused himself and drifted away. His drink was almost finished and he would not mind another. He went over to the bar, which now had a short line.

"Lovely evening," he said to an attractive woman also waiting for a cocktail.

"It could hardly be lovelier," she said, her eyes turning to him and lingering.

"May I get you a drink?"

"Thank you. Chablis."

Pendergast ordered her a Chablis and another Sazerac for himself. He handed the wine to her. "Pendergast," he said, extending his hand.

"Olivia," she said, taking it. "Last names only?"

"My first name is not worth mentioning," he said.

"Well, *Pendergast*," said the woman, "what brings you here?"

Pendergast moved closer to her and let his FBI badge show for just a moment. Her eyes widened. "I'm an FBI agent," he said. "Investigating a murder. I could use the temporary assistance of a clever, self-possessed woman."

She took a step back but was obviously intrigued nevertheless. He'd pegged her as a woman who liked an adventure, and he was about to give her a little one.

"You don't mean me, do you?"

"I most certainly do."

She smiled jauntily. "What kind of assistance?"

"I need to get close enough to Dr. Magnus to exchange a few words with him unheard—but, as you can see, he's surrounded by his people."

"What can I do about it?"

"He's coming to the bar now. Make sure he's looking your way, and in the process of taking off your gloves, drop one."

"And?"

"He'll come rushing over to pick it up for you—and that will give me a moment to speak to him without the others overhearing."

"Well." She looked at him slyly. "Tell me, Mr. FBI agent: is he a crook?"

"When is a New Orleanian being awarded the Huey P. Long Medal *not* a crook, my dear Olivia?"

As Magnus and his entourage made for the bar, Olivia accomplished her task with skill, catching the man's eye and then dropping her glove in a slow movement that seemed possibly deliberate, even enticing.

As expected, Magnus came rushing over, leaving his entourage, then bent down and scooped it up, offering it back to her. Giggling, she reached out to take it, and he bowed and kissed her hand. Pendergast, who had lingered next to the woman with his back turned, now swung around. "Ah, Dr. Magnus," he said in a low voice, "I want you to know that you are in grave danger."

"Danger? How?"

"Because I see through you—and your charade."

Magnus did not react as Pendergast expected. Instead, the man gave him a smile almost as if he'd anticipated the comment, then gently took his arm. As his entourage caught up, he turned to them with a smile. "Excuse us for a moment—my dear friend *Pendergast* and I have a small private matter to discuss."

This was hardly the guilty reaction Pendergast had anticipated. Nevertheless, he went along with it, as Magnus led him to a quiet spot beside a potted palm. Still smiling cordially, he bent close to Pendergast's ear. "And I see through you, too, *Aloysius*."

"And what do you see?" Pendergast asked.

"I see the Pendergasts of Dauphine Street: a strange, sad family. Parents burned to death by a mob, great-aunt a poisoner of her own children, grandfather killer of thousands with his quack medicines." He leaned closer and said in harsh whisper: "And I see a dear brother, well on his way to becoming a monstrous criminal." He straightened up with a laugh, as if they'd just shared a private joke, and concluded sotto voce: "Indeed, Aloysius—I see through you as one sees through a thin pane of glass... *And I'm carrying a rock.*"

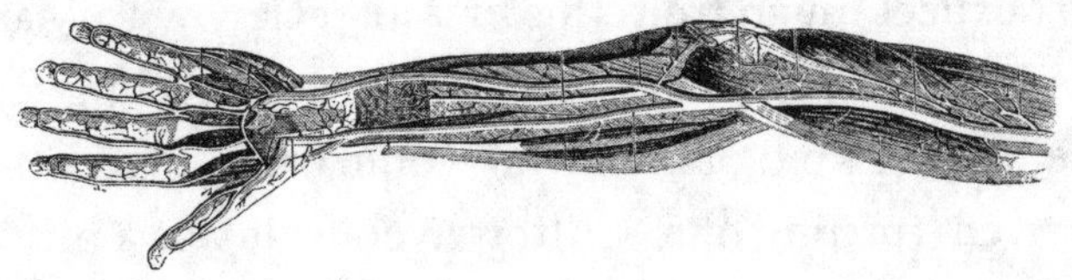

45

PENDERGAST HADN'T SHOWED UP at the meeting they were supposed to have had the evening before. Just blew it off, going instead to some ridiculous black-tie affair. As a result, Chambers had not been able to rope his partner into coming along to pay a visit to Lucius Mabley, his prime suspect. But that was okay with him: Chambers was tired of Pendergast and his argumentative, superior ways. In contrast, Fleury was an easygoing and compliant partner who put up with Chambers's shit while dishing out very little of his own.

Thankfully, Lucius Mabley had agreed to meet them voluntarily, saving them the wringer of having to get a warrant. They were now driving north on 61 from Baton Rouge to Natchez, Mississippi. Natchez was a place that Chambers and his wife had visited often—a place she adored, a lovely old town set on the Mississippi River and full of grand antebellum mansions. Her favorite had been the Rosalie Mansion and Gardens, right on the river, which they visited every time they went to Natchez. Chambers felt a certain creeping anxiety about how he was going to feel returning to a place that had once been a scene of happiness for both of them.

He was about to tell himself to stuff the sentimental bullshit when he realized that was the wrong attitude. Better to be grateful for what he—what they—had had. Easier said than done, but he was working on it.

He didn't expect much from this first interview with Mabley, but it would give him a chance to assess the guy, get a feeling for him, see whether he was the kind of man who would order a hit on someone.

They arrived, turning onto Clifton Avenue. It was a nice neighborhood, perhaps a bit run down, but set alongside a bluff with amazing views of the river below. They were early, so Chambers asked Fleury to pull over to the side of the road and wait. It was seven minutes to nine.

"Killer view," said Fleury.

"Yeah. I wonder what these houses cost." Chambers looked around. "Some look a little ramshackle, but the view is a million bucks." He glanced at Fleury. The guy was so eager. "I'm going to do the questioning, okay? When I'm done, if there's anything you want to ask, go ahead."

"Yes, sir." Fleury swallowed. "May I ask, sir, what the routine is going to be? I mean, are we going to do the good-guy, bad-guy thing?"

Chambers shook his head. "No. Someone like Mabley would see through that in a flash. We're just here to take stock. Best thing is to start out nice and friendly, then narrow the questioning. Just follow my lead."

"Right, sir."

Chambers had liked the frequent "sir" in the beginning, but now it was starting to wear thin. He had the creeping sense Fleury wasn't the brightest bulb in the box. Still, he was a lot better than being showered with Pendergast's deductions, quips, and affectations—or, on the other hand, interminable enigmatic silences.

When nine o'clock rolled around, Chambers started the car and drove up in front of the house. They parked and walked up to the door, rang the bell. Low chimes sounded inside. A moment later, a woman in a crisp domestic uniform answered.

"Mr. Mabley is expecting you."

They entered the house. It wasn't shabby inside, but it wasn't a rich man's digs, either—more like tasteful upper middle class. They followed the domestic into the living room, furnished with a nice cherry coffee table, some comfortable sofas and chairs, shelves with real books on them, a rubber plant in the corner, and some Chagall prints on the walls. All in all, not really a mobster's digs. But you never could tell.

A moment later a man came in, wheeling himself in a wheelchair. Despite the chair, he radiated strength: stony face, shock of thick black hair swept back, pale-blue eyes. Chambers wondered what had happened. He knew Mabley was only forty—perhaps a stroke.

Chambers proffered his badge. "Mr. Mabley, thank you for seeing us. I'm Agent Chambers, and this is Agent Fleury."

"Sure. What's it about? More news on Nick's murder?" His voice was gravelly and broadcast a no-nonsense attitude.

Chambers slipped out a handheld cassette machine. "May we record?"

"No. Sorry."

"Right." Chambers put it away. "So, I'm assuming you heard the news—that your brother was the victim of a serial killer?"

"I certainly did. I mean, back when I first heard about it, I told the sheriff it wasn't a mob killing, but he wouldn't hear of it."

"Why didn't you think it was a mob killing? It had all the earmarks of one."

"First of all, damn it, because we're not mobsters!" His voice rose. "Is everyone in the cigarette vending business a criminal?"

Chambers hesitated. "Yes, I believe they are," he finally said.

Mabley stared at him and then laughed. "You're a funny guy. Okay, fine. But here's the thing: the whole setup of the murder was fake. The torturing of Nick wasn't serious; it wasn't how wiseguys do it. It was all superficial—for show."

"Did you or your brother know of, or have any contact with, Parker Wickman before the killing?"

"Was that the guy's name—Wickman? Piece of shit. Not me. And I'm pretty sure Nick didn't, either. When I heard the news about him, I couldn't believe it. It doesn't make sense. I mean, serial killers target the weak and defenseless—right? My brother was in great shape. He carried a piece. He was alert. I couldn't—I *can't*—believe a serial killer could've gotten the drop on him. Why would this Wickman have even *considered* him a target? With all the slope-shouldered girlie men wandering around, why go after a guy like Nicky?"

"That's a good question. We don't have an answer on that yet."

"You should look into it."

Chambers tried to move the interview back on track. "So when you heard about Wickman, what was your reaction?"

"The sheriff sent some dipshit over here to tell us the news. He asked a few questions, but he didn't seem too interested."

"And when you heard your brother was the victim of a serial killer, what was your reaction?"

"I wanted to find out who the guy was and kill him."

"Really? You wanted to kill him?"

"Hell, yes! Wouldn't you? But that fire got him first. Good riddance—the bastard."

"Did you know that the person who killed Wickman cut off his arm, just as Wickman cut off the arms of his victims?" This, along with Wickman's name, hadn't been reported in the papers, and Chambers wanted to see his reaction.

At this, Mabley's heavy eyebrows rose. "Good for them."

"It means whoever killed him knew he was a serial killer who cut off people's arms. In other words, Wickman's killer knew who he was *before* law enforcement identified him."

At this Mabley looked at him steadily. "Okay, so now I get why you're here. You think it was me or someone in my family. We found him ourselves—and killed him for revenge."

"We're looking into the possibility," he said, careful not to react to this observation, "that a family member or friend of one of the victims was able to identify Wickman and took action on their own. Understandable, when you think about it." He tried to sound sympathetic.

Mabley pondered a moment, his craggy forehead creasing. "You know," he said, "Wickman probably *was* killed by someone as payback. Let me ask you a question: in addition to having his arm cut off, what else did they do to him?"

"You mean, how did they kill him?"

"Yeah. And what did they do *before* they killed him?"

Chambers decided to tell the truth. "They killed him while he was under anesthesia, by cutting off his flow of air or something similar."

Mabley nodded. "And before that?"

"Nothing."

"So they cut off his arm while he was asleep?"

"No, they cut it off after he was dead."

"Just to make sure I have this right: they put him under, and then suffocated him *while* he was under anesthesia?"

"That's what the ME determined."

At this, Mabley laughed again: a big, booming sound. "Agent Chambers, right there you have proof I didn't do it."

"And what proof is that?"

"The way you describe it, Wickman's killer offed him as sweetly as if he were dying in a hospice. If I'd gotten my hands on him, I'd have tortured the motherfucker within an inch of his life. I would've made his last moments a perfect hell on earth. And most of all, I would have cut off his arm while he was wide awake—and could appreciate the message. Otherwise, what's the fucking point?"

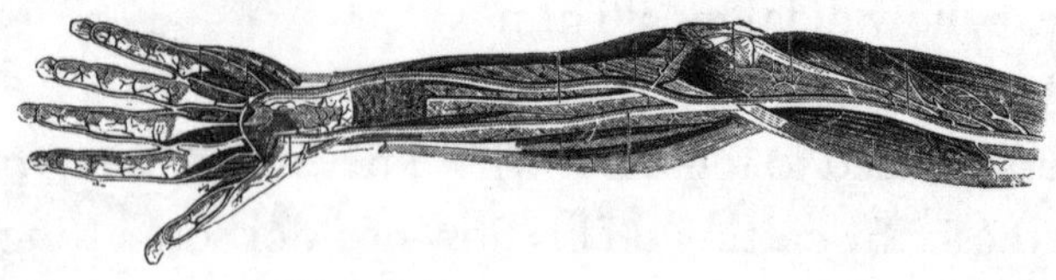

46

NORTHWEST OF TULANE'S CAMPUS, a warren of narrow, picturesque streets lined with brick houses served as an informal community for university faculty. The neighborhood, filled with mostly retired professors, was quiet, but after 8:00 or 9:00 PM it grew practically somnolent. The occasional car would pass, lights striping the crape myrtles that lined the curbs; less often the laughter of adolescents on their way home from the gym might be heard. At other times, the playing of a piano, or the sound of a violin, might issue faintly from a house. Other than that, silence reigned.

Except for the occasional barking of a nearby dog.

A lone figure stood in a pool of darkness next to a tall hedge that served as boundary between two such houses, dressed head-to-toe in black and carrying a black shoulder bag. He had been there for several hours, with infinite patience, waiting motionless, all his senses alert. He knew about the dog and had been waiting for it to be put to bed, but apparently that was not going to happen. Not a problem, however: he had come prepared.

At ten fifteen, finally, the lights in the upstairs bedroom directly above were extinguished. This was the bedroom of Dr. Neil Slocombe, retired professor of comparative literature: never married, no family to speak of, still in decent health and without need of a live-in nurse.

The man waited. The dog maintained its vigil in a nearby front window, occasionally barking in fury at random sounds or a passing vehicle. Now that the professor had gone to bed and been allowed fifteen minutes to fall asleep, it was time to act.

With consummate stealth, the figure left the cover of the hedge and crept up to the side of the house. There he waited below the windowsill of what he knew to be the living room. A few minutes later, when the dog once again resumed his angry barking at some external outrage, he took advantage of the animal's noise to slip the window lock free, then raise the sash roughly three feet. And then he knelt beneath the window, waiting once again.

When the dog barked next, he rose quickly and silently and made his way over the sill into the house, leaving the window open. Then he crouched again, preparing for the next step.

He could hear the dog huffing and grumbling two rooms away.

When all was quiet, the dark figure made a faint scratching noise with his finger on the fabric of a chair—undetectable to a sleeping human, but not to the sensitive ears of a canine.

The grumbling stopped, and a moment later came the sound of nails clicking over a hard surface. They came closer, still closer, until the figure could see an animal framed in the doorway of the room: a Belgian Malinois, as strong and fierce as it was ugly.

For a moment, it stood in the doorway, stock-still, its ears erect, staring into the darkened room. Then—as the man reached into the shoulder bag—the dog saw the movement and quickly swiveled its head at him.

There was a millisecond or two during which the animal, so accustomed to barking out the front window, was temporarily stunned by the sudden appearance of this trespasser inside the house itself. The man used this brief instant to fling an apple slice, coated with peanut butter and wrapped in bacon, at the dog's feet just as it opened its jaws to sound the alarm.

The beast stopped in mid-bark, sniffed at the snack, then ate it. Another followed, which was just as quickly consumed. Then it came forward, slowly, growling with suspicion. As it did so, the dark figure displayed no emotion of any kind, simply spreading his arms in a calm, non-threatening manner. In short order, the dog was close enough to tear the man's throat out, still growling—hair along its back sticking up.

Quick as lightning, the man grabbed the animal around the neck, squeezing its collar tight and using main force to throw it on its back. As it began to struggle from the awkward, defenseless position—paws flailing and jaws snapping at the air—the man placed one hand over its eyes, put his mouth near one furry ear, and began to half chant, half sing in some old and half-forgotten language. The dog writhed, its growls and yelps cut off by the tightened collar, as the man continued his strange singsong. As the animal fell under the spell of the chant and ceased struggling, the man released the collar. In a minute, it was calm, almost soporific.

Gently, the man loosened his grip on the dog, easing its head to the ground, and then rose, checking his watch. He had about fifteen minutes until the mesmerizing technique wore off.

He took a flashlight from his bag, switched it to the lowest setting, and used it to survey the room. What he saw was exactly what he expected: a space frozen in time like the period room in a museum. It was the unused room of an old bachelor fixed in his ways, who ate his meals in the kitchen and spent his evenings reading in his library or writing in the study—who never entertained. Protective plastic covers had been placed over the chairs and sofa. The flashlight beam licked around, illuminating framed paintings, heavy dark furniture. A breakfront contained unread books and knickknacks, probably given as gifts by students. Some fine-looking pieces of Dutch delftware, covered with dust, were displayed on a sideboard. He stepped closer and examined them. Judging by the tin glaze, they were indeed antiques, not replicas—worth a few thousand dollars each, perhaps. The man in black shook his head. The professor would have shown greater taste had he collected porcelain.

Finding nothing else of interest, he passed into the front hall, taking a glance back at the motionless dog. An open door on the right side of the opposite wall led to the professor's study, tucked into the far front corner of the house. This room was different—it displayed evidence of considerable use. A rolltop desk was covered with bills, a rarely inked appointment book, a month-old invitation to a faculty tea. On an adjacent table was a manual Olympia typewriter of ancient vintage with a yellowing piece of paper in it, with only one line typed on it.

But it was the surrounding walls that interested him. These were stuffed with books—thousands of them—precisely the kind one would expect a professor of comparative literature to have read, taught from, and still cherish. It was a forlorn display: these books and perhaps the delftware were the chronicle of a narrow, lonely life—the two things he loved most. One could only hope they loved him back.

"I said good-bye to Chips the night before he died," the dark figure murmured to himself as he scanned the shelves.

And there they were: exactly what he expected to find. He stepped closer, glancing at the spines, checking off the bound catalogs mentally against the list maintained in his head. Quickly, he took the ones he needed—there were only three not already acquired—and put them in his shoulder bag. He then arranged the shelf so nothing looked out of place. The old professor would probably never notice: these old course catalogs, not even from his own department, were the least interesting of his totems of the past; fragments shored against his ruin.

Quickly, he left the study, crossed the dining room, and stepped back into the living room.

To his dismay, he could see the dog was already coming out of its spellbound state, becoming aware of its surroundings. Its eyes opened; their glazed look began to fade. The ears pricked up.

Stepping over the half-conscious dog, the man reached for several pieces of delftware—then, taking pity on the old professor, grabbed a handful of knickknacks instead. Then he mussed up the area around the open window a little, slipped through it, closed the sash, backed away into the darkness—then picked up a large stone and heaved it.

With a shiver, the glass broke, the stone leaving a hole the size of a bowling ball. A roar of frantic barking sounded within. But already the dark figure had moved through the backyard and was crossing a neighbor's property, pulling off his mask and gloves as he did so and stuffing them into his shoulder bag. When he reached the adjoining street he slowed to a walk, smoothing down his clothes as he made for the car waiting a few blocks away. The barking had faded with distance, but it had not stopped. Professor Slocombe would find the broken window, notice the missing items, and congratulate himself that the thieves—probably some darn kids—had not taken anything of real value.

At the next intersection, the man dumped the knickknacks into a storm drain, then continued on.

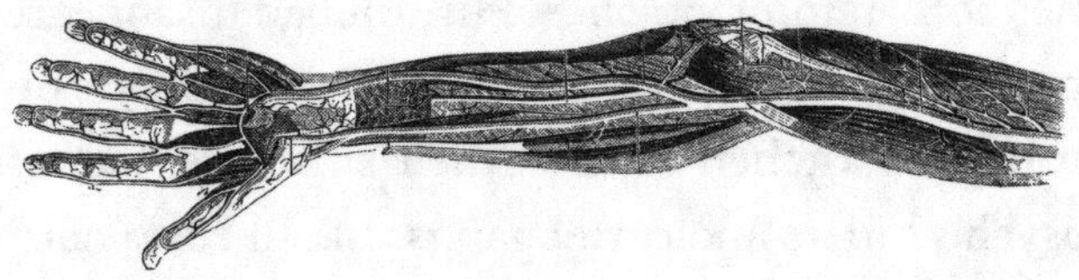

47

Chambers looked up at the clock and sighed. Quarter to seven. Almost the entire floor was deserted save for the night staff. Thank God Estevez had left for the day. He'd only popped his head in twice, while Chambers was either typing or else on the phone. Pendergast had been absent both times. The SOC had frowned but left without a word.

The fact was, Pendergast had been absent—period. In the daily reports Estevez had demanded, Chambers had been forced to be a little vague with the personal pronouns he used. He felt bad about not backing his partner in the earlier meeting and was now trying, against his own better judgment, to cover his ass—which annoyed him no end. Still, that blond-haired, black-suited enigma was a grown man, and beyond goosing the daily reports, Chambers wasn't going to nursemaid him anymore. He'd left a note for Pendergast to meet each evening to compare progress. And if Pendergast ignored the warnings and kept running around on a fool's errand—well, that was his lookout. Chambers had done all he could.

Except Pendergast hadn't shown the first night.

The only thing that mollified Chambers slightly was the thin police report he'd found on his desk this morning, left for him by Pendergast only God knew when. It was a police report from Pearlington, its subject a man who lived on Bali Road who had recently been heard several times threatening violence. His son had disappeared a month ago and the father blamed "those meth cookers down by the river" using "that big old kitchen to cook their shit." He had also rambled on about psycho killers and cartel gangs that liked to cut people into pieces. Clipped to the folder was an expensive sheet of monogrammed notepaper, containing a single large question mark, drawn with a flourish. Chambers wondered what Pendergast could possibly see in this missing person case that connected with Wickman, but at least the guy was doing something.

His musings were suddenly interrupted when the figure of Pendergast appeared in the doorway.

Chambers sat forward at his desk. "Damn it, Pendergast, where the hell have you been?"

"I'm quite well, thank you for asking." He sat down and put the leather case he'd been carrying on his desk.

Almost an hour late. "Well, let's get to it," Chambers said. "I started the last meeting. Why don't you start this one by bringing me up to speed on *your* progress?"

"I was hoping for that opportunity. You see, I've hit—what is the expression?—pay dirt."

Chambers sat back again and folded his arms. He hoped to hell this was going to be good.

"I've uncovered what Dr. Telligren was so obviously trying to keep secret," Pendergast announced.

So he was still at that old game. "Pendergast, you listen to me—"

"You asked me to go first," Pendergast interrupted. "Please allow me the opportunity to finish. I promise to be brief. You see, I have uncovered a series of graduate courses whose aim was to use medical techniques to not only detect but also enhance PSI abilities. Not only were the course catalogs that listed these removed—as you know—but all information *on the courses themselves* was deliberately expunged from the university's records. I checked with our friend in the registrar's office, and she could find no evidence of any of these courses having existed—none at all."

It sounded like the bastard had been spending all his time back at Tulane. Chambers looked at him, feeling a strange combination of annoyance and weary indifference.

"How is this relevant?"

Instead of answering, Pendergast reached into his leather case, pulled out half a dozen catalogs, and passed three of them over to Chambers. The titles were all similar: *Tulane University, Graduate School of the Sciences Curriculum*. Each volume covered a single semester: fall 1985; spring 1986; fall 1986.

"So if these were expunged," he demanded, "where did you get them?"

"Old course catalogs and syllabi are a common thing for professors to keep."

"Some professor gave you these?"

"Certainly not. Going around asking professors for old course catalogs would only arouse curiosity and gossip. I... appropriated them."

"What the fuck? Did I just hear you say you *stole* these?"

"It took me a total of three insertions to find what I needed."

"'Insertions'? Burglaries, more like!"

Pendergast shrugged.

Chambers picked up the catalogs and flung them across the room at Pendergast. "Fuck you and your euphemisms—this is stolen property! You *can't* use them as evidence, jerkoff. All you can do is get us cashiered!"

Pendergast nimbly snatched the three volumes flying in midair and restored them to the table. "I don't plan to use them as evidence."

"You still haven't explained how this is relevant!" Chambers found his mind going blank. This messing around of Pendergast's wasn't as bad as he feared—it was worse.

Pendergast spoke smoothly. "Agent Chambers, please: just listen to the names of these courses." He leafed through the books to pages he had bookmarked. "Neuroelectrical Stimulation of Precognitive Receptors, Neuroanatomy of PSI Limbic Structures, Surgical Interventions in PSI Medial Temporal Regions, Studies in DMILS

Feasibility—*DMILS* being an acronym for 'direct mental interactions with living systems.' These are not about *investigating* PSI activity: these are about *enhancing* PSI activity through surgical and electrical intervention. And look—" Pendergast pointed at a paragraph in one of the catalogs— "each class description is followed by an asterisk, viz.: *Please consult Dr. Telligren, Head of the Biopsychical Research Laboratory, for eligibility.* And do you see here? There's a notice from Dr. Telligren, calling for volunteers as experimental subjects."

And he put the catalogs down on his desk with something like triumph.

There was a silence that was ultimately broken by Chambers. "Good for you," he said. "I'll bake you a cake. You've illegally seized inadmissible evidence of no relevance while chasing a wild goose."

Pendergast fell silent.

"You've been wasting your time."

"Apparently you're not interested in considering who those volunteers might have been—or, for that matter, what the results of the experiments were." Pendergast gathered up the catalogs, face unreadable, and put them back in the leather pack. "So, Agent Chambers: perhaps it is your turn to relate what progress *you* have made since last we met."

Chambers rubbed his jaw. "You know what? It's late. I'm tired, and I'm going home. Any further discussion of this case with you tonight would be a waste of breath. So would you mind tossing me my jacket? And for the love of God, don't break into any more houses."

And he reached out his hand.

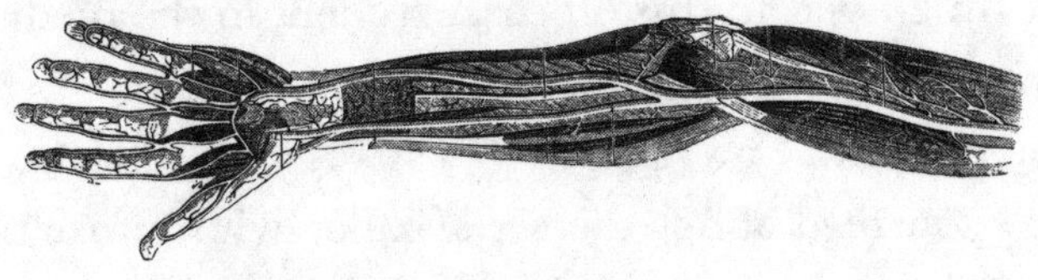

48

Pendergast gave a light knock on the partially open office door. When he heard a pleasant "Come in," he eased the door open and stuck his head in. "Dr. Telligren?"

The gray-haired man behind the desk looked at him. "Yes?"

At this, Pendergast slid out his wallet and opened it to the badge. "FBI," he said, without entering, standing at the threshold.

"FBI? Oh yes. You were here once before. And I recognize you from the ceremony. Magnus's friend, I guess—I don't see how you could have gotten into the faculty offices otherwise. But never mind that—come in."

Pendergast came in and waited.

"Sit down."

Pendergast sat down, his hands clasped almost submissively in front of him.

"So what can I help you with now?" Telligren asked, a note of impatience in his voice.

Pendergast fumbled out a tape recorder. "May I?"

"No."

Pendergast put it away. "I had a few more questions," he said, "about Parker Wickman."

When Telligren didn't reply, Pendergast added: "His name came up the last time I was in this office. A student in the medical school. Studying neurological psychology."

"What about him?"

"Perhaps you read about the serial killer who himself was murdered and his house burned, off the Chef Menteur Highway?"

"There were some reports about it in the papers."

"That was Wickman."

"As I told you already, I don't recall much about him."

"But you should. He was a student associated with the PSI lab."

At this Telligren seemed to go quite still. "Ah yes," he said. "But that was years ago. As I told you, he dropped out."

"Eight years ago."

"If you say so. Agent Pendergast, may I ask where is this interview going? You've taken up my time once before, and we've already gone over this."

"Tell me about the PSI research."

"Not much to tell. Nothing came of it. It was eventually an embarrassment to the university and it was canceled, the lab closed."

"But you were in charge of it."

A silence. Then Telligren sighed. "I don't like to think about it, much less admit it. I was young and green, and eager like most research MDs. I believed there might be something to it. There wasn't. Sometimes that's how it works in science. Thankfully, my career survived that youthful scientific misadventure."

"Do you recall what Wickman's proposed dissertation thesis was?"

"No, I don't."

"Or why all the course files are missing from the archives?"

At this, Telligren leaned back in his chair and tented his fingers. "They were tossed. As I said, the research field of PSI was discredited and the Tulane lab closed. Look, Agent Pendergast, I'm trying to be patient and cooperate, but these questions don't seem to be going anywhere. Is there something specific you want to know?"

Pendergast's voice changed timbre. His whole demeanor and body language altered. He stood and loomed over Telligren, invading his personal space, and spoke so quietly his voice could barely be heard. "What happened to Wickman? Because something happened to him during the PSI research he did under your tutelage. It turned a fine young student into a serial killer. *And you, Dr. Telligren, know all about it.*"

"I know nothing of the sort. I hardly remember the fellow, and I resent your accusation. Now, I'm through talking to you. If you want to question me further, find yourself a judge who will sign a warrant. Good day."

Pendergast straightened up. "But, Doctor, I'm not yet done. I'm certain you have much to tell me about your experiments, possibly even PSI surgeries. And, no doubt, how they went awry—with poor Wickman and who knows how many others? You did something to his brain, did you not? And that *something* turned him into what he eventually became."

At this, Telligren rose from his chair, gripping the arms with white knuckles. In a voice of barely suppressed rage, he said: "Get out."

Pendergast replied, in a voice so abruptly cheerful it was chilling, "Of course I'll leave. But I *shall* be back." He paused, lowering his voice once more. "And I will find out what you know, Dr. Telligren. All that you know. *I will break you.*"

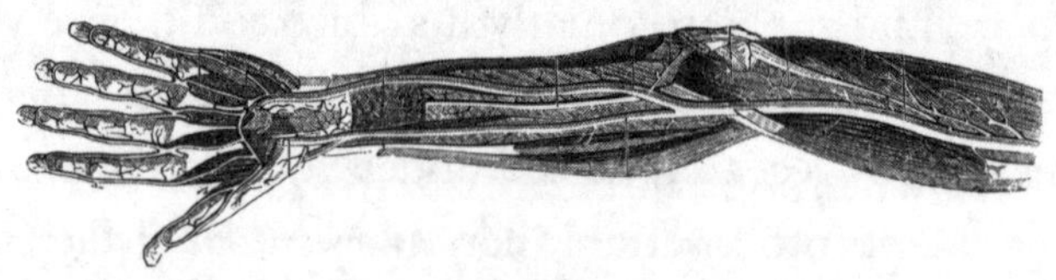

49

West from the academic enclave in which Dr. Slocombe resided—he who had so recently had a rock thrown through his window—lay another neighborhood even more lovely. It was at a somewhat greater elevation above the levees; its lawns were broader; its houses mostly older and larger, with higher ceilings; the canopies of trees lining its lanes were statelier. This was the retreat preferred by bank presidents and important officials in local government. An occasional Tulane professor or dean did live here, having accumulated wealth in some manner other than teaching—but this was a rarity.

Behind the main streets onto which the mansions fronted were narrow alleyways: relics from the antebellum South, now serving mostly as places to keep garbage cans, park vehicles within retrofitted garages, or—in the case of the largest houses—used as servant entrances.

At eleven o'clock precisely, a man entered from one of these alleys and walked down the cobblestoned surface. Despite it being August, he was wearing a long, dark coat with an anachronistic yet stylish homburg. His destination was a large Gothic Revival house halfway down; its rear gate and back door were illuminated, but the residence itself was mostly dark. The man stopped at the rear gate, pressed its code while casually looking up and down the alley, then stepped through. Closing the gate behind him, he followed the uneven stone path that made its way between the hibiscus and bougainvillea.

Mounting the steps to the rear door, he took a key from his pocket, noiselessly unlocked the bolt, and let himself in.

The interior smelled like pine and rose hips—the cleaning lady had been there earlier in the day. The man glanced around for a moment, then—without removing his coat or hat—made his way confidently through the house and up the stairs to the second floor. A door at the southern end of the upstairs hallway was ajar, light streaming from it. Other doors in the hall opened into dark, unoccupied rooms.

The man made his way to the open door and, with his knuckles, pushed it wide.

The room beyond was an elegant corner bedroom, with three-sided bay windows; a rich mahogany dresser, armoire, and bookshelves; and heavy tapestried curtains for privacy. An antique ceiling fan of wicker and brass turned in a lazy, counterclockwise direction.

A four-poster bed sat against the wall across from the covered windows. Dr. Telligren lay in it, sheets up around his waist, drinking a glass of sherry and reading the *Times-Picayune*. Roused by the sound of this new arrival, he glanced up. "Oh, it's you," he said with evident relief, looking at the man over his reading glasses. "I'm glad you've come—we need to talk about that devil Pendergast."

Now at last Magnus took off his coat and hat, placing them carefully on a sofa in such a way that his fingers did not brush the polished wood. Then he turned back, walked toward the bed, and took a seat in a chair opposite its nightstand.

"No," he said, smoothing down his elegant, mustard-colored suit. "Actually, I've come to talk about you."

Telligren's brows knitted in puzzlement. "Me?"

"Agent Pendergast gave you quite a grilling—didn't he? At least according to your secretary, who then told my secretary. You know how they can't resist gossip." Magnus shrugged.

"That's what I just told you—we need to talk about this damn Pendergast. Somehow, I can't imagine how, he's uncovered a lot of things that were supposed to have disappeared a decade ago."

"Such as?"

"The research lab, and the fact I ran it."

"Does he know what its purpose was—its ultimate purpose?"

"It's hard to say."

"Or who besides yourself participated?"

"I don't know, but he seems to know about the experiments!" Telligren exploded, shaking his head decisively. "He threatened me!"

While the older man spoke, Magnus looked on attentively. "Yes," he said at last. "And I am very sorry he did." He paused. "This won't do—I'm afraid this just won't do."

"Of course it won't do!" Telligren said, his eyes widening somewhat as he realized the conversation had veered away from Pendergast and was now fixed on him. "What's our next move? I mean, I told him nothing of importance; nothing he didn't already know." He paused. "We've gone over this kind of thing, time and time again." His voice became almost reproachful. "We've even practiced it, right down to the way your PSI abilities could render Wickman's blackmail threats useless. Ever since we learned about these atrocities he was committing, we've lain low, knowing he'd probably come to us when he needed his operation, and that would be a perfect opportunity to get rid of him."

"And now, it seems, that day has come," Magnus replied. "Only it's brought with it someone we never bargained for. Pendergast has learned a great deal about the things we'd buried. And at the same time, *I've* learned quite a bit about Pendergast. He's not going to give up until he's uncoiled this riddle . . . and he's too smart to be satisfied with our circumlocutions and evasions. It's gone too far for that. In time, he'll learn the details of the experiments—your role as professor, and our roles as students. Given more time, he'll learn about *me* and my own special . . . needs. And that would never do."

Telligren, sitting up straight now and putting the paper on the nightstand, returned Magnus's gaze. He seemed to be experiencing a mix of apprehension and indignation. "I didn't even mention your name, if that's what you're concerned about. Not once."

"I know," Magnus said. "Nevertheless, thanks to today's inquiry, you've become the weak link in the chain. Pendergast will be back, and then back again—and sooner or later, you'll fold."

"Never! I have as much to lose as you do!"

"I said you'll *fold*. I can see it. Which is why, regretfully, we must now bring this friendship of ours to a close." And with this, Magnus brought a 1911 semiautomatic out of his jacket.

"What the *hell*—?"

"Don't worry," Magnus told Telligren as he pulled back the slide and checked the chamber. "I'm not going to use this. It's only to keep you from trying to escape or some other impetuosity."

"Dorion—"

Telligren shut up when Magnus pointed the gun at him. "Let me finish. Just because you'll betray me doesn't change our past history—you've been good to me, and I'm genuinely fond of you. So I'll give you a choice of how to die. The first option will be quick, without pain—and by your own hand."

"Dorion, for God's sake—!"

Magnus stopped this gush of words with the raising of one hand. He placed the .45 in his lap. "Please don't degrade yourself with entreaties—you of all people know how I am when my mind's made up. Now: you have a bad heart, bad enough that you're now considering a Watchman implant." As he spoke, he pulled a pair of thin latex gloves from one pocket and snapped them on. Then he withdrew a small lozenge-tin of pills, leaned forward, and placed it on the sheet beside Telligren. "The compound in here will initiate a painless myocardial infarct. It will take perhaps fifteen or twenty minutes at most for the arterial thrombosis to form. But as I promised, when it happens, it will be almost instantaneous and you'll die with no pain."

By now outrage and fear—and disbelief—had left the old professor's eyes, replaced by desperation. As the arguing and begging began, Magnus remained patient. When Telligren had exhausted both himself and his arguments, Magnus went on. "The other option," he said in a colder voice, "should you refuse to cooperate, is this. We'll go out to my steamship—my man is waiting around the corner in his car. There's a skeleton crew aboard. Now that the pilothouse controls are fully operational, I've been eager to take a midnight cruise on the river. There's a picturesque, remote bayou that I'd love to explore. My vessel is fully stocked with everything I might need for such a cruise, including a burlap sack, ropes, lead weights . . . and a forty-foot chain."

He raised the gun as Telligren sat as still as a statue. "You've always had a fear of water, haven't you? I seem to remember you had a close call with drowning when you were six. I think you mentioned it once. Or maybe you didn't—it doesn't matter. I don't think you can even swim. Is that right . . . ? Ah, I see that it is.

"I'll describe this second option as briefly as I can. Once we are out in the main flow of the river and away from traffic, you will be blindfolded, hog-tied, and placed in the sack with a lead weight or two. The sack will be tied to one end of the chain, which will then be tossed over the transom to avoid the paddle wheel. I have a good imagination, but nevertheless I find it hard to fully picture the horror of your predicament—especially given your phobia of drowning. You will be dragged behind the boat. Water will seep in through the burlap. The pilot will hold the vessel at a few knots, enough to keep you at or below the surface of the water. Perhaps you will rise once or twice to the surface and manage to catch a choking gasp of air. In any case, depending on your endurance, I'd imagine it would take between five and ten minutes to bring this slow drowning to completion. From there, you will be towed into my midnight bayou, the chain will be released, and you, the sack, and the chain will sink, first into black water, then finally muck—far away from any commercial channel."

For a minute, two, the bedroom was silent. Neither stirred. Then Telligren's trembling hand began to move toward the pillbox.

"Two tablets, please," Magnus said.

He handed Telligren the glass of sherry and made sure both tablets were swallowed. Then he replaced the pillbox in his pocket and sat back with a sigh. "I'll just wait while you drift off," he said, picking up the newspaper and, still wearing the gloves, leafing through it until he reached the crossword puzzle. Magnus took a pencil off the nightstand and began filling in the blanks with block letters, now and then turning to ask Telligren for help with a clue—meeting, however, only silence. This went on for about twenty minutes. For a time, Telligren stared at the drapes of the window opposite the bed. Then he slowly shut his eyes.

Magnus was examining the last clue when he stopped abruptly—chuckled in delight—and, instead of filling it in, made a careful mark on the newsprint. *"J'ai fini!"* he exclaimed, holding up the paper.

At the same moment, as if in grisly congratulation, Dr. Telligren gasped; gripped his chest; then slumped over in the bed.

Magnus waited out the next few minutes, to be sure of cardiac death. Then he tossed the newspaper onto the bed. Pocketing the gun, he rose, checked Telligren's pulse, or lack thereof, went over to the sofa where his coat and hat lay, put them on, and walked out of the room.

As he moved through the first floor toward the back door that led to the alley, he slipped off the gloves and put them in one of his pockets. He was a frequent visitor to the house, after all; even if foul play was suspected, his fingerprints and DNA would be everywhere as a matter of course. It seemed most unlikely he would ever be questioned.

He walked down the back steps and along the path. It had grown rather chill for August, and he found the coat and hat suited the night air. After stepping through the gate and closing it carefully behind him, he glanced nonchalantly in both directions, then started walking briskly down the alley, back the way he had come.

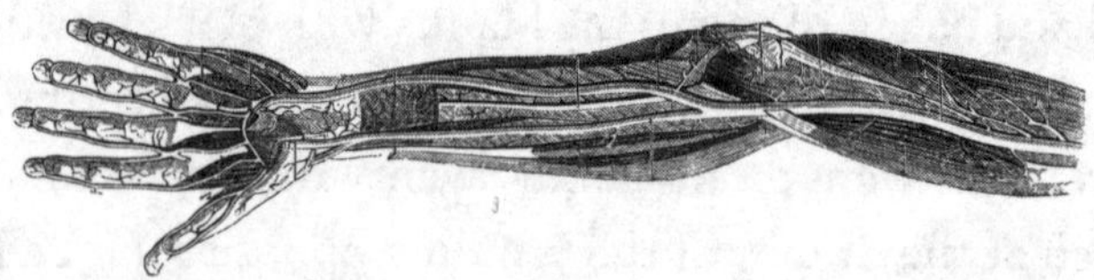

50

A. X. L. Pendergast arrived at the bedroom door just as the medical team was taking out the body. It was zipped into a white bag set on a stretcher, being carried by two bored EMTs. Pendergast stood aside to allow the body to pass by. Then he turned and entered the room, pausing to cast his gaze around, his silvery eyes taking in the details. The morning sunlight illuminated an elegant and spacious bedroom, with an antique four-poster bed, wood-paneled walls, and a brick fireplace flanked by bookshelves. In front of the fireplace was a sitting area with two brocaded armchairs and side tables. The wall to the right had shelves displaying a collection of antique Chinese jades and snuff bottles, and resting on the mantelpiece was what Pendergast recognized as an antique Tibetan silver-inlay Kangling trumpet made from a human femur bone.

The room was crowded with people. No crime scene perimeter had been erected, and no CSI measures had been taken to exclude visitors. There were two police officers who had nothing to do, standing around looking uncomfortable and out of place. The attending physician, Pendergast knew, had swiftly concluded that Telligren died of natural causes—cardiac arrest.

Many of the people in the room were clustered around a grieving man whose back was turned, head bowed, offering him their condolences and sympathies. Pendergast recognized the curly yellow hair of Dr. Magnus. He was once again wearing a beautiful suit and, even bowed by grief, he maintained an aristocratic mien.

As Pendergast circled around closer to the group, he could see the doctor struggling to maintain his composure in the face of his mentor's sudden death. The attending physician had left when the body was taken away, but Telligren's friends, along with the mayor and the district attorney, remained in the room, comforting Magnus in his hour of grief.

Pendergast, drifting still closer, picked up murmured phrases: "We know how much he meant to you... A good life, well led... A fine man... Not altogether unexpected, but still a tragedy... At least he didn't suffer... I feared for him, weak heart and all... Heartfelt condolences..."

Pendergast, drawing his face into a mask of sympathy, approached Magnus and held out his hands. Magnus turned toward him and accepted the proffered handshake of sympathy, clasping Pendergast's hands with both of his. "So good of you to come," he said.

"I'm so sorry for your loss," said Pendergast.

"Thank you."

"I know how close you were, how much Dr. Telligren meant to you."

"He was like a second father to me."

"It seems he died alone," said Pendergast. "Poor man. I hope he didn't suffer."

"The doctor assured me it was instantaneous—like falling asleep. Nobody had any idea until his housekeeper found the body, two hours ago."

"That must have been a shock," said Pendergast.

"A shock for us all."

Pendergast released the hands and stepped back, his glance falling on a side table, where a folded section of the *Times-Picayune* and a glass of half-consumed sherry could be seen. "I observe," said Pendergast, "that Dr. Telligren's last moments were taken up with a crossword puzzle."

"He was so fond of those," said Magnus. "It was part of his routine before bed—a glass of amontillado and the *Times-Picayune* crossword."

Pendergast casually picked up the folded newspaper while glancing at Magnus, who was watching him keenly, and glanced over the block letters filling the crossword squares. "It seems he almost completed it—save for a single clue." Continuing to hold Magnus's eye, Pendergast casually folded the section of newspaper containing the puzzle and slipped it into his suit coat pocket.

"Delightful to have seen you again, Agent Pendergast," said Magnus, taking his hand once more.

"I offer you my most sincere condolences at this difficult time."

"Thank you, my friend."

Pendergast turned and walked out of the bedroom and down the stairs to the street. The curb in front of the house was lined with black cars. At the far end stood an idling Rolls, which when Pendergast appeared moved away from the curb and drove up abreast of him.

Pendergast got in and eased himself back into the buttery leather, his face a mask of ice.

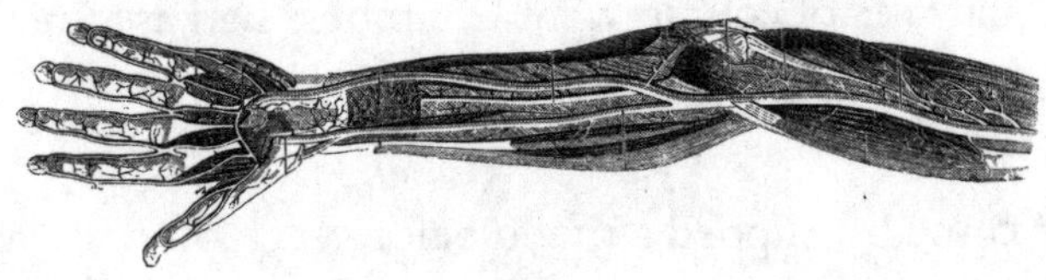

51

Chambers had never dined at Sous la Mer—it was three or four degrees above his restaurant affordability scale—but he'd certainly heard of it. The best seafood restaurant in New Orleans. And Pendergast had called him, conciliatory and apologetic, and invited him to dinner there at seven. Finally, Chambers thought, Pendergast was coming around. Maybe it was Telligren's death, coupled with the benign autopsy, that caught Pendergast up short. Maybe just the four days of fruitlessly exploring the rabbit hole was all that was needed for the guy to realize what a fool he was making of himself. This could be his come-to-Jesus moment. Pendergast was probably feeling a little humiliation along with regret. Not that he'd ever admit it, but a gesture like this, inviting Chambers to dinner at a fancy restaurant, spoke louder than words.

He entered the restaurant at five minutes after seven, and the maître d' ushered him to the back—all dark paneled wood, framed photos of bygone days and menus signed by celebrities, game fish mounted on plaques—to a corner banquette of red leather, far from the kitchen and the noise of other diners. He found Pendergast already seated, a brimming martini glass before him.

"Evening," Chambers said as he took his seat. "Thanks for the invite."

"Dinner's on me, by the way—just so there's no objectionable scene later on."

"Fine." That was of course what Chambers had assumed. He nodded at the glass. "Vodka?"

"Beefeater."

A waiter came by, slipped a menu before each of them, and Chambers asked for a Heineken. "You grew up in New Orleans," he said to Pendergast. "In a climate like this, you tend to live longer if beer is your beverage of choice. As for me, I'm off the hard stuff."

"I commend your self-discipline. I have not drunk beer since my brother forced one upon me when I was twelve."

This was interesting. Not only was Pendergast buying dinner, but he was opening up about his past... a little. "Guess I can see how that would put you off it."

"I don't recall many details, except that it had a ridiculously anachronistic pedigree covering the entire label, more appropriate for *Debrett's Peerage* than a domestic beer."

"Sounds like a Budweiser."

"You may be correct." The Heineken arrived. "In any case, cheers."

They quickly ordered, then relaxed in the snug booth while Chambers briefly brought Pendergast up to speed on the most recent events. He'd been making slow and steady progress, mostly eliminating possibilities. Good police work was often incremental. He'd pulled in more manpower to help, and while Fleury was no genius he was a fine and steady plodder. As he described his work, it wasn't hard to put an enthusiastic spin on things. He played up the investigation a little but was careful not to brag or inject any I-told-you-sos into the recap... after all, he had Pendergast's pride to consider. He avoided mentioning the file Pendergast had left on his desk; that, he'd decided, did not look promising and he had not pursued it.

"So," Chambers said in an offhand tone as a waiter brought their appetizers—steak tartare and toast points for Pendergast, smoked grouper for Chambers. The senior agent's pitch was delayed by the waiter's fussy preparation of the tartare, but eventually it was set before Pendergast, and he began again. "So I was hoping that, considering Dr. Telligren's unfortunate death, we could join forces again...

beyond these evening meetings. It would get Estevez off my back—and more to the point, off yours. We work well together. You helped me during a tough time, and…and I'd like to think I've taught you a few pointers about being on the job." He paused to drain his beer. "What we're doing right now with these meetings… It may have been my suggestion, but after these last few evenings it's begun to feel like a divorce." He laughed, trying to make it sound unaffected. "Anyway, with Telligren dead, there are some things I've learned about that second armless body that you'll—"

"Dr. Telligren did not die of natural causes," Pendergast said, placing a mound of steak tartare on an impossibly thin slice of toast.

"I'm sorry?"

"He was murdered."

"Didn't you see the autopsy report?"

"The medical examiner was wrong."

Chambers, who had speared a piece of smoked fish onto his fork, let it fall to his plate with a clatter, then sat back against the worn leather. He felt like a balloon that had been filled with air but never tied off and was now deflating. This was a nightmare that wouldn't end. He resisted asking Pendergast why he thought so. He just waited.

"Magnus did it," Pendergast said.

Magnus again. Oh Jesus. He let out an irritated exhalation of breath. Again, he resisted asking why Pendergast thought so. That never went well.

He watched Pendergast slip one hand into the pocket of his suit coat with a feeling of dread.

Pendergast withdrew a piece of what looked like newsprint. He unfolded it, smoothed it, then placed it on the table between them.

It was a crossword puzzle.

Suddenly, a field of red swam before Chambers's eyes. This prick Pendergast was like a demon, summoned from hell with a single purpose: to drive him crazy.

A crossword puzzle.

Without realizing what he was doing, he rose like an erupting volcano, reached across the table, and wrapped his hands around Pendergast's neck. "You mother*fucker*!" he nearly hissed, pressing down with his thumbs, his abrupt movement spilling Pendergast's martini.

Pendergast reached up, put his own thumbs under Chambers's palms for leverage, wrapped his fingers around the senior agent's wrists, gave a slight twist... and suddenly a stab of agony shot up his forearms. He let go immediately, but Pendergast did not—keeping his hands on his wrists and using the leverage to guide him back into his seat. Only then did he release his hold. Luckily, with the location of their booth, and the fact that Chambers had kept silent while being manhandled, they had attracted only the attention of the waiters. Chambers breathed hard, wondering what had driven him to the point where he actually wanted to strangle his partner. A long silence ensued as the plates were discreetly taken away and the table laid out for the main course.

"I can see now this is all my fault," Pendergast finally said. "I have not sufficiently explained myself. I have not acted the role of a junior partner. I've embarrassed you in front of Estevez."

"Go to hell," Chambers growled as he massaged his wrists.

"Let me tell you what I held back before. Are you willing to listen?"

Chambers said nothing. He briefly considered asking the waiter for a champagne bucket of ice to dip his hands into, then dismissed the idea.

"There is a rare psychosis known as 'body integrity disorder.' It's so rare that it's not in *DSM*—the diagnostic bible used by psychiatrists. The clinical features of this disorder present as a person believing some part of their body—leg, arm—is not their own. It is foreign. Alien. Even evil."

He paused, studying the look on Chambers's face.

"I initially believed Wickman might be suffering from some variant of BID. Many people with this psychosis actually arrange to have the limb surgically removed. And when they do... their symptoms clear up. Even though they are mutilated, they are relieved, if not actually happy, to be rid of the offending limb. And yet Wickman didn't fit the BID profile. He was amputating the limbs of others... many others. There was no precedent for this in all the annals of psychiatry. Ultimately, I came to the conclusion he suffered from BID in that he not only wanted to be rid of his right arm... but *he wanted the perfect replacement*. What precisely constituted the 'perfect' replacement I didn't know, although those pinpricks were clearly part of his testing process. He was searching, killing, testing arms, and discarding. His frustration grew as he failed to find the perfect replacement, and he tried different techniques, different methods. So you see, Chambers, this is why he set up that operating room. And it explains the role of Telligren and Magnus.

"I asked myself: where did this bizarre psychosis come from? His early life and college years showed no evidence of it. When I heard about his PSI studies—and later, when we first met Telligren and Magnus after investigating the fire—I knew the answer *had* to lie in the two years Wickman spent in graduate school. That was when he changed, when the grip of psychosis took hold. Telligren was his professor, and Magnus one of his fellow students. That, my dear Chambers, is what links them all, and I have no doubt Telligren and Magnus were the ones in that operating room on the Pearl River."

He signaled the waiter for another martini to replace the one that had been spilled. "When you met them, that day in Telligren's office, didn't your investigator's sixth sense tell you something was just a little bit off? That perhaps something was being concealed?"

It was true, Chambers had felt a prickle of suspicion—but this was no more than a heap of supposition built on speculation propped up by inference.

"Think of the way Magnus, in particular, toyed with us: offering cigars; using clichés involving arms; letting it slip that he'd known Wickman before—that they were classmates."

Chambers remained silent.

"Something happened to Wickman in that PSI lab. Something that was covered up. And that 'something' affected Wickman for the rest of his life—afflicting him with a psychosis heretofore unseen."

"Pendergast, get to the point."

"I am."

"Please."

"There was a PSI laboratory at Tulane, run by Telligren, that surgically and electrically experimented with volunteers in an attempt to enhance their ESP abilities. Wickman was a graduate student in the department; so was Magnus. They both volunteered to undergo a procedure—what kind, exactly, remains to be seen. But it turned Wickman into a serial killer. Magnus... no doubt he was affected as well, although in precisely what way I don't yet know, though I think it gave him a certain degree of extrasensory abilities. Such abilities may well have been the aim of those experiments. But what I *am* sure of is this: Magnus killed Telligren to silence him. Just as the two of them killed Wickman to silence him. I was going to break Telligren—and Magnus knew it. Behind the rather fey facade, he's a fiendish and deviously clever man. Now, given this, we need to get Magnus downtown if we're going to make him talk. He's always had everything his way—it's vital we pull him out of his cocoon. We need a judge and prosecutor who'll cooperate, and then we can hold him for seventy-two hours without formal charges. That would give us time to use measures I might suggest to sweat him—"

Chambers had finally had enough. "What have you been smoking?" he said angrily. "This is all the most ridiculous speculation. Magnus is a pillar of the community. He'll probably be Tulane's next president... if he doesn't win a Nobel Prize first. How are you going to get a judge to sign a warrant? Where's your evidence?"

Pendergast pointed to the crossword puzzle. "This was found on Telligren's bed after his death. Note that it's been filled out in block letters—and completed, save for one clue."

Chambers glanced at the puzzle without interest. The edges were torn, not neatly cut. He wondered when Pendergast had found the opportunity to covertly snatch it during evidence collection. One more transgression of the rules.

"The incomplete clue may be the easiest of the entire puzzle. It calls for a four-letter word meaning 'maneater.' Can you guess the answer?"

Chambers stared. Another bat-shit crazy theory was coming down the road.

"It's *lion*, of course. Yet those squares are the only ones in the puzzle remaining unfilled. And now: look at the clue."

Chambers looked. Whoever had filled in the rest of the puzzle, almost certainly Telligren, had deliberately crossed out the first three letters of *Maneater*, leaving a different word: *eater*.

"It's a message to me, specifically," said Pendergast.

Chambers said nothing.

"My wife was killed by a lion in Africa—killed and eaten. That is why *man* is crossed out."

Holy Mother of God. To think Pendergast had kept this to himself the whole time, even after commiserating with him over his own wife's death. "I'm sorry," he said automatically, even as he thought that the death didn't excuse Pendergast's wild accusations.

"Thank you. Right before that expedition, Mike Decker—whom I'd worked with closely in the military—asked if I'd like to join the FBI. I'd made up my mind to turn him down. But after my wife's death, I... changed my mind."

Chambers did not know what to say.

Pendergast spoke again. "You ask for evidence?" He stabbed the puzzle with an index finger. "A provocative, taunting message—obviously directed at *me*."

Another silence followed—much longer. Chambers wondered: could it possibly be true? No. Of course not. It was too crazy, too much of a stretch. He took a deep breath and tried to sound reasonable. "Look, Pendergast, there's no way you're going to get a judge around here to sign a warrant to bring Magnus in for an interrogation. The best you can hope for is a voluntary interview."

"All right. I shall ask for one."

Chambers was surprised. Not that it mattered: he knew Magnus would never consent to the interview, and that would put an end to this crazy line of investigation.

Their main courses arrived—smelling heavenly—but Chambers

just pushed the food around his plate. He had been truly sorry to hear about the loss of Pendergast's wife. And the crossword was undeniably strange. But as his mind went over the events of the past few days, of Pendergast's theories and ideas, and now this paranoia that he was being taunted by a killer, he felt a growing sadness. Crossword puzzle clues were the kind of thing you'd read about in an Agatha Christie novel. Stuff like that didn't happen in real life. Pendergast was going down another rabbit hole, and Chambers was not going to follow him. Not anymore.

It was then, quite suddenly, that Chambers made up his mind: whatever information Pendergast did or didn't get from Magnus—if he could even get an interview—Estevez would need to have a new mentor ready and waiting for this junior agent when he got back to the office.

He was done with Pendergast.

PART FOUR

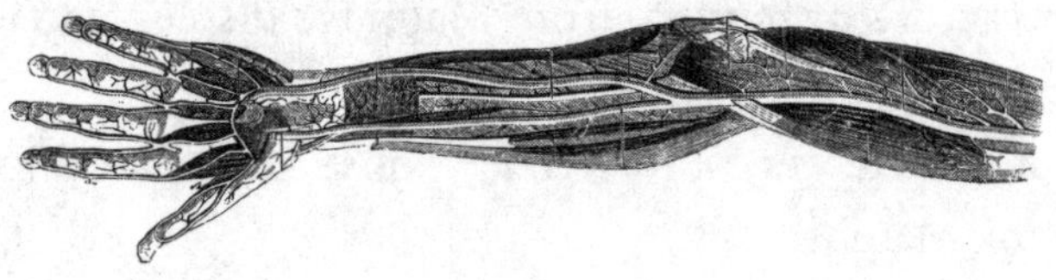

52

"Ah, my dear Leo," Dr. Magnus said to the contractor at his side—wearing a white jumpsuit and holding a notepad on an overstuffed metal clipboard box—"you've outdone yourself again."

"Thank you, sir."

Magnus took a moment to bestow a look of approval on the contractor, which he could see had the desired effect. And the approval was, in fact, genuine: the man was the finest contractor one could find in Louisiana. Such individuals were rare as hen's teeth, and they needed proper tending and care.

Magnus was wearing a straw boater, a jacket striped in fawn and ivory, and pleated linen pants. He looked and felt the part of riverboat owner as he stepped into the saloon of the steamboat, followed by the contractor. He paused and cast his eye around, admiring the beautiful way in which this old room had been brought back to life. The portholes gleamed in their brass fittings; the built-in mahogany bookcases shone like gold, already filled with rare bindings. The zinc bar was without blemish and period-perfect, framed by antique oaken scrollwork, laurel leaves, flying putti, and other classical motifs. He gave a sigh of contentment as he strolled here and there, running his finger over the satinwood, inhaling the scent of varnish and tung oil. He came to a halt in front of the porthole closest to the bow. He stopped, stared, and then turned to the contractor.

The contractor's gaze went from Magnus's displeased face to what he had been looking at.

"Damn it to hell," Leo muttered. "Those snakewood joints aren't properly book-matched."

Magnus gave a small smile. "I knew *you* would notice."

"I'll have it fixed right away, Dr. Magnus."

"As I know you shall."

"And I'll give the subcontractor a piece of my mind."

"Thank you. If you feel it appropriate, you might consider giving his fee a modest haircut."

"Yes, sir. Absolutely."

Magnus privately felt the culprit should be given the sack, but he knew the best results would be gotten by leaving the hiring and firing to Leo.

He strolled on, stopping to gaze languidly up at the coffered ceiling, which like the rest of the cozy space was being restored in period authenticity to perfection.

"Leo," he said, "I must say your people have done a truly excellent job, laying that purple heartwood over the cross members." He hesitated just a moment before the final word.

The contractor followed Magnus's gaze. "Thank you, sir. It's difficult wood to work with—I'd be lying if I said otherwise—but my men put in 110 percent."

"I'm sure they did," Magnus mused, still staring at the ceiling. The ornamentation of the cross members was complete, but the niches between them were still bare—the African padauk wood Magnus had selected for them being very hard to come by and, as a result, late in arriving.

"I got a call on my way over here that the shipment of heavy veneer just arrived from the Port of Dar es Salaam," Leo said, as if reading his mind. "My team will get it installed by midafternoon—perhaps even by lunchtime."

"Thank you, Leo, that would be outstanding."

It pleased Magnus that even though he had shown only the tiniest degree of disappointment at the porthole molding, Leo was frantic at the thought of disappointing him in even the smallest way. This was, Magnus mused, how one got the best out of people: not by bullying and fear, but by instilling in them an overwhelming desire to please. An example was how, without being told, his worker bees all seemed to intuit that they should begin work on the Magnus project at 7:00 AM. And despite the clang and buzz of machinery at that early hour, nobody within earshot seemed interested in complaining. Of course, Magnus paid generous overtime; he had a horror of being thought of as stingy. There were even days when he strolled through the ship, handing one-hundred-dollar bills to everyone as he went along. That, more than anything, brought him their love.

"You're a good man," he said.

Leo smiled as if he'd just been granted a boon, put on his paint-splattered cap, touched its visor deferentially, then turned and left. Magnus watched the man head aft down the central corridor of the stateroom deck.

Magnus settled into a banquette of polished red leather. With the simultaneous activity of half a dozen contractors, all just as eager to please as Leo, it truly was remarkable how quickly and masterfully the saloon had been redone. He could, of course, have handled things differently: fuming and fussing, nickel-and-diming his suppliers, yelling and threatening when things didn't go right or mistakes were made—but that wasn't the way he chose to use his gifts. Much better to employ empathy, offering a luscious carrot while allowing only the hint of a stick to be visible in the background. As a result, a few gentle suggestions was all it took to get fifty blue-collar workers slaving over one thing or another, as gratefully as if he'd been tossing them pearls.

Machiavelli, he was sure, would approve.

There had been a point years earlier when Magnus realized that—instead of going into politics, in which he would almost certainly have won high office—he would be happier limiting his ambitions. The mistakes so many made involved overreach, greed, and not appreciating the diminishing returns of power. Twice five miles of fertile ground, in the words of Coleridge, allowed him to be the toast of New Orleans, admired and loved by all, even as he flew under the radar that would expose a more grasping nature. It didn't matter, really, how big one's pleasure dome was, as long as it was feathered to perfection...and tenanted with people who, like innocent lambs, doted on his every word; flung themselves at him; worked for him; vouched for him; bowed to him; or fucked him—and always with an outpouring of gratitude.

At times like this, while enjoying the luxurious vessel, every whim of his quickly fulfilled, it amused him that not a single citizen of the Big Easy, from the bluebloods on Audubon Place to the struggling workers on Old Gentilly Road, realized how much he disdained their affection and servility.

Yet despite being so careful to limit the scope of his ambitions, Magnus had become aware of occasional periods—more frequent in recent years—when along with its perfect safety, that very scope also felt slightly stifling. He found relief in the secret consolation known to no one but himself—and on a whim, by taking up a pet project when the opportunity presented itself.

This steamboat he'd purchased was just such an opportunity—a perfect one, at that. It had never originally been in Magnus's grand scheme of things. But when he'd been invited to a party aboard one three years before, the germ of an idea had been planted. The vessel he'd boarded, of course, would never have done—it was a cheap, gaudy casino, with a stationary paddle wheel only for show—but nevertheless it struck an unexpectedly deep chord in him. New Orleans and steamboats went together like Echo and Narcissus. What a shame so few of them survived, and fewer still in good operating condition.

A little research revealed that those still in existence were largely decomposing at wharves or serving as two-bit museums. But there were a few that had been maintained through at least the first half of the twentieth century, and it was on these he focused his attention.

Ultimately, he came across the *Fantôme*. Its keel had been laid in 1880 by a wealthy inventor eager to apply his new ideas to a commercial steamboat. He'd made the hull of metal rather than wood—a rare and costly option—and he'd designed the stateroom and hurricane decks with an eye to both luxury and functionality. Because he was an engineer by training, the usually shallow draft of riverboats—often as little as six feet—offended the man's sense of efficient design. He had no plans to take the *Fantôme* upriver, where it would compete with all the commercial traffic on the Mississippi—rather, he imagined selling one-week cruises along the coastline of the Gulf of Mexico, limited to wealthy and discriminating clients. So he'd built the vessel with a draft of eighteen feet, so he could put the boilers where they belonged—deep in the bowels of the vessel—rather than in the usual site on the main deck, where their heat was an annoyance to passengers. Just as important, this design allowed him to place the paddle wheel deeper in the water. On most stern-wheelers, only about a quarter of the paddles were underwater and doing the work of propulsion at any given time—a ludicrous waste of energy. By employing Charles Morgan's new "feathering" design, over half could be submerged and rotating when the boat was under power. The builder also placed metal bracers along the outer edges of each paddle, the sharp edges cutting into the water more cleanly, adding still more efficiency.

Unfortunately, the *Fantôme*'s innovations came about too late in the age of paddle steamers to make much of a splash. And it turned out the wealthy were not particularly interested in cruising the Gulf of Mexico. And so the builder went bankrupt and the *Fantôme* went through a series of owners—all of whom took good care of her. She'd spent the last forty years tethered at a slip, but she was still structurally sound.

And now she would become Magnus's home away from home—done up in the best of taste, completely reconfigured for one resident. He'd been quick to paint the boat when it arrived at the Port of New Orleans, and it was now as elegant outside—shades of white and black, with red trimming—as it was becoming inside. Magnus wanted a showpiece, not a tourist curiosity.

When completely restored, the *Fantôme* would be a perfect New

Orleans touch to burnish his reputation with; a retreat from his home near campus, where it was impossible to avoid the unexpected call of a well-wisher... and, most important, a seaworthy vessel where—when the desire for indulging his secret vices became overwhelming—he could simply slip anchor and head out into the Gulf of Mexico or down one of the innumerable side channels leading to it. This way, any left-overs, so to speak, from the satisfaction of his needs could be safely and securely disposed of... deep in the muck of a Mississippi tributary.

At that moment, his Nokia 2110—he'd just recently switched from cumbersome satphones to cutting-edge but still-buggy cell phones—sounded. He took it out, frowning with curiosity—very few people had this number.

"Yes?" he said, raising the antenna and bringing the phone to his ear.

"Dr. Magnus?"

He recognized the voice immediately. "Special Agent Pendergast. What an unexpected pleasure."

"Indeed. I was wondering if you would grant me the courtesy of an interview—at your convenience, of course."

"An interview, you say?"

"At your home or office, as you prefer—the location is up to you."

As usual, Pendergast—or at least, his voice—was neutral. This was a man who interested Magnus very much. "I take it this interview is voluntary? I have the right to decline?"

"Naturally."

"Let me check my schedule."

Magnus put down the phone. This was precisely the development he'd anticipated.

He checked his watch—just a few minutes past 8:00 AM. He picked up the phone again.

"I could make myself available later this afternoon—say, two o'clock? Would that be satisfactory?"

There was a pause on the line, during which Magnus imagined Pendergast recovering from his surprise at the acceptance. "It would be satisfactory, yes. At your office?"

"I don't keep office hours on weekends. May I suggest my steamboat, where I'll be spending the day? It's still being retrofitted, but my quarters are furnished and comfortable. Just come down to the port—where Henderson Street ends near the wharves—and turn right. You can't miss it. The *Fantôme*."

"Very well. Thank you."

"Not at all." He ended the call with the press of a button. Then he made a series of calls of his own. Once complete, he looked at his watch again. Quarter after eight.

With a sigh of both satisfaction and anticipation, he settled into the banquette.

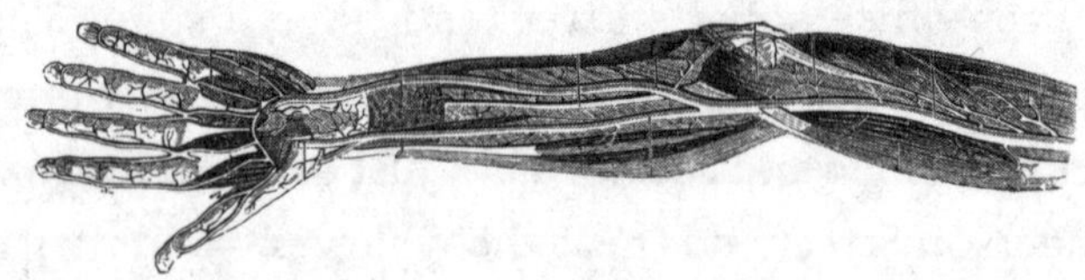

53

Agent Chambers yawned, then stretched luxuriously in his bed. Sundays had always been his favorite day of the week—sleeping in, puttering around the house, reading. Now that he was getting over the hump of his wife's death, and his mind had been put to rest with the decision to cut bait with Pendergast, it was gradually becoming his favorite day once again.

He yawned once more, spent another few minutes dozing beneath the covers, then rose and went into the bathroom to freshen up. And then—still in his nightwear—he descended the stairs, scratching himself absently, making for the kitchen.

As he did so, the phone began to ring.

He moved a bit faster, picked up the kitchen extension. "Chambers."

"Agent Chambers? I'm so sorry to disturb you on a Sunday. This is Dr. Magnus speaking."

Magnus? Chambers had been afraid it might be Pendergast. This was somebody he'd never expected to hear from.

"Yes, Dr. Magnus. What is it?" As Chambers spoke he went over to the cabinet and pulled down a container of ground coffee. Filling the coffeepot with water, then dumping it into the coffee machine, he had a vision of Pendergast showing up at Magnus's house, threatening him, maybe even manhandling him. God, he hoped this wasn't something like that.

"Well, I'm rather embarrassed to ask you a favor, but you see..." There was a pause. "Dr. Telligren, you know, was a dear, dear friend of mine. He was also my mentor. In some ways I owe everything I am today to him. And so, when I heard that the police and even the ME have ruled his death accidental—and apparently have no plans for further investigation—I realized you were the only person I could call."

"Me?" Chambers pulled a container of OJ and a pint of half-and-half out of the fridge and put them on the table, followed by a glass and a coffee cup. Coffee and juice had become the sum total of his breakfast and would remain so until he'd dropped fifteen pounds.

"Yes. Because his death wasn't accidental—I believe it was murder."

Chambers, now pouring brewed coffee into his mug, almost spilled it. "The police, the ME, have said it was natural causes. Cardiac arrest."

"The police are incompetent. As for the ME, I could probably perform a better autopsy myself. But I know my friend's heart attack wasn't accidental—it was provoked. It was murder."

Chambers poured cream into his coffee, stirred.

"Agent Pendergast is coming by this afternoon. He wishes to question me. I want you to be there, too, so I can explain what I know to be the truth—and *how* I know it."

Okay. That explains a lot.

"Frankly, Agent Chambers, there's a second reason for my request. I recall from our first conversation that you are an experienced agent. More so, I would guess, than your partner. The problem is that he's rather intimidating. For some reason, he seems to have taken an aggressive, even hostile attitude toward me. The fact is, I would feel much more comfortable... much *safer*... if you were there when I explain—"

"Don't say another word, Doctor. I completely understand. Given the circumstances, I'll certainly be there."

"Thank you. We're meeting at two PM on my steamboat, the *Fantôme*. It's down at the Port of New Orleans. Impossible to miss on the quay."

"I'll be there." Chambers hung up. It wasn't beyond credibility that Pendergast—with his crazy notion that Magnus was the perpetrator—might end up, one way or another, royally screwing up the case with crazy accusations and rash actions.

Chambers stood up, finishing first his coffee, then his OJ, and dumping the glassware in the sink. *So much for a quiet Sunday.* With a shake of his head and a muttered curse, he trotted back through the house and up the stairs to get dressed.

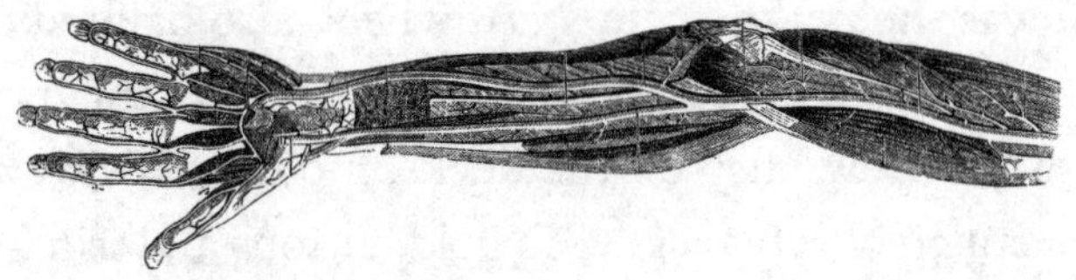

54

CHAMBERS KNEW THAT THE ports of New Orleans, given the snake-like bends and twistings of the Mississippi, were spread out rather than massed at one spot. He parked in a cracked asphalt lot at the end of Henderson Street and walked toward the warehouses that sat along the river. The nearest one had its huge doors, set on rollers, open to the heat, and within he could see shadowy figures of large floats, stored here by various Krewes to be brought out during the Mardi Gras parades. Turning right and walking to the end of the warehouse, he glanced southward. At the end of the short roadway between warehouses, the muddy brown of the Mississippi was clearly visible—along with a paddle wheel steamboat moored on the near side of the river.

He approached it slowly, intimidated by its opulence. Gleaming white with red trim, it was gigantic and imposing, with three decks and a pilothouse perched on top. The name of the boat, *FANTÔME*, was painted along the side in gold on black. Two tall stacks in glossy black, with petaled tops, rose amidships, from which twin trails of smoke lazily issued. Although it was obvious that retrofitting was still being done within the gleaming superstructure, it seemed the engine, or boiler, was already going. An oversize Stars and Stripes fluttered from a tall jack staff in the bow. High on the hurricane deck, forward of the two stacks, stood a brass bell, gleaming in the afternoon light. The final touch was the magnificent stern wheel, also painted bright red, that reposed beneath a brass-clad paddle box. Chambers could see members of the crew busy on the decks, moving this way and that, dressed smartly in blue blazers with gold buttons and trim.

He had been quite surprised by Magnus's call that morning inviting him to the interview. Even more startling was his insistence that Telligren had been murdered. After receiving the call, Chambers had not been able to get in touch with Pendergast to tell him he'd be coming along for the meeting. He wasn't sure how his unpredictable partner would react to it, so he'd arrived early to intercept Pendergast and give them a chance to talk briefly so they wouldn't be tripping over themselves. He was also increasingly concerned about how Pendergast would handle the interview, given his absurd declaration the night before that Magnus himself was the killer. This interview promised to be complicated—and quite possibly even ugly.

At that moment, in the distance, he spied the slender figure of Pendergast, striding along the wharf, his black suit jacket flapping behind him. Pendergast had already seen him, apparently. Chambers waited.

"Well," Pendergast said, coming up, looking as cool and inscrutable as usual. "If it isn't my partner, Agent Chambers—what an unexpected pleasure."

He held out his hand and Chambers took it.

"Am I to assume Dr. Magnus called you?" Pendergast asked.

"He did," said Chambers, surprised Pendergast had guessed. "He, ah, also seems to believe that Telligren was murdered."

"Does he indeed?" A troubled look briefly flickered across Pendergast's pale face before it returned to its neutral detachment.

"I thought," said Chambers, "we might take a moment just to get our questions in order. So that we present a united, professional front."

"An excellent idea," said Pendergast. He paused to make a brief but careful survey of the craft's superstructure. "Agent Chambers, would you be willing to allow me to lead the questioning?"

"I've got to be honest with you, Pendergast: I'm concerned about where you might go with the interview. I mean, do you still think he killed Telligren?"

Pendergast did not answer, and it was hard to tell what he was thinking.

"I'm concerned you might accuse him," Chambers said.

"It would be counterproductive to do so," Pendergast replied. "I won't level any accusations, I assure you. I will be most correct in my questioning."

"Good to know. But your questioning might still give him the idea he's under suspicion."

"He already knows I suspect him. But I promise you, Agent Chambers, I'll be respectful. I will ask him why he thinks Telligren was murdered and who he thinks might have done it, and we can hear out his explanation. I hope you'll listen to his answers and observe him closely." A hesitation. "You see, I believe Magnus intends to...how shall I put it?...*toy* with us."

Toy? Chambers didn't know what Pendergast was talking about. "All right," he said. "I'll let you take the lead. But if you start going off the rails, I'll cut you off fast. Is that clear?"

"Eminently so."

"Good." Chambers glanced at his watch. "Five minutes to two. Let's go."

A gangplank or stage had been swung out on a boom from the bow, ready for boarding passengers, and they walked toward it. Two crew members, who seemed to be waiting for them, stood at the railing and helped them aboard.

"We're here to see Dr. Magnus," said Pendergast.

"He's expecting you," said one. "This way."

They followed him along the deck and through a set of doors into an astonishingly opulent saloon, with rich brocaded wallpaper, cut-glass sconces, polished brass, and a brace of crystal chandeliers. A staircase led upward to higher deck. They ascended and followed the crew member to a stern cabin along an outside walkway, where he knocked at a small, unmarked door. A moment later the door opened, and Magnus stood there, also in crisp nautical dress, blue blazer, white pants, and a snowy captain's hat with a black brim decorated with gold laurels, braid, and anchors. Magnus's curls, equally gold, spilled out from under.

"Come in, gentlemen," said Magnus, stepping aside. They entered a snug little study, beautifully paneled in oak, with an elegant Persian carpet on the floor, a small chandelier above, and two walls of books in rare bindings. In an illuminated glass case at one end stood a violin with a bow and a label, in script too small to read at a distance, along with a few photographs and objets d'art.

"Welcome," he said as the crew member withdrew, shutting the door. "Please sit down." He took Chambers lightly by the elbow and steered him toward a plush red-velvet chair, one of a pair opposite an antique desk. Chambers sat and Pendergast took the other, while Magnus sat himself behind the desk in an old leather chair.

"I'm so glad you could come," said Magnus. "I've been terribly worried. I wanted to share with you my thoughts on the death of my mentor. I apologize for bringing you to my study with such haste; I would normally have preferred to give you a tour—of the private quarters, anyway; the rest of the vessel is still being heavily renovated. The electronics were the first thing to be updated—stuffing the bridge, in particular, with so much cutting-edge nautical equipment that a large crew is not needed—only a single helmsman, in fact, is necessary. And that is often me. But that also meant clearing out spaces full of antiquated equipment—and, more to the point, redoing the living quarters and staterooms."

Chambers removed a small tape recorder. "May we record?"

"Of course. Please."

Chambers pressed the button and quickly went through the preliminaries. "Now," he said, "I'd like to turn the questioning over to my colleague, Agent Pendergast, who's expressed an interest in asking you a few questions."

"By all means," said Magnus, turning toward Pendergast, a look of pleasant anticipation gathering on his face.

There was a silence, then Pendergast spoke. "Tell me, Dr. Magnus: what is *your* theory of Dr. Telligren's death?"

"Thank you for asking," he said. "I believe my friend was murdered."

"Indeed?" Pendergast asked.

"Yes. Someone was in the room when he died. Someone who filled out that crossword puzzle you took away."

"And how do you know this, Dr. Magnus?"

"The handwriting was not Telligren's. As I told you, the doctor was in the habit of completing the *Times-Picayune* crossword just before going to bed. But he never used block letters like that. Someone *else* completed it."

"And who was this person?" Pendergast asked.

"That's in fact the reason I wanted you both here—as law enforcement. To hear my suspicions as to who this person is and why I suspect him."

"Very well," Pendergast said. "Whom do you suspect?"

"I'm not quite ready to name him, I've got no proof. My suspicions rely on . . . a set of various observations."

"Such as?"

Magnus hesitated again, then turned to speak to Chambers. "There was a person at the crime scene whom I saw surreptitiously removing evidence. A person, moreover, who had no business being there."

"What evidence?" asked Chambers, deciding to take the lead.

"I'll get to that in a moment. This person, furthermore, had a strange and unaccountable antipathy toward Dr. Telligren. He'd recently accused the doctor of heinous criminal behavior."

"What sort of behavior?" Chambers asked.

"Of being no less than an accessory to murder. Not only that, but the day before Dr. Telligren's death, this person directly threatened him with personal violence."

"And how do you know this?" Chambers asked.

"Dr. Telligren told me."

"What about the autopsy?" said Chambers. "It was pretty conclusive that a heart attack was the cause. How do you explain that?"

"Agent Chambers, that is perhaps the most salient point of all. My suspect has deep medical knowledge. He knew Dr. Telligren had a weak heart. There are several drugs that could be administered to a person with a bad heart to induce a cardiac event—ergotamine derivatives, for example, or sumatriptan. My suspect came that night, administered the drug, and then did the crossword puzzle while he waited for Telligren to die."

"So how did Telligren ingest this drug?"

"I think the murderer had previously spiked Dr. Telligren's sherry bottle. He knew that he had a glass before bed, at the same time he did the crossword. Now tell me, Agent Chambers: what would you, as an FBI agent, conclude, given this evidence?"

"Your suspect would certainly be a person of interest."

Magnus turned. "Agent Pendergast, we haven't heard from you the last few minutes. What would your thoughts be on the suspect?"

Chambers turned to Pendergast expectantly and was shocked to see the expression of dark amusement on his partner's face. "Dr. Magnus," said Pendergast, "you certainly are a droll fellow."

"Why, thank you," Magnus replied.

Chambers felt confused. The exchange had suddenly gone over his head, as if Pendergast and Magnus had been sharing a private joke he'd been unaware of.

"So clever of the murderer himself to twist the facts in this way," Pendergast said, and then to Chambers: "Magnus is about to accuse me of this homicide, of course."

"*What?*" cried Chambers.

"He's right," Magnus said. "My suspect is you, Agent Pendergast. *You* visited Dr. Telligren that evening. *You* drugged his sherry. *You* waited while he died, coolly doing the crossword puzzle. And you did all this because you believed he was responsible for those horrific serial-killer deaths—deaths that Dr. Telligren somehow created with nefarious medical experimentation but would never, of course, be charged with. You decided to play the avenging angel, didn't you?"

Chambers stared at Pendergast, aghast, and then at Magnus, as he mentally ticked off each damning point the man had made. Could there be truth in such a terrible accusation? Chambers had known several law enforcement officers who'd taken their work so intensely and emotionally that at times they had been tempted to take justice into their own hands—especially if they suspected the suspect was getting away with it. None of them, of course, had followed through...

The voice of Magnus intruded into his thoughts. "It is a well-known phenomenon: certain law officers killing a suspect they feared would evade justice."

Chambers stared at Pendergast, who looked back with a neutral expression.

"How well do you know your partner?" Magnus went on. "As I understand it, he's new to the FBI."

Chambers tried to pull his thoughts together. It couldn't be true. But why wasn't Pendergast defending himself?

Magnus went on. "I looked into his background, Agent Chambers. It's the strangest thing—the last half a dozen years of his life are a blank. Not only that, but he comes from a family in New Orleans with a long history of mental illness and criminal behavior. His great-aunt poisoned her entire family, for example; she's currently locked up in an asylum in New York. And from what I could learn, his brother seems guilty of a long history of criminal acts—although he's a clever man, not to mention an elusive one."

Chambers stared at Pendergast, who remained unperturbed. "What have you to say to these accusations?" he asked.

"You may recall," Pendergast replied coolly, "that I warned you Magnus was likely to toy with us."

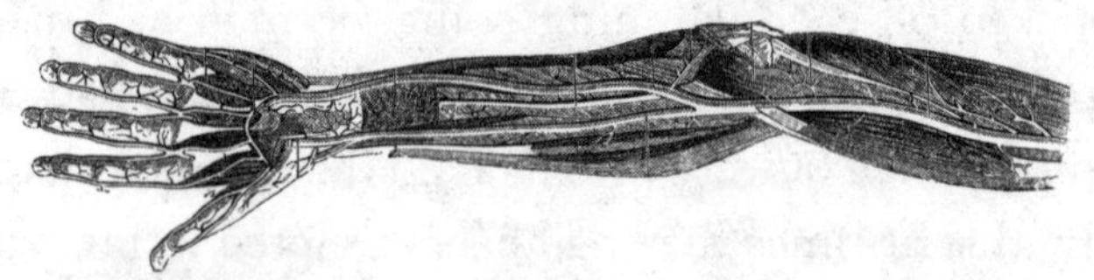

55

Dr. Dorion Magnus, having completed his premeditated parry and riposte, sat back in his chair and gazed upon the pale face of the FBI agent seated in front of him, mind filled with interest and speculation. This man was, quite certainly, the most unusual person he'd ever encountered, and he was intensely curious to explore his mind further.

Magnus was a passionate fencer, and he often employed fencing metaphors when engaged in a bout with another's mind as a way to express to himself what was happening. He glanced at the brass clock on the opposite wall, noting as he did so that the time for the flèche—the leaping attack—would soon arrive. Precisely how soon, he could not be sure, but in the meantime he would disengage and give distance... while amusing himself. He had observed that during their conversation Pendergast, ever alert to his surroundings, had been studying the contents of his glass cabinet. He could use that as a distraction to pass a minute or two.

"Agent Pendergast, I see you eyeing my display case. It contains a handful of mementos that mark the greatest turning points in my life. That Guarneri violin, for example, given me by the concertmaster of the New Orleans Symphony upon his retirement—it serves as a mordant reminder of my foresight in deciding to become a doctor instead of a musician. The scalpel lying next to it on a bed of felt, used in my first operation; the odd photograph and bauble—they all document, in one way or another, the steps that brought me to where I am today."

Another glance at the clock. He noted, with interest, that Pendergast's right hand had now shifted subtly so that it lay just inside the lapel of his suit jacket, where his .45 was holstered. The man knew something was about to happen.

And Magnus knew that he knew.

Pendergast turned to Chambers. "It's time to go." He said to Magnus. "We will see our way out."

"Not quite yet, sir," said Magnus, also turning to Chambers, his mind now catching the currents and eddies of thought from the senior agent instead... like a radio dial changing stations mid-song. "Agent Chambers, I request you arrest your partner for murder."

Chambers remained frozen in his chair. Magnus could see his mind swirling with warring beliefs, and—choosing his words carefully, so they remained in sync with Chambers's changing thoughts—he spoke in a low voice. "You've known for some time that your partner was abnormal. There is a genetic disposition in his line for violence and crime. Did you know a mob burned down his family's mansion on Dauphine Street, killing both his parents?"

More suspicions and doubts blossoming in Chambers's mind, and he watered them. "You must have harbored suspicions about his sanity before now."

"Agent Chambers!" said Pendergast sharply. "It is time to go."

Looking now once again at Pendergast, Magnus could feel the man's deep alarm. Without surprise, Magnus saw the man's hand had crept to a spot only inches from his hidden sidearm. Magnus knew that in any quick-draw contest, Pendergast would put a bullet between his eyes before he could even touch his own sidearm. Thankfully, that was not going to be a problem. The clock—his friend in this contest—was ticking. What Pendergast did not know, *could* not know, was that the terrible deed that filled the man's mind with anxiety was already done... and couldn't be reversed.

"Why so anxious to leave?" Magnus asked Pendergast, picking up on Chambers's thoughts of panic, alarm, and betrayal. "Is it the horror of being unmasked? Or the fear of punishment? Those aren't the kind of things, it seems to me, you'd recoil from. No: it would be the *disgrace* that would unman you most."

Pendergast had risen from his chair, but Chambers remained seated, his mind still in utter turmoil—grappling not only with his accusations but the even stranger, more outré exchange that was playing out between himself and Pendergast.

"Chambers," said Pendergast, a note of urgency in his voice, his hand now actually touching his holster and silently undoing the keeper. "Get up. We're leaving. *Now.*"

Magnus glanced again at the clock. The flèche was only seconds away. He could sense, almost as if it was his own, the consternation and confusion in Chambers; feel the rapid hammering of his heart....

Yes. Increase the blood flow, dial up the circulation, bring on the crisis that much quicker.

"Chambers!" cried Pendergast.

Chambers finally staggered to his feet.

Now: the flèche. "So, Chambers!" he said. "Your partner warned that I might toy with you. Is that right?"

Something new had entered Chambers's mind: the physical aura, the strange white glow, that precedes a seizure. There was no need to look into his mind any longer; that battle was already won. But it was no longer about need. It was about enjoyment.

Magnus tilted back in his chair. "And I have!" He laughed. "It's been amusing, toying with your miserably suspicious little mind. You see, Chambers, *I'm* the one who visited Telligren that night. *I'm* the one who administered the drug! *I'm* the murderer of Telligren! How delightful to make you think your very own partner might be the murderer—*or was that already a suspicion deep down?*"

Pendergast was about to draw his weapon, but it was too late. Chambers gave a guttural cry and clutched his chest. Abruptly, his body went rigid as a board, toppling over backward as the muscles of his legs seized up. He thudded to the floor like a fallen tree, and then his body bowed upward into a hideous, juddering arch, his head and heels hammering on the wooden floor in a lethal staccato. And in that instant of impeccable distraction, as Pendergast moved to assist his partner, Magnus drew out his .45 and took a brisk step forward, pressing it against Pendergast's head as his other hand pulled out the agent's firearm, conveniently unsnapped and half withdrawn.

He quickly stepped back, both weapons aimed. "Keep your hands in sight," he said quietly.

Pendergast raised his hands. The trap had been laid, and then sprung, to perfection. The agent's mind was now as dark as night—while his partner, Chambers, writhed and choked on the floor.

The door opened and three crew members entered, each carrying an AR-15. They spread out, covering Pendergast.

"There's nothing you can do for him," Magnus said. "I'm a biochemist, remember. Poor Chambers received fatal dose of a V-series nerve agent in his morning coffee, carefully calibrated to time his seizure to this *moment juste*." He glanced at his watch. "Twelve minutes to five—a few minutes later than estimated, but you must admit very accurate, nevertheless. After all, I had to approximate certain variables of his height, weight, and metabolism." He put the two handguns on the desk. "You see, Agent Pendergast, I realized it would not be an easy thing to get the drop on you—to evade your preternatural alertness and your innate caution. The seizure and collapse of your partner was one thing I realized I could count on to distract your attention—for just long enough." He turned to Chambers, who was now rigid on the floor, his eyes popping from his head, his face deep scarlet, the blood vessels pounding in his rigid neck. "Did you perhaps find that Guatemalan dark roast a bit rich this morning, Agent Chambers? Yes? No? Cat got your tongue, it seems?"

Magnus now brought his manicured fingers together with a self-satisfied smile as he watched Chambers expire, the agent's eyes filming over, the pulsing of blood in his neck fading away. All grew quiet in the little study at the stern of the boat.

Magnus enjoyed the silence, allowing it to linger for a moment before speaking again. "Jean-Pierre? Paul?"

Two of the three men came to attention, while the third kept his weapon trained on Pendergast. "Yes, sir?" one said.

Magnus waved at Pendergast. "Please escort this gentleman below-decks and lock him up in the darkest, filthiest, and most secure hold. There are several next to the bilges that should do: just make sure it's one he can't escape from."

The two men nodded.

"Jean-Pierre," Magnus said. "Take charge. The fellow's well trained at close-in military operations, so don't take any risks. Paul, you hang back just a little in case he causes trouble."

The man named Jean-Pierre slung his AR-15 over his shoulder, while Paul nodded and backed away, weapon at the ready.

"If there's any difficulty, shoot out his kneecaps—but don't kill him. I have a feeling I might want to *toy* with him some more... later. And then wrap some weights around his friend, here, and—once we're in the deep channel south of town—throw him overboard."

And as he spoke, the boat's great engine chuffed into life, a bell rang, and the creaking of the stern paddle started up, the sound of churning water coming through the windows. The great river steamer *Fantôme* began to move.

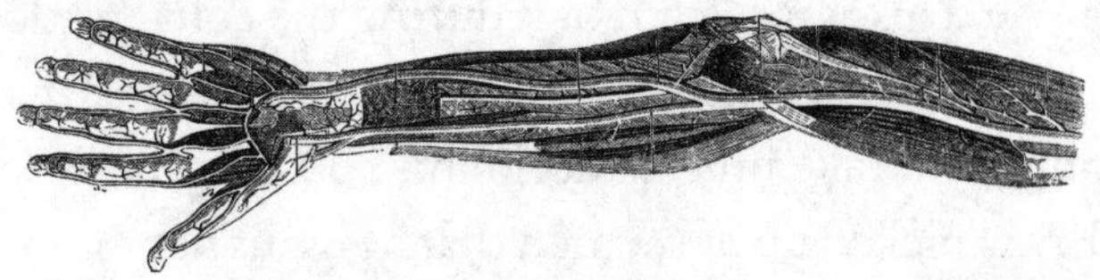

56

PENDERGAST SAT UTTERLY STILL in the darkness, his mind staggered by the cruel death of his partner and mentor. There would be time for recrimination—but now was the time for vengeance.

He made a quick exploration of his prison. The walls were of riveted steel covered with filth, and the single massive door fit tightly and was immovable. The floor was ankle-deep with a heavy layer of coal dust, grit, lumps, and fragments. He could hear the murmur of voices from somewhere; a laugh; the sounds of machinery—but so attenuated, he could not even be sure which direction they came from. His night vision was unusually sharp, and his stint training and operating with the Ghost Company had refined it further—but nevertheless he could make out absolutely nothing.

He tried his other senses. There was the faint smell of bilge and ancient urine often found in the bowels of old ships. There was a stronger, sulfurous odor as well. He was, it seemed, in the ship's original coal bunker.

Deciding he could make no further discoveries without a more detailed physical search, he nevertheless remained where he was, thinking. There were other matters to consider before trying to escape—primarily the nature of his adversary, Magnus.

Pendergast was now certain Magnus possessed some degree of telepathic or extrasensory ability. While this had previously been his assumption, he'd grown certain of it during the conversation that had just taken place, during which—as a test—Pendergast had allowed certain thoughts to take precedence in his consciousness, which Magnus had quickly picked up. It seemed that Magnus's ability was limited to the person directly in front of him and was inhibited by distance or intervening objects. It was not long-range, nor could it penetrate walls or other obstructions.

In his mind, he returned to a photograph he'd observed in the study's display cabinet. It was an old Polaroid, a blurry shot of four men. The younger three wore graduation robes, and all were kneeling in a jocular pose of obeisance to the older man—Telligren. Two of the three students he also recognized: Magnus and Wickman, along with a third student, named in the studies Pendergast had unearthed, who had later committed suicide. This was Telligren with his three cherry-picked graduate assistants who had volunteered to be guinea pigs in the PSI lab.

With Magnus, the experiment had apparently succeeded. The other two proved to be ghastly mistakes: one a suicide, the other transformed into a uniquely psychotic serial killer. Although, Pendergast thought grimly, it seemed likely that the PSI gift Magnus had acquired had not come without some dark or perverse side effect of its own.

How curious it was that Magnus displayed such a potentially damning photograph in plain view. But of course it was in keeping with his character. He was a man of whimsy and arrogance, who would smoke a cigar while watching an amputation and murder, who would cut off Wickman's arm as a sort of final joke on the serial killer who cut off arms. He was a man who liked leaving clues such as the crossword puzzle behind for his private amusement, to toy with Chambers for sheer entertainment before murdering him.

The outline of the situation was now clear. The PSI study had gone awry with the suicide of one of the subjects. Telligren—with Magnus's help—had erased all traces of the program's existence. But the medical experimentation had given Magnus a splendid gift, allowing him to become a brilliant young professor, a darling of society, and ultimately the king of his own little Xanadu. It also gave him power over Telligren. Whether Magnus was a sadist from the beginning or had become one due to the medical procedure on his brain was a moot point. However else he'd been changed, he was clearly a psychopath of far more refined nature than Wickman. *Did you perhaps find that Guatemalan dark roast a bit rich this morning, Agent Chambers? Cat got your tongue, it seems?*

Pendergast let his thoughts linger on Chambers for a moment. His death was one of the cruelest he'd ever seen. Pendergast had not been out of the military so long that the Ghost Company's creed had become anachronistic for him. *Fidelitas usque ad mortem*; Loyalty unto death.

There was unfinished business to attend to.

Most boys growing up in New Orleans had a fascination with steamboats. Pendergast was no exception, but his younger brother Diogenes had been truly obsessed. He designed his own paddleboats on paper, drawing all sorts of fanciful deck plans, engine blueprints, and interior decorations. The two of them had eventually built a four-foot working model of a steamboat. One night, they quietly took their craft to Big Lake in New Orleans City Park for its maiden launch. They had borrowed an elderly neighbor's Pekingese, Wiggles, to be the honored passenger. Unknown to Pendergast, however, Diogenes had secretly wanted to reprise, in miniature, the infamous 1865 explosion and sinking of the steamship *Sultana*, in which eighteen hundred lives were lost. So at the last minute, sending Pendergast away on the pretext of a diversion, he'd strapped a timer and a bandolier of M-80s beneath the model's waterline.

The miniature motor worked, the boat began sailing across the still waters of the lake, Wiggles barking joyfully in excitement . . . and then the boat was blown to kingdom come, along with Wiggles.

From his brother's point of view, it had been a spectacular success.

Pendergast shook off this memory and its aftermath. But there was a method to the madness of recalling it: Pendergast had an intimate knowledge of the typical paddle steamer.

Clearly, as evidenced by the empty coal bunker, Magnus had

thrown out the old boilers. He could feel the vibration of what were clearly modern diesels. While a portion of the boat had been elegantly restored—as he noted during the brief time he'd been escorted out of the study, belowdecks, and along corridors to this black empty space—it was obvious to Pendergast that much of the belowdecks interior spaces were still in their original state.

Pendergast sat in the darkness, still motionless. He could feel the diesels throbbing, hear the faint thrumming of water along the outside hull. Magnus was taking a little cruise.

Cat got your tongue?

Pendergast didn't know what Magnus had planned, and his desire, his rage, to avenge his partner could not wait. A second exploration of the coal bunker was in order. He moved at speed—keeping his arms ahead of him, feeling the walls, the floors, choking in the dust, memorizing every rivet and seam. The bunker was approximately ten feet by ten and featureless, beyond a steel truss of some kind. It had broken or been sheared off where it met the inner wall and now lay diagonally across the little room.

What was it? He sounded the deep past again in his brain. His brother, he remembered, had wanted to have their scale-model paddle wheeler burn coal for power instead of using batteries. He'd tried to convince Pendergast, but in the end it would have made the model too cumbersome and heavy for two young boys to fabricate. He thought about what he'd observed when he'd first boarded the *Fantôme*. It was the type of paddle steamer with the boilers belowdecks. The coal, he remembered, was brought by barges and loaded aboard into coal ports spaced along the hull. "Trimmers" inside the coal ports would send the coal down chutes to the boiler room, where it would be bunkered. All coal-fired vessels, large or small, had employed this technique. The *Titanic* might have had a dozen or more coal ports; the *Fantôme*, with only two boilers, would probably have had only one.

And he was inside it.

Immediately, he got down on his hands and knees and began searching the ancient metal floor, pushing aside the coal dust and debris and feeling the metal beneath. After a few moments, his fingernails caught on something and he felt around it: the outlines of a hatch in the floor. He wedged his fingernails underneath and pulled, but the cover didn't budge.

Standing up, he felt around and seized the broken spar. Feeling up and down it, he located a piece of twisted metal along the lower section of the broken edge. He wrenched it free and tried using it as a lever to raise the chute cover.

No good. A century of coal, rust, and disuse had sealed it fast against anything less than a jackhammer.

Pendergast sat down again, turning the piece of metal over in his hands. The vessel was at speed now, the water thrumming along the hull.

That broken steel truss, he recalled, had a name: it was a strongback, intended to keep the coal port closed and seaworthy when under way. Once all the coal had been loaded aboard, the ship's carpenter would seal the coal ports from water intrusion with red lead and fix the strongbacks against the ports. That meant there was another possible escape route—out the loading port in the side of the hull: disused, long forgotten, and no doubt painted over with the fresh coat Magnus had applied. And red lead, he knew, not only lost its seaworthiness over time . . . but it was soft.

He rose and, working quickly once again, felt along the inner wall of the hold until his fingers found the outline of the coal port. These edges yielded to his improvised prybar. He coated the hatch hinges liberally with coal dust to keep them from squeaking—and he also took the time to blacken his exposed skin with the same grime. He cautiously pushed the hatch open—dark water was rushing by just feet below him, the occasional spatter of bow wake hitting his face—and, using its upper edge as a step, hoisted himself up to the railing.

A quick look around in the golden evening light showed the promenade to be deserted. He pushed the coal hatch closed with one foot, then—stealthily, stealthily—eased himself over the railing and onto the cargo deck.

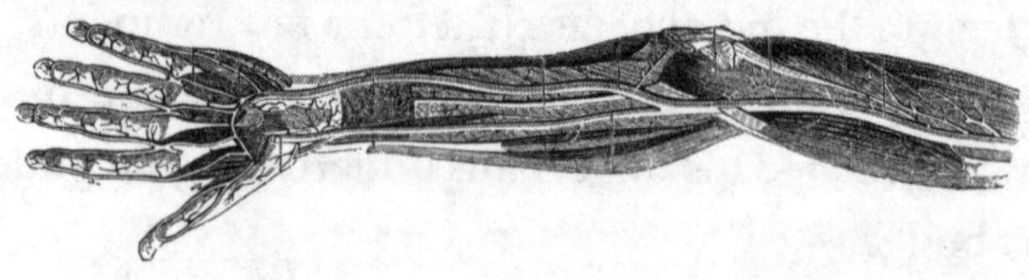

57

As THE *FANTÔME* MADE its way southward through the Delta, Dorion Magnus stood in the pilothouse—perched upon the highest deck of the vessel, like the top of a wedding cake—and watched the low-lying shores of the Mississippi slide by. They had just passed Venice to the starboard; beyond that small town, the Delta became a wilderness of twisting bayous, ponds, bays, islands, and marshland, where even a boat as large and conspicuous as the *Fantôme* could effectively disappear.

The river was muddy and brown, the surface smooth, not a breath of wind. The *Fantôme* was making good headway: eight knots, assisted by two knots of current. As the boat moved southward, the trees disappeared, and all that could be seen were dark channels winding among endless islands of cordgrass, cane, and bulltongue, with patches of black mangrove. It was a sultry, dead afternoon, the humid air smelling of salt and mud, the sun sinking into a bloody swirl of clouds over the Gulf. A few fishermen in johnboats plied the channel, becoming fewer as they continued southward. The shrimpers, who usually left in the early morning, had returned with their catch hours ago, and the main channel was mostly deserted.

It was chilly in the air-conditioned pilothouse, all the windows shut against the mosquitoes and muggy evening air. Magnus glanced at his captain: a stout, grizzled old Louisianan with pale-blue eyes and a perpetual squint. His name was LaGrange, and he was a man of few words and unquestioning loyalty, manning the helm as skillfully as if he'd been born with it in his hands. On his other side stood Magnus's right-hand man, Mako John, big, broad, and solid with a heavy face, mashed nose, and thick lips, the crude visage concealing a clever and nimble brain. John oversaw the small group of loyal men who protected him—and kept his secrets.

Magnus kept an eye out on the port side, and soon he saw what he anticipated: an opening in the main channel called Cubits Gap. The *Fantôme* slowed, the paddle wheel churning as the triple rudders began turning the boat's heading from the main waterway. Cubits Gap led into a maze of the deeper bayous and ponds among islands, continuing for many miles before emptying into the Gulf of Mexico. It was a place he knew well, having spent many an afternoon exploring these channels as a youth—before the big change.

Once in the gap, the current fell off and LaGrange slowed the engine as the channel narrowed. Magnus could see the low outline of Savage Island: first looming to port, then passing by as they steered into Brant Bayou. He remained motionless as the boat reached Octave Pass and slowed to bare headway, the paddle wheel turning more slowly. They were now entering the most remote and beautiful stretch of the Delta, the air wheeling with gulls and terns, black skimmers flying low over the water, the shorelines dotted with snowy egrets and wading herons.

He felt relief at ridding himself of New Orleans: leaving behind its chattering masses and banalities, exchanging them for the watery freedom of the Delta's wilderness. The PSI powers Magnus had acquired ten years ago allowed him to peer, albeit as if through a dark mirror, into the minds of others. His powers did not extend far in terms of space—no more than fifteen or twenty feet—and they could not penetrate walls or other barriers. Inside that limit, however, as others passed in and out of his psionic range, he unwillingly picked up, like stray broadcasts, the half-baked inanities rattling around in the hollow vessels of their minds. It was hard to tune out, not unlike a home in which the television is left on to blare incessantly in the background. After the novelty and first flush of acquiring this unexpected sixth sense had receded, he began noticing, with dismay, the appalling banality, the vacuity, the swamplands of thought he'd discovered inside the minds of most people he encountered. Before his awakening, he had had no idea how tedious the average human being was; how almost no one expressed a glimmer of intelligence or original thinking. In this one way, his gift had become a golden curse: giving him enormous powers to manipulate others while torturing him with their farcicalities at the same time. And there was another curse beyond even that one: an almost physical blow he had not been able to bear without reacting—by dealing fate an equal, but opposite, blow of his own...

He'd made his point—he could console himself knowing his response to the mocking, hateful universe had not been in vain. And the consolation itself would soon be aboard, almost directly below where he now stood. But for the time being, there were other matters to consider—and this pilothouse was the perfect place. Although he could not go among the throngs and still remain deaf to their contemptible thoughts and coarse notions, here in the Delta he could escape.

And yet...

From time to time, he'd encountered a startlingly original mind; a person whose thoughts took unexpected paths in the gardens of ratiocination. This fellow Pendergast was one of those...but he was even more. He had, it seemed, the ability to climb the hilltops girdling the gardens and take in the entire landscape, displaying powers that rivaled Magnus's own. He was sui generis—a man possessing one of the most intriguing and dangerous minds he'd ever encountered. Magnus felt uneasy about him, even troubled, questioning if perhaps he'd finally met his match or—more worrying—if his own PSI powers were fading. He wondered what Pendergast knew, or had guessed, about him—and whom he might have shared that knowledge with. Magnus sensed it would not be wise to keep the man alive on his boat for long: just long enough to plumb the depths of his mind more aggressively, get answers to the questions currently troubling him... before killing the man and disposing of the corpse.

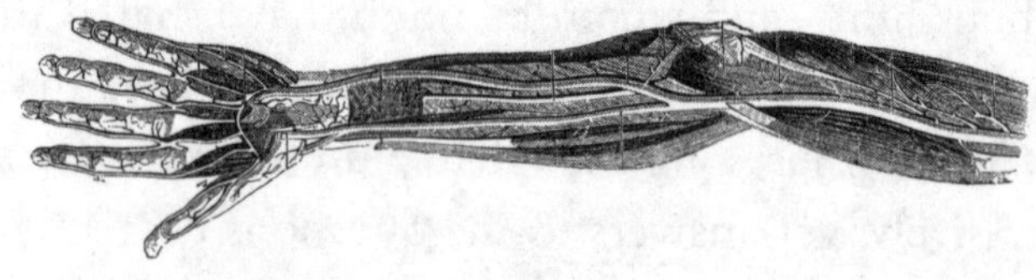

58

Lingering in a recessed hatchway of the cargo deck, Pendergast could see the boat was heading southward, traveling in a subsidiary channel and cruising among low islands covered with cordgrass. As the sun vanished into a pile of distant thunderheads, a reddish glow spread across the landscape, turning the muddy water the color of dark blood. The steamboat was moving slowly, the rhythmic splashing of the paddle wheel like a watery metronome underlain by the throbbing of the diesel engine.

Ensuring the deck was clear, Pendergast now moved rapidly past a series of doors, halting at one marked stores. He tested the handle: unlocked. He slipped in and eased the door shut.

A single porthole allowed sufficient light for him to see. As he'd hoped, this was the boat's main storeroom. Everything here was new and meticulously organized. Large machine parts were stacked on one side, fresh and gleaming, many still packed on pallets. There were smaller machine parts, wooden trusses, valves, spare rudders, bronze fittings, rods, as well as linkages, paddles, and cams for making repairs to the paddle wheel's feathering mechanism. Hawsers were coiled up in a far corner, while racks of tools and equipment occupied the rest of the space. The air smelled of machine oil and rope lubricant.

Pendergast went over to the tool cabinet. He scanned the neat labels on each drawer before easing one out. Inside, packed in foam cutouts, was a row of deburring implements of various sizes and shapes—instruments used to remove metal fragments from the edges of machined steel. Each had swiveled hooks with blades at one end, wickedly sharp.

He took one and tucked it into the small of his back. After a moment's thought, he moved to a second cabinet full of marlin spikes. After hefting a few, he selected one in six-inch steel, oiled and gleaming. He slid this up his sleeve, then made a small hole in his cuff and hooked the sharp end to it; this served to hold the spike securely, hidden but instantly available.

He completed supplying himself by selecting a coil of thin rope, a signal flare with a time delay, and a roll of gaffing tape. These all went into a haversack that he slung over his shoulder, silently congratulating Magnus on the diligence with which he was fitting out his boat.

At the farther, darker end of the storeroom was something else he'd been looking for: a metal cabinet emblazoned with hazardous warnings and flammable symbols. It was locked, but he hunted around for a few shims and pins and had the lock open within minutes. Inside he found what he'd expected: an array of toxic and flammable chemicals, antifouling paints, MEK, lubricating oil—and the two chemicals he was looking for in particular: acetone, used for degreasing, and spare cartridges of halon 1301 gas used in the vessel's fire-suppression system. He took a one-liter can of acetone and a pressurized halon cartridge. They joined the rest of the equipment in the haversack.

He tucked the lock-picking tools into his jacket pocket.

A large paddle wheel steamer in the nineteenth century normally required a crew of at least twenty-five. This one, he recalled from Magnus's bragging, needed far fewer—the equivalent of a skeleton crew. But that still meant half a dozen, at least, loyal and complicit.

At least six crew members—a lot of people to kill. But kill them he would. This situation reminded him of several others he'd been in during his days with the Ghost Company—days not so far in the past that he'd forgotten the pitiless violence, the cold-bloodedness, they had employed to bring those critically important, extremely dangerous missions to quick and successful completion. After the brutality and sadistic cruelty that his partner, Chambers, had been subjected to, Pendergast planned to even the scales in the manner of the Ghost Company. Nobody would leave the boat alive.

He closed his eyes, taking a long moment to assemble in his mind the likely layout of the steamer and fixing it in his spatial memory. The engine room would be far aft, containing the new diesel engine powering the paddle wheel. It would be difficult to get there without being seen, as the deck was open and unobstructed from bow to stern. But that must nevertheless be his main objective.

He visualized other rooms he would likely have to pass and perhaps hide in. There would be two cargo holds: one open, the other secure. There would be a kitchen, crew mess, workshop, stewards' cabin, laundry room—a cluster normally situated in the rear. Forward of that would be the boat's now-disused boilers. The pipes carrying steam to the engine, and the speaking tubes from the pilothouse to the engine room, had been spared in the renovation, perhaps for historical purposes. There was plenty of cover for Pendergast to move about, due to the stacks of debris, equipment, and other materials associated with the ongoing reconstruction of the vessel.

Equipped with everything he needed, save a firearm, Pendergast returned to the door of the storeroom and listened. All was silent. He carefully drew down the door handle, easing it open a quarter of an inch. Then he waited, once again listening acutely. Minutes passed—and then he heard a faint footfall approaching on the deck boards. A single person. He tensed. Using the instincts of stealth combat he could never lose, at just the right moment he flung open the door and, like a trapdoor spider, seized the man around the neck and drove the marlin spike into his voice box. The spike cut off the man's incipient scream as Pendergast forced him into the storeroom, swiftly reclosing the door.

The man jerked violently, gurgling hideously as the two twisted around in a gruesome ballet, finally falling to the deck as a hard twist of the spike severed his carotid artery. Warm, thick spurts of blood struck Pendergast's face and chest, soaking him before the man's heart ceased beating. Rising to his knees and groping around the now-limp body, he found, then pocketed, a handgun. He pulled out the handkerchief he habitually carried, preparing to wipe his face. As he did so, shards of glass and a piece of vintage precious metal, winking in the dim light, came along with it—his pocket watch had been ruined in the struggle.

He cursed under his breath. Then, flapping the handkerchief open, he cleaned his face and snorted out the blood that had squirted up his nose. Hauling the body to the far side of the storeroom, he stowed it behind a coiled mass of hawsers. Regaining his breath, he took a moment to consider his plan of attack. He realized his clothes and face, covered in black coal dust from the bunker, had now been decorated further by a great gush of clotted blood. He must look, he thought, like a monster.

Good.

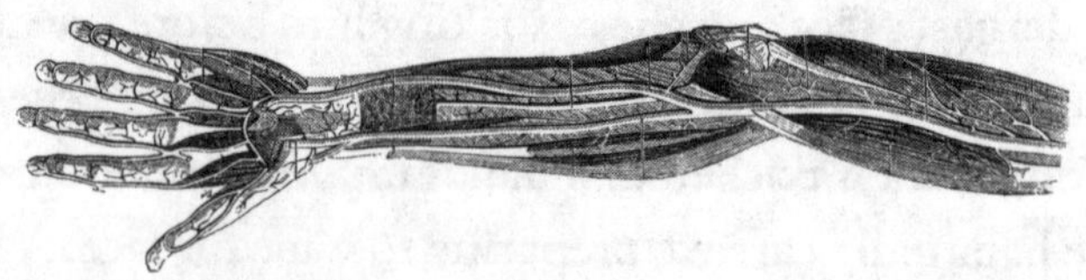

59

Now that they were well beyond civilization, Dorion Magnus exited the pilothouse and took the ladderway down to the hurricane deck. He strolled aft, arms behind his back, heading for the ship's bell. His mind was clouded with thoughts roused by this fellow, Pendergast.

He stopped beside the bell and gazed upon it abstractedly. It had been originally made for the famous SS *Robert E. Lee*, the steamer that had defeated *Natchez VI* in the legendary 1870 race from New Orleans to St. Louis. He placed his hands on the bronze slope of the bell—still warm from the sun—inhaled deeply, then paused to take in the view while organizing his thoughts. From this elevated vantage he could see across the low marshy islands to the distant Gulf. As he watched, a final gleam from the setting sun broke through distant thunderheads, flashing an ephemeral trail of gold across the water before sinking into an eddy of clouds, shrouding the Gulf in that special, haunted twilight found only in the bayous of the Delta.

The thunderheads, he noted, were boiling up rapidly. The weather report had predicted late-evening thunderstorms, and Magnus could spy some distant flashes of lightning, still too far away to hear. It certainly felt like one of those humid, still summer evenings that preceded a storm. He was not concerned: they were well protected from sea swell in these channels, and though refitting was still in progress, the boat was as tight and dry as on the day of its original launch.

He felt the boat begin a slow turn, heard the splashing of the paddle wheel as the three rudders swung to starboard, directing them into the channel leading to Goose Island Outside Pond. It was a tight channel, and LaGrange was taking it slow. Looking forward, Magnus could make out the channel that would take them to that distant pond, the water lying as still as a sheet of ebony in the darkening twilight.

...And now, glancing up, he noted the appearance of Venus in the western sky; the evening star, named after the goddess of love and beauty. It was indeed beautiful, the brightest object in the night sky after the moon. But even as he watched, the leading ledge of the storm blotted it out. A dark, stormy night was precisely what he needed to securely dispose of two bodies. On such a night, no stray fisherman would be lingering unseen in the distant channels.

He now strolled past a longboat and jolly boat stored near the stern under tarpaulin covers and took the ladderway down to the stateroom deck. He walked forward, admiring the glistening mahogany doors of the newly refurbished staterooms, past the grand dining room—yet to be completed—to the double doors to the glassed-in saloon. He entered the magnificent space and settled into the leather of his favorite banquette. Mako John, his first mate, was standing watch at one of the windows. Magnus signaled the man to bring him his usual from the bar.

He waited, tapping his finger on the mahogany table, until his drink arrived, and then took a deep draft. Pendergast. He had gone to some trouble digging into the man's past and had been astonished at what he'd found—as well as what he'd *not* found.

It wasn't merely this Pendergast of his acquaintance who was striking; his entire family, going back generations, was an assortment of mountebanks, criminals, quack doctors, madmen, and murderers. And his brother, Diogenes—there was surprisingly little hard information on the fellow, but reading between the lines Magnus could tell he was a piece of work, to be sure. It raised an interesting question: how in the world had a man like Pendergast become an FBI agent? And why? The man was rich as Croesus, with more money than even

Magnus himself. Yet here he was, toiling as a junior agent under the thumb of an unexceptional man like Chambers, who—while not stupid—had an intellect dwarfed by Pendergast's.

The man was a cipher... and a troubling one at that. Their conversation in the saloon before and after the death of Chambers, though it would have seemed civil enough to an onlooker, had been, beneath the surface, a most serious battle of wills. Magnus had never encountered a mind so resistant and devious, so slippery and evasive to his PSI powers—and it once again made him wonder if those powers might perhaps be waning. After all, there was no precedent for what that experiment had done to him, and thus there was no case history to go by. Either way, the confrontation had put him out of sorts. He needed some time with Pendergast in proximity, to probe, push, unlock the mysteries of his mind—and to reassure himself this was a unicorn; a singular event. But it could wait until he reached his destination; by then, his mind would be at peace again, and when the interrogation reached its end the body could be quickly and permanently dispatched.

Magnus turned his attention back to the passing landscape. Spanish Island was hard by their starboard side, and Goose Island was coming up. He could see the small notch that marked the channel leading to the isolated, rarely visited body of water called Goose Island Outside Pond: a perfect destination for the purposes Magnus had in mind.

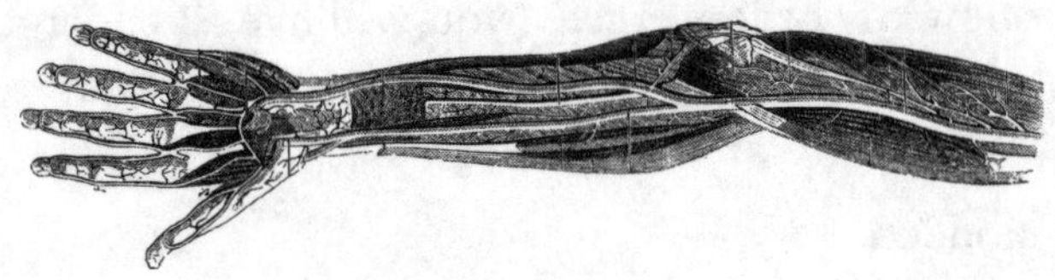

60

Leaving the dead man behind the stack of hawsers, Pendergast went back to the storeroom door and listened. He soon heard footsteps on the deck again, but he immediately realized there were two people, not one, and he let them pass. After waiting a bit, he eased the door open again, peering up and down the cargo deck. There was no one in sight. He eased out, then dashed silently down the deck. He stopped at the door where secure cargo would normally have been stored—except this new door was made of stainless steel, with a lock but no handle. He crept past it and, seeing someone coming down the ladder, ducked into the next door—the crew mess. He expected it to be empty, given the hour and the paucity of crew, but to his surprise a cabin boy was clearing the table. The youth looked up, freezing at the sight of a gruesome man covered in blood, gore, and caked coal dust.

Pendergast, too, momentarily froze, marlin spike in striking position. The boy couldn't be more than fifteen years old. Pendergast leapt on the terrified youth just as he was about to scream, locked an arm around his neck, and clapped a hand over his mouth.

The boy twisted and struggled, and Pendergast whispered in his ear: "Stop, or I'll drive this into your neck." He gave a little prick with the spike.

The boy fell still. His eyes were wide and Pendergast saw they were starting to leak tears of fright.

"If you follow my orders *exactly*, you will live," Pendergast continued. "When I take my hand away, don't make a sound. Nod if you agree."

The boy nodded.

"I have questions."

Another nod.

"How many are on board? Whisper the answer." He removed his hand so the boy could speak.

"Um, eight."

"Name them."

The list of names came out in a series of halts and stammers. "Dr. Magnus. Captain LaGrange. Mr. John, first mate. Manning, Rodney, and, um, Goins, crew. Mr. Robertson, chief engineer. And—and Mr. Dunning, engineer's mate."

"No pilot?"

"Dr. Magnus serves as pilot."

"Are they armed?"

"Yes, sir."

One of the three crewmen, Pendergast figured, must have been the man he killed. "Where are we headed?"

"Goose Island Outside Pond."

"And what will happen there?"

"That's . . . Dr. Magnus's special place. The boat's been there before."

"Why?"

"I don't know."

"What's behind the steel door that's locked so securely?"

"I don't know. No one's allowed in there but Dr. Magnus."

"Can you swim?"

"Yes," said the boy. His teeth had started to chatter the moment Pendergast mentioned the steel door.

"How well?"

"Good enough."

"Listen closely. We're leaving this room and going straight to the railing, where you're going over into the water. Swim away from the boat to clear the paddle wheel. The shore's only fifty yards away, and the boat's moving slowly. Understand?"

The boy nodded.

"If you cry for help, they'll hear you and pull you back on board—and then I'll have to kill you along with the others. That means no noise. And no talking to anyone—*anyone*—about you being aboard tonight, or what you thought you might have seen. I'm afraid that would land you in so much trouble that death would seem preferable. Understood?"

The boy nodded again.

"You're going to have to spend the night on an island. The early-morning shrimpers heading to sea will pick you up."

A final nod.

Holding the boy tightly with one arm, Pendergast went to the door of the mess, cracked it, and made sure the coast was clear. Then, hustling the boy across the deck passageway, he arrived at the rail and, in one smooth motion, heaved him over.

The sounds of the splash were masked by the noisy churning of the paddle wheel. Pendergast saw the boy swimming like mad for the nearby shore as the boat slid past him.

Nobody complicit would leave the boat alive.

It was almost dark, but there was enough light to see the boy reach the muddy embankment, claw his way up it, and slip into the tall switchgrass. In a moment he was gone.

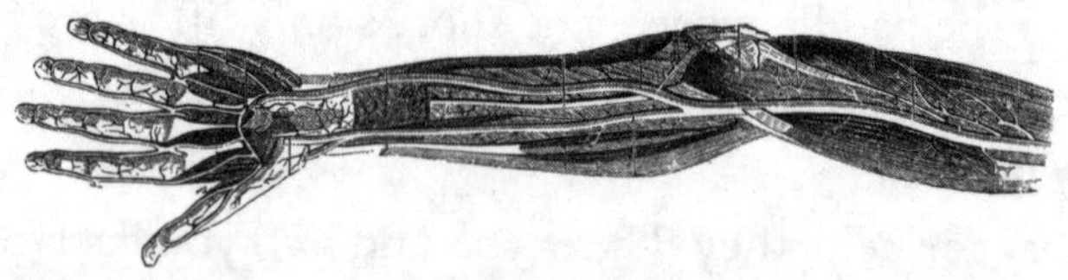

61

PENDERGAST TURNED AWAY AND let his mind dwell on the business at hand. The engine room—that would, in all likelihood, be where he'd find the chief engineer and possibly the engineer's mate. He began to head aft, away from the mess... but then stopped.

That stainless-steel door... Why so carefully hardened, and without a handle? It was strange. And the reaction of the cabin boy to the mere mention of it was telling.

Pivoting and moving stealthily forward, he stopped at the door and pressed his ear against it. Nothing. He took out his improvised set of lockpicks and, despite the sophistication of the lock, he managed to coax it open. Slipping inside, he closed the door behind him, flicked on the light switches with a sweep of his hand—

And stared.

An opulent bed occupied the center of the room, draped in rich brocaded material, standing on a splendid Aubusson carpet, with paintings on the walls of horses and dogs. Standing beside the bed was a stainless gurney, such as one might find in a morgue, surrounded by racks and bottles of what appeared, from their color and odor, to be formalin and ethanol. There were also steel medical carts holding a variety of needles, an angular spring forceps, a cavity injector, and several trocars—again, of the kind one would use in a morgue. Strangest of all, the bed was turned down invitingly, as if perhaps awaiting a tryst.

This bizarre room and its accoutrements, Pendergast suddenly realized, must be in some way the expression of Magnus's own special psychosis, caused by the PSI medical experimentation that had triggered suicide in one subject and made a serial killer out of the other. But what form that psychosis had taken in Magnus—he mused as he took in the inexplicable contents of the room—was still obscure.

He had no more time to spare; ducking out and relocking the steel door, he again headed for his original destination, moving swiftly down the cargo deck leading to the engine room. The hatch was closed, and the hammering of the engines behind it was very much audible. Convenient, should there be any screams from his targets.

If the engine room had a standard layout, it would be small and tight. This meant there was only one option for what he intended to do. He grasped the marlin spike in one hand and the deburring hook in the other. With his elbow, he eased down the engine room hatch handle until he felt the latch beyond free itself from the strike plate. He waited, took a deep breath, and then kicked open the door.

The chief engineer and mate were busy at work on the engine, bent over, heads close together. They started up as the door crashed open and stared, half paralyzed with horror, at the apparition that had just appeared. Taking advantage of both his appearance and the engine noise, Pendergast unleashed a Rebel yell and rushed at them, simultaneously driving the marlin spike into the chief engineer's eye while wrapping his other arm around the mate's neck, the deburring tool cutting into the skin beneath his chin. The chief went down with a gurgle, arterial blood drenching both Pendergast and the mate.

"Move and die," Pendergast said to the struggling mate—who immediately went still.

"I'm not going to gag you. Make a sound, you're dead."

A nod.

Pendergast removed the man's weapon and tucked it next to the other one in his waistband. Using the rope he'd taken from the storeroom, he tied the man to a nearby steel pipe. As he did so, he saw that the man's radio was hooked to his belt, apparently tuned to the open deck frequency. He let the man keep his radio, pretending not to notice it. He removed the man's watch and put it on his own wrist: timing would be critical.

And then he went to work. While the mate watched him balefully, Pendergast unslung the haversack, took out the cylinder of halon gas, and opened its valve. There was an angry hiss of escaping gas. He jammed the cylinder into the speaking tube connecting with the pilothouse and was pleased to note it fit snugly. Given the cylinder's aggressive rate of dispersion—it was meant for fire suppression, after all—he wouldn't have long to wait. The ship was air-conditioned, and while observing the vessel earlier that afternoon, he'd noted that the pilothouse, at the top of the ship in direct sun, had its windows closed. Halon was nontoxic, heavy, and odorless. Coming up through the speaking tubes, it would eventually displace the air from the deck up—asphyxiating the captain and anyone else in the enclosed space in the process. It would render the ship NUC—not under command—but still under propulsion.

He quickly searched the chief's body, taking his radio and weapon, a .45—more punch than the other two he had, and he only needed one. He discarded the other weapons. Slinging the haversack over his shoulder again, Pendergast took a moment to examine the engine. It was a Caterpillar V16, forty-four hundred horsepower, the drivetrain consisting of a crankshaft and pitman arms connected to the churning stern wheel.

He turned back to the engineer's mate and untied him. "We're going to the cargo hold."

The man glowered at him, and Pendergast raised the weapon. "My dear fellow—will it be necessary to kill you?"

The mate shook his head.

"Good man. Stand up."

The man complied.

Pendergast went to the hatch and—keeping the man covered—cracked it and peered out. All was calm; the deck was clear.

Pendergast motioned the man over with a wave of his gun. "Go out the hatch," he said. "I'll be behind you, gun aimed. Break into a run, shout, signal—instant bullet to the spinal cord." He paused to let that sink in. "You will walk casually forward to the main cargo hold. You will go inside and I will follow."

The man did as he was told, walking down the deck with Pendergast one pace behind, approaching the cargo room door, then opening it and going inside. Pendergast followed. It was a cavernous space that went up two stories, with a metal stair and catwalk above, punctuated by a door leading onto the stateroom deck. The cargo area was mostly empty.

It would serve its purpose well.

Pendergast tied up the engineer's mate—more securely this time, by both the waist and ankles—to some cargo braces, while allowing his hands to remain free. Then he ducked out of sight behind some supplies, delved into his haversack, took out the can of acetone, set it on the floor, and used the marlin spike to stab holes in its bottom. Liquid began gurgling out and spreading over the floor.

While this was happening, Pendergast's keen ears heard the faintest beep from his unseen prisoner's radio, followed by the man's voice—a mere whisper—speaking over the radio, he assumed, to Magnus. Pendergast allowed another moment to go by, then came back out from behind the supplies to see the man quickly put away his radio—which he pretended not to notice.

But the results of the call were nevertheless evident by the pounding of feet on the deck above; a chorus of shouts and then a whooping alarm sounding over the PA system.

All hell was breaking loose.

The cargo door burst open and three men rushed in carrying AR-15s. Pendergast sprinted for the metal stairs and leapt up them as the men fired their weapons, spraying rounds, even as Pendergast returned fire, spoiling their aim. Reaching the top, he pulled a flare out of the haversack, yanked off the cap, hit the igniter button, and gave it a long, lazy toss toward the spreading pool of acetone. Then he yanked open the door to the stateroom deck, dove through it, and slammed it closed with his feet just as it was raked by another burst of gunfire. A split second later, an unearthly *whoosh*, followed by a massive, shuddering explosion, shook the ship from top to keel.

Lying on the deck, Pendergast took a brief moment to tally the result: Manning, Robertson, Dunning, Rodney, and Goins, dead; John, dead. Cabin boy, gone. LaGrange, asphyxiated.

That left one man still alive: Magnus.

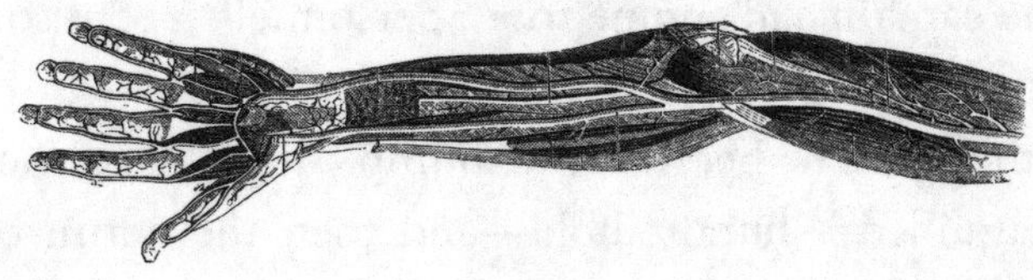

62

Magnus had just lifted his drink to his lips once again when his radio hissed and, a moment later, Dunning's low voice came through. *"Prisoner's escaped,"* he heard in a hoarse whisper. *"Tied me up in the main hold. He's still here. For God's sake, send backup now."*

Magnus leapt to his feet, spilling his drink as he gestured to Mako John. "You, Rodney, and Goins, get the hell down to cargo and kill that son of a bitch!"

"Yes, sir!"

Magnus lunged across the saloon to the boat's emergency comm system. He broke the glass with his fist and pulled the lever. Immediately, an alarm sounded and red lights began blinking in the ceiling. He raised his radio, tuned to the ship's frequency. "All hands to cargo!" he said. "The prisoner is at large, armed and dangerous—kill on sight!"

He changed frequencies. "Engine room, this is Magnus. Over."

Silence.

"Engine room, respond."

Silence.

Magnus switched to the helm frequency. "Helm, this is Magnus. Over."

More silence. "LaGrange, *respond.*"

He stared at his radio in disbelief. Could Pendergast have already disabled the captain *and* engine room personnel—and if so, how was it that the boat was still running? This was insane—

At that moment, he heard a low thump—like the lighting of a gas burner, magnified a hundredfold—and then the entire boat shuddered as if it had struck a reef, causing the chandeliers in the saloon to swing and rattle madly, bottles to fly out of the bar shelves and crash to the ground. The forward motion of the boat slackened, the vessel lurching to one side as the rudders were apparently shoved hard to port. A minute later the boat was churning around in a tight circle, not under command.

Magnus sprinted to the saloon staircase, leapt down it to the cargo deck. The cargo room hatch had been blown off its hinges, and a fire raged within. He sprinted past the conflagration and yanked open the door to the engine room. The chief engineer lay on his side, half decapitated, eyes wide open in the horror of death, the entire floor of the room awash in congealed blood. Magnus, who was almost never shocked, stared in stunned horror at what Pendergast had wrought. How had he done it, and so fast? It had been a colossal mistake not to dispatch him right away, thinking he could toy with a man like this. He lifted the radio and pressed the transmit button on the ship's frequency. "Anyone, respond. *Respond.*"

He released the button. After a silence, a low voice emerged from the hiss of static. "Greetings, Dorion! This is Pendergast responding from your saloon."

For a moment, Magnus—thunderstruck—was silent. His saloon? He'd been there himself mere minutes before.

"At the moment, I'm rinsing blood from my hands with some of your A. E. Dor Grande Cru Cognac—I find it makes an excellent cleansing agent."

It was a bad dream—it had to be. "Robertson," Magnus heard himself croak into the radio. "Dunning. LaGrange—"

But he was interrupted again by that cultivated drawl from hell that not even the wash of static could disguise. "They are gone, my friend. All gone."

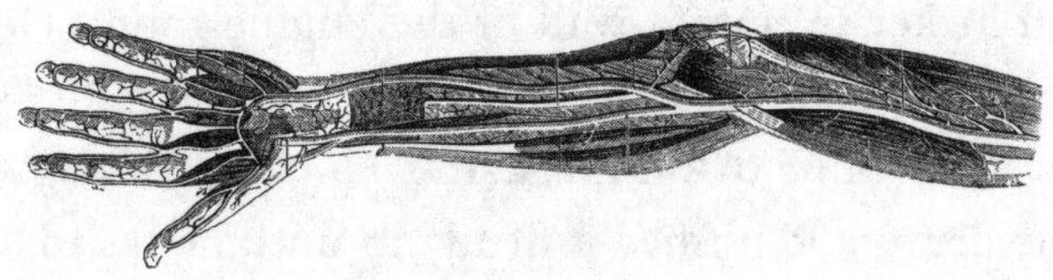

63

MAGNUS STARED AT HIS radio in a paralysis of disbelief.

A second, shuddering explosion in the cargo hold shook him out of his astonishment. And now an acrid smoke began filling the engine room, accompanied by the sound of fire: muffled at first, but morphing to a dull roar. The engine churned on, the boat yawing to port, and to his horror he felt the deck beginning to slant.

The boat was on fire and starting to go down by the head.

With a great effort he cleared his mind, remembering who he was and what he was capable of; and he concentrated on the consequences should Pendergast survive and tell the world the truth about him. It had become inescapably clear this was to be a fight to the end—one or both would die.

It had also become all too clear the kind of person he was up against: someone almost—or maybe even actually—his equal, perhaps endowed with the same powers he had. If it happened to him by a medical experiment, it could possibly happen to another by a freak of birth. Over the years, he'd grown soft and flabby by exercising his powers against the weak and feeble. Life without challenge had filled him with lassitude. But now, and for the first time, he had met the test of his life.

The thought was strangely bracing.

At least he was in the right place to arm himself. There was a hidden gun locker set into a wall of the engine room. He punched in the code, unlocked the panel, and pulled out an AR-15 and a preloaded, hundred-round drum magazine. Holding its magwell up, he inserted the drum and pushed it firmly in until he heard a click. He pulled the charging handle back to insert a round into the chamber, set the automatic lever to three-round bursts, then—taking a deep breath—kicked open the engine room door and exited onto the deck. Flames and smoke were roaring out of the cargo hold, and the deck was slanting farther toward the bow, paddle wheel still churning, the motion evidently forcing water in through a hole blown in the forward hull. Helmless, its rudders jammed to port, the boat was circling and essentially sinking itself in one of the deepest subchannels of the Delta.

Pendergast was in the saloon... or so he claimed. The grand staircase was forward and as Magnus ran, he saw water already surging across the bollards on the cargo deck. Wading through the rising water he reached the grand staircase, only to see Pendergast at the top, waiting for him with a handgun. He dove to one side, unleashing a burst from the AR-15 as Pendergast returned fire. The agent vanished and Magnus took the opportunity to scramble up the tilting staircase, pausing at the top to get his bearings. He caught a glimpse of Pendergast's black form disappearing out the saloon's aft exit. He fired a second, sustained burst in his direction, the rounds blowing out a row of frosted cut-glass antique windows.

He had, in that momentary encounter, captured a faint echo of the man's mind. This gave him a surge of encouragement and power. He'd learned that Pendergast had only a .45 handgun—hugely overmatched by the AR-15 and his personal sidearm, a Swenson custom 1911. If he could only get close enough, he could see even more fully into Pendergast's mind, "hearing" his current thoughts and thus achieving an almost insurmountable advantage.

He sprinted across the saloon toward the aft exit, then paused to glance down the stateroom deck; another mental flash—a glimpse of sixth sense—and he realized the man was close, intending to shoot through the wall; he took evasive action, and Pendergast's rounds burst harmlessly through the woodwork. Two could play at that game. With another spurt of gunfire, he raked the outer stateroom walls, knowing the AR-15's .223 high-powered rounds would go through the wood like butter. He unleashed another burst, lower this time, chewing up the antique beadboard, sending smoke and splinters everywhere.

The fire had spread forward and was now engulfing the stateroom deck. He figured he had less than five minutes.

Suddenly, with an almost bat-like fleetness, his opponent flew out of the grand stateroom window—the son of a bitch looked unscathed—and got off a double tap at him even as he dashed up the ladderway to the hurricane deck. But Magnus had again picked up the echo of his thoughts and was further encouraged. He added another fact to his growing collection: the mag in the .45 Pendergast had taken held only the standard ten rounds—all his crew had been issued the same sidearm package—and Magnus had counted six shots. That left no more than four plus one, or perhaps less if he'd used up shots before, and he could feel the concern in Pendergast's mind about running out of ammo and lacking either another mag or a second firearm.

Magnus leapt up the ladderway after him, aiming the AR-15 and unleashing a burst as he ascended, driving the man back. Poking the muzzle over the top of the ladderway, he swung it around and raked the deck, glimpsing Pendergast taking cover behind one of the longboats in the stern. The deck was now slanting badly, the paddle wheel churning, engine stuck on full throttle. The entire bow section was engulfed in flames, spreading burning debris on the water as it sank. He pulled open the door of the engineer's cabin and, using it as cover, fired a burst into the longboat, hoping the rounds would penetrate deeply enough to reach Pendergast. Two more shots came back—that made eight—which he answered with another burst.

In the wake of this brief exchange of fire, Magnus took the opportunity to slip aft to the deckhand's cabin. And now, at last, he was finally within full range of Pendergast's busy mind...and he picked up, almost like a radio broadcast, the raging thoughts of his adversary—from which he learned the man indeed had only two shots left in his magazine.

He could feel the heat of the fire at his back, feel the slant of the deck; something had to happen, and fast, or they both would be sucked down with the burning ship. The key was now to show himself, present the most tempting target possible, and waste the man's last rounds. He unloaded another burst into the tarp-covered longboat, splinters flying everywhere. As a sensation of panic and alarm reached him, he knew the rounds were making it through. Time to flush out his prey. Magnus now stepped partially into view; Pendergast fired a round, but Magnus had picked up on the man's intention to fire and was able to evade the blast. Otherwise, he'd have been dead—the man was a crack shot. He then showed himself again, a most tempting target—and in the same manner as before evaded Pendergast's final shot.

And now he got the message—half sensation, half thought—that he'd hoped for: Pendergast was out of ammo. All he had was a marlin spike and some sort of sharp tool.

Magnus prepared to step out and finish him off, but then hesitated. The man was damnably clever. He wasn't sure, beyond a shadow of a doubt, whether Pendergast had sussed out his special power—but if he had, he might be transmitting a counterfeit thought. No one had done it before—in the early days after the experiment, Telligren had tried a few times as a test, without success—but then, he'd never encountered anyone like Pendergast.

He waited, letting his brain soak in the steady stream of anger, chagrin, and helplessness, along with a burst of remarkably complex reasoning that explored, like a chess master, every possible strategic outcome. None of them were good.

Still, he must be cautious. He would test him; show himself again, confident he could anticipate any shot before it was fired and dodge it. He stepped out on deck and walked toward the longboat. No shot came; what did come was only further chagrin at the vulnerability of the man's position: no way to fight back except with a marlin spike. He could even see the man staring at his useless gun, slide locked back.

But now he picked up on a fresh idea of Pendergast's: the man had taken the bloody marlin spike from his belt and planned to throw it. Magnus assumed the man was an expert knife thrower. *Very well*, he thought with satisfaction, *let's see how this works out.* He continued walking down the hurricane deck, exposing himself completely. And then, in perfect synchronicity with Pendergast's thoughts, he deftly skipped aside just as the marlin spike whirled past him and embedded itself with a shuddering thud into the wall behind him.

The game was up. Magnus leaned back, breathing hard, and laughed. "I know you're out of ammo. Come out, hands up, or I'll perforate you."

A beat—and then the man stepped out. Christ, Magnus thought, he was a monstrous-looking son of a bitch: covered with black coal dust mixed with clotted blood and gore. Now they were face-to-face and Pendergast's thoughts were even clearer: fury, humiliation, mortification... and continued scheming. He held the useless gun in his hands, slide locked back.

"Drop it."

Pendergast complied.

"That tool in your belt—take that out and drop it."

He removed the tool and let that fall.

"Take a step forward. Just one."

Now, at this proximity, his thoughts were clear as a bell. He was completely unarmed, his mind overflowing with frustration, humiliation... and fear.

Magnus needed to know nothing more. "Step back again."

The man took a few steps back, and Magnus did the same. They were on opposite ends of the stern, the churning of the paddle wheel loud just below, mist and spray in the air. He could also hear the approaching roar of the fire, heading rapidly toward them from the bow.

"One question before you die."

The man said nothing.

"Do you have the gift?"

"No."

"Then—how do you do all this?"

"I am more observant than most. And what I observe—"

But in an instant, Magnus realized what it was Pendergast observed: it came like a silent emergency broadcast to his brain; immediately followed by the realization that he, Magnus, was doomed. Enraged and alarmed, he fired the AR-15 at Pendergast, the weapon bucking with recoil. But even as the roar of the weapon sounded, something like a black shroud descended upon him without the ghost of a warning *from behind*. He swung around, firing madly; he felt powerful hands grip both sides of his chest; there was a sudden jerk upward—and then, to his perfect astonishment, he was in the air, flipping over the rail and plummeting headfirst toward the churning, boiling paddle wheel below.

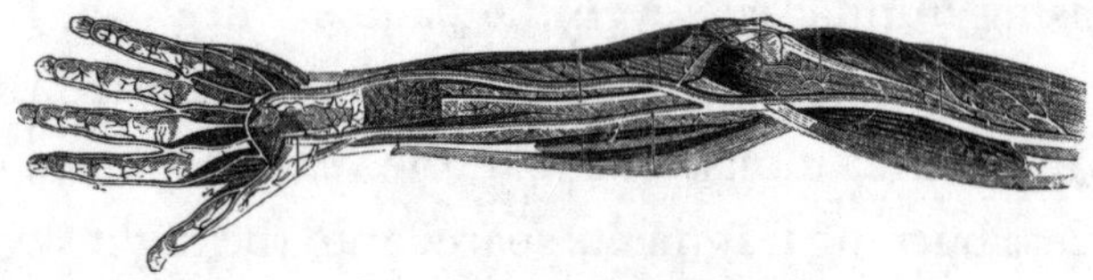

64

Pendergast righted himself and watched as Magnus disappeared over the railing, his body glancing off the paddle box and into the turning wheel—wedging itself into the iron feathering. With a hideous scream, Magnus was carried around and—stuck between the paddles—down into the boiling water, plunging below the moiling surface. Pendergast waited, and a moment later the body came back up still wedged in the paddles, tangled and bloody, like a medieval traitor being broken on the wheel—his face distorted in agony, a keening cry escaping from his lips before he was carried around and buried once again in the foaming wake.

Pendergast waited as the wheel made another revolution, but this time it came up empty: the body was gone, save for a few trailing clouds of blood in the water.

A fiery explosion from behind knocked Pendergast off balance, tongues of fire licking the deck around him. He snatched up the gun from on the deck and, with a backward glance at the raging inferno, dove over the railing, passing briefly through smoke and flame before plunging into the warm Delta water. He stroked up to the surface and swam toward the near shore. Reaching it within a few minutes, he made his way up the muddy embankment into the cordgrass, scrambled to his feet, backed off to a safe distance, and turned to watch. The air was aglow with a lurid ruddiness, the huge boat tilting ever higher, the stern rising until at last even the paddle wheel was fully out of the water, groaning and clanking in air. Then the blaze reached the fuel tanks and, with a monstrous roar, the vessel exploded in a ball of fire. Countless burning fragments soared into the night sky, a million orange arcs of flame that rose and spread and, losing momentum, at last fell back to earth. As the plume punched upward, it left behind a mass of burning flotsam, swirling and sinking in the black water, to the accompaniment of hissing and great clouds of steam.

Pendergast's unmoving, impassive face, lit by the glow of the fire, was punctuated by two glittering eyes that seemed illuminated from within.

And then he heard a sound—not from the ship, but from the tall grass in front of him. It rustled strangely... and then, like a ghost, a figure rose up from the vegetation: hideous, dripping gore, one hand hanging by a mere thread of flesh, an eyeball loose in its cracked socket—a body so broken it looked scarcely human.

"*You!*" breathed Pendergast in genuine astonishment.

The figure lurched toward him. "Me." A ghastly, gurgling laugh emerged from his chest. "How did you do it? I... must know."

"I was behind you the entire time."

"But I saw—"

"No. What you saw was a visualization in *my* mind, projected for your benefit."

"It was not a thought in your head. I *saw* you—for real."

"Are you familiar with the Tibetan discipline Chongg Ran? No? Visualization, or the simulation of it, plays a large role in their mental exercises. A pity you don't have the time left to hear more about it—judging from your condition."

Another mirthless laugh erupted from the man's broken chest. "You know, Pendergast, I should thank you. My life had grown dull to the point of deadliness. But you've revivified me—just in time, it would seem: that little merry-go-round ride you just sent me on is something I'll never forget." He giggled, his voice cracking. "I realize I've been living... well, in lockup, a tiny unlit space in the punishment block.

I'm a fifth grader in a kindergarten class—knowing all the answers, beating up the boys, taking all the toys I want. Only now it's all grown so tiresome. And yet I can't move on. Where would I go? And to think that all this time, I've been congratulating myself on how clever I was to keep my ambitions restrained—along with my sweet little secret."

"Is that secret connected to your locked cabin?" Pendergast asked.

"Ah! Did you see its splendors?"

"I did."

"You saw, but no doubt lack the refinement to understand. It is for a fragrant jewel, an impossibly rare truffle, its musk to be always enjoyed but never devoured. Not yet aboard, alas, but still in the cellar of my house, for you to seek out... if you can."

"I wish I could say I look forward to it."

"And *I* wish I could be there to see the look on your face." A silence—and now Magnus's face twisted in true agony, forcing him to drop the badinage. "The gun—was it really empty?"

Pendergast reached behind and withdrew it from his waistband. The slide was no longer locked back. He ejected a round from the chamber, caught it deftly in midair, held it up between thumb and forefinger in the dying glow of the burning boat for Magnus to see, then reinserted it and racked the weapon. Without a word, he turned the butt of the gun around and held it toward Magnus.

Magnus took it with a trembling hand and pointed it toward Pendergast. "You're a fool in the end, my friend. Say your prayers."

"There's only one round left," said Pendergast. "Either for me—or for you. Not both. Consider carefully."

After a long silence punctuated only by his wheezing breath, Magnus turned the gun around, tucked it under his chin, aimed skyward—mumbling under his breath something that, to Pendergast, sounded like a *l'envoi*—and pulled the trigger.

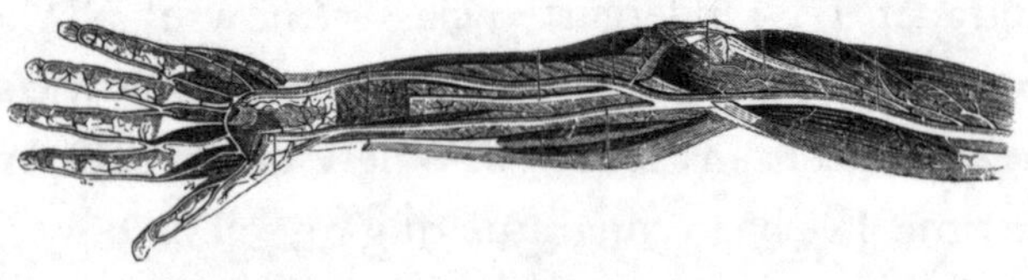

65

A. X. L. Pendergast, unshaven and dirty, dressed in a soiled suit coat and shabby tuxedo pants, carrying a bottle of Night Train in a stained paper bag, lounged in a doorway near the corner of Chestnut and Washington, observing the Garden District mansion with narrowed eyes. The mansion, surrounded by yellow crime scene tape, was swarming with NOPD and FBI agents. Estevez had arrived an hour before with two additional agents to join the search—a search from which Pendergast had been firmly and pointedly excluded. There was, of course, established procedure for taking him off the case; as the junior partner to an agent who had been murdered, he could no longer participate in the investigation: his objectivity, his credibility as a witness, and his emotional fitness had all been compromised—or so FBI protocol insisted. On top of this was the highly ambiguous role he had played in the previous night's destruction of the *Fantôme* and the shocking suicide of Dr. Dorion Magnus.

In his initial debriefing—which Estevez had silently listened in on but not participated in directly—there were a number of things Pendergast had failed to mention, not the least of which was the mysterious room Magnus had hinted would be found in his mansion. It was, apparently, to serve the same purpose as the highly secure one he'd built aboard his ship, but seemingly far more incriminating.

Pendergast had pondered what that purpose might be for some time but had been unable to draw any but the most grotesque and improbable conclusions. The secure cabin on the boat appeared to be a trysting hideaway of some kind—but for whom? And why the secrecy?

As he watched the FBI come and go, he had grave doubts they would be able to find the secret Magnus had hinted at. His was a big, beautiful antebellum mansion, thoroughly renovated—a renovation that would have given Magnus plenty of opportunities to create, somewhere in its depths, a well-hidden room.

But Pendergast knew he was damned if he would cede that coup to another agent who had just stepped into the case. It was a mystery that had not permitted him sleep the evening before.

Raising the bottle of Night Train to his lips, he took a small sip, swished it around like mouthwash, and spat it out. Then, pushing himself away from the doorframe, he wobbled down the street toward the front of the mansion. Several big-bellied NOPD cops were standing guard, and as he teetered by he paused in front of one, swaying.

"What's going on?" he asked, giving the cop a good blast of his alcohol-laden breath as he peered down the walk toward the open front door. He glimpsed Estevez inside busily directing his agents. The sight annoyed him.

"Move on, pal," said the cop.

"Has there been violence?" he asked eagerly. "A murder?"

"I said, *move on*."

Doffing his soiled hat, Pendergast staggered down the street and turned the corner. There was another cop guarding the far end of the building, but it was quieter on the side lane. He could see, halfway down it, a private alleyway blocked by a wrought iron gate, which had once been the carriage entrance to the mansion.

He headed down the lane, clutching the paper bag. The cop at the end gave him a quick glance and, seeing nothing of interest, turned away. Pendergast continued until he was opposite the iron gate; then, in a flash, he seized the bars, launched himself up and over the tall spikes, and clambered down the other side, discarding the bottle in a dark corner as he did so.

In seconds he had disappeared.

Now to get inside. The entrance to the old carriage house had been bricked over to create an additional space, but an old window remained. He peered in, discovering it was a small exercise room—empty. With his elbow, Pendergast gently broke a windowpane, reached in to unlock it, lifted, and entered.

His knowledge of antebellum mansions led him to believe that the staircase to the cellar would be found nearby, in the back of the house. After listening at the door and hearing nothing, he eased it open, entered a service hall—and there, at its end, was the door to the basement.

As he made his way down the hall, he could hear the heavy tramping of feet above and the muffled voices of the searchers as they went through the mansion. The suicide of Magnus; his grievous but strange injuries; the burning and sinking of the famous boat; and the discovery of Agent Chambers's waterlogged corpse had become an explosive—if still utterly confused—story, which Pendergast's obfuscations and explanations had done little to clarify.

He eased open the door to the cellar and paused at the top of the stairs, listening. Voices filtered up from below: it appeared a few cops were currently searching the basement. That would complicate things... but not unduly.

Slipping down the stairs, Pendergast kept to the darkest corners while the cops—he saw there were only two—talked loudly about the latest Saints game while shuffling and poking their way through the basement's many rooms and alcoves, flashing their lights around willy-nilly, turning things over, opening chests, and picking through heaps of decaying furniture. They had no idea what they were looking for, and it was immediately clear to Pendergast they would find nothing. Crouching in the shadows, he watched them work, waiting for his opportunity. It didn't take long. After twenty minutes, the two decided to conclude their search and returned upstairs, the conversation having shifted to a heated evaluation of the sudden size increase of the breasts of some country-western singer Pendergast had never heard of.

Hearing the door close above him, he took out his penlight and began moving through the dark spaces, playing the beam along the basement's brick walls. The mansion was, like many of its New Orleans counterparts, primarily an aboveground structure, but nevertheless the walls oozed niter and a frosting of crusted carbonate from the moisture of two centuries. The air was heavy with the smell of mold and rotting wood.

He slowly worked his way around the perimeter of the basement, convinced that the secret room would not have been built along the perimeter, but rather hidden somewhere in the vast labyrinth of the basement's interior spaces, taking full advantage of the reconstruction project. He began examining the interior walls as he slowly continued his search. Even here, his light glittered off a crust of many tiny crystals, built up over centuries of seepage—not as obvious as on the exterior walls, but evident nevertheless.

There. He paused his beam and peered more closely. There was a section of brickwork that did not look quite right. It wasn't cleaned—that would be too obvious—but his beam did not reflect the buildup of crystals in quite the right way, and on careful inspection Pendergast noticed that the crust on this section of wall was not real but cleverly painted onto the bricks in a faux approximation of actual seepage. An even closer inspection with a magnifying glass showed suspicious seams in the brickwork, which, when traced, outlined a door of sorts.

It had been clever to use an interior wall, where the lighter layer of crust would be easier to imitate. It would also have made his secret installation—whatever it was—that much easier to accomplish.

Pendergast gave the wall a push, but it did not budge. There would be a trick, of course; a hidden release somewhere. A quick search of the wall disclosed nothing obvious. However, standing against the wall was a bookcase stuffed with decaying tomes.

Surely Magnus wouldn't have gone for such an obvious trope, would he? Sounding the man's character, or what he knew of it, Pendergast decided he would: given Magnus's clear disdain for the intelligence of his fellow residents, it would probably seem a delicious irony to him.

The light passed along the spines, alighting on *Canon Medicinae Avicennae*, Avicenna's famous thousand-year-old textbook of human anatomy. *Ah yes*, thought Pendergast, no longer in doubt: that was just the sort of volume Magnus would select as a lever. He pulled out the book, to be greeted a moment later by a grating noise. Then a section of the brickwork swung open, revealing an inner wall—and, once again, a stainless-steel door.

This lock did not yield easily to Pendergast's tools, but after five minutes of coaxing it came open, swinging inward to reveal a dark space. Pendergast paused a moment. Then, finding the light switch, he turned it on—and stared in perfect amazement.

It was almost identical to, although rather larger than, the space on the boat: a beautiful, elegant, welcoming bedroom, with sporting prints on the walls, fine Persian rugs on the floor, a large Louis XIV gilt mirror, a ladies' side table overspread with bottles of perfume, a silver and tortoiseshell brush and comb set, jewelry, and what appeared to be a Fabergé egg. A matching side table and chair, beautifully inlaid, stood near the door; on the table was a silver salver with vertical panels holding soiled, much-thumbed letters. The room smelled strongly of formalin, methanol, erythrosin, glycerin, and phenols. The only thing that broke the illusion of past elegance was, apparently, a cryogenic chamber, countersunk into the brickwork, flush with the wall. And, as on the boat, a stainless-steel gurney sat next to a rack of chemicals, needles, tubes, and trocars.

In addition, it contained a large bottle of baby oil—opened and half full.

In the middle of this bizarre tableau was a bed—a beautiful bed draped in rich damask silks, satin, and gold brocade. But unlike that on the *Fantôme*, this bed was occupied. A woman lay within, her golden hair spreading fetchingly over the satin pillow, her eyes closed, her hands folded demurely upon the silk coverlet, a look of contentment and peaceful satiety on her face.

And she was dead.

As Pendergast leaned closer, he saw that she was not only dead, but very dead, severely decayed, falling apart—even though it was clear that much skilled effort had been made to keep her body as fresh and lifelike as possible, with makeup, emollients, oils, paint, preservatives, prosthetic inserts, embalming chemicals, and filler.

He grasped the edge of the covers and drew them back to reveal the entire body. The woman was nude. Pendergast stared, paralyzed with horror. For the first time in his life, he found himself forced to look away from a sight so ghastly it was unbearable. It was clear—clear as day—that the corpse had been *used*—repeatedly violated over many months... or, more likely, *years*.

Pendergast, head still averted, allowed the coverlet to fall back. Shocked to the core, he backed out of the room like an automaton, grasping only by instinct the sheaf of letters displayed on the salver. Leaving the door open, he stumbled across the cellar to the staircase. Voices filtered down from above. He had finally discovered Magnus's hidden psychosis.

He took several deep breaths, composing himself. He smoothed his dirty suit, tightened the knot of his tie, relaxed his facial muscles, and put his disordered mind into order. Then he ascended the stairs—to find Estevez in the kitchen with his two new agents and a gaggle of NOPD.

Estevez stared at him, eyes narrowing. "Who the hell are you, and what are you doing here?"

Pendergast took out a handkerchief and, with a shaking hand, wiped his face clean.

"Pendergast? What the devil? What are you doing here, looking like a bum? You were debriefed and taken off the case!"

"In the basement," Pendergast managed to say. "Something you need to see." He could utter nothing more.

"I'll be seeing *you* before a board of inquiry, mister...!" roared Estevez. But Pendergast, already moving unsteadily toward the front door—with its promise of freedom and oblivion beckoning from beyond—did not hear him.

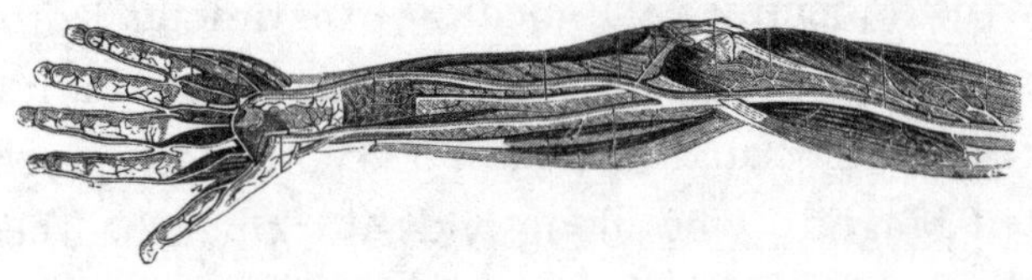

66

THE QUIET RAP ON the door to his office roused Estevez from a stupor. He'd been on his feet most of the last seventy-two hours. What a perfect storm of insanity this case had abruptly turned into. One of his senior agents sadistically poisoned. New Orleans's most respected doctor, exposed as a murderer and deviant—dead by suicide. The famous *Fantôme*—blown up and sunk. Seven corpses, burned beyond recognition, fished out of the Delta. And then, to top it off, the corpse of one of New Orleans's young socialites, tragically struck down by premature cardiac death, suddenly exposed as murder, not peacefully reposing in the family tomb as everyone supposed, but in a pervert's den of horror. All of New Orleans was in an uproar.

What had actually happened on board the *Fantôme* was still somewhat unclear, because no eyewitnesses had been left behind—except, of course, the one who'd just knocked on his door. In his debriefing, which Estevez had observed but not participated in, Pendergast claimed to have been imprisoned in a coal bunker, emerging only after the boat's explosion tore a hole in it that allowed him to escape—and for that reason he could shed no light on the events leading up to the explosion or the deaths of the crew. However, he'd witnessed Chambers's death and the suicide of Magnus: in his debriefing, he'd been careful to emphasize how Chambers himself had cracked the Wickman case; how he had saved Pendergast's life in the burning house; how he'd identified the medical experiments led by Dr. Telligren, which had resulted in irreparable damage to a little-known part of the brain associated with both perception and psychosis; how he suspected Magnus, who along with Wickman had been one of Telligren's students and a subject of the experiments, to be the doctor's killer; and how, finally, Chambers had gone to the *Fantôme* to question Magnus, only to be murdered by him—cruelly and with premeditation.

"Enter," Estevez said curtly.

Agent Pendergast walked in. Estevez purposely did not offer him a seat.

"Has the plaque for my partner on the Wall of Heroes been approved yet?" Pendergast asked.

"You don't have to worry on that score, Pendergast," said Estevez. "The recommendation has gone to the director, and I have no doubt, with your sworn affidavit, that Agent Chambers will be added to the DC memorial."

Pendergast bowed his head in satisfaction.

"But let's talk about you for a moment. In particular, your future." Estevez was shrewd enough to know that Pendergast had said all he was going to say, even though Estevez suspected he knew a great deal more.

"Sir."

"It's a rather short agenda—two items, merely. First, I'd like to congratulate you. Your probationary period will expire in six months, and I'm pleased to let you know I've recommended you be given full status as a special agent."

"I am glad to hear it. Thank you."

"We are all grateful for your part in assisting Chambers in his courageous and successful efforts in bringing Wickman to justice and exposing Magnus as the deviant murderer he actually was."

"I learned a great deal from Agent Chambers, and for that I will be forever grateful."

"Agent Chambers was a hero, and I'm pleased to hear that you learned much from him. And now for the second item. With your promotion to full agent will come reassignment to a new FO."

Pendergast raised one eyebrow in mute inquiry.

"To put it more bluntly—your tenure here is on a six-month timer, starting now." Estevez paused; when Pendergast said nothing, he continued. "I've already spoken to Executive Assistant Director Decker about it and secured his approval. You will spend the remainder of your probationary period here, per regulations—but on light desk duty only. You might wish to work on a cold case or two, just as you were doing when you first arrived—I understand one or two were of particular interest."

"That's true. One such case, although six years stale, struck my interest. In particular. It involved a freighter washing up in Bayou Grove, with—"

"Very good. I encourage you to spend as much time as possible in the basement archives looking into that as well as any other old cases that might interest you. Meanwhile, Decker is sending me a list of field offices for you to choose from. The decision is yours—just so it's not in Louisiana."

"I believe I understand." And Pendergast nodded slowly.

"That makes everything easier. The fact is, we've had the benefit of your, ah, skill set long enough." Pendergast was a rogue agent and would never change, and Estevez couldn't wait to get him out of his hair and let some other unfortunate FO deal with him. The way Pendergast had willfully disobeyed almost every order Estevez had issued following the burning of the Wichman mansion had been outrageous—and his showing up in the Magnus mansion after being taken off the case was the straw that broke the camel's back.

"Thank you, sir. And since we may see little of each other in the months to come, may I take a moment to observe that it's been an honor working for you?"

"You may. Thank you, and dismissed."

Estevez watched the slender figure, dressed in his signature black, leave his office, and only then did he dare breathe a huge sigh of relief.

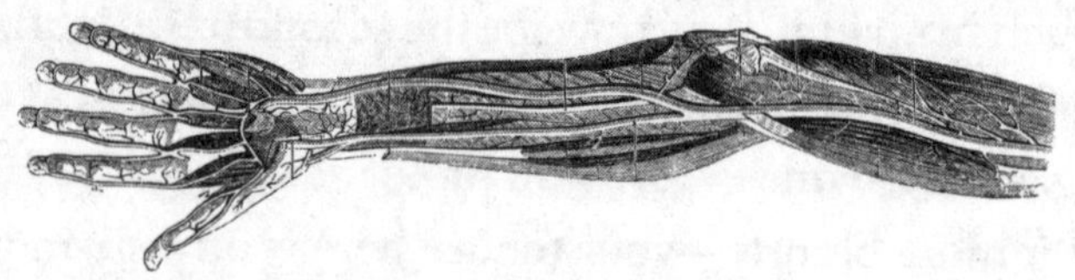

67

Agent Pendergast walked down the hospital corridor. The room that had previously been guarded now looked like the others, the policeman removed when it was clear that Proctor had been the victim of a kidnapping and not an accomplice.

Pendergast entered the room to find Proctor sitting in a chair dressed in a hospital gown and slippers and reading a paperback. The color had returned to his skin, and the powerful muscles beneath it rippled faintly as he turned a page. Although Pendergast had appeared silently at the door, he noted with approval that Proctor seemed to have already known he was coming—his instincts were still sharp.

"Sir!" Proctor said, putting the book aside and preparing to stand.

"Rest easy," Pendergast said, closing the door behind him. "In the unclassified world out here, you're not a sergeant major and I'm not a colonel. We're just shades in the memories of Longstreet, Michael Decker, and others who aren't the kind to reminisce." He took a chair beside Proctor. "We're civilians now—although one of us is still actively working for the government." At this, he pulled the FBI badge out of his black suit jacket and showed it to Proctor.

"What? You're working for *those* candy-asses?" Proctor said.

"The analogy I'd prefer is that I'm a diner, and they are the restaurant. They offer up many interesting and mysterious sauce piquante dishes, of which I may sample."

Proctor nodded as Pendergast peered at the book in his hand. "Don't tell me you're still reading Trollope."

"Why not? The books suffice for an extended op. The world they describe is so strange and distant they make hours pass quickly when you're waiting for a go-sign. And if you lose one somewhere, it's easy enough to replace."

This sounded like Proctor's logic. Pendergast remembered him, crouched behind a Jerusalem thornbush in the Middle East, or a Manchurian fir in a colder climate, reading a battered paperback by Gen 3 night-vision goggles. "I should have thought you'd have finished all his books by now."

"They're just as serviceable the second time around." And Proctor held up the cover of *Barchester Towers*.

There was a brief silence. "I understand you're being released tomorrow," Pendergast asked, in a somewhat different tone. "How good is your memory of my first visit?"

"I told you all I knew about my captor."

"I assume you were officially debriefed?"

Proctor smiled mirthlessly. "I received a visit from two humorless men in sweatsuits. They took copious notes. But I was left unsatisfied. They didn't tell me squat about the case—all I know is what I've read in the papers."

"Well, I will certainly fill you in." And Pendergast began to tell Proctor all about Wickman, the PSI experiments, and his demented search for the proper limb to replace his own evil one; how he died; the roles of Magnus and Telligren; and all the rest of it. Proctor listened intently and, when it was over, gave a dry chuckle. "I suppose I owe you thanks for saving my life."

"Agent Chambers saved your life—not me."

Proctor looked skeptically at Pendergast. "So that's the official version?"

"Indeed so."

"I've been wondering what happened with my job, that day I didn't show up for work—"

"I can enlighten you," Pendergast said. "The arrangements were shifted to a backup plan, and it went through without a hitch. Foreman was correct, though, about the two workers he suspected of being rogue agents. He found additional confirmation, allowing him time to dispose of their services before they could compromise future operations."

"How did you learn all that?"

"I knew you'd be curious, so I did a little investigating on the side."

A pause. "I suppose old Foreman is wondering what the hell happened to me."

"The whole team is—or rather, what's left of it. I know they would take you back, if you wished."

Proctor shook his head. "No," he said. "Thanks, but no thanks."

There was another silence—longer this time. While they'd been speaking, Pendergast had been scrutinizing Proctor. The Ghost Company had been dissolved suddenly and indecorously during a change in administrations, and Pendergast had seen almost nothing of Proctor since. In every way that mattered, however, he still seemed to Pendergast like his old steady self, showing no signs of depression, hyperarousal, intrusion, or the other symptoms of PTSD that had plagued other members of the Company.

"Expedited Medical Transport," he said. "Why?"

"Why not?" Proctor asked in return. "I needed a job." Proctor shrugged. "When I was young, I'd always known I would end up in the military. But I never figured on being tapped for anything like the Ghost Company. The places we were dropped into, the unsanctioned liquidations, the rogue operations..." He shook his head. "If you wrote a novel about it, nobody would believe it. And then some politician or bureaucrat decided we were a liability—and boom, we were disbanded."

"You could have had your pick of postings in the armed forces," Pendergast said.

Proctor nodded slowly. "Yeah—but no." Another pause. "I had

had enough of that. Look, I know that some—maybe a lot—of the things we did were . . . well, dirty. Brutal. But they served a purpose. We didn't undertake a single op unless our entire chain of command, from Longstreet on down, believed it was right. We risked our lives to make a difference. Sometimes, a *huge* difference." He toyed idly with the paperback, then tossed it on a nearby table. "They offered me a posting in the SEALs. But—I don't know how else to put this, sir—how can you be satisfied with a ground assignment once you've made a trip to the moon?"

This was perhaps the longest, most personal statement Pendergast had ever heard Proctor make. But he understood only too well what he meant. Their secretive years in the Ghost Company had been made up of long stretches of a terrible kind of excitement: balanced on a knife's edge, existing in a strange twilight where death surrounded you and life seemed far away. Even for the healthiest mind, being dropped back into civilization after that, with those memories, forbidden to speak of it ever, to anyone, made for a disquieting existence. It was no wonder Proctor had taken up a nomadic life, getting one job after another just to stay busy, moving around, changing cities, never settling down. Pendergast said, *"A good traveler has no fixed plans, and is not intent on arriving."*

"We are both travelers, sir, are we not? And I guess it's time for this 'good traveler' to get back in his Land Rover, pick a direction . . . and drive."

"I must tell you, Proctor, that my ride is a lot smoother than your old Rover."

"*Your* ride?"

"A Rolls-Royce Silver Wraith."

Proctor whistled.

"It seems I am in need of a driver."

"A driver? You mean . . . a *chauffeur*?" The tone of skepticism was unmistakable.

"Have you forgotten your operating brief already? You might wear, from time to time, the outfit of a chauffeur. But there will be more to the job than mere driving—a great deal more. Your very special skills, my friend, will be put to most excellent use: in my employ this time, rather than under my command."

And, listening, Proctor smiled—if a faint twitch at one corner of the lip could be called a smile.

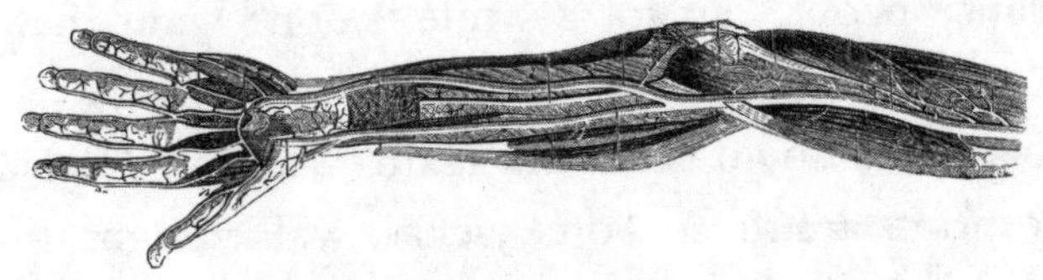

EPILOGUE*

New York Museum of Natural History
7 Months Later

D'AGOSTA JUST COULDN'T GET used to the Hall of the Great Apes. All those big grinning chimps, stuffed, hanging out of the fake trees, with their hairy arms and hilarious realistic dicks and big human hands with real fingernails. He wondered why it had taken so long for scientists to figure out that man was descended from the apes. Should've been obvious the first time they clapped eyes on a chimp. And he'd heard somewhere that chimps were just like humans, violent, excitable, always beating hell out of each other, even murdering and eating each other. *Jesus,* he thought, *there must be some other way to get around the Museum without going through this hall.*

"This way," said the guard, "down this stairway. It's pretty awful, Lieutenant. I was coming in at—"

"I'll hear that later," said D'Agosta. "You say he's wearing a guard's uniform. You know him?"

"I don't know, sir. It's hard to tell."

The guard pointed down the dim stairs. The stairway opened onto some kind of courtyard. The body lay at the bottom, in shadow. Everything was streaked and splattered in black—the floor, the walls, the overhead light. D'Agosta knew what the black was.

"You," he said, turning to one of several policemen following him, "get some lights in here. I want the place dusted and swept for fibers pronto. Is the SOC unit on its way? The man's obviously dead, so keep the ambulance people out for a while. I don't want them messing things up."

D'Agosta looked down the stairs again. "Jesus H. Christ," he said, "whose footprints are those? Some jackass walked right through that pool of blood, it looks like. Or maybe our murderer decided to leave us a fat clue."

There was a silence.

"Are those yours?" He turned to the guard. "What's your name?"

"Norris. Eric Norris. As I was saying, I—"

"Yes or no?"

"Yes, but—"

"Shut up. Are those the shoes?"

"Yes. See, I was—"

"Take the shoes off. You're ruining the carpet." *Fucking doorshaker,* D'Agosta thought. "Take them to the forensics lab. Tell them to seal 'em in a crime bag, they'll know what to do. Wait for me there. No, don't wait for me there. I'll call you later. I'll have a few questions for you. No, take the fucking shoes off right here. You'll have to walk in your socks."

"Yes, sir."

One of the cops behind D'Agosta snickered.

D'Agosta looked at him. "You think it's funny? He tracked blood all over the place. It's not funny."

D'Agosta moved halfway down the stairwell. The head was lying in a far corner, face down. He couldn't see it all that well, but he knew that he'd find the top of the skull punched out, the brains floating around somewhere in all that gore. God, what a mess a body could be if it wanted to.

A step sounded on the stairway behind him. "SOC," said a short man, followed by a photographer and several other men in lab coats.

"Finally. I want lights there, there, and there, and wherever else the photographer wants 'em. I want a perimeter set up, I want it set up five minutes *ago*, I want every speck of lint and grain of sand picked up. I want TraceChem used on everything. I want—well, what else do I want? I want every test known to man, and I want that perimeter observed by everyone, got it? No fuck-ups this time."

D'Agosta turned. "Is the Crime Lab team on the premises? And the coroner's investigator? Or are they out for coffee and croissants?" He patted the breast pocket of his jacket, looking for a cigar. "Put cardboard boxes over those footprints. And you guys, when you're done, squeegee a trail around the body so we can walk without tracking blood everywhere."

"Excellent." D'Agosta heard a low, mellifluous voice behind him.

"Who the hell are you?" he said, turning to see a tall, slender man, wearing a crisp black suit, leaning against the top of the stairwell. Hair so blond it was almost white was brushed straight back above pale-blue eyes. "The undertaker?"

"Pendergast," the man said, stepping down and holding out his hand. The photographer, cradling his equipment, pushed past him.

"Well, Pendergast, you better have a good reason to be here, otherwise—"

Pendergast smiled. "Special Agent Pendergast."

"Oh. FBI? Funny, why aren't I surprised? Well, how-do, Pendergast. Why the hell don't you guys phone ahead? Listen, I got a headless, de-brained stiff down there. Where're the rest of you, anyway?"

Pendergast withdrew his hand. "There's just me, I'm afraid."

"What? Don't kid me. You guys always travel around in packs."

The lights popped on, and the gore around them was bathed in brilliance. Everything that previously appeared black was suddenly illuminated, all the various shades of the body's secret workings made visible. Something D'Agosta suspected was Norris's breakfast was also visible, lying amidst a wash of body fluids. Involuntarily, D'Agosta's jaw started working. Then his eye caught a piece of skull with the dead guard's crew cut still on it, lying a good five feet from the body.

"Oh Jesus," said D'Agosta, stepping back, and then he lost it. Right in front of the FBI guy, in front of SOC, in front of the photographer, he blew his own breakfast. *I can't believe it,* he thought. *The first time in twenty-two years, and it's happening at the worst possible moment.*

The coroner's investigator appeared on the stairs, a young woman in a white coat and plastic apron. "Who's the officer in charge?" she asked, sliding on her gloves.

"I am," said D'Agosta, wiping his mouth. He looked at Pendergast. "For a few more minutes, anyway. Lieutenant D'Agosta."

"Dr. Collins," the investigator replied briskly. Followed by an assistant, she walked down to an area near the body that was being squeegeed free of blood.

"Photographer," she said, "I'm turning the body over. Full series, please."

D'Agosta averted his gaze. "We got work to do, Pendergast," he said authoritatively. He pointed at the vomit. "Don't clean that up until the SOC has finished with these stairs. Got it?"

Everyone nodded.

"I wanna know ingress and egress as soon as possible. See if you can ID the body. If it's a guard, get Ippolito down here. Pendergast, let's go up to the command post, get coordinated, or liaised, or whatever the hell you call it, and then let's return when the team is done for a look-see."

"Capital," said Pendergast.

Capital? thought D'Agosta. The guy sounded deep South. He'd met types like this before, and they were hopeless in New York City.

Pendergast leaned forward and said quietly, "The blood splattered on the wall is rather interesting."

D'Agosta looked over. "You don't say."

"I'd be interested in the ballistics on that blood."

D'Agosta looked straight into Pendergast's pale eyes. "Good idea," he said finally. "Hey, photographer, get a close-up series of the blood on the wall. And you, you—"

"McHenry, sir."

"I want a ballistic analysis done on that blood. Looks like it was moving fast at a sharp angle. I want the source pinpointed, speed, force, a full report."

"Yes, sir."

"I want it on my desk in thirty minutes."

McHenry looked a little unhappy.

"Okay, Pendergast, any more ideas?"

"No, that was my only one."

"Let's go."

In the temporary command post, everything was in place. D'Agosta always saw to that. Not one piece of paper was loose, not one file was out, not one tape recorder sitting on a desk. It looked good, and now he was glad that it did. Everyone was busy, the phones were lit up, but things were under control.

Pendergast slipped his lean form into a chair. For a formal-looking guy, he moved like a cat. Briefly, D'Agosta gave him an overview of the investigation. "Okay, Pendergast," he concluded. "What's your jurisdiction here? Did we fuck up? Are we out?"

Pendergast smiled. "No, not at all. As far as I can tell, I would not have done anything differently myself. You see, Lieutenant, this case has been on our radar from the very beginning, only we didn't realize it."

"How so?"

"I've been transferred from the New Orleans Field Office. Before I joined the Bureau, they'd investigated a series of killings down there: some very odd killings. Not to get into specifics, but the victims had the backs of their skulls removed, and the brains extracted. Same modus operandi."

"No shit. When was this?"

"Several years ago."

"Several *years* ago? That—"

"Yes, they went unsolved. First it was the ATF, because they thought drugs might have been involved, then it was the FBI when ATF couldn't make any progress. But we couldn't do anything with it, the trail was cold. And then yesterday, I read a wire service report about the double murder here in New York. The MO is too, ah, too peculiar not to make an immediate connection, don't you think? So I flew up last night. I'm not officially here—although I will be tomorrow."

D'Agosta relaxed. "So you're from Louisiana. I thought you might be some new boy in the New York office."

"They'll be here," said Pendergast. "When I make my report tonight, they'll be in on it. But, as I said, I've been transferred. And I will be in charge of the case."

"You? No way, not in New York City."

Pendergast smiled. "I will be in charge, Lieutenant. I am, frankly, interested in it." The way Pendergast said *interested* sent a strange sensation down D'Agosta's back. "But don't worry, Lieutenant, I am ready and willing to work with you, side by side, in perhaps a different way than the New York office might. If you'll meet me halfway, that is. This isn't particularly my turf, and I would welcome your help. How about it?"

He stood up and held out his hand. *Christ*, D'Agosta thought, *the boys in the New York office will take him apart in two and a half hours and ship the pieces back to New Orleans.*

"Deal," said D'Agosta, grasping his hand. "I'll introduce you around, starting with the security director, Ippolito. Provided you answer one question. You said the MO of the New Orleans killings was the same. What about the bite marks we found in the brain of the older boy? The claw fragment?"

"From what you told me about the autopsy, Lieutenant, the ME was only speculating about the bite marks," Pendergast replied. "I'll be interested to hear the salivase results. Is the claw being tested?"

Later, D'Agosta would remember that his question had been only half answered. Now, he simply replied, "It's being done today."

Pendergast leaned back in his chair and made a tent of his fingers, his eyes looking off into space. "I'll have to pay a visit to Dr. Ziewicz when she examines today's unpleasantness."

"Say, Pendergast? You aren't by any chance related to Andy Warhol, are you?"

"I don't care much for modern art, Lieutenant."

The crime scene was packed but orderly, everyone moving swiftly and speaking in undertones, as if in deference to the dead man. The morgue crew had arrived but was standing out of the way, patiently observing the proceedings. Pendergast stood with D'Agosta and Ippolito, the Museum's Security Director.

"Indulge me if you will," Pendergast was saying to the photographer. "I'd like a shot from here, like this." Pendergast demonstrated briefly. "And I'd like a series from the top of the stairs, and a sequence coming down. Take your time, get a nice play of line, shadow, and light going."

The photographer looked carefully at Pendergast, then moved off.

Pendergast turned to Ippolito. "Here's a question. Why was the guard—what did you say his name was, Mr. Ippolito, Jolley, Fred Jolley?—down here in the first place? This wasn't part of his rounds. Correct?"

"That's right," Ippolito said. He was standing in a dry spot near the entrance to the courtyard, his face a poisonous green.

D'Agosta shrugged. "Who knows?"

"Indeed," Pendergast said. He looked out into the courtyard beyond the stairwell, which was small and deep, brick walls rising on three sides. "And he locked the door behind himself, you say. We have to assume he went outside here or was headed in that direction. Hmm. The Taurid meteor shower was peaking at about that time last night. Perhaps Jolley here is an aspiring astronomer. But I doubt it." He stood still for a minute, looking around. Then he turned back toward them. "I believe I can tell you why."

Christ, a real Sherlock Holmes, thought D'Agosta.

"He came down the stairwell to indulge a habit of his. Marijuana. This courtyard is an isolated and well-ventilated spot. A perfect place to, ah, smoke some weed."

"Marijuana? That's just a guess."

"I believe I see the roach," said Pendergast, pointing into the courtyard. "Just where the door meets the jamb."

"I can't see a thing," said D'Agosta. "Hey, Ed. Check out the base of the door. Right there. What is it?"

"A joint," said Ed.

"What's the matter with you guys, can't find a fucking joint? I told you to pick up every grain of sand, for Chrissake."

"We haven't done that grid yet."

"Right." He looked at Pendergast. *Lucky bastard. Probably wasn't the guard's joint anyway.*

"Mr. Ippolito," Pendergast drawled, "is it common for your staff to use illicit drugs while on duty?"

"Absolutely not, but I'm not convinced it was Fred Jolley that—"

Pendergast shut him up with a wave of the hand. "I assume you can account for all these footprints."

"Those belong to the guard who found the body," said D'Agosta.

Pendergast bent down. "These completely cover any local evidence that may remain," he said, frowning. "Really, Mr. Ippolito, you should have your men better trained in how to preserve a crime scene."

Ippolito opened his mouth, then closed it again. D'Agosta suppressed a smirk.

Pendergast was walking carefully back underneath the stairwell, where a large metal door stood partially open. "Orient me, Mr. Ippolito. This door under the stairwell goes where?"

"A hallway."

"Leading to—?"

"Well, there's the Secure Area down to the right. But it's not possible the killer went that way, because..."

"Excuse me for contradicting you, Mr. Ippolito, but I'm sure the killer *did* go that way," Pendergast replied. "Let me guess. Beyond the Secure Area is the Old Basement, am I right?"

"Right," said Ippolito.

"Where the two children were found."

"Bingo," said D'Agosta.

"This Secure Area sounds interesting, Mr. Ippolito. Shall we take a stroll?"

Beyond the rusty metal door, a row of light bulbs stretched down a long basement corridor. The floor was covered in shabby linoleum, and the walls were hung with murals of Southwestern Pueblo Indians grinding corn, weaving, and stalking deer.

"Lovely," said Pendergast. "A shame they're down here. They look like early Fremont Ellis."

"They used to hang in the Hall of the Southwest," said Ippolito. "It closed in the twenties, I think."

"Ah!" said Pendergast, scrutinizing one of the murals. "It *is* Ellis. My heavens, these are lovely. Look at the light on that adobe facade."

"So," said Ippolito. "How do you know?"

"Why," said Pendergast, "anyone who knows Ellis would recognize these."

"I mean, how do you know the killer came through here?"

"I suppose I was guessing," said Pendergast, examining the next painting. "You see, when someone says 'it's impossible,' I have this very bad habit, I can't help myself, I immediately contradict that person in the most emphatic terms possible. A very bad habit, but one that I find hard to break. But of course, now we *do* know the killer came through here."

"How?" Ippolito seemed confused.

"Look at this marvelous rendition of old Santa Fe. Have you ever been to Santa Fe?"

There was a momentary silence. "Er, no," said Ippolito.

"There is a mountain range behind the town, called the Sierra de Sangre de Cristo. It means the 'Blood of Christ Mountains' in Spanish."

"So?"

"Well, the mountains *do* look quite red in the setting sun, but not, I dare say, *that* red. That's real blood, and it's fresh. A shame, really, it's ruined the painting."

"Holy shit," said D'Agosta. "Look at that."

A broad streak of blood was smeared waist-high across the painting.

"You know, murder is a messy thing. We should find traces of blood all along this corridor. Lieutenant, we'll need the crime lab people in here. I think we have your egress, at any rate." He paused. "Let's finish our little tour, and then call them in. I'd like to go ahead and look for evidence, if you don't mind."

"Be my guest," said D'Agosta.

"Careful where you walk, Mr. Ippolito, we'll be asking them to check the floors as well as the walls."

They came to a locked door marked RESTRICTED. "This is the Secure Area," said Ippolito.

"I see," said Pendergast. "And what exactly is the point of this Secure Area, Mr. Ippolito? Is the rest of the Museum insecure?"

"Not at all," the Security Director replied quickly. "The Secure Area is for storing especially rare and valuable objects. This is the best-protected museum in the country. We've recently installed a system of sliding metal doors throughout the facility. They're all linked to our computer system, and in the event of a burglary we can seal off the Museum in sections, just like the watertight compartments on a—"

"I get the picture, Mr. Ippolito, thank you very much," Pendergast said. "Interesting. An old copper-sheathed door," he said, examining it closely.

D'Agosta saw that the copper covering was riddled with shallow dents.

"Fresh dents, by the look of them," Pendergast said. "Now, what do you make of this?" He pointed downward.

"Jesus H. Christ," breathed D'Agosta, looking at the lower section of the door. The wooden frame was scored and gouged into a welter of fresh splinters, as if something clawed had been scrabbling at it.

Pendergast stepped back. "I want the entire door analyzed, if you please, Lieutenant. And now to see what's inside. Mr. Ippolito, if you would be so kind as to open the door without getting your hands all over it?"

"I'm not supposed to let anyone in there without clearance."

D'Agosta looked at him in disbelief. "You mean you want us to get a damn warrant?"

"Oh, no, no, it's just that—"

"He forgot the key," said Pendergast. "We'll wait."

"I'll be right back," said Ippolito, and his hurried footsteps echoed down the corridor. When he was out of hearing D'Agosta turned to Pendergast. "I hate to say it, Pendergast, but I like the way you work. That was pretty slick, the painting, and the way you handled Ippolito. Good luck with the New York boys."

Pendergast looked amused. "Thank you. The feeling is mutual. I'm glad I am working with you, Lieutenant, and not one of these hard-boiled fellows. Judging from what happened back there, you still have a heart. You're still a normal human being."

D'Agosta laughed. "Naw, it wasn't that. It was the scrambled eggs with ham and cheese and ketchup I had for breakfast. And that crew cut. I hate crew cuts."

About the Authors

The thrillers of **Douglas Preston** and **Lincoln Child** "stand head and shoulders above their rivals" (*Publishers Weekly*). Preston and Child's *Relic* and *The Cabinet of Curiosities* were chosen by readers in a National Public Radio poll as being among the one hundred greatest thrillers ever written, and *Relic* was made into a number-one box-office hit movie. They are coauthors of the famed Pendergast series and the newer, popular Nora Kelly series, and their recent novels include *Badlands, Angel of Vengeance, Dead Mountain, The Cabinet of Dr. Leng, Diablo Mesa, Bloodless, The Scorpion's Tail*, and *Crooked River*. In addition to his novels, Preston is the author of the award-winning nonfiction book *The Lost City of the Monkey God*. Child is a Florida resident and former book editor who has published eight novels of his own, including such bestsellers as *Chrysalis* and *Deep Storm*.

For more information you can visit PrestonChild.com

RAISING READERS

Books Build Bright Futures

Thank you for reading this book and for being a reader of books in general. We are so grateful to share being part of a community of readers with you, and we hope you will join us in passing our love of books on to the next generation of readers.

Did you know that reading for enjoyment is the single biggest predictor of a child's future happiness and success?

More than family circumstances, parents' educational background, or income, reading impacts a child's future academic performance, emotional well-being, communication skills, economic security, ambition, and happiness.

Studies show that kids reading for enjoyment in the US is in rapid decline:

- In 2012, 53% of 9-year-olds read almost every day. Just 10 years later, in 2022, the number had fallen to 39%.
- In 2012, 27% of 13-year-olds read for fun daily. By 2023, that number was just 14%.

Together, we can commit to **Raising Readers** and change this trend. How?

- Read to children in your life daily.
- Model reading as a fun activity.
- Reduce screen time.
- Start a family, school, or community book club.
- Visit bookstores and libraries regularly.
- Listen to audiobooks.
- Read the book before you see the movie.
- Encourage your child to read aloud to a pet or stuffed animal.
- Give books as gifts.
- Donate books to families and communities in need.

BOB1217

Books build bright futures, and **Raising Readers** is our shared responsibility.

For more information, visit **JoinRaisingReaders.com**

Sources: National Endowment for the Arts, National Assessment of Educational Progress, WorldBookDay.com, Nielsen BookData's 2023 "Understanding the Children's Book Consumer"